ABOUT THE AUTHORS

HRISTINE DAIGLE IS A NEUROPSYCHOLOGIST, COFFEE AFICIONADO, AND SCRABBLE DEMON LIVING IN THE GREAT WHITE NORTH (IN SOUTHERN ONTARIO, WHERE IT'S ACTUALLY QUITE SUNNY). Her short works have most recently appeared in *Apex* Magazine, *Grievous Angel*, and the *Automatons & Airships* anthology, under Christine Purcell which was her name before she got hitched. She is an active HWA member.

TEWART STERNBERG LIVES OUTSIDE DETROIT, MICHIGAN, AND IS A RETIRED EDUCATOR INVOLVED IN STATE POLITICS AND ISSUES RELATING TO CHILDREN'S WELFARE. *The Emerald Key* is his second novel, the first being *The Ravening*, published by Elder Signs Press. He and Christine Daigle are also putting the finishing touches on the next book in the Ember Quatermain/Peter Styles series, *The Magic Trap*, and are planning book #3. Stewart's shorter works have appeared in various anthologies available through Chaosium, Elder Signs Press, Mythos Books, and *White Cat* Magazine. Visit his blog at House-of-Sternberg.blogspot.com and travel over to his website, stewartsternberg.com.

The EMERALD KEY

Also by STEWART STERNBERG

The Ravening

CHRISTINE DAIGLE AND STEWART STERNBERG

T℡
p℡
Ticonderoga
publications

To the ever patient Jamie, my loving wife
—SS

*To Sean and William (for living with my
weirdness everyday)*
—CD

THE EMERALD KEY by Christine Daigle and Stewart Sternberg

Published by Ticonderoga Publications

Designed and edited by Russell B. Farr
Typeset in Sabon and Mesquite Standard

A Cataloging-in-Publications entry for this title is available from The National Library of Australia.

ISBN 978-1-921857-79-9 (limited hardcover)
      978-1-921857-80-8 (trade hardcover)
      978-1-921857-81-8 (trade paperback)
      978-1-921857-82-5 (ebook)

Ticonderoga Publications
PO Box 29 Greenwood
Western Australia 6924

www.ticonderogapublications.com

10 9 8 7 6 5 4 3 2 1

The authors would like to thank everyone who read this in the early stages; Joe Ponepinto, Dora Badger, Steve Tschirhart, Helen Pattskyn, and the late Jon Zech and Justin Purcell.

Deep love to our families, for allowing us to dedicate exorbitant amounts of our time to finishing this book.

Our heartfelt thanks to Ticonderoga Publications, especially our editor, Russell B. Farr, for his skill and patience.

PROLOGUE

Wherein a merchant completes a deal with a powerful and mysterious Italian

THE GREEK COUNTRYSIDE, 1859

A LOG COLLAPSED IN THE HEARTH, STARTLING THERON GIANNIS. It wasn't the knock on the door he'd been expecting. His heart raced even as he realized his mistake. He grimaced and massaged his chest. Theron accepted mortality, but he didn't have to like it. Still, eighty years was long enough for a man to live. At least he would die with coin in his pocket. God willing, he might have a little time to squander it. That would be nice.

Theron struggled to his feet with a groan. He checked the window for the fourth time that evening, swinging a jug of wine as he walked. The road was empty.

He turned from the glass and faced the innards of his crumbling confines. Then, he approached a shelf containing four dolls. A sad light shone from his eyes, but he smiled and wet his lips. He took a poppet from the ledge and walked back to his chair, tenderly propping the figurine on the table.

His fingertips, which had widened and rounded over the years, caressed pretty brown locks tied in a gingham bow.

Little Agata.

He glanced lovingly at the other dolls on the shelf, each a totem to perfection, and spoke their names: "Kristabelle, Layna, Vienna." And sweet Agata. Posing her on the table made him feel almost neglectful of the others.

A pounding at the door brought Theron to the present. The old man considered putting the doll back on the shelf, but instead left her on the table to greet the late night visitor.

He opened the door and admitted a tall man, with the back and shoulders of a laborer. The guest lowered his head to slip into the dark cottage and pushed past Theron. He was fluid in movement and, in a sense, cruel of face. Shockingly pale skin highlighted pronounced lines about the forehead and at the corners of the eyes. His sullen mouth was full; his brow heavy and expressive.

The man paused to inspect the cottage, amusement lightening his features.

Theron made to close the door when another figure filled the frame. This one wore a hooded robe, face hidden in the shadows of the cloth. Theron worried he might be a monk. The possible presence of a devout individual disturbed him, but refusing entrance was impossible. Robes swirled around a stiffly moving form as the man assumed a post in a corner.

"You are Giannis?" the visitor asked. His Italian accent sounded odd, like a traveler long removed from home.

"I am."

The Italian moved about the room, as if committing the surroundings to memory.

"You are quite isolated here, Mr. Giannis. It's charming though. That little cemetery down the road had such an ethereal air. It reminded me of a painting by Lorraine."

The visitor picked up the doll, his face darkening as he studied it. He stroked the hair with the back of a hand before untying the little gingham bow. The ribbon floated to the dirty floorboards. He cradled the doll in the crook of his arm as if it were a child.

"What a sad reminder to find on an old man's table," he said.

Theron shrugged, too shamed to find insult.

"Trappings of youth are fodder for corruption," the Italian mused. "What is the nature of sin, Mr. Giannis? Is youth to blame for its corruption when it has yet to know the burden of choice?"

Theron's face flushed. He didn't like the accusation in the man's words. Or maybe he was being overly sensitive, fabricating a condemning tone where none existed. Swallowing was difficult, his mouth suddenly dry. Theron's gaze swung to the hooded figure in the corner. He wished he could see the man's face. The features remained obscured by shadow, except for a strong jaw marred by a sickly complexion.

A thought struck Theron. Robes and hoods sometimes concealed disfigurement, or worse, disease. What if the man was a leper?

"What beautiful craftsmanship," his visitor said. "What is the name of this charming poppet?"

Struck mute, Theron chewed his lip in response. When he found his voice, it was heavy with resentment. "It's a doll," he said carefully. "Why would it have a name?"

The Italian stroked the poppet's hair and turned dark eyes on Theron. The man's gaze chilled and fascinated him with an intimacy that made Theron blush. This was power. He broke contact, his fragile heart beating too rapidly within his chest.

"Everything has two names," the man offered. "One kept hidden and one worn about in public."

"Like the two faces of Janus?"

The Italian's black eyes flashed, shaming Theron and making him feel he had somehow committed heresy. The stranger shook his head slowly, still petting the doll in the crook of his arm. Abruptly he tossed Theron's treasure into the fire.

Theron bitterly watched the flame consume Agata. The guest held out pallid hands as if to warm them.

"I don't disapprove," the man said. "Your distractions are of little consequence, yes?"

With an abrupt businesslike air, the Italian sat down in one chair and gestured Theron to sit in another. The old man warily obeyed. The knife on his table was his only weapon. He reached for it and drew comfort from the feel of the hilt against his palm.

"Would you like some cheese?" Theron asked. "Or bread? I have wine, but it is spoilt. I could get you some water from the well."

The visitor smiled, the expression uncannily feral.

"I make you nervous," he said and waved a dismissive hand. "Perhaps it would be best if we simply complete the transaction. I'll leave, and you can finish your dinner and perhaps entertain your other dolls."

Such a statement would have provoked a younger Theron. Now, he held his tongue and instead lurched to his feet, taking the knife with him. He worked loose a stone above the shelf and from a space within retrieved a wood box, approximately the length of his forearm.

He should have gone with the Englishman. That was who first tasked him with finding the document. The Englishman told him where to start searching and promised tremendous reward. The Italian promised more.

"I'm eighty," Theron thought, the age an often repeated rationalization for inaction.

Returning to the table, he slid the bowl of olives to the side and placed the box on the greasy ring left behind. One hand firmly on the prize, the other hand tightened about the knife's hilt.

The visitor's face remained calm and unreadable. He reached into his cloak and withdrew a heavy bag that he dropped on the table.

Theron couldn't resist saying, "I almost sold it to someone else."

"How fortunate you made the right decision," the man responded.

"At some point, you may have to deal with him."

The Italian nodded thoughtfully. "Your other bidder intrigues me. He is able to mask himself well. I suppose he's been too careful to supply you with an identity?"

"I only know he has vast resources."

"Patience will bring him to me," the man said, throwing a glance at the hooded figure. "And perhaps patience will determine who is the better."

Theron's clumsy fingers lifted the bag. The weight thrilled him. Tomorrow morning he would flee to Liopessi and never return.

The Italian pried free the top of the box and extracted a scroll tied with a leather string. An infectious smile stretched his lips. He undid the string and placed it aside. He unrolled the parchment with care and studied the scrawls and diagrams scribbled on its face.

"Phoenix," the man said. "What conceit!" He tapped the document and laughed with pleasure.

Theron had no idea what his guest referred to, nor did he care. This transaction was complete, as far as he was concerned, and the sooner the man left, the better.

"You have no idea what this truly is, do you?" the guest asked. "See this word here? It is what Lysimachus of Arcarnania called himself from time to time. The Phoenix. An arrogant man, Lysimachus, but he knew things, my friend. He knew things."

While the Italian perused the document, Theron opened the bag of coin and inspected its contents. He didn't want to count out the amount, fearing it would be construed as insult. Instead he contented himself with quietly removing one coin and warming it within his palm.

"He was one of Alexander's tutors," the Italian continued. His tone was that of a teacher entranced by the sound of his own voice. "I liked him enormously. Do you know what he once wrote, Giannis? *'Knowledge is an aphrodisiac.'*"

"It is also a knife in your enemy's hands," Theron added. He hadn't meant to say the words. His visitor's brows rose and his eyes glinted with pleasure. With a laugh, he returned to studying the document. He stopped with an exhalation of surprise and tapped the parchment with a fingertip.

"Britain?" he said. "One never knows where irony will be found."

Rolling the parchment again and once more tying the leather string, he returned it to the box before secreting it within a fold in his cloak. At last he offered Theron a hand.

"You've done well, Theron Giannis, I'll leave you with your poppets. Nothing sweetens old age like the memory of warm unblemished flesh against cold decrepit skin."

Unsure how to answer, Theron remained silent.

"Well," the man said, "our business is done."

The words brought relief. Theron wanted him gone. There was something wrong about the man that eluded him. He smiled politely and gestured his guest toward the door.

"If there is anything else I can do for you . . . " The words were merely a courtesy.

The Italian waved him off. They exchanged a handshake and Theron again experienced the man's power. It was difficult to let go of the hand, so appealing was the touch.

Instead of moving for the exit, the stranger turned his gaze to the corner of the room; to the hooded figure whose presence had been almost forgotten.

Theron watched as the hood was slowly pulled backward to expose a desiccated face. The flesh on one side was stripped, exposing gray tissue from mouth to forehead. Eyes smoldered deep within their sockets, the hate so profound it electrified the room. They were not the eyes of the living.

Theron's hammering heart seized. The old man sucked in air, trying to keep from collapsing. His legs were straw, barely able to support him. Time cruelly slowed to prolong his agony as he struggled to keep his head. He couldn't fight this thing, this nightmare.

The figure approached, an inevitable force.

The old man cried out and lunged feebly at the creature. He struck, relying on neglected skills learned in the poorer sections of Athens. Feinting with one arm, he lashed out with the other. A lucky strike drove the blade home. Theron ripped through the abdomen with surprising ease, giving the blade a final twist before yanking it free.

No pain registered on the dead man's face. No blood issued from the wound. Theron stared at his weapon, eyebrows raised in confusion at the black ooze staining the steel. He groaned as hopelessness rushed over him.

The attacker paused, perhaps waiting for another strike, and loomed over him.

"I have nothing!" he cried. He jabbed at the air with his free hand, the gesture a protection against the Evil Eye. "I'm a poor man."

The statement sounded absurd, even to Theron. It was a whistle in the night to trick the darkness and bolster bravery. This brute didn't want coin.

Theron's weapon-hand trembled violently. He clenched his jaw shut and fought back tears as he ignored the tremendous pressure gripping his chest.

"I don't want to die," Theron whimpered. His knees trembled and his shoulders slumped forward. He used a forearm to wipe away tears. "I'm not ready."

"It is better this way." The Italian's voice floated from the shadows. "At least you won't die alone." The man stepped forward, the hearth illuminating the amusement on his cruel features.

"When you're finished," he commanded the creature, "bring him along. We can use him to find the Brit."

The Italian strode to the exit and a blast of cold air hit Theron as the door swung open.

The dark form closed on him again, the smell of moss and fresh turned earth assailing Theron's nostrils. He heaved himself upward, throwing a shoulder into the attacker's sternum. It stumbled back, taunting him with the possibility of escape.

He tried hurrying past. The monster responded with surprising speed. Gripping his arm, it flung him into a wall, the impact knocking the dolls from their perch and sending them sprawling across the cottage's floorboards.

Dead eyes turned first to the dolls, then to Theron, now on his hands and knees.

"Scream," it hissed. The voice wasn't human. It was a thousand flies buzzing over rotting meat.

Theron rose, ignoring the agony that spread from his chest to his arm. He staggered with the knife still in his hand and raised an exhausted arm to strike. The monster effortlessly shoved him back.

"Scream," the thing said again.

"No," Theron shouted, the defiance surprising him.

A long arm flashed out, and splayed fingers sunk through his soft belly as though it were dough. The hand closed into a fist with inhuman strength, ripping skin and muscle. Theron almost passed out.

It pulled the flesh from his abdomen, bringing with it his intestines.

Theron screamed.

And having started, he couldn't stop.

CHAPTER I

Wherein the remarkable daughter of a famous adventurer fends off an attack and investigates a mystery

THE MEETING OF THE SOCIETY OF WOMEN WAS MORE THAN A DISAPPOINTMENT TO EMBER QUATERMAIN, IT WAS AN INSULT. Ember hastened across mist covered cobbles, weary for the comforts of home, but too riled up to relax. As she walked the thoughts of the meeting consumed her.

If the male establishment knew the superficiality of the Society's radicalism, the old blowhards would sleep well at night rather than post the occasional attack in the *Illustrated London News*.

"We want progress, but certainly not at the expense of propriety," Charity Colridge chastised.

The foremost issue tonight had been hats! Was headgear becoming more than a fashion statement reflecting station and taste, or was it possibly something women could exert more influence on as part of a political identity? It had been difficult for Ember to conceal her frustration at the absurdity of it all.

"You don't change minds by offending people," Charity said in response to Ember's demand for a more active agenda. "You persuade people, win them over to your point of view. One needs to be non-threatening. Feminine. Look at the queen, no one would ever accuse her of lacking femininity."

To her credit, Ember maintained a sober expression.

"You annoy people," her father habitually warned. "I should bring in a tutor, someone who understands etiquette." The irony of such a statement coming from Father was not lost.

She exhaled, expelling her thoughts with a foggy breath that hung in the cold air. Ember turned a corner and paused. This wasn't right. The stench of the neighborhood, the depressing miasma of the Thames—somehow, she made a wrong turn, and now stood in an unsavory neighborhood as the shadows of evening darkened.

Despite a heavy overcoat, a tingling ran up her spine and goose pimples formed across her neck. Raising a collar to the cold, she shoved papers from the meeting into a pocket. Moving serpentine through the streets, she avoided vendors and the occasional carriage that clattered along the narrow thoroughfare. Her father would advise more caution and greater respect for what crept from the poverty and meanness of these streets.

"The city has its own savages," he'd said.

Ember considered her temper. If she hadn't been fuming after her encounter with Charity Colridge, she would have taken a hansom after the meeting, or at the very least given more attention to the street signs and changing neighborhood.

The echo of footsteps gave her pause. They slowed and hastened when she did. Someone kept pace, but advanced cautiously—as if a predator enjoying the chase more than the kill.

Ember relaxed her breathing, calming herself as the pungent reek of the city stung her nostrils. Eyes moving, checking the shadows ahead, she sought out the familiar and comforting shape of a constable on his rounds. The streets lay empty, as if people knew something horrible was about to happen. Costermongers melted into darkness to avoid witnessing the impending event.

Ember wasn't sure if fear governed her now, or anger. Or perhaps both. Quatermains weren't victims. Her back straightened.

The trap closed.

A tall man stepped out of shadow at the end of an alley. He was clumsy, with a red, bulbous nose. He wore a stained and patched linen suit. Were it not for the violent flame burning in his eyes, she would have been disposed toward charity.

Someone else tried moving silently behind her. She backed into the wall of a building as the two men approached. They reminded her of gulls about to dive on market day spoils.

Ember inched sideways, looking for an exit.

"Hello, Miss," the big man said. His voice was deep and unpleasant. Stepping closer, he scratched a rough chin and squinted an eye in appraisal.

"Don't be afeared, Miss. We didn't mean to startle you. Things can be tough here after dark and we thought we might offer ourselves to see you safely to your doorway. Ain't that so, Albert?"

"That's so," the other man said. His voice was soothing.

The first man reached for her arm and she instinctively pulled back.

"Nothing to be afeared of," he grumbled.

Ember searched the street for someone. She considered screaming, but sensed it would only initiate violence. Her heart pounded now and her mouth was dry.

The man moved again, this time a cold flash of steel glinted in his hand.

"It's not always the lions one has to worry about," her father once said. "Sometimes the jackals can be just as dangerous. Don't show them weakness, it only makes scavengers hungrier."

She repressed the panic that crept up her throat. She kept a clear head and opened her petit point handbag.

"If I give you some coin, will you leave me be?"

The taller of the two shrugged.

"Maybe it would be better if you just hand over the entire purse."

"What if she's hiding something on her person?" the other said with a sick giggle. "What if she's hiding something?" he said again. His eyes shone with excitement until his companion silenced him with an impatient gesture.

"She's a pretty thing," the tall robber said. "A bit skinny for my liking, but still a woman for all that."

Ember pulled an egg-shaped crystal from the purse, hating herself for the tears starting to form at the corners of her eyes.

"Here take this! It's worth a great deal. Just leave me alone."

The taller man's eyes widened. Nodding approval, he held out a hand. "Now, that's more like it! What a pretty bauble!"

"A bauble," the other fellow agreed, still cackling. He stepped closer and peered at her. "Still, maybe it's not enough. Maybe we want more."

"Just leave me alone."

The man grinned as his hand closed over her wrist. She fought the instinct to jerk. Instead she slid a thumb over a stud set into the egg's surface. At the same time she turned her head and shut her eyes hard.

The egg popped open, splitting the insulating crystal in half. Brilliant white seared out through the crack and into the night, momentarily banishing darkness and exposing the street in unreal detail.

Her attackers dropped to the ground, grabbing their eyes and screaming in surprised pain. Quickly shoving the egg back in her purse, Ember went to the smaller man.

"Not laughing now," she murmured.

"You think I won't remember you, witch? You think I won't?" Nasty words from a man grabbing at empty air.

"If I were you," she said, "I would be more concerned about me remembering *you*."

Ember might have felt sorry for them; this was the first time she used the device for self-defense, and she had no idea whether or not the incapacitating blindness was permanent. She suspected not. It was stupid to be concerned for them after what they had in mind for her.

Ember assessed the street ahead, struggling to keep a tight hold on her fear. There were surely people watching, but still no one surfaced. She moved swiftly, careful to present a confident gait, but desperate to be inconspicuous.

When Ember drew close to her father's front door she stopped to fix her appearance. She straightened her clothing, hoping to avoid questions or concern. A lock of hair had come free and hung down one cheek, but she could do little without a mirror. She squared her shoulders and approached the ornately carved tamboti-wood door. Before she could ring the bell, the sound of footsteps made her turn. Her hand closed around the crystal egg within her purse.

"Hello then," someone called.

Chief Constable Baker hurried up the walk, his posture so formal one might wonder if his movement was restricted. He was handsome, she supposed. Chestnut hair fell into curly bangs above his brow and he had the sort of boyish face that would stay young even as age slowed his step. His eyes were friendly, but judgmental, if not mocking.

"Out late," he commented.

"I'm just coming home from a meeting."

"Are you?"

His eyes strayed to her hand, still buried in her small cloth purse. "What have you there?"

The tone irritated her and Ember was tempted to show him.

"Have I done something wrong?" she asked.

Her statement appeared to amuse him. Baker toyed with a corner of his moustache. The gesture seemed pretentious; the handlebar worn as evidence of his qualification for leadership and responsibility.

"If you have, I'm sure it's more your father's business than mine," he said. "I'm actually here to see him."

No longer concerned with being accused of anything, Ember bristled at his abrupt manner. It was hardly keeping with the deference he should be giving someone of her class. He reached past her and yanked the bell pull. Another examination of the constable showed strain at the corners of his eyes and a tightness of the jaw. He looked uneasy.

The door swung inward before Ember could confirm her observation. She smiled at the short man standing there, his presence immediately comforting. He looked barely thirty rather than his true age of forty, with smooth dark skin and hair cropped close to his skull.

He frowned at the constable, then peered at Ember with a discerning eye.

"*Jambo bwanas,*" he said in Swahili.

The police officer waved an impatient hand at the African.

"I sent a message that I would be coming. Mr. Quatermain should be expecting me."

"And you've brought Miss Quatermain? How thoughtful."

"We arrived at the same time," Ember said. Her cheeks warmed. Her reaction tickled Hans, the Bantu servant, to the point of laughter.

"So I see," he said.

Ember pushed past Baker and Hans stepped aside to let her pass. She hastened into the long hallway, intending to get upstairs quickly to avoid an encounter with her father. Still, Baker's presence had piqued her curiosity.

She paused on the bottom step. Her hand rested on the banister while she considered how she might discover the nature of his business without sparking scorn.

"Ember."

She turned, head slightly bowed. Allan Quatermain stood outside his study, peering at his daughter with scrutinizing blue eyes. He was a short man, but his wiry frame and powerful shoulders suggested great physical strength.

"You are rather late returning home," Quatermain said. He didn't sound judgmental or critical.

"I suppose I am," she agreed guardedly.

Quatermain's head dropped. A yellow sheet of paper lay on the floor where it had fallen, unnoticed, from Ember's pocket. He pointed to it and snapped his fingers. The police officer, who had now been allowed entrance, quickly bent and handed it to the older man.

Ember knew what was coming. She removed her overcoat and hat, handing them to Hans. Her bodice hung close to a boyish frame and a long skirt fell limply, evidence she'd once again forgot to wear a crinoline.

Her father's friend, the self-important Edward Masterson, emerged from the study. Seeing him, Ember wished herself elsewhere. She felt his gaze and tried to offer a courteous smile. His frosty eyes narrowed as they took in Ember's spoiled appearance. Most of her strawberry hair now swirled wildly about her shoulders, knocked loose from its coiffure.

"'How to make a pressurized canister for the delivery of emulsified chili powder'," Quatermain read. "'Subtitle: safe travelling for the unescorted woman.' Really, Ember? They ran this bit of subversive writing in *The Englishwoman's Review*?"

"Women should be able to protect themselves."

"If women weren't walking the street at night, they wouldn't need protection," Masterson intruded.

Ember's face reddened, but she bit her tongue. Of course, he had to speak his mind. A dozen quick retorts passed through her head, but she knew her father would frown on any rudeness. Especially to one of his oldest friends. Instead, she offered a plaintive expression and prepared for his disapproval.

"We'll talk later," Quatermain said. He shook his head and gestured Masterson back into the study. He remembered Baker and waved at him to join them.

"That's what comes from educating women," Masterson said over his shoulder. "Insubordinate thought, then action."

"Ember is fine," Quatermain countered, his tone cool. "Anyway, she's not your concern."

"I don't mean to offend, but people talk, Allan. That thing she's built on your country estate, when people see that, they'll laugh you out of the club."

"Let them laugh," Quatermain grumbled. "The thing flies. I've flown it myself."

"It's nonsense and you encourage it. You should be a grandfather. Marriage would be the best thing for her. Settle her down."

Masterson's words made Baker's face flush slightly. Seeing this rankled Ember. She wasn't sure if he was embarrassed for her or just a prig. Either way, she resented his presence.

"Come along, Baker. Don't dawdle," Quatermain said.

Playing the good blue coat, who'd been waiting for such acknowledgement from his superiors, he hastened forward. The conversation between Masterson and Quatermain continued.

"I've left her alone too much," her father sighed. "Too many years in Africa. Still, she's quite remarkable; you should see what she has in her workshop."

"No young woman should have a workshop," Masterson protested.

The den's door closed. Shut out again. She sat on the steps, deflated, chin cupped in her palms. Hans pattered over, eyes offering gentle support.

"We control what people think of us," he said. "If you don't like the impression people receive, then change the impression you give."

Ember shrugged. "Masterson is quite right. I'm an odd one. I'm not apologizing for it, but it makes things difficult. My father understands. Sometimes."

Ember's mind strayed to a desk in the workshop she maintained below and the many projects still down there. She wanted to continue work on the egg. It had been surprisingly effective, but the intensity of the burst was greater than anticipated. The white phosphorus proved a success, but it was impractical. She ticked through alternatives and means of controlling the substance's volatility.

"Your father loves you," Hans offered. "You are very much alike."

She looked up at the man, grateful for his effort. No one was as kind to her. Only a foreigner could so freely display emotions.

"I'm not at all like the great Allan Quatermain."

"No, of course you aren't."

"I'm sorry, Hans. I didn't mean to snap at you. I suppose my father and I are somewhat similar. We're both stubborn, both driven. Sometimes I think he only keeps me around because I amuse him so."

"You should not talk this way," he said. "Your father has known great loss and treasures you."

She nodded, warmed by his words. "I suppose you're right."

"He is a lonely man, Miss Quatermain. You are evidence of his humanity and what is best in him."

She stood.

"You come and eat," Hans said. "I'll go ahead and warm something for you."

Ember watched him depart and weighed his words against Masterson's cold assessment. She stared again at the door to the cozy den her father kept. When the meeting within ended, her father would surely confide in her what the police officer was doing here. It was of course none of her business.

She should stop worrying about what didn't concern her and instead have a bite before heading upstairs for bed.

Ember approached the wall beside the door. From her cloth purse she pulled a device—a piece of copper coil wrapped around a magnet and attached to the end of a metal cup. She pushed the cup against the door and amplified the conversation on the other side.

Baker said something about the Underground. Ember moved the cup slightly and his voice came in more clearly.

" . . . as far in as the excavation's progressed. The body was burned beyond recognition, though nothing around it was touched by fire. We think it was one of the workers."

Hearing about the Underground rankled her. That was John Fowler's project. Fowler also announced recent plans to build a fireless locomotive, an idea he stole from Ember, though she couldn't prove it. The engine used steam generated with the assistance of heated bricks. What the dullard didn't realize was the bricks had to be mixed with a catalyst of her invention; otherwise they wouldn't do the job. His design was flawed.

She heard a match being struck and the smell of phosphorous leaked through the doorjamb and keyhole.

"There were some strange artifacts found at the dig," Baker continued. "Some of them were the typical Roman things you'd expect, but others seemed out of place. We know your expertise, Mr. Quatermain, and hope you will come take a look."

"You're worried about some Roman coins and pottery fragments?" her father asked with amusement.

"No, it's just the death was so queer we want to be sure we've taken everything into consideration."

"Baker, you astonish me," Masterson broke in. "What a romantic! How could one be related to the other?"

A finger abruptly tapped Ember on the shoulder. "It's rude to listen in on conversations, Miss Macumazahn," Hans said.

Ember lowered the cup and adopted a properly chastised expression.

"I will put your food in the dining room," he said sternly.

Ember waited for him to go away, and then pressed the device to the wall once more.

"This is really too inconvenient. However, if you are willing, I'd be happy to have my daughter go in my stead. She can record her observations and bring them back."

"You see," Masterson said, "you encourage her."

"She's an amazing young woman, don't you think so, Baker?"

Her father chuckled at what Ember assumed to be embarrassed acknowledgment by the Chief Constable.

"She knows Roman antiquities and she's fiercely intelligent. If something stands out, Ember will pick up on it quickly. She'll do well."

Masterson snorted. "At the very least send Hans as an escort. Don't let her travel down there alone. She's liable to assault someone with pressurized chili powder."

As if she were in the same room, her father spoke without raising his voice.

"Did you hear that, Ember, darling? Of course you did. You'll go first thing in the morning. Baker, do be prompt."

CHAPTER II

Wherein the enigmatic Mr. Styles makes an enemy and is sent on a dark errand

SMOKING WAS A VILE HABIT. The hypocrisy of such a thought brought a slight smile to Peter Styles' well-formed lips. He glanced through his oversized snifter as the man rounded his mouth in an attempt to form rings of smoke. Seen through the amber cognac and the curved glass, Phillip Glaston's already small forehead shrank further and his mouth lengthened so he resembled an ugly red fish.

Peter sipped the cognac and then lowered the snifter. The alcohol warmed him. He reached across the table and picked up one of Glaston's carefully laid out cigars.

"You don't mind, do you old boy?" Peter said.

"I'd rather—"

Peter pinched the cigar between his lips. It had been poorly cut, and bits of dried leaves stuck to his tongue.

"Light?" Peter said out of the corner of his mouth.

The reliable Avery Tressler offered up a flame. Being more of a pipe smoker, Avery held the match too close to the cigar's end.

The taste of burnt smoke mingled with the chocolaty leather of the fine cigar. Despite Glaston's bland personality, he'd chosen flavorful tobacco.

Peter ran a hand through curly black hair and glanced at his cards. Three fives and two fours. A full house.

He studied Glaston's face; one didn't need to be a mind-reader to see the man was pleased at his hand. An image of a card suit teased Peter, but he drove it away. Damaged as his moral compass might be, he wouldn't stoop to use his powers to see what Glaston had. He may be a philanderer, but he was no cheat.

Peter put up a wall between himself and Glaston, who rapped the table with irritation.

"Do you always have to be the center of attention, Styles? Be an adult. If you have the cards, play them. If you don't, get out."

Peter's back stiffened at Glaston's words. So much for his moral compass. Peter opened his mind and picked up the image of a healthy flush—hearts.

Peter casually tossed several chips onto the pile on the table, raising the bet. He turned and smiled at Avery. "I hear you're planning on heading to India," he commented.

Avery raised an eyebrow at the question, obviously surprised at Peter's choice of timing to initiate a discussion of this nature.

"Well, the family business is picking up," Avery said. "I need to make sure our supplies are set at a reasonable price."

"Excellent," Peter said. "Me? I've never had a head for business. I'm a disappointment to my poor father, don't you know? Have you ever been to India, Comstock?"

Joseph Comstock, the fourth man at the table, grunted and stuck out a lower lip as he realized this last question had been addressed to him.

"No," he responded after some time. "The only place I ever travel is to Paris."

"*On m'a dit que les françaises et les anglaises sont pareilles au lit, non?*" Peter quipped.

"Don't be crude," Avery responded. "Someday your indiscretions will be your undoing."

"What man doesn't enjoy a good conquest? Right, Comstock? I've never found platitudes about moderation satisfying."

Glaston shifted in his chair. He had studied his hand this entire time and now stared at Peter with daggers in his eyes.

"Perhaps your obsession with women is a form of compensation," Glaston remarked dryly. He finally pushed several chips into the center of the table to meet Peter's raise. He flipped over his cards like a general declaring war.

Comstock shook his head and exposed a losing hand.

"If my hunger for women is a flaw of character," Peter countered, "then may my flaws continue to aggregate until they supplant any crippling remnants of decency."

Comstock stared at the ceiling while Avery coughed to cover a laugh.

Silence reclaimed the table.

Peter placed his cigar on the edge of the glass ashtray. With Glaston leaning forward in anticipation, he flipped his cards over, one by one, in a display even he would admit ungentlemanly.

Avery rolled his eyes and pushed back from the table. He played with his thick and well-groomed moustache. "Here, here. I can't believe you weren't bluffing. After all this time, you would think I would know you better."

"I've never seen such luck," Comstock drawled good-naturedly.

Glaston hadn't yet moved. He watched Peter scrape the pile of chips to his side of the table. Peter didn't need to read Glaston's mind to pick up on the man's loathing for him.

"Maybe it isn't luck," Glaston said.

"Bad form," Avery murmured. The middle-aged military man rapped the table with his knuckles.

"Are you calling me a cheat, Glaston?" Peter asked. He was amused—insult could only be given if one still had honor to besmirch, and he had lost the last shreds of that long ago.

"No," Avery responded for the other man. "Tell him, you meant nothing of the sort, Phillip."

"I meant precisely what I said."

Glaston sneered at Avery's attempt to intercede. He deflected his fury back at Peter.

"You're an embarrassment, Mr. Styles. I pity your family. The fact your father hasn't cut you off entirely is a testament to his Christian nature. However, other people in our circles won't be charitable. Take care, I think you'll find more and more doors closing to you, until the only ones remaining belong to those already fallen from favor."

With this last comment, Glaston cast a menacing eye on Avery as well.

Peter exhibited complete calm, as if taking Glaston's words to heart for self-improvement.

"That's kind of you to be concerned about my popularity, Glaston," he said at last. "However, I suspect people will continue to invite me to their parties, if only because I am the only person able to keep dinner guests from falling asleep whenever you open your mouth."

Avery turned his head, but his lips pressed hard together to stifle a laugh.

"Mr. Styles, my charity has run out," Glaston said. "I think it best if you leave."

Peter gathered his winnings and tossed them back at Glaston. "Here you go, old man," he said. "You obviously need this more than I do. You might want to pick up something nice for your wife. I think she's developed a taste for lace collars, although I am not sure why she would want to hide such a lovely neck."

Glaston jumped up, knocking over his chair. He approached with hunched shoulders, his posture tense and threatening. Peter put on his hat, displaying lack of concern.

With his teeth clenched, Glaston produced a leather glove from his pocket and struck, slapping Peter first across one cheek, then across the other.

"I demand a chance to defend my wife's honor," Glaston pronounced.

"That must be an exhausting enterprise."

Avery leapt up and interposed himself between the two men. He made clicking sounds with his tongue to keep Peter at bay.

"No one is dueling anyone else," Avery said.

"I accept," Peter announced. He leisurely poured another glass of cognac and threw the liquid back, enjoying its sweet burn.

"No, you do not accept," Avery cautioned.

"I will send a second to make arrangements," Glaston said. "Joseph, would you do me the honor?"

Joseph Comstock shut his eyes at the request. When he opened them again, he sighed and nodded, a defeated expression on his face.

Peter stood and clapped his hands.

"Good. Tressler here will be my second. Now, Mr. Glaston, considering what has passed between us, I suppose I should leave."

Peter strode from the room, Avery Tressler at his heels. The butler handed the gentlemen their coats and hats.

Outside, the cold sobered Peter. He stood at the gate of Glaston Manor and glanced down the narrow boulevard in search of a cab. A hoary frost coated the pavement and London moved in slowed motion. Avery wrapped a muffler about his neck. Sensing a lecture, Peter put his head down and started walking, long legs taking great strides.

"Were you cheating?" Avery asked, keeping pace with him.

"To be honest I don't remember. I might have been," Peter

acknowledged.

"Your abilities obviously don't come from The Lord," Avery griped. "Surely, He would have seen how you abuse them and taken them away by now. I can't believe you would cheat at cards. Bad form. Very bad form."

"Quite right," Peter said, lowering his head.

"Don't you dare look penitent. I won't be mocked. I'm quite probably your only remaining friend," Avery scolded.

Peter put on a properly chastened expression.

Abilities, talents, gifts—all inadequate to describe what Peter did. He saw and heard things others couldn't, channeling impressions from outside the natural world, or at least outside contemporary understanding of that world. A few years ago, some might have burned him for being a witch. In Rome, he would have been called a heretic and then purified.

He always intended to keep the curse to himself, but in time his family found him out and did their best to help insulate him. Thinking of his family made him dour. He walked faster, ignoring the coldness of the night and the heavy breathing of his friend working to keep up with him.

He had cheated.

The more Peter drank the less self-control he exerted. There was no excuse.

"And Glaston's wife?" Avery inquired.

"What about her?"

"Your comment. What it suggested. What you said."

Peter grinned at the embarrassment in his friend's voice.

"If the answer to a question makes you uncomfortable, then perhaps you shouldn't ask in the first place."

"What cheek!"

"What am I supposed to do, Avery? I'm unworthy of your friendship."

Avery folded his arms and grumbled to himself. "One is a child and the other is a horse's ass. However, I have no intention of allowing you and Glaston to fire pistols at one another. We're calling this off. I'm not letting it happen."

"Of course you won't, why else do you think I chose you as a second?"

"You never meant to go through with it?"

"Do you blame me? The man has a reputation."

"*Some tricks, some quillets, how to cheat the devil,*" Avery replied snidely. He tapped the street with his cane for emphasis. The quote was a game they played. How angry could Avery be with him if he issued such a challenge? Peter searched his memory and came up with the solution.

"*Love's Labour Lost.*" Shakespeare. He came back with a challenge of his own.

"*Has friendship such a faint and milky heart?*"

Avery considered this but signaled surrender.

"*Timon of Athens,*" Peter said, identifying the quote.

"Really? Nobody reads *Timon of Athens.*"

"And you call yourself a scholar."

"You're an ass," Avery said, and Peter didn't have to search his mind for the origin of the quote.

⚷

A shade waited for them at Peter's apartment. A darkness unmoving. The man pressed close to the brick building, impossible to find unless he chose to be seen. He manifested by stepping out as the two gentlemen sought entrance.

"Mr. Styles? I've brought a message."

The voice was horrible. A tortured hissing. The words that followed formed slowly, as if each syllable produced tremendous pain for the speaker.

Peter stopped, throwing up an arm to hold Avery from advancing. He braced himself and let the mind of the shadowy figure touch him.

"Who is it?" Avery asked.

"I think it best if you go," Peter warned him.

"I'm not leaving you to this cutpurse."

"I can handle him," Peter said. "It would be best if you left, but at least keep your distance."

Avery wasn't satisfied, but advanced no further. Although the reek of the charnel house threatened to overwhelm him, Peter closed on the wretched man.

"Eastbourne Terrace," the man rasped. "Tomorrow, the new tunnel for the trains."

Anger crackled through Peter's mind as the monster came closer. The eyes were sunken, almost useless within their sockets. Gray skin cracked at the cheek and split open at the forehead. Black lips peeled back revealing dark gums and yellowed teeth.

Avery gasped and raised his cane as a weapon. "What are you?" he cried.

With dazzling speed the thing came under Avery's defense, knocking the cane aside and throwing an arm about his neck. Peter knew the monster would kill him in an instant.

"Don't!" Peter commanded. "If you want my cooperation, you'll let him go."

It freed Avery with a push and turned to face Peter. It swayed from side to side, like a giant ape.

"What am I supposed to find there?" Peter asked. "What does your master want?"

The thing reached out, dirty fingers painfully gripping his shoulder. Its strength was inhuman.

"I was told to tell you, you'll know when you find it. It is very old, and it has power."

"Why doesn't Virgil go himself? Can your master hear me?" Peter challenged.

The horrible face pressed closer. "You have no idea how hard this is for me. This close, all I can think of is crushing your skull."

Peter's demeanor changed. He stood erect and squared his shoulders. His inner vision expanded so he could see the connective energy glowing between the walking corpse and its necromancer. The thaumaturgical signature was unmistakable—Virgil.

He didn't know the man's identity, each face-to-face meeting was carefully arranged and Virgil always remained hidden behind a pair of masks, one physical and one psychic.

Summoning power, Peter lifted a hand and closed his fingers, imagining them crushing the filaments between necromancer and puppet. The messenger's knees bent and its head rolled back. It staggered, a death rattle emanating from its throat. Clawing the air, batting at an unseen enemy, the monster fell back into the shadows.

Peter released it.

The dead man leaned against the wall and hissed at them. "You're hanging over a cliff, Styles. Be careful you don't fall."

The tone of the voice had changed. He knew he heard Virgil. Having issued such a warning, the messenger pushed away from the building and pivoted into the blackness.

"What was that?" Avery croaked.

Peter didn't want to say anything; he worried about unnecessarily exposing his friend to danger. He also didn't want to share his shame. However, he owed Avery the truth. He knew his friend a believer who wouldn't dismiss him with a skeptic's sneer.

"He was one of the '*nekroanypomonos.*' The restless dead."

Avery considered his words and stared after the thing. Fear and disapproval shaded his friend's features.

"It's been years since I've felt such evil," he said. "It's been years."

Peter didn't respond. He put an arm around his friend's shoulders and guided him inside the building.

"You told me you were done with this," Avery said. He rapped his cane hard against the tiled floor of the foyer. "You promised."

"I am."

"The walking corpse below would suggest otherwise."

"I didn't conjure that monstrosity, Avery. I had nothing to do with it."

Peter unblocked his mind, expanding awareness and sensitivity, looking for the presence of other threats. He felt Mr. Hogan on the floor below. Abandoned a month ago by a shrewish wife, the man now wallowed in the meaninglessness of life. The pain awakened Peter's own miseries, memories best left set aside.

With a shudder, he retreated and put back the walls, not wanting to see her face or hear her name.

Satisfied there was no other threat, he opened the door and gestured Avery in before him.

"I'm a former seaman, Peter. I know things. I've seen things. I learned the hard way to turn my back on the stuff of nightmares. You continue this path and it will end badly. It's one thing to sully a reputation, but a sullied soul is less easily mended."

"Stop lecturing me."

Avery sat in his usual wing-backed chair, a disgruntled expression on his face. Although slightly overweight, he still had broad shoulders and a barrel chest. Youthful eyes stood out against age lines scored across his forehead and on either side of his nose.

The two friends sat quietly. Peter contemplated Virgil. Just when he thought he had closed the book on that part of his life, it blew open with a vengeance. Maybe Avery was correct, maybe the only way this could end was "badly."

"What are you planning?" Avery asked.

"I don't follow?"

"Are you planning on going to Paddington? Are you going to see what Virgil wants?"

Peter didn't respond. Virgil knew he would find the lure of such a challenge irresistible. The necromancer wanted it badly, but sending a lackey was risky, and the man wouldn't come himself and risk discovery. Virgil obviously thought he still controlled Peter to some degree, or hoped involving Peter in this enterprise would rekindle their relationship. The man was in error. Virgil's path was too dangerous and too corrupt.

Bad luck having Avery present as Virgil played his card. His friend was precious to him, and the man had exposed himself to too much danger in his life. He didn't deserve to be cast once more into a cauldron.

"Do me a favor," Peter said. He reached behind him and removed a sheathed blade from his belt. He carefully handed it to Avery. "I want you to take this."

"I have a blade, thank you." Avery raised his cane and nodded at its handle. "And should that fail, I have my revolver."

"A revolver will do no good against what you saw tonight. Nor will just any blade."

Avery reluctantly accepted the weapon and examined it. His brow furrowed with disapproval and Peter feared he would reject the gift.

"You've etched in some symbols," Avery said. "You know I don't approve of this sort of thing."

"Humor me, Avery."

His friend held the blade to the light and turned it over. "Is this silver?"

"If you drive the blade into one of the *nekroanypomonos* with enough physical violence, you can sever the tie between the necromancer and the risen."

Avery stashed the blade into the folds of his coat.

"You never answered my question. Are you planning on going to Paddington? What will happen if you don't go?"

Peter shrugged and slouched further in his chair. He studied the window, lost in thought, and tried remembering when life became so complicated.

"I'm sure I'm not the only one in the game," Peter said at last.

"Meaning?"

"Meaning Virgil has other plans and I'm more than likely an afterthought. It shows how little regard he has for me."

"Do you want me to go with you?" Avery asked.

"I don't think so. It won't be much. I'll nose around and see what he's worked up about."

"And if you find something?" Avery inquired.

"I'll make sure I keep it from him."

"I wish you would tell me his name," Avery grumbled. "If this Virgil is such a threat, we should deal with him."

Peter spread his arms. "I don't know who he is."

Avery scoffed, but Peter leaned forward with a stern expression.

"Seriously, Avery. I've only known him by the one name he gave me when we first met, at a masquerade in the countryside. The less said about that the better."

"Virgil," Avery mumbled. "And you're his Dante?"

Avery stood and walked to the window to peer into the street, perhaps to see if the restless dead still lurked in the shadows. Avery seldom spoke of the things he'd seen in the war against the Sikh, and later while serving as the first mate of a slave ship, but those experiences had transformed him. Avery believed in the uncanny, no matter what face he put on when exposed to the dark.

"We live in perpetual shadow," Avery once remarked, while in his cups. "We're tied to our propensity for cruelty and self-destruction. I've seen the things that go bump in the night and they pale beside the personal demons we accrue and the sins we tally."

Avery continued staring out the window now, his face forlorn. The only sound in the room was the occasional sputter of candle wax.

"I'll see Glaston tomorrow," Avery said.

"To what end?"

"To see if his temper has cooled and what might be done to avoid this absurd duel."

"He'll want a public apology," Peter cautioned. Avery turned and raised his eyebrows. Peter smiled grimly and stood. He clapped a hand on his friend's shoulder.

"Don't worry, if he so demands, I'll oblige. I have no pride to defend. If he insists on following through, I'll do the honorable thing. Put on a good show. Maybe even point my gun in his direction."

Avery remained silent. He looked as though he might chide Peter for his response, but instead gave a nod of acceptance.

CHAPTER III

Wherein Miss Quatermain and the Chief Constable go to Paddington where they encounter another mystery, and Miss Quatermain meets the striking Peter Styles

TROUBLE SLEEPING BROUGHT EMBER TO THE WORKSHOP BEFORE THE SUN PIERCED THE THICK CLOUD COVER. An uncharacteristically chilly May heralded the threat of a storm and the tension in the predawn air matched her uneasiness. Within the workshop though, many of Ember's cares dimmed; this sanctum was her world and she was entirely in control.

The bazaar of vials, beakers, crystal globes, loose quartz, mirror fragments, and other breakables reflecting the muted lantern light, created a strange landscape of her crafting. She liked glass. Glass and crystal embraced change. Glass shielded and threatened, it allowed in light and at the same time could manipulate it in so many ways. Glass was illusory. Glass was misunderstood and fragile.

Ember leaned over the workbench, distracted. The violence of the night before still haunted her. She thought of the danger and considered what might have happened had the crystal egg not worked. Remembering the two men dropped to the cobblestones in blindness, she didn't feel at all sorry for them. Such predators got what they deserved.

Masterson might disapprove of young women walking the streets unescorted, but even he would have been impressed by how she got herself out of a bad situation. She recalled his words about her airship and bristled.

Ember placed a leather strap about her head, monocles of varying magnification dangling from the band on delicate chains. She ignited a burner and went to work on a present for her nephew Harry. With a squint, she held the most powerful lens in place and spun a miniscule metal rod tipped with hot glass. When the glass was a perfect sphere, she dipped the glowing ball in a barrel of water. It hissed as it cooled from red to icy blue.

She cracked the tiny orb from its stem, setting the fragile piece down gently next to its twin. Examining her handiwork, she scooped up the tiny orbs and went to the next workstation.

Gears and metal pieces littered the surface of another bench. Among the mess sat a small, copper horse. She picked it up, and with steady fingers, slipped tiny eyes into their respective sockets before securing metal slivers of eyelids to hold them into place.

The horse stared at her vacantly.

"Harry will love you," she said.

She turned the windup mechanism protruding from its back. Gears whirred as the head tossed and the equine legs kicked into a prance. Perfection.

What had her father thought when hearing Masterson's chiding the night before? "You should be a grandfather."

That stung.

So had Chief Constable Baker's sympathies. The man's sentiments made everything in the workshop seem a selfish indulgence. Worse, they implied she was deficient and either unwilling or unable to attract a man.

When the gears wound down and the mechanical horse stalled she tucked the miniature treasure into her purse. She progressed toward the lantern, but stopped to study herself in the cheval glass.

Not bad to look at. Perhaps a bit underfed. She imagined a man's kiss at the silky alabaster nape of her neck, and shivered. Could Mr. Baker be interested in someone as unconventional as herself? Ridiculous. The Chief Constable would want someone less challenging and perhaps malleable and old-fashioned.

"I should have been born in another time," she said to the mirror. "I surely don't belong here."

Hans' voice tumbled down the stairs. "Miss Macumazahn, the Chief Constable is here for you."

She checked herself in the cheval glass. The reflection returned the image of a pale woman with humble beauty. She lingered for a last look before she blew out the lantern and hurried up the stairs.

Squeezed between Hans and Baker on the small seat of the hansom cab, Ember was barely conscious of the crowding or the distraction of the driver, James, who jostled in the sprung seat behind them. Instead images of a horseless carriage passed through her mind, the vehicle careening along at breakneck speed as steam-powered pistons turned the wheels. Ember pressed back in the seat as her invention accelerated.

"Is there a limit to how fast we go?" she asked herself. "Is it possible accelerating at too fast a rate would be dangerous?"

"Do you do that often?" Baker asked.

She opened her eyes and stared at him. "What?"

"Talk to yourself?"

Ember's face burned.

"Miss Quatermain is a brilliant woman," Hans replied. "Sometimes all that brilliance just overflows."

The coach turned onto Eastbourne Terrace, west of the dig site. Baker pointed a long finger toward a sign for Praed Street.

"Not far now," he commented.

They were an hour into their journey, and Ember was of the opinion they could have run to Paddington faster. Through the window, she watched the smear of buildings in the damp, foggy air. The gaslamps, which should have been doused at dawn, remained lit to combat the bleak drizzle. They were little more than dreary spots of orange in the persistent gray. As they passed St. Mary's Hospital, tiny puddles formed on wet cobblestones.

Ember produced a box the size of a deck of cards. It was made of polished cherry wood and copper with a hole cut out in the center. She fiddled with it, effortlessly slipping thin glass panels from their light-proof fabric wrappings into a shielded slot.

"What's that?" Baker asked.

"It will create an image of the site for father."

"Like a camera? It's so miniscule. Where's the tripod?"

Ember smirked, pleased at his wonderment. "It doesn't need one."

"How does it work?"

Baker leaned in to inspect the device, and his closeness surprised her. She spoke quickly, suddenly embarrassed by the attention, and pointed out the different components and how they worked together.

He laughed and gave his head a shake. "I'm sorry," he said. "It's still mostly incomprehensible to me. Where did you get such an idea?"

"I don't quite know what happens," she said simply.

She thought about it and almost remained silent on the matter. He watched her with an encouraging expression.

"I see things in my mind," she said haltingly. "The pieces are there, patterns emerge, and suddenly it all comes together. Puzzle solved. What was difficult to imagine is suddenly clear."

"You make it sound like something mystical."

Verbalizing her ability made her aware of how unsatisfactory the explanation was. Her ability, whatever it was, wherever it came from, was the thing that most often made her feel like an outsider. And yet it also gave her a sense of pride.

Seeing admiration spread across Baker's face deeply pleased Ember. She openly studied him, forgetting modesty and social etiquette. He was attractive, though not in a rugged fashion, but rather in a quiet, respectable way. This one was a man at peace, a steady man, and a leader. She could sorely use a kind, stable man in her life.

The cab bounced over a patch of uneven road and their fingers brushed. She caught the scent of cologne and beeswax pomade. Ember's hand lighted on his, her boldness surprising her.

"Miss Macumazahn?" Hans said deadpan.

Baker jerked upright. "Sorry," he mumbled.

Ember stuffed the camera box in her purse. Her posture became rigid once again and she raised an eyebrow at her father's manservant. He smiled back, but his eyes disapproved. She was about to say something, then decided to avoid the humiliation.

"Macumazahn," Baker said. "You've called her that before. What does it mean?"

"It means *Watcher-by-Night*," Ember said.

"That's an unusual name."

"Miss Ember is a most unusual woman," Hans said, a wry grin turning the corners of his mouth. "The name alludes to her keen instincts."

James tugged the horse to a halt in front of a cut-and-cover tunnel and scrambled down from his perch to open the cab's door. Hans stepped out first, feet squishing in the mud. He offered Ember his hand, and bore her weight while she descended gracefully. Baker placed a hand on each side of the door and used a sliding technique to avoid splashing. He turned and marched into the lead, leaving Ember to swallow a snicker at the dirty streaks smearing the lower half of his trousers where he'd rubbed against the cab. Hans noted the object of her humor and frowned.

"James," Ember said pressing a coin into the driver's hand, "we'll likely be quite a while. I saw the baked potato vendor half a block back if you're hungry."

He removed his hat, bowing slightly. "I'll be here when you get back."

"Come on, Miss Macumazahn, we're falling behind."

Ember hurried to catch Baker. Around her, the sprawl of demolished ghetto properties lay in ruins as the area was transformed for the creation of the Underground. A long section of trench was fully excavated and roofed over, and there were already several ventilation shafts installed. At the furthest end, the trench forked. On the left branch, men with wheelbarrows pushed loads of covering materials while balancing on overhead support beams.

Baker stooped and retrieved a lantern from the ground, lighting it before strolling through the entrance.

"Stay close to me," he said.

Hans followed immediately after Baker, leaving Ember to trail behind as the mouth of the tunnel swallowed them. She nearly trod on Hans' heels. It wasn't just the darkness, but the feel of the tunnel. The air here made her uneasy. Hair along her arms and the back of her neck tingled as it rose.

The underground silence swallowed them. Strange it had that effect; Ember followed her father into many underground digs and never felt such uneasiness. Mr. Baker still moved ahead of them, but his steps seemed more cautious now.

"It's not far now," he said softly.

The flickering lantern light bathed the newly exposed roots and rocks in an eerie glow. A piece of bone jutted from the dirt, a femur partially ground away by the excavation. It should have been extracted and properly laid to rest. Perhaps no one else had spotted it. Or perhaps no one had wanted to.

Baker stopped suddenly.

"Miss Quatermain, I must once again caution you that what you are about to see is quite ghastly. I question the wisdom in allowing you down here."

Ember considered the patronizing statement, but instead of being insulted, she almost agreed. The air here pressed against the skin and reinforced the mounting sense of claustrophobia.

"I appreciate your concern, Chief Constable. However, my father would be extremely disappointed if I didn't complete the task assigned me."

"Hans?" Baker implored the manservant.

"Sir, as soon as you questioned her, you ensured her determination. We will go on."

The police officer grimly examined both their faces before turning and holding out the lantern. They advanced slowly on the site.

"*Wallah*," Hans muttered, pressing a fist to his forehead.

A charred corpse stretched on the ground in tortured sprawl. The soil beneath the body appeared fused, as if melted from a discharge of tremendous energy. Ember pictured the man those petrified remains represented and fought a sudden bitter taste at the back of her mouth. She froze, seeking calm for the task at hand. This was a puzzle to be solved. Each bit of information needed to be stored and reorganized until a pattern emerged where none was yet visible.

"It's ghastly, yes?" Baker asked.

"It is," she agreed.

Ember kept the horror from her face. Mindful of her mission, she lifted the camera and aimed it at the dead figure. It took tremendous effort to keep her fingers from trembling as she exposed one of the small gel plates. She changed the device's settings to compensate for lack of illumination and slipped in another plate for exposure.

"Poor soul," she said. "I hope it happened fast and that he did not suffer."

"The workers in the area insisted there was no fire," Baker said. "Only a flash of light and the smell of ozone. Only seconds passed before they saw the light and headed down here to find him."

"Like lightning?" Ember asked.

Baker grunted. Ember approached the wall of the Underground and ran her palm along the exposed earth looking for evidence of scorching. Nothing.

"I've heard of this sort of thing before," Baker continued, "but I always thought it so much doggerel. People don't spontaneously incinerate."

Something metallic caught Ember's attention. She crouched to examine a small collection of coins only a yard from the dead man's feet. She bent down and lifted one of the coins. She turned it in the lantern light and ran a thumb over the embossing. It was definitely Roman.

Baker hastened to her side to cast lantern light further down the tunnel.

"These are the items the workers uncovered," he announced. His tone sounded absurdly formal, but his eyes were wide with uncertainty. He met her gaze and quickly looked away.

Ember returned her attention to the grisly scene. Near the coins, previously cloaked by darkness and a bit of soil, sat a *pugio*, a Roman dagger. Rust or something else stained much of the ugly weapon's blade.

Hans instructed Baker to hold the light source nearer. Ember took a few more images before spying something interesting among the small collection of Roman objects.

She reached out and closed her fingers about a strange triangular stone fragment. Under the thick patina, it was green, almost jade-like. While most of the carvings were rubbed away, she could make out a small sun, with sixteen rays emanating from its center.

What was familiar about this? Ember remembered another symbol from a book in her father's impressive library. Only that one had eight rays. She must consult someone with greater arcane knowledge about its meaning, doubting that even her father would know what the sixteen rayed sun symbolized.

Next to where she found the fragment was a rectangular patch of loose soil, as if a box of some kind had been sitting there. She re-examined the small triangular stone, wondering if it might have come from the missing box. She scanned the area a second time to check for any other odd shapes or fragments.

Ember turned to Baker. "I'd like to speak to the workers who were present."

Baker shook his head. "There's no need. I already have their statements. Besides, I'm interested to know if these Roman artifacts have any value, if they might have served as a motive for murder—"

"You can't be suggesting this poor wretch was murdered," Ember said incredulously. "According to your description of the testimony of the workmen—"

"I'll admit this is an odd case," Baker interrupted. "However, I won't rule out any possibility until I'm satisfied it's been disproven."

"What?" Ember asked. "Did someone strangle this man and then hurl a lightning bolt to make it seem like an act of God?"

"Miss Quatermain," Hans said sternly.

"Begging your pardon, Chief Constable," Ember said, her tone far from repentant. "Were this a murder and acquiring the artifacts a motive, then wouldn't the person committing murder know the artifacts were here, underground, waiting to be discovered? How does that make any sense?"

Before he could answer, the sound of quickening footsteps and the visage of another constable bathed in the glow of a lantern closed on them. He was a barrel-chested man with eyes set too close together and a tight mouth. He appeared nervous, his eyes darting back and forth, but conspicuously avoiding falling on the corpse.

"What is it, Cornwall?" Baker asked.

The officer lowered the lantern and chewed his lower lip.

"I don't want to say in front of the lady."

Ember scoffed at the absurdity of the statement in light of their present surroundings. "What is it?" Baker asked again, this time his tone conveying an order.

Cornwall nodded deferentially and gestured the way he had come.

"I came to tell you we found another body. Burned. Like this fellow. I thought you would want to know immediately."

They followed Cornwall from the tunnel and down Bishop's Bridge Road. Baker tried persuading Ember to return to the cab and wait there with James, but she brushed off his arguments, pointing out the two incidents were more than likely connected. That, and her expertise with the miniature camera, along with her investigative prowess at the earlier scene, made her indispensable.

Baker gave up with a disgruntled expression. Ember found herself once more at the rear of a procession. As she hurried to keep up with them, she thought about the rectangular depression in the dirt and hoped the artifact would be at this next site.

She remembered James.

"Constable Cornwall? Could you have someone tell our driver where we'll be? He's on the other side of the excavation."

"I'll send someone." The man sounded irritated.

As they moved away from the excavation, they passed along a narrow street toward the still intact neighborhoods of Paddington. A gray drabness characterized the buildings here; factories, public houses, and individual dwellings crowded together and gave testament to the area's poverty.

At the end of one street they found several constables milling about and keeping the curious at a distance.

Ember turned in time to see Baker receive a business card from a tall policeman. She waited as he studied it, his mouth drawing downward in distaste.

"Who does it belong to?" Ember asked.

"Miss Macumazahn," Hans scolded. "Where are your manners?"

"It's from a Peter Styles," Baker said. He glared at the constable who had given him the card.

Ember knew of him. London society gossips never tired of stories about his rakish behavior and how his conduct was quickly stripping him of the considerable power of his station. Styles could easily have risen to a position of power in the government if he had chosen, but instead his charms were wasted on hedonistic pursuits. Ember's curiosity piqued. What was someone like Peter Styles doing here?

"Don't stand there," Baker snarled. "Send him over."

"Yes sir."

The constable hurried away and returned a moment later with a handsome man in a dark overcoat wrapped tightly around a narrow frame. He leisurely made his way to Baker, giving the Chief Constable a condescending nod. When he spotted Ember, one eyebrow arched and his lips slid into a broad smile. The man's gaze swept provocatively over her frame, amazing Ember with its intensity and pull.

Hans scowled but remained silent.

Ember did not return his stare, waiting until he'd turned his attention back to Baker before studying him in quick, covert glances.

Baker's face remained expressionless in response to the man's caustic presence, no doubt a political skill the Chief Constable learned in dealing with his betters.

"Mr. Styles, may I help you?" Baker asked.

"You're in charge here, Chief Constable? I'm surprised Detective Branch didn't assign a detective to the case."

"I'm from Detective Branch."

"Indeed? Then you must know Commissioner Maine gave me access to this site."

Baker's face reddened.

"Why would you want access?"

"I am representing a personage who finds the facts thus reported to be of extreme interest."

"May I ask, sir, who this personage might be?"

"No, Mr. Baker, you may not."

Styles smiled again, this time a cold warning. Ember didn't like this bullying manner. She stepped closer and he looked her way again, his shadowed eyes a dark contrast to his fair skin. Intrigued and chagrined by the man's tactless impertinence, she boldly challenged his gaze. Styles looked away and leaned into Baker, addressing him with placating familiarity.

"I have no intention of becoming a nuisance," Styles said in a soothing voice. "I respect the work you do and the challenges you must face. However, I assure you, the strangeness of this death is within my realm of expertise, and perhaps in that respect I can be of assistance to you."

"Are you a physician then?" Ember asked.

Styles returned his attention to her, eyes crackling with mischief.

"I apologize," he said. "I've been unforgivably rude, Miss Quatermain. You are Ember Quatermain, yes?"

Ember smiled curtly in reply.

"Your most recent writings caught my attention. Using compressed chili powder—quite ingenious!" He produced a business card and slipped it into her purse. Hans's eyes widened, but Ember turned her back to his scrutiny.

"Very well, sir. Very well," Baker stammered. "I think it best if we continue about our business then. We've just left the first body."

Baker's rudeness surprised her, although she could understand it given Styles' demeanor.

"Two deaths? Well, that would seem to rule out a coincidental act of God, don't you think?" Styles asked.

"I never speculate, Mr. Styles."

Baker further stiffened his posture and led the way to a shabby house. He paused at the front door to examine the hinges, running large hands over the wood. Mr. Styles stayed close to Ember, his face expressionless save for his constantly moving eyes.

"What do you make of that?" Ember asked. She directed attention to an adjacent window that was pried outward.

"I would say someone used a crowbar to force the window open," Baker remarked.

Styles approached and ran a finger along the sash. He removed his hat and scratched at the back of untidy midnight curls.

"I don't think someone used a crowbar," Peter observed. "It looks like someone pried the window open with their fingers instead."

"What?" Ember asked, stepping closer.

"Impossible!" Baker interjected.

"Yes, I suppose you're correct," Styles said. He stepped back and gave Ember a quick nod. "Miss Quatermain, I think I'll head in and watch the Chief Constable at work. I'm always fascinated by the law."

"I'll join you momentarily," she said.

As the men proceeded into the house, Ember hung back to comment to Hans.

"This Styles is a bit full of himself, don't you think?"

Hans considered her words with a furrowed brow and raised his index finger for emphasis as he spoke. "Be careful around that one. There's something about this Mr. Styles, something I do not like. There's darkness in him. Trust me, Miss Macumazahn."

"I think you overstate things," Ember said.

"No. I've seen this in people back home. He has an unhappiness which makes him dangerous."

She weighed Hans' words against her own impression of the man as she paused to capture an image of the windowsill. The idea of someone using their fingers to pry it open struck her as absurd. She peered closely at the wood and noticed something dark smeared into the grain. Along with something else. Ember leaned closer and uneasily recognized a bit of fingernail wedged under a splinter.

Ember put another lens on her device and moved the box close for a picture.

Good eyes, Mr. Styles.

Ember left the window and gestured for Hans to accompany her into the house. When she stepped inside, she had to struggle to catch her breath. The thick air choked her and her stomach rebelled at the overwhelming stench of ozone, and something else: putrefaction. "You feel it, don't you?" Hans whispered. He touched his chest, pressing his fingers to a charm worn under his shirt. "Kufa Hakwishi," he uttered. *Dying never ends.*

Despising her own weakness, Ember straightened, and walked stiffly into the other room where Baker and Styles leaned over the blackened remains. She watched them, taking heart in the fact that both men looked as though they too fought the rancid air about them.

Ember had one gel plate remaining. She steadied the box, but decided at the last moment not to capture the image of this tragedy. Instead, she handed her invention off to Hans and circled the dead man. She hoped he had no wife or children who would be forced to mourn his loss or struggle to support themselves in his absence.

Looking at the deceased, she noticed scorched wood about the body and thought of the amazing amount of energy necessary to do this to a human. How had the house not burned to the ground around him? A small change purse lay nearby, the leather still smoldering.

Ember gathered strength and stooped beside the burnt remains. The corpse's arms and legs bent at awkward angles where no joints existed, and blackened lengths of splintered bone protruded from melted skin. Only an unimaginable electrical discharge could produce muscle contractions strong enough to snap bones. The organs surely burned within as the energy crackled through him.

She picked up the purse and dumped out the fused coins. In her mind, a pattern formed, like the pieces of a puzzle snapping into place. In spite of the horror that lay before Ember, she innately processed the scientific realities suggested by the plight of the two charred corpses—that light, electricity, and magnetism were all manifestations of the same thing.

She stored the hypothesis for later examination.

"Miss Macumazahn." Hans shook her gently.

"I'm fine," she said with an emphasis to discourage further inquiry.

She collected herself. Since childhood, when in the midst of stress, her mind lapsed into a machinelike state where she emotionlessly gathered information and processed it. Many of her inventions came to her this way. The design for the prototype of an airship was born when she and her father heatedly argued over her brother Harry.

She watched Baker scribble notes. Styles remained at the opposite end of the room, an expression of intense concentration on his face. He abruptly strode to Hans and presented him with his walking stick, which her father's manservant accepted as if it were capable of coming to life and striking him.

Styles closed his eyes and stood still. Baker became aware of his inaction and approached.

"Are you quite all right?" Baker asked. His voice expressed concern.

"Three men broke into the house, Chief Constable. They forced the window and made their way to the corpse. The man was dead when they entered. They stole something from the corpse's hand."

"Three men?" Baker asked with a patient smile. "How do you deduce this?"

Styles pointed to the windowsill.

"One of them had to boost the other over the sill."

"And the third?"

"The third stood guard."

Baker rolled his eyes. He turned from Styles, but stopped and came back a step.

"And how do you know the one who boosted the other didn't just stay outside as sentry?"

"Footprints here. Two men."

The Chief Constable snorted. Styles shut his deep-set eyes and expelled a long breath. When he opened them again, he directed a finger at the corpse.

"If you look at the man's hand, you'll find a portion of the palm has been only slightly singed," Styles said. "The area suggests he held something about three inches in width and just over four in length. It had to be small enough for the man to secret it from the dig site."

Baker looked at Ember askance, but she continued watching Mr. Styles. He shut his eyes again. "But it's all conjecture, of course."

"Of course," Baker sneered.

Styles opened his eyes. He grinned wolfishly and strode across the room, snatching his cane back from Hans. Ember watched him with amusement. She considered whether Mr. Styles naturally cultivated a sense of mystery, or whether it was merely an affectation. Rude, self-absorbed, arrogant; Styles was all these things, and yet she confessed, she couldn't help being drawn to him.

"Three men, Chief Constable," Styles said. "You don't need me after all."

"And what about the object in the dead man's hand?" Ember asked.

Styles gave her a penetrating glance and she felt her modesty stripped away. She almost turned, but didn't want to belie her discomfort.

"Yes, what about the object?" Baker seconded.

"You're the one from Detective Branch, Chief Constable."

With that, Styles headed briskly out the front door.

"What cheek," Baker muttered almost too softly to be heard.

Ember decided to follow Mr. Styles, but found Hans blocking her way after a couple strides.

"No, no, no . . . " he whispered. "That one is an agent of *weusi*,"

"I'm sure I don't understand your meaning," she responded.

"You know my meaning, Miss."

Ember did not engage him in debate.

Another policeman entered the house.

"Chief Constable, there's been another murder. Three bodies, about a block away."

Baker straightened, brushing dust from his uniform. "Burned?"

"Oh no, sir. I'm not sure how these chaps died, bludgeoned or knifed perhaps. Maybe both, by the look of them. But I'll tell you this, their bodies are quite ripe."

"*Weusi*," Hans uttered.

CHAPTER IV

Wherein Mr. Styles investigates and attracts nefarious attention

IMMEDIATELY OUTSIDE THE HOUSE, PETER LEANED AGAINST A LAMP POLE. He gathered his wits, glad to be done with this errand. His senses had been assaulted not just by the stench of seared flesh, but by the rot of the restless dead and a throb of psychic energy greater than any he'd ever felt before.

It took strong hands to damage the windowsill, inhumanly strong and aided by supernatural powers. The aura left behind by the three *nekroanypomonos* he detected was vile. It hung in the air like a cloud of pure hatred.

If the victim in the house hadn't been blasted by some mysterious energy, he surely would have been torn apart by the restless dead whose presence overwhelmed him.

As for what actually killed the worker, Peter didn't have a clue. If given time and left alone, he might sift through the psychic imprint left behind by such violence, but Baker would hardly give him room to maneuver. Of course, Baker wasn't the issue. The man was a victim of his own skepticism and rigidity. Miss Quatermain, on the other hand, might start asking pointed questions.

He liked her tremendously. She had spirit that one, and a quick intellect. Miss Quatermain had approached the crime scene with an eye which missed little. With a grim smile, Peter remembered her stooping over the dead man, trying to make sense of the strangeness of the death.

Recalling the scene, Peter considered the dead man's palm. What had he been holding? Obviously the prize that interested Virgil.

Peter considered the mystery at hand.

The dead man in the tunnel must have found whatever artifact Virgil treasured and somehow unintentionally released its power.

The second fellow likely spied the item beside his fallen fellow and absconded with it before the arrival of the authorities.

Since it didn't destroy the chap immediately at the dig site, the artifact either had to re-energize, or something the man did set the thing off.

A dangerous relic was now loose in London, made worse in the hands of whoever summoned those corpses. Worse, the summoner hadn't been Virgil. So who?

Peter turned and studied the street, uneasy as he watched the people milling about. Since setting out for Paddington, he felt someone following him. It wasn't Virgil—the necromancer was an impenetrable blank zone. Nor was it one of Virgil's summoning. Peter would know if he were being shadowed by one of the restless dead. This was someone else or something else.

He checked the street again and pushed his consciousness into the shadows. This game had two players he could see, Virgil and the one who had summoned the three dead men to retrieve the artifact. The involvement of a third party stretched credibility.

The prize must be great to draw so many flies.

There.

A matron with winter blue eyes and silver hair caught his attention. She looked away quickly, a playful smile on her lips. Peter reached out psychically, but before he could focus attention, the door to the front of the house opened and Ember emerged, behind her Hans, then Baker. The matron was gone, lost to him.

Peter considered going after the woman, but he didn't have much hope of success.

Baker approached and laid a hand on Peter's back. The police officer leaned forward with concern.

"Are you still here, Mr. Styles? Is everything all right?"

"I'm fine, Chief Constable. The smell was a bit much for me."

Ember Quatermain's pale gray eyes probed him. He was tempted to collect her thoughts, but stopped himself, not certain if he wanted to know what he would uncover. Flirtatious or disapproving thoughts would both be equally unsatisfying. Or worse, he might find she was not thinking of him at all. Baker gave him a reassuring pat. Perhaps seeing Peter in discomfort made his unexplained power less threatening to the Chief Constable.

"If you're up for it, there's been yet another development," Baker said.

Peter stepped away from the lamppost. He waited for Baker to continue.

"Three more bodies in a field not far from here. I doubt they're connected, except for their strangeness." The sun was high in the sky, hidden behind a dense cloud cover. Peter glanced up, thinking how far from darkest night they were. Daylight dimmed Peter's thaumaturgical abilities.

"Three more bodies? Quite the scandal, Chief Constable," Peter proclaimed. "What an opportunity for advancement."

Peter approached Ember, and extended the crook of his elbow in offer of escort. With a sunny smile, she ignored him and instead followed the Chief Constable. Her servant brushed past Peter, eyes cast downward.

Tapping his cane against the pavement, Peter joined this strange parade.

⚷

The three corpses were in a field beside a modest apartment building. Crowds of the curious gathered, kept back by a handful of constables.

Peter studied the group, half-expecting to see the old woman he spied earlier. Instead his glance fell on an old man with wild snowy hair and bright blue eyes. The old gent gave him a nod and faded back into the gathering. Peter considered following him, but his attention was diverted by Baker, who was shouting instructions to police officers at the scene.

With a humorless smile, Peter inspected the faint line of footsteps leading to the corpses. Although partially obscured by subsequent traffic, enough of the originals remained if one looked hard enough. He lifted a hand and hailed Baker.

"Mr. Styles?" the Chief Constable responded. Peter gestured at the tracks.

"These are similar to the ones outside the window of the house we've just come from," Peter said.

The constable knelt down. He scratched his jaw and studied them with a troubled expression.

"You could preserve the footprint and make a comparison," Ember suggested.

"Preserve it?"

"With plaster."

Baker looked like he was about to dismiss the suggestion but instead elevated an eyebrow and smiled broadly. "What an ingenious idea."

Peter agreed, but withheld saying anything complimentary for fear the praise might be misconstrued by Miss Quatermain. Instead, he approached the corpses and grimaced at their mangled appearances. One lay with a broken neck and the side of its face crushed in. Beside that one, a painfully thin old man rested on his back. The loose flesh about the arms and legs suggested some disease had devoured him.

This poor soul should have been allowed to rest instead of being horrifically dragged back across the threshold to do someone's cruel bidding.

The third of the dead was long and thick of form. His lips and cheeks were grotesquely swollen. Bending over, Peter ripped open the shirt and exposed a distended belly. The man's flesh was gray with purple-black streaks.

Peter needed a moment alone with the corpses. The energy the necromancer had used to animate them was dissipating fast. If he could tap into it, he might be able to learn something of the spellcaster. The odds widened with each passing moment, especially as daylight continued to deaden the emanations.

Peter shut the man's shirt as Baker approached. "These men have been dead for some time. Why would someone keep three corpses and dump them in the middle of a field?" Baker asked.

"Maybe they walked here themselves," Peter answered.

As Ember drew closer, he wanted to stand and shield her from the grisly scene. She shouldn't be allowed here. He didn't doubt her courage or tenacity, but he didn't want her exposed to the carnage. The puzzle presented here might prove irresistible, and Miss Quatermain was the sort not to be blinded by skepticism. He had seen the way she studied the second worker from the Underground. She was a terrier who would keep digging until something broke from hiding.

Before Peter could object, Ember held a handkerchief over her nose to filter the smell, and stooped down, leaning close to one of the dead men in the muck. She used the handkerchief to lift the corpse's hand and made an exclamation which brought Hans to her side.

"Miss, perhaps it would be a good idea for you to step to the edge of the field and wait for us there," Baker suggested.

Hans nodded and said, "We came for the dig, not to stand in cold grass and see things that aren't fit for our eyes."

Ember stood and stared at Peter with a suspicious expression. She pulled away from Hans. "My eyes are seeing things just fine. Check the man's fingers."

"Come, Miss," Hans urged.

"Check them," she ordered.

Baker grunted with exasperation and moved to humor her. He squatted by the corpse and held up the hand. Peter felt Ember continuing to peer at him.

"What am I looking for, Miss Quatermain?" Baker asked.

"Do you see the wood slivers embedded in the skin?"

"What of it?"

"Those slivers match the window sill in the house we just came from."

Baker dropped the hand and stood. He shook his head and threw Peter an accusatory glance.

"That's a working man. Working men get slivers. You can't suggest a dead man broke into the house."

"You're the experienced criminologist," Peter said. "I warrant that if you removed some of those slivers and compare them with the wood from the windowsill, you'll find they match."

"The impossible is impossible, Mr. Styles."

Baker glared first at Peter, then over at Ember, as if trying to determine whether or not they were making him the butt of a joke. He clenched his jaw.

"I may be just an officer of the law, Mr. Styles, but I am a man to be taken seriously. I'll grant you, this case is strange and promises to become stranger, but I'm not about to become a laughing stock."

Poor Baker. A loyal civil servant who labored to better himself deserved more. If the police officer presented the case to his superiors as the facts delivered it, they would use him as a scapegoat rather than exposing the department to the ridicule of a disbelieving public. Or the government would merely shut the door on the investigation for fear of the effect of such dark discoveries on the general population.

Peter turned his attention again to the corpses and once more gave consideration to the problem of how to pursue his special line of inquiry in the presence of others. There was no other option. He avoided Miss Quatermain and stepped next to Baker.

"Chief Constable, if my words have upset you so far, you're not going to like what I am about to request, and I will first remind you I'm here with the Commissioner's authority."

Baker waited.

"I want a moment with the corpses. Alone. I need you and your men to step back to the edge of the field there and to keep people away."

The Chief Constable's eyes bulged. He thrust his face close to Peter. "What are your intentions?"

"I want to study the scene more carefully, without distractions."

The answer did little to pacify the Chief Constable. His face continued to darken and the veins along his neck stood out. "You're lying," he hissed.

"I am," Peter agreed.

Things were going poorly enough for the Chief Constable without challenging orders from his superiors. Baker didn't say anything further, but instead stood and ordered his men to back away to the end of the field. There was some grumbling, but in the end the policemen respected their commander's orders.

"What is it you're up to, Mr. Styles?" Ember asked.

"Never anything reputable, Miss Quatermain, I assure you."

"Will you be direct with me, sir?"

"I will not," Peter said.

Someone in the crowd waved. Peter looked past Ember and directed her attention to the manservant, who stood at the edge of the field flourishing a handkerchief for her attention. Sparing him a last disapproving glance, the young lady started across the muddy grass. Peter admired her from behind.

When he was alone, Peter dropped to a knee beside the corpses and steeled himself for a miserable experience. He gave a final glance at the faces peering at him with curiosity from across the field and shut his eyes.

Opening himself to the living was one thing, using the dead as a channel through the aether, the shadow world beyond the material plane, was insufferable agony.

This went beyond anything Virgil might expect of him, so why do this? He knew the necromancer was like a blackmailer, always returning for one more payment. Virgil would ever be there, pulling, threatening, cajoling. However, if Peter could find something to give him the advantage, putting himself at risk was worth it. Even if it meant having to face another necromancer, one who was capable of animating three corpses at one time.

Peter relaxed his muscles with a sigh. He blocked out the stray thoughts from the crowd gathered at the edge of the field and focused on teasing out the remnants of magical energies left by the necromancer.

"Where did you hide it?"

He almost missed the question. It passed through his mind as an unimportant thought, a daydream. *"Where did you hide it?"*

Peter grasped at the thought, traveling into himself to follow the thread. The power of the one issuing the question grazed his mind and spun after it until the stern visage of a man with a high forehead and intense, hypnotic eyes crystallized. A regal face. Without pausing to consider the wisdom of his act, Peter increased his effort and reached toward the necromancer. Unlike Virgil, this man had no magical barrier protecting him from discovery, and as the man turned inward and peered at him with curiosity, Peter considered with alarm—*neither do I.*

⚷—⚸

The Italian stood at a table, peering at an old map stretched out before him. Dark skin, heavy brow, a pointed chin—the features distinct and memorable, handsome if not for the cruelty they expressed. The only outward feature that betrayed his true nature were his black within black eyes; the eyes of the lamia.

The man leaned over and ran a finger along the map, tracing an energy line across the contour of the Isles. This was one of Jupiter's markers, an impressive stream pooling between realities. Seeing it brought the General to mind. How many years had it been since he had thought of him? Poor Publius Aelius Hadrianus.

He hadn't been serious when suggesting the wall to him. He brought up the idea as a lark, a clownish suggestion to help instill discipline among the men and to intimidate the local population. So absurd a concept. The General, however, hadn't laughed. Instead, he implemented the construction of the barrier as a way to "focus" the military, and as a marker establishing Roman dominance. And its limitations.

He puzzled over the map. Each time he saw his old friend and tutor, Lysimachus of Arcarnania's markings on the rendering, vindication surged through him. The scribbles had led him to the key, now they would lead him to the location of the green tablet. This mystery was far from solved, but the answer danced closer to him than at any time in the last hundred years.

He tapped the map at the spot from which Hadrian's Wall had been built and slid his finger along the wavy energy line to the location where Lysimachus chose to secret the key. The two spots were part of a pattern formed by the energy streams. This wasn't coincidence; this was the will of the gods!

He turned from the table and approached the object delivered by the dead men, a fractured container about three by four inches. Within was a cylindrical green soapstone. Only it was no longer soapstone. It may have started as such, but once the tiny characters were carved into its surface, it had transformed so the secret writing would never be lost. The message inscribed on the key wasn't the work of Lysimachus, but the effort of someone far cleverer, and therefore much more difficult to decipher. It was said Hermes himself dictated the creation of this stylus.

The writing mocked him. Without the tablet, the key itself was relatively worthless.

A chill caused him to raise his head.

Something touched the aether, along the thread he'd opened when he raised the three corpses. It moved toward him, like a blind man clumsily feeling his way through a narrow passage.

Someone was close to his risen poppets, someone with talent. He smiled and stole a quick glance at Theron. The old Greek stood against the wall, a simple brown robe hiding the gaping wound that ended the man's life.

The presence intruded again.

He opened himself to the aether and welcomed the will pushing its way through, until he touched the presence of the intruder. A young man; a tormented individual whose arrogance too often clouded his judgment. The young man also knew pain. He had experienced the loss of a loved one, a young beauty, a first love, and her loss blended with shame and guilt to form a bittersweet nectar.

Poor fellow; forever the outsider seeking entrance and forever sabotaging it.

Having tasted the young man, he didn't think him much a

threat. Nonetheless, it wouldn't do to allow him this close without consequence.

Bowing his head, he reached through the aether, stirring one of the three poppets he animated earlier. Released back into oblivion only a few hours before, it resisted, screaming through the blackness as it battled the command to enter cold flesh and become once more the *nekroanypomonos*. "Hello, Peter," the Italian spoke through the corpse in a loving tone. The response startled the young man, who sent back a wave of wariness and uncertainty. The upstart questioned himself, unsure whether the words came from the cold lips or had sounded within his mind. The Italian stayed quiet as the young man puzzled over this.

Peter made up his mind and pushed back at him through the aether.

The Italian, surprised by this inexperienced necromancer's intensity, let slip a glimpse of his obsession—the green tablet and the sweet power it promised.

The young man peered at his goal with a child's ignorant eyes.

Angry at his own weakness, at his uncharacteristic lack of discipline, the Italian let the fury build and fuelled it into the *nekroanypomonos*.

"Very clever, Peter," he whispered. "You know a few tricks."

Who are you?

The question delivered became a demand, but the Italian shoved it back.

"You're not that talented, Peter, and I am far too busy for games. I shall let you live this time, but you must fight for the privilege."

Peter Styles shuddered and pulled back, desperate to break the connection between them.

He returned to himself, disoriented from the experience. Someone had pushed him out and Peter felt as though the thrust took no more effort than it would to flick a finger. In the face of such power and malice, Peter's self-confidence wavered.

The icy air made him shiver. He swallowed quickly to keep from retching and longed for the shelter of the dark corners of London where he enjoyed anonymity. Still squatting by the dead men, Peter glanced at the edge of the field, where the hard faces peered in his direction. Baker stood with arms folded across his chest and his jaw set in disapproval.

He spied the matron seen earlier by the house where the dead man had been discovered. She stood whispering into the ear of the old man he noted earlier. Who were these people?

The elderly couple appeared excited. The man gestured toward Ember and moved in her direction. The woman pushed back through the crowd and Peter lost sight of her.

A hand wrapped around his wrist.

Peter started but the *nekroanypomonos* held him fast. Lifeless eyes opened and the face twisted in brutal malevolence. He couldn't help crying out, and the alarm in his voice emboldened the monster.

The thing rose to one knee.

"Non est satis callidus," it hissed in Latin. "Clever isn't enough. Clever is for lost boys, not for men with ambition."

Peter battled back the panic and struggled to remember what paltry knowledge Virgil had meted out. He drew in energy from the field animating the unclean entity that held him.

The corpse now stood. Its other hand lashed out and closed on his neck, compressing Peter's windpipe.

He continued to gather energy and sought his inner rage. It took anger to raise the *nekroanypomonos* and only a greater fury could control them.

"You'll be with us soon enough, Mr. Styles. Soon enough."

The dead man now spoke in English. The other presence had moved on.

Peter dove into the darkness, confronting the abhorrence before him with his own shadow self. His bile fed from the death of loved ones and from his own guilt and self-loathing. Bitterness fed his rage, which crackled within like a wild animal seeking release and destruction.

His jaw clenched and with a painful blast of effort, he expelled the energy into a single burst and channeled it into the *nekroanypomonos*.

His will ripped through the dead man, following the path used for animation, and severing the tie through the aether.

Cut free from its husk, the restless dead returned screaming back into oblivion.

Peter stood over the rotting cadaver, breathing heavily, and rubbing at his throat. He shook his head in appreciation of the necromancer's power. The man, if he was a man, was more powerful than anyone he had ever known or imagined. He may not have been able to pierce the man's defenses, but if only for a moment, he had linked with him, and had seen something the man hadn't wanted him to see—the bit of green stone stolen from the dead man's hand.

Baker was now at his side. The Chief Constable gazed at the corpses, eyes wide, face fixed in horror. When he at last raised his gaze to Peter, it contained a hint of accusation and fear.

"What happened? What did you do?"

Baker and the other police officers waited, their countenances grim. Peter remained silent as he straightened his jacket, tugging at first one sleeve, then the other. He used his palms to smooth back his hair.

"The corpse stood and gripped your throat," Baker charged. "I saw him. We all saw him."

"Did you?"

Peter's head hurt and, as his heart slowed, his hands trembled slightly. He turned and started across the field, the police following him, some at a distance. Baker kept pace, his voice hushed and urgent.

"You owe me an explanation."

"I have none. You saw what you saw, Chief Constable."

"I'm going to find out more about you, Mr. Styles. I'm going to ask around. I don't care whose protection you claim."

"I'm an open book, Chief Constable."

"What happened back there? It was a trick, wasn't it? You're using this to further your ambition. You're trying to perpetuate some outrageous hoax."

Peter stopped and stared at the apoplectic Baker. He suppressed a smile and continued on to Ember, who stood waiting beside a hansom. The old man with the unruly white hair stood next to her. His crinkled smile widened like the opening of a yellowed hymnbook. By the time Peter reached them, the man was gone; his exit so fast it was as though he simply vanished. Peter stopped and scanned the crowd for him.

He hailed Ember.

"There was someone standing next to you, Miss Quatermain. An old man?"

She appeared confused by his question.

Peter slapped his thigh in frustration and shut his mouth to avoid saying anything offensive. Instead he started into the hansom.

"What are you doing?" Hans asked.

Peter paused on the step and gave the African a broad grin. "I am not well," Peter said. "I need to collect myself."

"Then let the police assist you until a physician can attend to you," Hans sputtered.

Peter shut his eyes for a moment, and in truth he did feel spent. His shoulders sagged and he spoke with sincerity. "I should like a moment to sit until I gather my wits."

"You're being rude and un-Christian," Ember chided Hans. She waved Peter into the cab and settled in next to him.

"Wait!" Baker called. "I'm not satisfied."

"Can't you see Mr. Styles is ailing?" Ember said. "You can talk to him later. Mr. Styles, may we transport you home?"

"That's most generous of you, Miss Quatermain."

"Your father will be most unhappy," Hans warned. "He will not like it you rode with a stranger."

"My father is leaving for Africa today," she said. "Where shall we drop you, Mr. Styles?"

"It's not terribly far." His voice sounded distant. "I'm not going directly home, but to a friend's lodging near Queen's Park. His name's Avery Tressler."

Baker put his face to the hansom's window, speaking through clenched teeth.

"I'll be by later, Mr. Styles. I know what I saw with my own eyes."

"If you do, Mr. Baker," Peter responded, "Then you are one up on the rest of us."

CHAPTER V

*Wherein Allan Quatermain leaves for Africa and
Miss Quatermain visits a secreted family member*

IT WAS MID-AFTERNOON WHEN EMBER ARRIVED HOME. Returning from the excavation, she felt let down; the images of the burned corpses and the ones discovered in the nearby field flooded her. She didn't want to think about the other thing; her mind refused to accept the dead had risen. She tried applying herself to the problem, but rebelled at the coldness of it. It was a matter to be considered in sunlight.

Entering the house, her father bellowed for Hans. The unflappable manservant bowed gracefully.

"Your father sounds impatient," Hans said. "I'll see what I can do to calm him. He is always difficult before a trip."

Ember watched Hans depart. Her father's journey brought the shadow of loneliness to her shoulder. Every time he disappeared, she felt this way. She should be used to it; most of her childhood was spent with surrogate parents.

Ember slunk off to her workshop.

When she emerged a few hours later, she was still in a dark mood. Her father hadn't called for her yet, and she suspected he wouldn't, preferring to slip off without an emotional farewell. She decided to seek him out; why make his departure any easier for him.

The trophies of exotic beasts brought home by her father greeted Ember as she entered the great room. She kept her head down, not wanting to see the ferocious countenances of the now dead animals. Her attention was instead drawn to the tidy piles of luggage ready to be loaded into the carriage that the driver would bring about shortly.

"It's almost night," Ember said mirthlessly. She turned a face to the window. "By the time you're ready to ascend, there will be no light."

"I'm seaman enough to navigate by the stars," her father replied. "I'm too anxious to wait until morning."

She wanted to object, but held her tongue.

He put the paper down and presented his cheek. Ember crossed to where he sat and kissed him. She almost expected him to flinch.

"There's a good girl." Allan Quatermain stood and threw the paper onto a table. She could feel his nervous energy and found it irritating. Her father vigorously rubbed his hands together and then clapped them three times, a sign he was ready for action.

"Do you want me to accompany you to the airfield? Run through the operations again?" she asked.

"I think your old father can handle it". His tone was condescending. "Our last trip to Scotland was not so long ago."

Mention of Scotland made her bristle. She recalled his impatience as she tried showing him the rudimentary mechanics of piloting the airship. He ignored her words, of course, and instead threw himself into the task of using trial and error rather than the listening to her offered instruction.

What a miracle they hadn't crashed.

She thought of Masterson's reference to her invention. What had he said? "When the club sees that thing, they'll laugh you out of the club." She suspected the newspapers would be onto her soon; enjoying the curiosity of a woman inventor and her freakish creation. Thank goodness Father would be in Africa when that happened.

"Did Hans tell you anything about this afternoon?" she asked, quick to change the subject.

A guilty expression on Quatermain's face showed he knew little about it.

"He said you took pictures. I trust you were extremely helpful to Chief Constable Baker."

Hans lowered his eyes. The servant had probably communicated little of what had transpired; or else, her father's apathy deafened him.

She offered him a paper package containing the glass photographs. He stared at them for a moment, as if not sure what they were, but then shuffled through the bunch, pausing to scratch his beard and grunt approval.

"Well done," he said, and handed them back.

They looked at one another. Her father pursed his lips and his heavy eyebrows drew together. A long moment of silence ensued, but the tension resolved itself as Ember reached into her purse and withdrew the green fragment taken from the tunnel.

"What do you make of this shard?" she asked. "I think it might be part of a container. It's quite tough. It took considerable force to break it off, I'm sure."

He turned it over in his palm.

"I'm not familiar with this kind of stone." He squinted, taking in the smooth texture. He scratched at the side of his nose and shrugged.

"Take this," he said, scribbling onto a sheet of paper. "It's a note for Masterson. He'll know what to do. Just give it to him."

She accepted the paper but had no intention of asking Masterson for help.

"Are you familiar with Peter Styles?" she asked.

Her father cleared his throat in disapproval. He exchanged a look with Hans that suggested the manservant had neglected to mention the rake.

"His family is titled," he said. "Their wealth is well known. Yes, Mr. Styles' name occasionally appears in the society column. Why?"

"Someone sent him to the site. That's all he would say."

The mention of Styles attracted his interest more than anything else she had brought him.

"Someone sent him?" he asked.

"He was quite mysterious about it."

Her father considered this new development with a snort. He nodded and placed a heavy hand on her shoulder.

"Stay away from *that one*," he instructed. The phrase used to refer to Styles surprised her. It was how he referred to her brother, Harry. Allan Quatermain fell silent, his expression troubled.

"Hans, where's the blasted carriage?" Quatermain snapped his fingers. The manservant hastened to the door.

"If you need someone reliable, you can turn to Masterson. He has influence," he said. "Don't let his exterior dissuade you; he may be old fashioned by your standards, but he has a keen wit and a good heart. He's marriage material. You could do worse."

Her father's statement shocked her. Masterson?

"If he should approach you and offer a more direct friendship, I hope you won't rebuff him. I think he's a good man. I like him."

He had discussed her with Masterson. Perhaps she was a housekeeping matter to be put in order before departing. Ember calmed herself, not wanting to get into a full-blown row.

"What will you be doing with yourself in my absence?" he asked with the tone of afterthought.

"Waiting at the door for your return," she said, still smarting from his earlier statements.

He froze her with a stare.

"You have so many interesting mirrors in your workshop," he countered. "You might consider actually looking into one of them."

"And you might consider looking away from one from time to time," she snapped back.

Allan Quatermain laughed at the jibe and turned his head at the sound of the door opening. Hans waited for him. Outside, a horse whinnied as the hansom cab stood at the ready.

"Well, girl, I can't say you haven't come by your cruelty honestly," he said.

Ember followed him out of the great room and arranged herself on a sofa in the foyer. She watched as they finished securing the bags. Her father moved with the athleticism of a man half his age as he roared instructions to the driver and to his manservant. He was a whirlwind, sending anyone within his influence spinning off in confusion. How ironic he was the one person who understood her.

Allan Quatermain took measure of his home, proud chin raised and eyes flashing with excitement at the prospect of being off. He was a heroic figure, a grand presence. With a perfunctory wave, he settled into the cab and the new adventure began. He was reborn.

Ember listened to the sound of the hansom fade. She sat a while longer, waiting for her pain to ebb, certain her father banished her from his thoughts as soon as the hansom jerked into motion.

Killing a few lions didn't make a hero.

Tears began at the corners of her eyes. She hated crying, and her father was one of the few people who could upset her.

Cramped but cozy, Josephine's sitting room gave her more welcome than her own home. Father paid for the upkeep of the cottage, but Josephine was the one who furnished the place with bright flowers and plush cushions.

This woman was the closest thing Ember had to a mother, her real mother having died giving birth to Ember and her twin brother.

The aroma of bitter tea leaves and sour yeast drifted from the kitchen as Josephine hummed a tune and rattled plates. A kettle began to whistle. In a moment, Josephine ambled out of the kitchen, a cup and saucer in hand.

"It was getting late, I didn't think you'd be coming around," she said. The older woman handed Ember the cup and moved to the fire to stir the coals. She breathed heavily.

"My father left today," Ember said.

"He did," replied the old woman. She was heavyset, with broad shoulders and wide hips. Her eyes were kind, although they bulged slightly.

"I sent him away with an argument."

"Then all is well," she said.

Ember smiled at that. She settled back in her chair and studied the flames as she thought about her father's reaction to her account of the day's events. He hadn't given her serious consideration. He was dismissive of the photographs and relatively uninterested in the stone.

However her reference to Peter Styles certainly got his attention.

"You should move in here," Josephine said. "There's nothing for you at that house, and Little Harry Junior would get the attention he deserves. I can't chase after him like I did your brother and you."

Ember wanted to believe that her twin would surface in time. The last anyone heard of Harry Senior was in Kenya, where the story was that he worked offering medical aid to smallpox victims. Such a noble lie.

"I might take you up on your offer," Ember replied.

A sound attracted her attention. Little Harry appeared in the doorway; her nephew possessed the Quatermain look; lively gray eyes set beneath a high forehead framed by curly red hair. It flowed down almost to his shoulders, making him look more like a girl than a boy.

The toddler held his arms open for his aunt, then rushed to her lap with a cry of elation. She scooped him into an embrace and held him against her.

"You've grown in the last few days, I swear," she said, tilting him back to get a good look at his face. Her broad smile tightened as she took in the change of eye color from baby gray to frosty blue. Her brother lurked behind those piercing eyes. She'd make sure this one chose a happier course than his absent father.

"Look at him," Josephine said with contentment. "There's beauty for you. Why can't we keep some of that as we get older? Where does the child in us go?"

"Some of us don't ever grow up. Me? I don't remember ever being this young," Ember said.

"I don't think you were," Josephine said playfully. "You were always too smart, always too eager to push people away and do for yourself and others."

She set Harry on the floor, and ruffled his fine hair. "I've brought something for you."

Producing the copper horse from her purse, Ember held the toy aloft and winked conspiratorially at her former nanny. The little boy jumped up and down until made to stand still to receive his gift as a proper gentleman. Into his mouth went the horse, where Harry contentedly sucked on its muzzle.

Ember laughed. "It's not for chewing," she admonished gently. Extraction of the horse from Harry's lips brought grunting protest.

"Wait. Just watch."

She wound the gears and set the contraption parading across the wooden floor. Her nephew clapped his hands, loping and stomping after it.

Josephine applauded, then, still laughing, headed into the kitchen to retrieve supper. Ember followed, putting on an apron and pulling dishes from the cupboard. She lifted a spoon and began to stir a pot of rabbit stew. The aroma made her stomach growl.

"For Heaven's sake, dear, haven't I taught you better?" Josephine hurried to her side. "Don't ever stir *widdershins*. It's bad luck. You know that."

"Every year you get more superstitious."

"Every year is a step closer to the end. Why tempt fate and hurry the journey?"

Ember smiled and passed the pot to Josephine. She bent over and retrieved a fresh loaf of bread from the oven. "You used to be a better Christian," she teased.

"What a mouth on you," Josephine chided. "I'm still good enough a Christian to remember Ecclesiastes. 'To everything there is a season . . . ' Seems to me you're at an age where you should be thinking about meeting someone. Hiding in your smelly workshop is no way to attract a man. You're too good with Little Harry not to have one of your own."

"You, too?" Ember asked. "Only last night father's friend, Edward Masterson, brought up maternity."

Josephine laughed.

"Oh my, is Mr. Masterson still coming around then? He's such a somber man, I sometimes wonder the weight of his own seriousness don't topple him."

"He doesn't approve of me."

"One hears things about Mr. Masterson and company he keeps, from time to time. I don't pay attention to gossip."

She glanced at the old woman; Josephine loved societal gossip. A thought occurred to Ember. The next question came with casual air. "What do you know of Peter Styles?" she probed.

The woman put her spoon down and became contemplative. She shook her head with disapproval. A nervous old habit surfaced as the nanny fiddled with a loose hairpin, pushing it deep into raven tresses heavily peppered with gray.

"Why are you asking?" Josephine said.

"I met him this morning. He's attractive."

The old maid agreed with a glint in her eye. "That one's bad," she said. "You stay away from him, Miss Ember. He's too free with his drink and his family's money. He likes to gamble. Although he doesn't lose much, he wins few friends. People say things about him, but you know me, I don't listen."

"I think there's more to him than people give him credit. He's perceptive. The man sees things. I had difficulty keeping up with him."

"Where were you meeting such a character as Mr. Styles?"

"Paddington."

The old woman frowned. She leaned forward and shook a biscuit at Ember.

"I read about it in the papers. That poor worker. Burned. You shouldn't have gone. It wasn't proper. Your father doesn't think!"

"I wanted to go," Ember objected.

"Well, of course, you would. What happened then? What *really* happened?"

The paper's account attributed the tunnel worker's death to a fire resulting from a spark igniting a gas pocket. The second death and the three corpses in a field weren't mentioned at all. Thankfully, her name was omitted, as well as Styles. Baker received praise though.

At Josephine's insistence, Ember related what occurred, but left out the discovery of the three corpses in the field, and what transpired there. Josephine listened with macabre satisfaction and when the tale was concluded, she patted Ember's hand.

"Be careful," she said. "There's darkness afoot. Whatever was in that tunnel was best left undisturbed. Put there for a reason, it was."

"Don't you think it was a tremendous coincidence the tunnel was planned where the object was hidden?" Ember asked.

"The earth is magical," Josephine said in a hushed tone. "Some spots are hot with magic. Makes sense, don't it? Look at Stonehenge. Tell me the druids didn't put those rocks there for a reason. And there are other spots where the wall between worlds is thin and things slip through. Magic woods and glens and such. Faeries are real. So are darker things. I'm wise about these matters. Grew up near Holywell, I did."

Ember kept quiet so as not to encourage her former nanny. She didn't want another lesson in folklore. Having said her peace, the older woman grew thoughtful. A playful smile appeared at the corners of her mouth.

"Did you like Chief Constable Baker? Is he a looker?" she asked.

The context and presentation of the statement wrought a laugh from Ember.

"I haven't given it much thought, but I assume you would consider him so."

Josephine cackled. "Well, there's nothing wrong with that. He's handsome, isn't he?"

"Baker? He is."

The older woman winked.

They ate their dinner and enjoyed one another's company, with Josephine making an occasional allusion to the Chief Constable, more often than not as an opportunity to say something off color. Both women laughed until tears came from their eyes.

Little Harry, excited by the mirth of his elders, rapped the table with a spoon, scattering crumbs all over the floor. Ember rose to attend to the mess and knocked a knife from the table.

"That's an omen," Josephine said. "Expect a male stranger."

Ignoring her, Ember cleaned the corners of the little boy's mouth and set him on the floor. Harry ran and retrieved the horse. She wound it again and he took off after it with a wobbling gallop.

"Do you know what my father is planning on doing?" Ember asked rhetorically. She watched Harry sit down to play with his toy. "He intends to eventually bring Little Harry into London Society as my brother."

The older woman scoffed half-heartedly, but her manner suggested she already knew his intent.

"No one will believe him. At his age?"

Ember shrugged. "He's started shaving off a few years, tells people he's forty. I suppose he'll be forty again next year."

"Well, that's one way to fool The Reaper. Whatever your father's intentions are though, I know he means right by the boy."

When Ember returned to the table, she found Josephine had taken her cup and was peering intently into the dregs. Since she was a girl, her nanny had done this to her.

"A man," Josephine announced playfully.

"You always see a man," Ember complained.

"Maybe this one's for me."

"Highly doubtful. What else?"

Josephine's brow furrowed as the old woman bent in concentration. She abruptly slid the cup back across the table. Ember wouldn't admit it, but since childhood, Josephine's divinations made her uneasy. Coincidence or not, they often proved true. Maybe it was their generality, but the nanny's belief in them unnerved her.

"You're seeing gloom again, aren't you?" Ember asked, trying to make light of it.

"Dark things."

Ember thought of her father and the old fears returned.

Josephine, seeing her expression, waved a finger. "A man, someone young and foolish. He's heading for disaster."

Ember thought of her brother and glanced at Little Harry. Young and foolish, heading for disaster, that sounded like her twin. She was grateful she kept her nephew from his libertine influence and the conceited self-indulgence of her father.

"Who is this man?"

"Someone who has brought misfortune upon himself."

"Don't we all," Ember uttered. For no good reason she remembered a card secreted in her purse. Impulse struck. Her anxieties always made her eager for action.

"I have to go," she said, trying to make her voice light.

"Are you all right, dear?"

"Yes, yes. I just remembered something I need to do."

Josephine tried dissuading her, but in the end the old woman enfolded Ember in fleshy arms and rocked her for a moment. Breaking the old woman's embrace and the illusion of safety it gave, she knelt and hugged Harry.

"Ber-ber!" her nephew cried in distress.

"I'll come visit soon," she said gently. "It's time for bed."

As if the words were hypnotic, Harry bobbed his head sleepily. She hoisted him up before releasing him into Josephine's cradling hold.

"I won't be away long," Ember assured them both.

"I can always tell when you are about to do something unwise," Josephine chided. "And right now I know you've got an itch you're mad to satisfy. Only this one might be better off left unscratched."

"Don't be foolish. I'm only interested in gathering more information about the day's events."

"If you were a smart girl, you would go straight home and let the morning rather than the night rule you."

Ember kissed the old woman again and hurried across the threshold and down the street. She was tired, and Josephine was probably correct, still she wanted to strike while her curiosity championed over good sense.

A block away, Ember hailed a hansom. The driver, a man of wide girth, with tremendous jowls and a prominent overbite, acted in a differential and considerate manner. As the clock tower chimed, he consulted a pocket watch. She gave him her destination.

"That's a rough part of the city," he said with a frown.

"You mean for a woman?" she bristled.

"Begging your pardon, Miss, but I mean for anybody."

CHAPTER VI

Wherein Miss Quatermain seeks out Mr. Styles and finds her intentions woefully misinterpreted

THE ADDRESS AT THE STRAND WAS LOCATED ON A ROUGH BLOCK. The houses crowded together, many of them in ill-repair. Garbage littered the street, and a horrible stench suggested a slaughterhouse nearby. She couldn't imagine the sun ever shining here. This was another world, a sphere of ash and mud, where life was all too predictable.

The hansom was a rarity, and people watched it arrive with eyes of quick resentment. As the carriage stopped, three boys poked their heads in to gawk at her, unruly children with grimy skin and rushed voices slurring words in an almost alien dialect. The driver called out to them, whipping the side of the vehicle with a crop.

Ember sat for a moment, gathering courage and trying to understand why a person with Styles' wealth wished to live in this dark neighborhood. A shadow drifted from one building to another. She feared it might be someone repositioning himself to accost her as she descended from the cab. He stepped into light and she saw an old man.

He leaned against a dirty wall, a great, out-of-fashion overcoat draping his slight frame. His hair, a shock of blinding white, was combed straight forward, partially obscuring blue eyes.

With a start, Ember recognized him from the empty lot where the bodies were discovered. Keeping one hand within her purse, she stepped from the hansom.

"Can you wait for me?" she asked the driver. He winced at the question, but doffed his hat.

Ember turned from the cab, ready to hail the old man, but he was nowhere to be seen. She frowned, biting a lower lip, and searched the shadows, looking first one way, then another. Either he was a spry old fellow, or else he knew a door or path not immediately visible. He certainly hadn't disappeared into thin air.

The driver gestured to her.

"Miss, I just don't feel right about letting you wander. Let me escort you to the address where you're expected."

She shook her head. The horse stamped its foot impatiently, eager to be away.

Before the driver could protest further, she walked toward Styles' apartment building, still keeping an eye open for the strange old fellow. She stepped over discarded refuse that littered the gutters, as well as the fouler stuff of slop buckets. She held her chin up, trying to present a confident air to anyone who might be spying on her.

A dun colored mastiff lying beside the front steps raised its head at her approach. Its ears slipped far forward. She noticed bare skin marring the animal's sides, and dried blood on its snout.

With a growl the animal rose.

Ember didn't make eye contact. She slowed her pace slightly, but continued toward the entrance. She hoped the beast would give way.

Another growl, this one sustained and more threatening.

"Easy now," Ember said in a soothing tone. "Nothing interesting here."

Despite her words, the mastiff crouched, hackles raised. Its hind legs trembled slightly as the beast prepared to attack.

She pulled a glass globe from her purse and sprayed its contents downwind while continuing to make gentle admonitions. The animal froze, sniffing the air with a puzzled expression. Its tail began to wag. Abruptly it trotted after the breeze, eagerly following the scent. Ember indulged in a self-satisfied nod before returning the bottle to her purse.

A dark patch beyond the apartment stairs materialized into Peter Styles, brown eyes bright with amusement.

"That was impressive," he said with a clap.

"Were you planning to watch the hound devour me? Or were you preparing to intervene?"

"Ogre's all bluff," he said with a shrug. Styles gave her a long look and she stared back. He was a handsome man, the sort who didn't have to work at it. He pointed at her purse and asked, "What was that you used so aptly?"

"A perfume I created. Animals respond to smell. All animals."

"Men?"

"Especially men, Mr. Styles."

He leaned back against the building, once again nearly invisible in shadow. She could sense his smile, the thought of it hanging in space disconcerting.

"What are you doing hiding outside your own residence?" she asked.

His eyes were hooded, and a collar stuck up on one side. In the evening light Styles' shade looked ghostly.

"I've had the unsettling sensation someone was following me. I've felt that since early this morning. So, I've been keeping watch. And here you are."

"Me? Why would I be following you?"

"Excellent question."

Ember wasn't sure how to respond. She eyed the street, alert for the old man she noted earlier.

Styles stepped out of shadow again, deep in thought. He ran his hands through lustrous black hair.

"You've been drinking, Mr. Styles," she said, careful to make it an observation and not a judgment.

"A little absinthe," he said dismissively. Styles closed his eyes. When he opened them again, his expression changed. He was suddenly more feral looking than any dog. His voice lowered and his words were gruff.

"What do you want from me, Miss Quatermain? What brings you sneaking around here to spy?"

"I'm not spying."

He moved quickly, clamping a hand over her purse. "None of your tricks. Don't think of using your arsenal on me. I heard about your antics the other evening."

His action and tone frightened her.

"Heard what? From whom?"

"Never you mind, Miss Quatermain. Tell me what you want. Tell me why you're here."

Ember slapped his hand away. Her fear resolved into anger as she realized she wasn't the only one afraid.

"I want to know what I saw today. I need to understand."

He laughed too loudly at her words, the sound cut through the night, accentuating the silence swallowing the city streets.

Styles turned his back to her and headed up the steps of the apartment building. She stared after him with uncertainty. He wasn't dismissing her; this felt more like a challenge. He paused at the top of the steps and held the door open for her. His lips curled into a wolfish smile, and she understood the invitation. Irritated at his presumptuousness, she almost went back the way she came, but then she blanched at giving him that satisfaction. She could handle Mr. Styles.

They proceeded up a narrow flight of stairs. Desperation and poverty permeated the air; too many people living too close together. The wall along the stairs showed rings of water damage and mold grew near the ceiling.

Again Ember considered her wisdom; she didn't really know Mr. Styles, and thus far no one had vouchsafed for his reputation. In fact, quite the opposite.

She reached into her bag, fingers closing around another of her eggs. Ember thought better of it, and snapped it closed.

"Miss Quatermain, you're an intriguing woman," he called over his shoulder. "I could tell from watching you this morning that your intellect matched your beauty."

His compliment both flattered her and reminded her to keep up her guard.

"You haven't answered my question about the field," she said in a hushed tone.

He opened a door into a spacious front room, its cleanliness and comfort a surprise. The wallpaper was lilac, with a calming floral pattern. Dignified white muslin curtains hung before a large window. The furniture in the room, dominated by two comfortable chairs, each with an oversized ottoman, and a sumptuous sofa, were arranged informally. Opposite the window overlooking the street was a large fireplace, above which hung an enormous mirror.

Mr. Styles was a man of functional taste.

"Can I offer you refreshment? A brandy? Wine? Perhaps *Le Fee Verteé?*"

He gestured her to the sofa and then hastened to a cabinet near the window.

"Nothing, thank you."

Their eyes met and she experienced a moment of vertigo. His brown eyes were darker than she thought. Styles' features were sharp and expressive; he had the face an artist would render not in careful lines, but in passionate sweeping strokes. He was leaner than he should be, and he exuded the air of a man always in midstride.

"Miss Quatermain, so you want to know what happened today?" he asked, mirroring her earlier question.

"I need to talk about what I saw," she said carefully.

"Women always do," he uttered.

Ember decided to push him, but feared sounding foolish. Gathering courage she went ahead and said: "I stood at the edge of a field and watched a dead man rise."

The statement sounded absurd, and she flushed having said it.

"And?" he responded.

The answer surprised her. She frowned. He should have denied it, or at least passed it off as her imagination. She almost wanted to help by suggesting the possibility that some electrical energy perhaps built up around Styles when he had entered the house, had discharged in the field and produced an automatic muscle reaction from the corpse.

"You're saying the dead man rose," she said.

Styles peered at her with grim eyes. He crossed the room and sat beside her on the couch. She noticed the bruises on his neck where the corpse had gripped him.

"What is it you require?" he said, his voice suddenly tired. "Miss Quatermain, what you saw, you saw. You believe, or you do not believe. As Shakespeare might offer, 'There are more things in heaven and earth, Horatio, than are dreamt of in your philosophy.'"

"I don't understand," she started to counter, but he cut her off.

"Why does everything have to be explainable? Because that's the way your mind works? Some things can't be rationalized. Some things shouldn't be explained."

Shallow words. She studied him with a contemptuous eye.

"This is beyond your science, Miss Quatermain," he continued, "but you're one of those logical ones aren't you? You like to collect things and arrange them in neat piles. Cause and effect. But not this."

"You're patronizing me."

"I'm protecting you."

"I don't need protecting."

"I do," he said with a bitter laugh.

Styles leaned back, and let out a long sigh. He covered his eyes. Ember sensed his exhaustion and felt suddenly intrusive. She waited, listening to the quiet of the apartment. She would have sought an unobtrusive exit, but the question that brought her here demanded satisfaction.

"How can the dead rise up?" she asked.

"Miss Quatermain, you should take my words and use them as they were intended, first as a warning that this is beyond your ken and second as a caution against trafficking with these forces."

"You aren't answering me."

"You are correct."

She tried another approach, remembering the other mystery.

"I want to know what went missing from the tunnel and again from the hand of the second dead man in Paddington."

Styles shrugged. "I have no idea."

"Then why were you there?"

He took one of Ember's hands, the boldness of his touch disconcerting. Spreading her fingers out, he ran his fingertips along each one, as if discovering something exotic. She pulled her hand back, but he took it again, this time watching with amusement.

"You're presumptuous," she mustered.

"You come to my apartments, unescorted, at night."

"The cab is waiting."

"Would your father approve such a chaperone?"

Styles surprised her by bowing his head and pressing his lips to her palm. She snatched her hand away as if his touch seared her flesh. He was trying his best to ruffle her feathers, and doing a wonderful job of it. Ember resisted the urge to slap him. Instead she took back control and boldly met his gaze.

"Who sent you to the tunnel?" she demanded. "Who were you working for this morning?" Styles' eyebrows rose. He laughed and settled back with an air of resignation. When he looked at her again, it was with new interest. She felt herself being reassessed. His eyes left her face and moved slowly along the lines of her form. She didn't flinch at his inspection.

"I don't have an employer," he said in earnest. "I was doing a favor for someone, Miss Quatermain. Ember. You don't mind if I use your first name, do you?"

"Who?"

"An excellent question, Ember. I wish I could answer it, but I'm afraid I don't know him. He's never approached me directly. He works through intermediaries."

"So he sent you to the tunnel?"

"He did."

"You sound resentful."

"Do you know what this man is, the one who would command me? He is a necromancer."

His words were surely meant to shock and offend, not to be believed. And yet in light of what she had seen earlier, they couldn't be dismissed out of hand. Somewhere in the ludicrousness of his statement there was something truthful.

"Is that what happened? Someone raised the dead?"

"What do you think? Perhaps you have a scientific rationalization for what you witnessed?"

"I know I wasn't hallucinating."

Her words elicited a grin and she found herself joining him. For a second it was as if both of them had dropped their guards. When the moment passed, Styles let out a long sigh and clapped his hands against his knees, as if a matter had been settled.

"And now Miss Quatermain, I think it best if I escort you to your waiting carriage. I have things yet to accomplish this night."

Ember refused to move. Styles started to rise, but she surprised herself by grabbing his arm and forcing him back onto the sofa. The mischievous smile that came to his lips confirmed the action had been a mistake.

"Ember?" he asked. His tone was suggestive. Before she could brush him back, he leaned forward and pressed his mouth against her throat, and then against her lips. The kiss intensified and his hand moved along her waist.

Ember pushed him, but Styles leaned forward and grabbed a handful of strawberry hair to pull her head back. The kiss became more passionate. Although she struggled against him, she didn't want it to stop. His touch was electric.

Ember disengaged and turned her head. She wanted Mr. Styles to kiss her again, to push her back against the sofa and press against her with his lean torso. If he continued persuading her, she feared she might surrender. As he bent to kiss her once more, she held up a fist and flipped open the top of a signet ring. She held it to his temple.

Styles paused to wrap a hand around her wrist.

"You'd be wise to let go," she said.

"I've never been wise," he replied.

He leaned in and tasted her again. Instead of activating the ring, she slapped him. They both blinked in surprise. Ember scrambled back on the couch, not sure if she feared reprisal, or if she was preparing for another advance. Styles rubbed his cheek and laughed ruefully.

"I can understand now why I've heard such awful things about you," Ember said. "Your behavior is appalling."

"That's not why you slapped me," he said. "You were quite a willing participant."

Styles rose and opened a cabinet, from which he retrieved a bottle of green liquid. He held it up, appeared to think better of it, and instead selected a bottle of whisky. He poured a drink for himself and turned to face his guest.

"You're a beautiful woman, Miss Quatermain. You're bright, lively, and unpredictable. That is perhaps your best trait; I find it provocative."

Ember hated herself for smiling. She stood and smoothed the front of her dress. Styles watched as though she did this for his entertainment.

"I should never have given in to impulse," Ember said.

Styles tipped the remaining amber fluid into his mouth. He held out the crook of his arm for her and smiled with such charm that Ember once again felt a pull in the pit of her stomach.

"Miss Quatermain, I think it best if we call an end to this evening. In a few minutes, I'm not going to be of much use to anyone, especially to a woman of such good breeding and sensitivity."

When she didn't move, he approached and said, "I apologize for being forward. I want you to go now. There's nothing else I'm going to tell you."

"I'll come back when you're sober," Ember said. She started for the door.

"Sober or drunk, I've told you all I can. I have nothing for you. Or anyone. Quit this line of inquiry, Miss Quatermain. You're too smart, too gifted, and too pretty. You don't belong on this side of town. Go back to your own world and stay there."

"You don't know me," she said. "I won't stop until I get the answers I seek."

"Don't denigrate ignorance," Styles said. "It's nature's protection against things we're not prepared to handle. It's the foundation of faith."

"I'll be back," she said.

Before Ember shut the door, she caught a last look at Styles. He stood with his legs slightly apart, and his arms crossed against his chest. His countenance was dark. Seeing him, she thought about the truth of his statement and knew he wasn't cocky, but rather struggling to maintain a façade she didn't understand.

***

Outside, Ogre had returned to his post. The animal raised its head as she passed, attentive but no longer threatening. She walked down the block to the waiting hansom.

"Everything all right, Miss?" the driver asked.

She spoke through gritted teeth. "Just drive me home."

Ember gave Styles' building a last glance before the carriage rolled away over smog-cold cobbles. She sought his window, looking for some sign of him. Her gaze fell instead on a male figure moving stiffly along the sidewalk. He stayed within shadow whenever possible, hurrying and cringing in pale moonlight.

A growl drew her attention to where Ogre stood on the porch. The mastiff bared its fangs and snarled; this wasn't the intimidating rumble with which he had greeted her earlier, this was a frantic response. The snarling stopped and Ember marveled at the sight of the dog slinking away.

"Driver, stop."

This person was up to no good. He obviously had been spying on Styles' residence. Perhaps she should warn him. Mr. Styles stayed in a rough neighborhood and ran with unsavory company; she didn't think it her business.

The figure paused and slipped into shadow, almost invisible. He approached the front door and swayed like a drunkard. She thought of the thing in the field and recalled Styles' explanation with a shiver.

Against her better judgment, Ember again left the safety of the cab. She slipped open her purse and withdrew the most powerful weapon in her small arsenal, a ceramic egg.

"Get back in the cab, Miss," the driver urged. His voice was strained.

Ember ignored him and instead approached the mysterious figure; her egg clutched in one fist. She had to see his face; more than likely it was just a beggar or a drunk on his way home. She would hail the figure, asking if he sought Styles' residence. Once she saw his face, she would laugh at herself for being swayed by Styles' fantastical statements.

Behind her the driver uttered an expletive.

Ember paused and again glanced at Styles' window, but saw nothing.

The figure turned to confront her. The eyes were dead.

Ember choked back a cry and froze. Up until this moment, her skepticism protected her from what she had seen in the field and from Styles' mysterious proclamations.

A leer crossed the lips of the dead man as he approached. Ember threw the egg. It smashed at the man's feet and released a cloud of yellow powder capable of immediately incapacitating someone for hours.

The corpse stood in the midst of the chemical haze, but showed no ill effects. Instead it continued approaching, its grim features now twisted with hatred.

The hansom's mare whinnied, a painful sound. She checked over one shoulder and with alarm watched the animal try to rise in protest. The driver leaned back, with the reins gathered in his large hands. He struggled and shouted commands at the poor beast.

Ember backed up, but the dead man was suddenly within reach. She tried batting away its cold hand, but it shoved aside her defense and closed on her. The smell of decay threatened Ember's sanity.

"You have no place in the dark," it said, the words sounding strained. "You living, you things of light. You deserve nothing."

The hansom's driver gave a shout. The horse and carriage rattled away at a breakneck speed. Hope slipped from Ember and she knew her life balanced on an edge, close to tipping.

Her eyes met the dead man's and she saw his rotting skin and remembered how he moved along the face of the building, staying in darkness where possible and hurrying through the moonlight when necessary.

Her slender fingers slipped once again into the purse.

"Don't hurt me," she whispered. She gripped the crystal egg from the other night. There wasn't much left within the glass shell, but she wouldn't need much.

The dead man shook her like a dog might a small animal. The rotting face pressed closer, touching her skin. It wanted her afraid; her terror was nourishment.

Ember concentrated. She used her thumb to change a setting; she didn't want an explosive flash of light, but a strong fountain of brilliance that would last several minutes. She flipped the plate separating the chemicals within.

White light washed over them, driving away the shadows.

With a shriek the dead man released her. It stumbled beyond the small circle of illumination, finding the protection of the doorway on the stoop outside Styles' apartment. She feared the light merely startled the thing, and cast about for a path to escape. Her stomach contracted and her fear shamed her.

"Well done, Miss Quatermain."

The voice came from behind. She whipped about, fearful of the new danger. The old man she noted earlier stood with arms spread to show himself no threat. Ember's glance bounced from the new presence to the thing sheltered in the doorway.

"The light is starting to fade," the old man said. "You'll have to make a decision quickly. Come with me."

"Why should I?"

The old man nodded and stepped back. "I can give you the answers you came looking for. Want to know why those two fellows died? Want to know what they found that was so valuable?"

The light diminished until it was almost a candle's glow. The dead man hissed and moved from the doorway.

"Miss Quatermain, I'm leaving," the old man said. "If you're coming, then you'll need to come now. The breach is closing."

She wanted to argue, to ask him what he was talking about. Instead, she took a leap and held out her hand. He clasped it and with an encouraging glance, led her swiftly away.

CHAPTER VII

Wherein Miss Quatermain meets Timothy, who drags her to an odd neighborhood and divulges astounding information

THE CITY MELTED AWAY AS THE LONDON MIST INTENSIFIED. Her body felt strangely suspended, and she thought of the sensation experienced long ago when she'd brashly smoked her father's opium pipe. She wondered if the intense blast of phosphorus had affected her senses during the stand against the dead man.

Time sped up. Despite trying to hold the seconds in her head, she could not count them.

Voices greeted her guide as they moved, coming from all angles in contrasting volumes. She saw shapes and felt the presence of those she couldn't clearly see.

"Good evening, Timothy," rumbled a deep voice. An impossible-to-determine time later, a woman sang in Cockney, "'Ello squire."

Consciousness wavered as Ember floated, feeling barely attached to the hand clamped around her wrist. She tried to drive off the effects of the drug; there was no other explanation for her sudden disorientation.

"Mr. Tim, good to see you," the accent Scottish.

"Buona sera, Signore."

After what seemed like an age, she stood before a tall wrought iron gate, its hinges pitted with rust.

"What did you do to me?" she asked, fighting to keep the words from slurring.

He took her chin and lifted it. Their eyes met and she saw concern in his gaze. His sallow eyes seemed to change color, from a pale blue to a pale gray. They were kind eyes, set beneath unruly white brows.

"You're not drugged. Stand still for a moment, your head will clear. We'll wait."

"I don't know where we are."

The mist swirled and obstructed the street. They couldn't have gone more than a few blocks, yet she had the sense they had traveled a long distance. Ember gazed up at the gate and composed herself with wary eyes.

"That's better now, isn't it?" he asked.

They passed through the gate and across an entryway. The haze ebbed as an odd collection of wondrous lodgings came into view. The structures were too close together, the streets too narrow. The neighborhood was a hodgepodge of architecture: Gothic, Renaissance, Tudor, Baroque, Rococo. Looking about, she knew of nowhere in London where they might be, and certainly not within walking distance of Styles' apartment.

"Almost there," Timothy cooed.

Ember stopped.

"We're just up here," he said, indicating stairs to a small apartment. Ember again fought to orient herself to the strangeness of their surroundings. Seeing her hesitate, Timothy gave her shoulder a gentle squeeze and pointed up the steps.

"Please" he said with an encouraging lilt.

His voice soothed her fears enough to allow Ember to follow him inside. He had saved her, after all. He had taken her hand and led her away from the dead man.

As they entered a set of comfortably decorated rooms, a tall woman turned to face them. She was middle-aged, with a high forehead accentuated by frosty eyes. Seeing them, her mouth opened slightly and those eyes seethed with disapproval.

"You brought her here," the woman said.

"Miss Quatermain had an unfortunate brush with one of the dead, Adala," Timothy replied. He shook his head and narrowed his eyes.

"*Nekroanypomonos.*" Adala pronounced the word as if it were painful. "Why bring her here?"

"I think she has something to offer. Miss Quatermain has abilities she's only just begun to discover about herself."

"I thought we agreed on the other."

"The other lacks stability. He is unreliable."

"That wasn't entirely your choice to make, Tim."

Adala waved Ember into a chair and her body responded before her mind could catch up. She fell heavily onto soft cushions and partly closed her eyes in comfort.

"She's so young," Adala said.

"Don't underestimate the girl," Timothy countered. "And the other isn't much older."

"The other has experience in the dark realities."

"This one held her own against one of the restless dead."

Adala gave her an appreciative glance. "How did she accomplish that?"

Timothy grunted and took Ember's hand. He patted it and smiled encouragingly. "Would you like tea, Miss Quatermain?"

Ember opened her eyes and accepted his offer. While she waited for her host to bring refreshment, she studied her surroundings, noting the amazing number of mirrors hanging on the walls and standing free. Here were glasses of all shapes and sizes, ancient ones dulled under thick patinas, and sparkling geometric ones. In one mirror she beheld a desk in the corner with a brass globe perched on its surface. Several copper rods were soldered together at the poles, and an equatorial band bearing strange markings wrapped around the frame. Gears clicked as the globe rotated on its axis.

Ember looked over her shoulder to see the actual globe, but the corner was empty. She stared back at the glass with wonder.

The clockwork innards continued to tick, producing a predictable pattern as the orb spun around its base. Sprouting from the top pole, little crystals danced on fine chains. Diamonds perhaps. She suspected they represented the stars, but something about them looked strange.

"Here you go, Miss Quatermain," Timothy said as he returned. He set a silver tea service down on a glass table and poured three cups, handing the first to Ember and another to Adala before taking one for himself.

"I still don't know where we are," Ember said.

Coming here, allowing herself to be led by an old man, even one as harmless looking as this one, was a foolish act. At the time, with the hansom long gone, stranded in an unfamiliar neighborhood, it seemed like a fair gamble.

"Who are you two?" Ember asked. She was determined to share as little information as possible until someone started answering questions.

The old man sighed and sampled his tea. The flavor evidently pleased him, for he sat back in his narrow chair and took several sips before answering.

"Sometimes I'm not sure," he said playfully, but there was a hint of weariness in his voice. "You know, the name Timothy comes from the Greek; it means 'in God's honor.' I've always liked that. Do you know the meaning of your name? Ember comes from the Latin: '*urere*,' meaning 'to burn.'"

Adala shifted impatiently. The old man nodded and pulled a folded sheet of foolscap from his overcoat. He carefully spread it onto the table. It was a map of Europe, detailed with intricate scrawling.

"I've drawn this up. Is it at all familiar?" he asked.

Ember shook her head, but thought somehow she should know this. Her curiosity fired, holding wariness at bay.

Timothy looked solemn.

"Several people have died for the information contained here," he said. "One old man, a sadistic pedophile named Theron Giannis, cheated someone seeking to buy this and instead sold to a higher bidder. He should have kept with the original deal."

His finger followed several lines running over the familiar landscape of Great Britain and Europe. He paused at Paddington and tapped the page.

"This is the site of the Underground diggings. Here. This is where those two unfortunates were struck down by an electrical charge."

His eyes left the map and fixed on Ember.

"These lines," he said, "represent manifestations of where planes intersect. These are places where energies gather and disperse, where a wall is built between different possibilities."

Ember pinched her chin, trying to piece together what Timothy suggested. "By energies, you mean both electric and magnetic?"

"And light. Light is made of rapidly changing electric and magnetic fields, you know."

"So if electric fields and magnetic fields are both part of light, then if you change one field you also change the other by proxy."

Timothy leaned back in his seat, his fingertips forming a tent. He laughed and addressed Adala. "You see what a quick study she is? I told you."

Ember considered the logical conclusion—if light always moved, the fields were constantly in flux. It meant there might be places where the energies were stronger, and places where they were weaker. If someone could exploit such a weakness, the wall between the planes might be pierced or even collapsed.

He drew her attention back to the map.

"See this line," he pressed down a thin finger, "the tunnel excavation intersects here . . . that's where it was hidden."

"What?"

"A key to something old—something that is said to once have belonged to Hermes. Have you ever heard of the Emerald Tablet? It is a relic of the gods, Miss Quatermain."

The Emerald Tablet. Ember's head swam. This must be a dream.

"Lysimachus of Arcarnania himself hid the tablet's key here," Timothy continued. "It was Alexander the Great's tutor, The Phoenix, who fashioned this map."

"Alexander's tutor was Aristotle," she said.

"He had several tutors. Aristotle was wise in the ways of the material world, though he perceived the puzzle of the aether. Lysimachus, on the other hand, was a spiritual man. He was a guardian of arcane knowledge."

She returned to the idea of the energy lines separating the immense planes of conflicting realities. If this was true, the natural world was vast beyond all comprehension. She didn't know what might be possible. The immensity of the implication tumbled down on her, and anxiety gripped her chest.

"It would serve you well to memorize this map," Timothy instructed.

"Why?" she demanded. She didn't like the feeling that the old man was playing games.

"Because it's important. The map will give you a clue as to where the relic might be found."

"Why not get it yourself," she challenged.

"I used to know where it was. But I was unable to trust even myself."

"And now?"

"I still don't trust myself. That is why I will never physically touch the tablet. I'll once more shield it and send it where no one will touch it again."

"And you were so successful the first time," Adala said.

He let his head hang for a brief moment before continuing. "Please trust me and study the map. If nothing else, it will give you the same information your rival has."

"My rival? Who is that?"

"Not now," Timothy replied and tapped the map again.

She laughed weakly. "I can't memorize this," she insisted. "Maybe if I had the time and the inclination."

"Give it hard study," Timothy urged.

She looked at the miniature details, seeing the carefully rendered lines sweeping along, some running parallel and some intersecting one another. Dots appeared at different sites, many following the lines, others randomly dispersed. Seeing them, she thought of the diamonds dancing above the brass globe in the mysterious mirror across the room.

And just as she'd begun, Timothy folded the map back up, once again tucking it in the folds of his overcoat.

This time, Ember's laugh was strident. "You're having at me."

Timothy's eyes were stern. "You've memorized it," he said. "You may be skeptical, but you haven't yet touched your potential."

Adala, still silent, regarded Ember. Timothy noted his companion's apparent doubt.

"I'm not exaggerating," he said. "If her abilities were to be known, they would place her in danger from those who would fear her and resent her for it. Some might even question her humanity."

The words disturbed Ember, tapping her desire to be accepted.

With a kind smile he added, "You haven't even begun your journey."

Ember's expression sobered. "I don't understand what you want from me."

"I'm just an old man, Miss Quatermain. I don't want anything. I'm content in my little corner. However, there is someone who is not content with his little corner, a dark man who traffics with the dead. He also seeks the relic. With it, he could draw enormous powers through the barriers, becoming godlike, transforming matter in horrible ways, perhaps changing the nature of reality itself.

"I see my words cause concern. Good. Be frightened, Miss Quatermain. If he doesn't know about you, he soon will. Once he does, he will seek you out and either claim you, or destroy you."

Ember pressed her hands to her temples, her head throbbing in protest as it processed the information. She thought of the animated corpse outside the Strand apartment. Was he referring to Styles?

"Right now, he has the key he recovered from the excavation at Paddington, but he is still unable to read it. The key, however will lead him to the relic—the Emerald Tablet. You find it first."

"How?"

"Use the map. The answer is hidden in the lines."

Timothy opened his mouth to say more, but was cut off by the ringing of a church bell. Its clamorous cry rattled the mirrors within. He stood and a thousand Timothys stood with him.

"Is it an alarm?" Ember asked.

"It's a summons," he said. The ringing unsettled Adala. She stood, nervously smoothing her dress.

Ember rose as well.

"Don't worry, Miss Quatermain, it's merely an abstraction. It's all just abstraction."

Adala pointed toward the door. "I'll go. You take her back."

Again the church bell sounded.

"Come on, dear, we should be going. It's not good to mix realities too long, it upsets the balance of things."

"What about the other?" Adala asked.

Timothy gave it thought and shook his head. "There is no other."

Ember followed Timothy's exit from his little rooms, down the front steps, and in the opposite direction of the way they first came. Outside, she again became disoriented. She put her head down and took little note of the strange structures they passed. Her guide led her through a small stone arch with a wooden door. Ember stepped through, her body tingling as she crossed the threshold, and passed into a clinging fog.

A familiar carriage sat in front of her father's home. She stared at it for some time before finally dragging herself from the hansom and letting herself in. Weary and exhausted, her mind reeled trying to process the events of the last twenty-four hours. So much had changed in such a short a time. Her entire belief system trembled under the burden of the new knowledge she had gained.

A servant named Lucy met her in the hall, taking her coat and hat.

"Mr. Masterson is here," Lucy said.

"So I see."

"He's been waiting for at least three hours," she said.

"Tell me he hasn't," Ember groaned. She considered sending Lucy in with an apology. Instead, she gathered her strength and went to meet him.

Masterson sat by a comfortable fire, a book open in his lap. His deep-set eyes were half-closed and his huge frame appeared relaxed.

Ember put on a false smile.

"Mr. Masterson, I hear you've been waiting for hours. My apologies. I didn't realize you were stopping by."

Her presence startled him. The book dropped from his lap to fall loudly on the floor. He recovered it and stood stiffly. He greeted Ember, eyes scrutinizing her in an uncomfortable manner.

"You've been out late," he said, as if he expected her to respond with an explanation.

Ember went to the fire and extended her palms. A log settled and the flames brightened for a moment.

"Would you like something? Tea? Perhaps something from my father's cellar?"

"That's kind of you, but no."

He sat back down and pulled a cigar case from his pocket. Ember settled into a comfortable chair opposite him and watched as he fiddled forever with the cigar, trimming the edge, rolling it over a flame, sucking in smoke to get it just right.

Ember removed a pipe from the small table next to her chair and mimicked Masterson's fastidiousness, tamping down the strong tobacco with a practiced motion before finally striking a match.

"Are you really going to smoke that?" he asked. She rankled at the disapproval in his voice.

In answer, she drew in a mouthful of smoke and leaned back as she exhaled a pale blue cloud.

"Now, Mr. Masterson, is there anything I can do for you? I assume you waited all this time for a reason."

He used his thumb to remove a bit of tobacco from his lip. His eyes fixed on it and he wiped off the offending particle on the rim of a nearby ashtray.

"I was interested in what you found at the excavation," he said. His voice was casual.

"Why?" she asked.

"When your father and I discussed it last night, it roused my curiosity. A dead man in the Underground at the site where ancient artifacts have been unearthed—it ignites the imagination."

His enthusiasm shouldn't have surprised her. Although Masterson was a crushing bore most of the time, he was a scholar and an expert in Greek and Roman mythology. He had generously funded expeditions into unfamiliar territories. Most recently, he gave money to her father for a journey to the Nile. Maybe his perspective on the strange events in the Underground would be useful.

Ember launched into a quick narrative of her experiences at the Paddington excavation, describing in detail the unearthed Roman artifacts. Masterson listened without moving a muscle, but when she mentioned the soapstone, he begged to be allowed to examine it.

He took it into his hands and ran his finger over the surface. His mouth opened slightly and he whispered something to himself she didn't catch.

"Do you recognize it?" she asked.

"No," he said, and Ember felt he wasn't being forthcoming.

Masterson leaned forward and frowned. He took a moment before speaking. "What was it that killed those poor men?" Masterson asked. "They didn't show signs of violence, did they?"

It surprised her that he should ask her opinion on anything.

"I think they were exposed to a sudden tremendous discharge of energy," Ember replied.

His posture changed slightly at the answer. He relaxed his shoulders and drew another mouthful of smoke from his cigar.

"What would bring about such a discharge?" he asked.

"That's the mystery, isn't it?" she said.

Masterson turned the soapstone over, sliding a well-manicured fingernail along its edge. His hands were almost delicate in appearance. Styles' fingernails had been ragged, and his hands had scars on them. Not the hands of a gentleman, but not the hands of a workman, either.

"What do you know of Peter Styles?" she asked.

The question startled Masterson.

"I've heard nothing good about him," he blurted. "Not that we've been properly introduced; I've only met him in passing. We've attended some of the same affairs."

"He was at the site, as well, carrying on his own investigation."

"Was he? Stay away from him, Miss Quatermain. He's a hedonist of the first order. The man's burned through London like a comet, but his brilliance is fading. It may come to a complete end tomorrow."

"What happens tomorrow?"

"The rake was caught cheating at cards and compounded his crime by insulting his host. He has a quick wit and a stinging one. I have heard there will be a duel at dusk."

It disturbed her to hear this; she didn't like the idea of Styles coming to harm. She loathed admitting it, but he had made a strong impression.

"I met someone else who warned me away from Styles. He said he was engaged in other things that would bring him to ruin."

"I can't imagine what more he could do?" Masterson brayed.

"This person said Styles was involved in the occult."

Her father's friend stopped laughing. Instead he studied his cigar and finally turned a serious eye on her.

"If I were you, Ember, I would put Mr. Styles entirely from your mind. He's a bad egg, and people who associate with him run the risk of having their reputations tarnished as well."

"You know more than you're telling."

"I know more than I'm willing to tell," Masterson admitted. "You're Allan Quatermain's daughter, and you've been exposed to enough that you should respect such matters."

"Is Peter Styles a necromancer?" she asked.

Masterson's eyebrows rose and he blinked rapidly. He laughed, but he didn't sound amused.

"Where did you get such an absurd notion?" he asked and Ember felt suddenly quite stupid. "Ember, while superstition and magic may not be restricted to the jungles of Africa and the Arabian deserts, I think one would be hard-pressed to find someone practicing necromancy in London."

"It is an absurd notion," she said.

"I'll grant you Styles is rude and something of an imbecile, but he still comes from a good family and has many honorable friends. His father is a respected country squire."

Masterson extinguished the stub of his cigar and rose to leave. His face showed signs of agitation and weariness. Ember stood out of courtesy, emptying her pipe in the hearth.

"Ember, do you think I could take your soapstone with me? I'd like to show it to some people. I promise its safe return."

She complied without question. He pocketed the stone and

paused again, still troubled by something. A sheepish expression appeared.

"I have one last thing before I go. It's the real reason I came by tonight."

His manner made her suddenly uncomfortable. She couldn't read his face, but she felt his embarrassment. Masterson grinned sheepishly and tugged at his sideburns.

"Ember, I am a man of property, respected in the community," he began. He paused and she could tell he was considering his words carefully. "Perhaps you think a man in his late forties is past his prime, and you may be right, although I would argue otherwise.

"I said something to your father before he left, last night to be exact. I'm not known to be impulsive, but I couldn't help myself."

He pulled a polished wooden box from his pocket, removing the lid to reveal a little gold pocket watch.

"With your permission, I'd appreciate the opportunity of becoming your suitor. We'll be quite proper about it, of course. From here on, I'll only visit when an appropriate chaperone is present."

He turned her hand over, resting the open box in her palm. A knot coiled inside Ember's stomach.

"I can't accept this."

He shook his head. "The watch is yours, either way. When I saw it, I thought it suited you. All I ask is that you don't take it apart and use it in one of your inventions."

He smiled self-consciously and shifted his weight, as if hoping she would say something meaningful or offer him some encouragement. She carefully thanked him for the gift, but said little else; fearful he might misconstrue her words.

Masterson acknowledged the lack of enthusiasm with a red-faced nod and shrugged on his coat. He avoided eye contact as he walked to the doorway.

"Just consider it," he called over his shoulder. "Your time would be better spent with me than with some self-indulgent engaged in futile pursuits."

He stalked out of the room.

Ember stared after Masterson. She felt sorry for the man since she could never accept him as a serious suitor, but she also felt angry at her father for having agreed to Masterson's intentions without even consulting her.

The fire crackled comfortably, warming and lulling her. She relaxed her shoulders and settled into the enormous chair once again. She lifted her feet to the ottoman and placed the watch on the table beside her. What an awkward gift, but then Masterson was an awkward personality.

The ticking of the watch's second hand reminded Ember of the globe spied within the mirror in Timothy's apartments. She thought about the strangeness of the experience. Her hand strayed to the watch and she ran a finger over its surface. The slender second hand continued its sweep, like the diamonds suspended over the brass globe, following a predetermined path and altering slightly with each pass.

Her eyes narrowed as the fire continued to lull her. She drifted off winding along lines where reality intersected as bright sparks marked where breaches opened from one reality to the next.

Heading into sleep, she heard Timothy whispering, "As above, so below."

CHAPTER VIII

*Wherein Peter Styles encounters the restless dead
and discovers the existence of yet another influence*

ETER STYLES LISTENED TO THE SOUND OF EMBER QUATERMAIN HASTENING DOWN THE STAIRS OF HIS APARTMENT BUILDING.

He shook his head and dropped into an easy chair where he threw a leg casually over one of its arms and contemplated his rude behavior toward the woman. The intriguing Miss Quatermain, a head strong woman, but obviously brilliant, if not lacking common sense. What a lapse in judgment coming alone to this neighborhood after dark. A twinge of guilt stung him. He should not have treated her like one of the bored housewives he regularly bedded.

He should go after her and make sure she made it safely across the street to the waiting hansom. Peter crossed to the window and stared down at her retreating form, noting the rear view Miss Quatermain presented had an alluring shape. The driver of the hansom came down from the cab to open the door for her.

This woman brought trouble. He would do well to avoid becoming ensnared. That long graceful neck and those reddish curls; her captivating gray eyes, quick to express pleasure and passion—bait for someone else, but not for the savvy Peter Styles.

He turned back to his room and rested a moment against the window sash. The light from the street changed.

A chill ran through Peter. He cast his mind and knew the presence of the *nekroanypomonos*.

Peter gripped the windowsill for support and again stared down at the street. A rag-draped form staggered away from blazing white light. It headed into the shadows, arms raised protectively. The person bearing the light source was invisible in the brightness, but he knew Ember's presence.

Peter whirled around and charged from the room. He pounded down the narrow steps, slipped near the bottom, and slid the rest of the way. Pain shot from his ankle.

He ignored the stinging and limped into the cold night, grateful for the sobering effect of fear and pain.

Abruptly the light went out and he heard a pair of steps hurrying away. Peter cast about in the darkness for Ember, calling out to her. Someone else was there, someone who emanated power.

"Miss Quatermain!" he shouted.

The air crackled and Peter felt a disturbance in the aether. Her presence abruptly vanished, as if she stepped through a door and pulled it shut behind her.

He let his awareness flow and tried to find a thread to follow. There was nothing.

He was about to move down the block, when something grabbed his arm and flung him into the brick wall of the apartment building.

In his concern for Miss Quatermain he had forgotten about the *nekroanypomonos*.

The cadaverous face twisted with horrible rage. It leaned against him, pinioning him to the brick. This was the same dead man who had visited him the night before to deliver the threat from his former mentor.

"I want to bleed you." It almost wept the words.

The thing's rage passed through him, igniting his own self-loathing. "Then bleed me!" Peter shouted.

"Tell me what you found. Tell Master," it rasped. "Or I will hurt you."

Peter snarled and shoved back at the corpse. He peered through the darkness, searching the aether for the path between this bag of rotting flesh and its animator.

The cadaver made a murderous lunge. It shoved him against the wall and closed a hand over his throat. Rage roared through Peter's mind.

"Master doesn't need you alive," it hissed. "Master can make you one of us, and you'll tell him everything."

The waiting maw of death closed on Peter. The part of him that still clung to life sorted through the complicated strands of energy passing through the *nekroanypomonos*.

He only had seconds before he lost consciousness.

Peter saw the energy strand fashioned by Virgil. As always it was distinct, crude and awkward in fashion, but strong in its simplicity.

Compared to the more practiced and powerful hand of the Italian he'd danced with earlier in the small field in Paddington, this was the work of a talentless amateur. Yet, the strand was buffered so the identity of the one wielding it remained hidden.

He would have only one chance. Peter directed his energy into a blade to sever the connection between the necromancer and its puppet. By the cadaver's silence and its sudden cessation of movement, he guessed the thing knew what he was doing.

"Free me," it whispered, the voice suddenly too human.

He could break the bond, but not truly free servant from master, not as long as Virgil maintained some relic of the dead man—a lock of hair, a remnant of the burial shroud, an item the thing found important in its human existence.

"Free me," the thing said again.

Peter felt his strength returning. He seized the opportunity and again exerted himself, weakening the necromancer's hold. The cadaver's head lolled obscenely.

"Who is he?" Peter demanded. "Who is Virgil?"

The thing sobbed, but no tears ran from its dead eyes.

"Who is Virgil? Tell me and I'll let you go."

"I can't." The answer was given with profound regret.

"Tell me. How does he mask himself?"

Its silence wrenched Peter's heart. The thing pulled in air in a struggle to fill its diaphragm. It spoke with tremendous effort, the sound thick with emotion.

"I do not know him," it wept. "I know he'll kill you and make your body his own."

"You know only that he will try," Peter corrected.

"He hates you like the dead hate the living. He thinks you would be his master, Peter Styles. He hates you as much as he fears the other."

"You know of the other?"

"I know you are caught in a trap between the two of them."

Peter felt Virgil through a ripple in the aether; the necromancer observed him through the dead man's eyes and ears.

With his teeth clenched in anger, Peter threw his will through the aether and shredded the tether. The cadaver's hand went limp and the body dropped to the cobblestones.

Still gasping for air, Peter sank back against the wall and stared down at the body.

The time would come when he and Virgil once again met face to face. He looked forward to paying the man back.

The cold of the night made him shiver. The drop in temperature was a byproduct of both the necromantic spell that animated the corpse, and his own manipulation of energy. His breath hung in the air as mist.

Peter checked his surroundings, watching for anyone in shadow. He didn't want to be found beside a corpse; his father would not again intercede if the authorities came to call. And Scotland Yard had no fondness for him since the scandal with the commissioner made the newspapers.

Peter reached down and gripped the wrists of the dead man. He would drag the body down the block, stay close to the shadows, and leave it in an alley.

"Mr. Styles, you need not concern yourself. Leave him and I will see he is tended to."

Peter whirled about in a defensive posture, his back pressed to the apartment wall. He wasn't prepared for any form of supernatural battle, and he was too tired to flee. He drew in what power he could and searched the night for this new threat.

Ogre appeared, the great mastiff padded silently in his direction, head down, tail waving back and forth. The animal showed no signs of alarm. The beast rubbed its muzzle against Peter's leg as he smoothed the hair behind its ears and kneaded the loose skin. All the while, Peter waited, listening for footsteps, not daring to drop his psychic defenses. He considered feeling for the presence of another, but worried in doing so he might make himself vulnerable.

"It's not enough to break the bond," the voice said. "You need to bury the body with salt and stick iron nails about the grave at the points of a pentacle."

A woman stepped from the darkness. He recognized her from earlier this day. She had been in the crowd surrounding the field.

"Finally," she continued, "you should pray. It doesn't matter to what deity, as long as your intention is pure."

Peter noted Ogre still wagged a tail and sniffed the air with interest but no concern. He stayed against the wall of the building and acknowledged her.

"The prayer keeps the necromancer from reclaiming what he owns," Peter said.

The statement brought a wry amusement to the woman's face. "The necromancer never owns the dead, and the prayer is for you, so obviously in deep need of it."

She came closer, and he smelled lavender laced with vanilla. It had a calming effect. Peter studied her features. She was in her late fifties, but her smooth skin gave her a youthful appearance. Her silver-streaked hair was combed back, accentuating a strong face with deep set eyes and thin, well-formed lips.

"You can call me Adala," she said, and for the first time Peter realized they had been speaking German to one another.

He looked at her with trepidation and sampled the energies in the air.

"Where did you come from?" he asked.

She ignored his question and approached the body. Her face saddened as she stood over it. "I weep for the *nekroanypomonos*. They are so angry and lost. You know, each time one of them is dragged across the aether, there is a terrible price to pay. I don't think your Virgil understands the real consequences of his actions."

"Who is Virgil?" Peter demanded. He watched her face, still trying to gauge the threat she posed.

"He'll reveal himself, and when he does, you'll be ready. Be aware though, Mr. Styles, that there are several players in the game."

"Like yourself?"

"Like myself. And others."

Adala knelt beside the corpse and pressed her hands together in prayer. Peter waited respectfully, but again checked the street. He wanted more answers, but any moment he expected to hear the shrill cry of a police whistle.

"Not all dead who walk are what you have termed the *nekroanypomonos*," she said. "There are others who come willingly, who make the journey peacefully. Life and death are part of the same reality."

Ogre whined, smelling the night air. The mastiff casually trotted off after something.

Adala nodded and stood. She squeezed Peter's arm. "We cannot finish our conversation now, Mr. Styles. You should go, too. As I said, we will take care of this."

"Who will?"

"Go, Herr Styles. Discovery is near. You do not want to be approached by the law."

"Why should I trust you," Peter asked.

She smiled at this. "You don't have a choice. Go now!"

She spoke with the tone of someone used to being obeyed. Peter was about to challenge her, but a stir in the breeze gave him pause. Energy built nearby, running along the street, and growing in intensity. An unpleasant buzzing filled his ears.

He raised his eyebrows and glanced at Adala, who gazed at him with amusement.

"I'm being manipulated, and I don't like it," he said.

"Too many puzzles, Mr. Styles. Too much at stake."

The buzzing grew louder and the temperature continued to fall. Peter reached for Adala's consciousness, in hopes of discovery, but she blocked him. Her eyes turned icy.

"Your talent doesn't always match your swagger, Mr. Styles. One last thought; self-punishment isn't the path to redemption. I'll see you again soon, my lovely boy."

A crackling in the air startled Peter. He jerked back and pressed against the wall. The rush of energy crippled him with vertigo. He drew a protective shell about himself and turned to challenge Adala, positive this was her doing.

Peter pivoted and found himself alone.

The buzzing ended as if sliced away. He shook his head in amazement and felt around for any remnant of the woman's presence. Nothing. Where had she gone? Was this an illusion? Had she somehow dazed him?

Peter drew his coat close about him and started off down the street, moving with long strides. Adala had helped him out, to be sure, but her presence raised many questions, and the possible answers made him uneasy.

If the woman knew Virgil's identity, why hadn't she just told him? She was playing games. She had offered him help, but he sensed there was a price.

"Not all dead who walk are *nekroanypomonos*," he said, repeating her words. "Others come willingly."

Peter was in over his head. He had been since the day he allowed Virgil to seduce him.

His father hoped time spent in Germany, deep in academic pursuit, would help Peter find maturity and temper his hedonistic behavior. He returned from Europe gaunt, moody, and reclusive. He had written his father about Maddalene, a young woman he intended to bring home as a bride. However Peter returned to England alone and unwilling to talk about his loss, other than to mention the drowning in hushed, bitter tones before quickly changing topic.

His behavior worsened, and he resumed his hedonistic pursuits, only now they were joyless, extreme, and self-destructive.

At one dinner party Gabriel Montresor, an eccentric inventor, mentioned an event he was hosting at a hunting lodge in the north.

"You must come, Peter," he urged. "I promise you the most libertine experience imaginable. We'll redefine sin."

The party was to be a masquerade, of course. Anonymity protected identities and released inhibitions.

He arrived after midnight, and instantly wished he hadn't come. He would need to wear more than one mask.

The guests lounging about gave little notice. A malaise seemed to have gripped most of the party goers, and their revelry was forced and shallow. Perhaps the shock or the novelty of the evening had worn off, and what remained was the desperate ludicrousness of their gathering.

A woman wearing a white ceramic mask intercepted Peter and pressed his face between gloved hands. The smell of honeysuckle overwhelmed him.

"You're a pretty one," she cooed.

Peter hid behind a narrow band of black silk with two eyeholes. He took her hands away from his face and kissed both her palms.

"Use me," she said. "As you will."

He ignored her offer and instead pushed past the woman. She accepted rejection without protest, but Peter could hear her inner pain and the consideration of the effort required to make a suitable scene. In the end it wasn't worth it.

The masked woman instead eased her arms around another individual, rubbing lasciviously against a heavyset individual wearing a papier-mâché *hound's face*.

Peter entered a small room where a figure in black held audience with three people lounging on divans. They urged the man on, laughing with delighted disgust at his description of necrophilia.

"I've often felt some of my partners weren't quite among the living," one wag said.

"What's the allure?" one woman asked.

"Role-play?" someone offered.

"It isn't role-play if your partner is unmoving dead flesh."

"Not all dead flesh is unmoving," the man in black responded.

"I don't see too many corpses dancing about, except perhaps in the House of Lords."

The statement provoked the expected mirth.

"We know little of the natural world," the man in black said. "We play at being enlightened, but we have little understanding of the true nature of life and death. Or of the nature of reality itself."

"And you do?"

"I know the dead can rise."

The statement brought a lull in conversation.

At the University of Bonn a student who claimed knowledge of thaumaturgy, later kicked out for his beliefs, sought to ease Peter's grief over Maddalene's death.

"Death is a doorway, not a destination," the disgraced student had said. "One can step across a threshold and return, but the experience of the journey is transformative."

Perhaps the *nekroanypomonos* were transformed from what they had been in life.

"I'm not religious," the reveler said to the man in black. "The nature of reality is far too deep a subject for me."

The fellow put his arms around the two women and they rose. With shrill laughter, the three unsteadily slipped from the room.

Peter remained, gazing at the black draped figure, trying to feel the person behind the mask. A null field surrounded the individual. Peter increased his focus, trying to pick out something about the man's personality, or a hint about his identity. Nothing. He had never encountered anything like it.

He sat down opposite the fellow and they examined one another in silence. Again Peter tried piercing the veil and again came up empty.

"You speak like someone familiar with necromancy," Peter said.

"Do I, Mr. Styles?"

The use of his name was meant to disarm him, but Peter only shrugged. "I have no reputation to preserve."

The gentleman leaned forward in an act of intimacy. He put a hand on Peter's arm and squeezed. "I've heard things about you, sir;

things you do and say which make people uncomfortable to be in your company. It seems you have talent.

Peter didn't speak.

The masked man gave a grunt of satisfaction and sat back. "I think certain meetings are fated, don't you?" he said.

"Remove your mask," Peter demanded.

The man's laughter filled the room.

"You want to know who I am, use your ability."

"You're blocking me," Peter said.

The stranger rose, smoothing the black cape he wore. He pulled a cigar from a pocket and spent several moments trimming the edge, obsessing over it before striking a match.

"I think it best if I keep my identity closed to you, at least until we know one another better. If you'd like, you can call me Virgil."

"Are you here to guide me through Hell?"

Virgil laughed and stepped closer.

"I could be your guide, Mr. Styles."

"And show me what?"

"How to see beyond the ordinary. Life doesn't end when our bodies cease to function. There is so much more. Do you want to raise the dead? They have many secrets they can tell."

"Is raising the dead the key to bringing back the living?"

"The only way to know that is to do it," Virgil replied. "Do you want to raise the dead, Mr. Styles?"

He couldn't answer.

"Think it over," Virgil said. "A man with your abilities could do amazing things with the proper guidance, maybe even bring back the living."

He and Virgil met clandestinely through the following year while the man continued guarding his identity, both physically and magically.

It was their last meeting which haunted him most of all. Virgil led him through an alley and into a narrow entranceway. The man unlocked a door and waved him in.

"I have a friend whose work in anatomy has helped the medical profession wonderfully," Virgil proclaimed as he went about the room lighting candles. The pale orange light illuminated a figure stretched out on the wood floor, covered by white linen.

"I no longer have the desire to see you raise the dead," Peter said.

Virgil ignored him and continued speaking. "My friend once invited me to his workshop for a demonstration and I suspect to convince me to fund some of his work. I'm a rich man. There, now you know something about me, Mr. Styles.

At any rate, one such demonstration involved the vivisection of a canine. The animal whined and howled piteously. My friend assured me the animal didn't actually experience pain. We were merely displaying anthropomorphism; much as we attribute to other races and civilizations sensibilities and intelligences that are uniquely British."

"Animals feel pain," Peter objected, thinking of the oafish Ogre.

"Do they?" Virgil said dismissively. "Well, I won't question your excellent education. But I assure you, Mr. Styles, the dead can't feel pain if they are no longer human. Their display of anguish is a memory and nothing else, like the raging cries of the *nekroanypomonos*. It's hollow.

Virgil ripped the sheet from the corpse of a young woman. He stepped back and summoned Peter closer.

"Isn't she lovely? I brought her for you."

"I don't want to do this. I don't want to raise the dead."

"You don't have to raise the dead, Mr. Styles. You know that. There are other uses for necromancy."

The statement hung between them, a tease Peter couldn't ignore. He gazed at the corpse and a sad smile formed.

"Goddamn you," he said.

He accepted the small sack of salt Virgil offered, and poured out a handful. The crystals ran through his fingers.

He moved slowly, spreading a narrow ring around the body. When the circle was complete, Peter raised his head and peered at Virgil. They locked eyes, and the older man looked away first.

Peter spoke the words, the invocation stumbling over his lips. He concentrated, drawing the energy from the air about them. Power surged through the aether and flowed into the corpse.

He waited.

Awareness came with a rush and the presence of many drifted through his mind, distinct entities passing from one reality to another. Their yearnings, their pain, their elation, all transformed into acceptance and peaceful unity.

No, not all.

Others winked out; some returned, some twisted and changed into something obscene.

The temptation proved too great, as Virgil knew it would be. With mounting anxiety, Peter tentatively reached into the darkness and sought Maddalene.

He didn't expect anything. Yet, he suddenly knew the path, and traveled it as if having done so a thousand times.

Her presence flowed about him and the memories rushed at him too quickly to seize and appreciate any one, so instead Peter opened himself to their totality. For a brief moment he knew peace.

His joy abruptly dissipated like dandelion seeds caught in the wind.

Maddalene shunned him. Her bitterness flung Peter into the darkness of the moment of death.

"I hate you," she uttered.

Peter recoiled, but she took him back to the Aussee River and he watched himself dive in after her, struggling with the icy current as it sought to trap him as well. He felt Maddalene's panic as the cold water claimed her. He felt her lungs give out.

Here, she offered, is where you left me. Here is the void. Here is my loneliness and the harsh disappointment.

He could have fallen to his knees and begged forgiveness, but this echo of Maddalene offered no respite from his shame and guilt.

Peter let the tie between them unravel and she disappeared back through the aether.

The masked man now stood across the room and watched him with wary eyes. Virgil had known what Peter would find.

CHAPTER IX

Wherein Mr. Styles pleads his case and keeps a grim appointment

THE CHIMING OF THE PARLOR CLOCK DREW PETER'S ATTENTION. He stood and stretched, tired but knowing he would not sleep tonight, he considered losing himself in alcohol; however, that route meant maudlin introspection, and he'd had enough of that.

Maybe he should head over to Avery's apartments. His friend might be asleep, but he thought not; like himself Avery kept strange hours. He would chance it. Poor Avery; Peter wondered if the man realized what a bundle of headaches he took on when he accepted him as a friend.

After a tiring walk through the London streets, he thumped on Avery's door. His friend appeared in a blue dressing gown and peered at him with concern.

"You look hideous," Avery said.

"And yet, irresistibly puckish?"

His friend grumbled and led him into a room filled with the unusual souvenirs of a life well-lived. On the wall above the fireplace was a large model of a three-masted barque christened *The Dolphin*. Many of the other items in the room followed a nautical theme, including a grotesque wood carving of Neptune; the sea god's face twisted in an exaggerated scowl as he poised to strike with a brass trident.

Peter slouched into his usual seat as Avery retrieved a decanter of brandy and a sturdy glass. He offered a drink to Peter, who waved it aside. Avery's eyebrows rose.

"That bad?" he asked.

Peter avoided answering by letting his gaze dart about the familiar surroundings. Although Avery was slow to discuss his colorful history, so many of the accumulated items testified to his time at sea and some of the unfortunate choices he had made. None spoke as loudly as the model of *The Dolphin*, the slave ship Avery served on first as a mate, and then as captain. The model filled Avery with loathing, and Peter supposed his friend kept it not as a token of his past, but as punishment.

Once they passed a group of children reciting a silly bit of nursery rhyme. "From ghoulies to ghosties, to long-legged beasties . . . "

The bit of doggerel caused Avery's color to drain. His friend fended off communication, and when pressed on the subject, he would only offer, "I saw things on *The Dolphin* that made the battlefield pale in comparison."

Few would guess Avery harbored such bleak despair. People knew him as a jovial and a dependable person. He was well-liked. Only Peter saw through the cracks, and he never shared what he saw, even with Avery.

"Might I stay the night?" Peter asked.

Avery gestured toward a door. "You know the room is always yours."

Peter nodded. He wanted desperately to tell Avery about today, but his friend frowned on Peter's forays into necromancy. And Peter didn't want to admit the extent of his ties. Besides, how did one raise the possibility of having had communication with someone who advised the Roman Emperor Publius Aelius Hadrian without sounding like a madman?

"I spoke to Joseph Comstock earlier," Avery remarked.

"What about?"

"Our friend Glaston. I hoped to stop this absurdity, but Glaston has been running his mouth and is determined to see the matter through."

Peter faced Avery. "What are you talking about?" he asked.

"The duel. Tomorrow. Dusk."

"Ah, the duel."

Avery finished his brandy and poured another glass for himself. Peter felt the man's anger and fear and experienced a twinge of guilt.

"Glastons's purely bluster. The idea of the duel excites him, but I can't imagine he has any enthusiasm about seeing it through."

Avery rapped the arm of his chair and his thick eyebrows dropped in a frown. "He means to kill you, Peter."

"He *says* he means to kill me. To be honest, I haven't had time to worry about Mr. Glaston. I've been engaged with other matters, activities which will make you think less of me."

Avery's expression softened. He sighed and spoke with weariness.

"I heard your name in relationship to those bodies discovered in Paddington. People are talking and some are afraid. You told me you would try and put this aside. Necromancy isn't the end of the darkness, it only opens the door a crack. Be careful you don't throw it open all the way and get sucked in."

"I feel as though my whole life has been spent on the other side of that door," mused Peter.

"You've had your share of misfortune," Avery acceded.

He stared at Peter for a long time before leaning forward and speaking in an earnest, endearing tone. "Seriously, about tomorrow. What do you intend to do?"

Compared to the shadows flitting through Peter's mind, Glaston was a minor concern. He clapped his hands together and said, "I think I'm going to join you in a glass after all, and then go to bed."

In the morning he breakfasted with Avery, marveling at the old soldier's appetite. How did his friend not balloon? Peter seldom ate breakfast; food in the morning always tasted disagreeable.

They sat in silence. Avery read through the pages of a morning newspaper. "This article's about the affair at Paddington," he grumbled. "Fortunately, you aren't mentioned at all. Chief Constable Baker is featured prominently."

"What about Ember Quatermain?"

"They had the good sense to omit her as well," Avery said. He put the paper down and smiled. "I met Miss Quatermain once, a year ago. She's energetic, brilliant, and brimming with personality. Not your type at all."

"All women are my type," Peter said. He wiped his face and pushed back from the table.

"Are you leaving?" Avery asked.

"I have an apology to offer the woman in question."

"You mean to apologize? To a woman?" Avery rubbed his chin.

"I'm not as beastly as you make me out to be," Peter said with some annoyance. He stood and cast about for his coat, not sure where he let it drop last night. He found it hung up neatly by the door, obviously Avery's handiwork. Securing his hat, he headed into the bright May morning.

He found the Quatermain residence without too much difficulty. A servant allowed him entrance and bade him to have a seat in the hall. Peter did so, taking a moment to glance around at the masculine trappings. The décor was stylistically an abomination, but it captured Allan Quatermain's reputation for self-centeredness and horrific egotism.

A bold painting looked down on Peter, an imagining of The Great Hunt. He moved closer and noted the artist was Millais. He met Millais once, dearly admiring the man's boldness and disregard for the sensational. Millais, unfortunately, hated him.

Peter explored further down the hall, appreciating a collection of swords. These weren't clean museum pieces; all showed signs of wear. He was about to run a finger along a blade when a voice froze him.

"Mr. Styles, I would not assume you to be the sort to be out and about before noon."

Peter turned and grinned broadly. Ember Quatermain approached him with an expression of uncertainty. Her strawberry blonde hair was tied back from her face and protective eyewear rode high on her forehead. A smudge of dirt marred one smooth cheek.

"I stopped by to apologize for my behavior last night. It was unforgivable. You came to me in good faith and I abused your generous nature."

She eyed him critically, and for a moment he feared rebuke. However, she showed him into a large room whose walls were thick with trophies of her father's visits abroad. An enormous lion's head glared down, daring him to imagine the danger of facing such a beast.

Peter gave Ember his best smile and waited for her to be seated before settling himself. He kept his smile as she continued watching him.

"Last night you had questions," Peter offered. "As a way of making amends, I'll answer them fully now."

In a cold voice she said, "I think I may have found the answers since then."

"Have you?"

"No less than two people have warned me away from you, Mr. Styles, and both of them good judges of character. Of course, their appraisals only made me more curious about who sent you to Paddington and what you hoped to achieve there."

"I'd try and narrow down who might have told you such things about me, but that would be too lengthy an enterprise."

Ember smiled slightly at his response.

"Miss Quatermain, I don't deny being a cheat and a philanderer. I'm a child in a man's body and not fit for polite company. However, as for my motivation for being at Paddington yesterday, I can assure you I was only doing someone else's bidding. I had no agenda."

"Whose bidding?"

"I don't know," Peter answered. She flashed him an expected disapproving look. He held out a hand in protest. "However, he bids me call him Virgil."

"As in the poet?"

"Perhaps more as a character in Dante's *Inferno*."

Ember's hands twisted nervously in her lap. There was evidence of a poor night's sleep about her eyes. He sensed she weighed whether or not to reveal something to him and knew she needed to unburden herself. Before he could offer encouragement or pave the way for disclosure, she blurted it out.

"I encountered something outside your apartments last night," she said. "It almost killed me."

Her words stabbed him. If she had crossed the restless dead, she was fortunate to be alive. Peter studied her with new appreciation.

"You said the dead could be wakened," she prodded.

"I never said 'wakened.' The dead are dead. However, one can commune with the spirits of the departed, and if one is corrupt enough, one may raise the dead."

"Have you raised the dead?" she asked.

Peter shook his head.

"I won't deny having dabbled in necromancy. I'm not proud of it. However, I never raised the dead."

"Why should I believe you?"

That always seemed to be a stumbling block between him and the fair sex. Her glance held contempt for him. A pity, especially since it came from such beautiful eyes. Thinking of last night, he leaned forward in his chair and considered how much he ought to disclose. If she was in danger, and if he was in any way responsible, then he needed to be forthcoming. The words stalled in delivery; asking people to take the leap into acceptance of the dark realities around them seldom resulted in appreciative responses. Peter leaned back in his chair, hoping his grim face would mirror the seriousness of his explanation.

"Miss Quatermain, I will be straight."

She leaned back as well, in imitation of his posture.

"First, Virgil sent me to Paddington because he is seeking something and believed whatever was unearthed in the tunnel might help him find it. Second, another desires the same item. As fearsome as Virgil might be, he is nothing compared to this individual."

"Who is this other one?"

Peter struggled to find words to communicate the strangeness of the man he encountered. He plunged ahead, deciding to risk further derision.

"He is a foreigner. Perhaps Italian. He's quite powerful, and maybe not even human, as you and I might define that word. I would say he is not."

Having stated this, Peter watched her face and knew she analyzed his words in light of other available information. He pressed a bit, trying to see the context of her understanding, but only received jumbled images, distorted as shapes seen through uneven glass.

"He was the one responsible for the animation you witnessed," Peter continued. "It was a lark for him. He did it with little effort. Now, that is someone worthy of fear *and* respect."

Peter stopped and studied Miss Quatermain's face. Did she believe him? Having already ventured into impropriety by trying to pick up surface impressions, he now further breached personal boundaries and expanded his mind, this time giving it some effort. Usually awareness of another person's thoughts and emotions came in a trickle, giving bits and pieces to either discard or latch onto, but without warning a battery of information assailed him.

Snippets of conversation and apparently unrelated images of familiar and unfamiliar objects exploded into his consciousness. Streams of information dashed first one way, then another, following incomprehensible patterns. Her mind was a maelstrom, unlike any intellect he had ever encountered. The speed of thought and the complexity of the ideas given birth drained him and made it difficult to breathe.

He looked out over a cliff and feared diving without control. Peter shut his eyes and broke the connection. He clutched the arms of his chair and sought to calm himself.

"Mr. Styles? Are you quite all right?"

Ember stood and approached him, pressing one hand to her bosom as the other reached out for his shoulders. "Would you like something to drink? Your face is red."

His heart slowed and a dull pain pulsed through his temples. He forced a smile and shook his head.

"My apologies," he said.

The woman had no idea of the ability she possessed, of the sheer intellectual power at her disposal. At least not yet. That wasn't something easily harnessed; it would come slowly, in small steps. Perhaps it would be better for Miss Quatermain if it didn't come at all. A person who suddenly waded in too deeply would go mad.

Miss Quatermain returned to her seat. Peter didn't speak. Miss Quatermain had her own abilities, and he feared her and feared for her. She had a greater role in this mystery than he had imagined.

She dug into the pocket of her leather apron and withdrew an attractive pocket watch. The gesture's meaning was obvious; Ember Quatermain was dismissing him. Peter rose.

"Is there anything else, Mr. Styles?" she asked.

He shook his head and made to leave, but the object in her hands arrested his attention. He stopped and stared at the watch, his breathing quickening.

"Mr. Styles?"

Peter quickly recovered and masked his disquiet. He smiled broadly and casually gestured to the watch.

"That's a lovely work there," he said.

She ignored him for a moment, but finally glanced up. "It was a gift from a friend."

"I do hope it wasn't from a suitor," he said with forced amusement. "Still, it certainly is more practical than roses, or chocolates. May I see it?"

He extended his hand, knowing the gesture was rude and intrusive. Miss Quatermain bristled, but held it out to him.

As soon as the item touched his palm, a shudder of revulsion ran through him. Had the watch not been attached to a chain, it would have fallen to the floor. It dangled from the bracelet, now wrapped about her fingers.

He knew its owner.

"Can I be forward and ask the identity of the friend who gave this to you?"

"If you must know, it came from one of my father's associates, a Mr. Masterson, not that it's your business. Now please go."

"Masterson?"

Peter recalled the face; the coarse sideburns, the heavily hooded eyes, and the thick lower lip that often seemed to frown. The man had influence in London's banking community, and according to rumor used his wealth like a club. When Mr. Masterson entered a room, he took control, even though his pompous and bullying manner put people off.

How had Peter not seen this before?

"I know him, Miss Quatermain," Peter said carefully. "If I may give you advice, I'd suggest care regarding what you do and say around him. I don't think you know him as well as you believe."

His statement made her eyes widen.

"I've never known anyone like you," she said in anger. "Do you have no boundaries?"

Peter resisted the urge to make a flippant response. He instead swept into a deep bow and strode from the room. He hastened out of the house and stood in the sunlight.

What a gift he had just been given.

After a year of guessing and probing, he knew the identity of Virgil! The necromancer's presence had lingered about the watch in Ember's hand. It was a unique marker.

For the first time in quite a while, Peter allowed himself hope.

Possessing Masterson's identity meant leverage. It would also make things riskier. Once Masterson knew himself revealed, he would want to take precautions against Peter. It didn't matter; he would accept the challenge. He was hungry to confront the man and put an end to the hold he had over him.

CHAPTER X

Wherein Mr. Styles keeps an appointment on the field of honor

FOLLOWING HIS VISIT TO EMBER QUATERMAIN, PETER'S FIRST COURSE OF ACTION WAS TO HEAD TO THE LONDON LIBRARY AND DO RESEARCH ON EDWARD MASTERSON. He entered the building and found a niche where he could study in privacy and peace. He shed his coat over the back of a wood chair and rolled up his sleeves.

After an hour, he knew that Edward's branch of the Masterson family was not faring well financially, and that Edward himself lost a crushing amount of capital through poor investments in Asian trade. Respected by the financial community, and accepted as one of their own, Edward was hardly deserving of such esteem.

Peter studied an article where Masterson was listed as a guest of honor at Windsor Castle and laughed at the effusive praise lavished on the man by the society column's author.

Edward Masterson apparently did little to distinguish himself other than lend his family's name to the rosters of party guests where the ruling class shook hands on quiet deals to solidify social standing.

Another article caught Peter's eye. Masterson was a patron of Gabriel Montresor, a man with a growing reputation within the realm for his work with the military, earning him the nickname "Her Majesty's Armourer."

It was at Montresor's country estate where Peter first met Virgil.

Peter pushed the newspaper away and gave solemn consideration to what to do about the man. Formal records and gossip in the newspaper provided a starting point, but hardly gave a complete picture. For that, Peter knew he needed to approach friends and family. They might not be willing to talk openly, but he didn't necessarily need their words to pick their brains. Few people probably knew Masterson well.

He thought of the watch. Perhaps Masterson had feelings for Ember Quatermain, or perhaps he was positioning himself to be able to manipulate her. If that was the case, she would be more of a challenge than Masterson bargained for.

Peter grinned. He flipped open another newspaper and scanned the pages for mention of Masterson, but half his attention remained on Ember Quatermain. She was the sort of woman who wouldn't tolerate the usual games; she knew what she was about. Her directness and unconventional views intrigued him.

Peter leaned over another article. The story flattered Masterson for an enormous gift to the Society of Antiquaries of London, the amount being given specifically for work being done on Roman society and culture. The Society was respectable, but Masterson's motivations were not.

Following a hunch, Peter headed over to the Society's headquarters and spent time perusing papers written by different members. The director of the Society, Mr. Cooper, was on hand; a short man with delicate features and soft handshake. Peter spent a few minutes being cordial, and then breached the topic of Masterson's gift.

"Quite generous, Mr. Masterson," Mr. Cooper cooed. "Quite. After Michael Salridge published his manuscript on the Apollonius legend, Mr. Masterson provided funds for further research by Mr. Salridge, who had announced his intention of running down the origins of the Emerald Tablet of Hermes Trismegistus."

"Are the legends of Apollonius and the Emerald Tablet connected?" Peter asked.

"Mr. Salridge believed so. He insisted Apollonius' disappearance was tied to the tablet. He believed records mentioned the tablet being discovered in a tomb in Egypt and that Apollonius had gone in search of it."

Peter smiled broadly. He would pay Mr. Salridge a visit.

Before he could inquire into how to contact the scholar, Mr. Cooper volunteered, "Poor Mr. Salridge never had the chance to follow up on his research," Cooper said. "He died recently. His heart. A pity. Quite young."

Peter sensed Cooper had doubt concerning Salridge's death. He felt the man's unhappiness and the discomfort over knowing that when they found Salridge, the man's face was contorted in horror, as if something had literally scared him to death. Cooper didn't know what could have had such an effect on the historian, nor did he want to. Masterson must have engineered it.

Peter thanked Mr. Cooper and left The Society of Antiquaries. He walked with his head down, his thoughts racing.

The Emerald Tablet of Hermes Trismegistus; alluded to throughout history as the Holy Grail of alchemy. The tablet was purported to contain the secret of transforming not just primordial matter, but perhaps reality itself. It contained the knowledge of the gods.

Peter rubbed his hands together and cautiously eyed the shadows in search of anyone taking an undue interest in him. He let his awareness expand, and listened for anything out of the ordinary. He had cause to be a little paranoid.

If Masterson and the other necromancer chased the Emerald Tablet of Hermes, then perhaps he needed to make it his goal as well.

Or at least, he needed to make it his goal to keep it out of the other's hands.

Peter remembered his other appointment of the afternoon. With Virgil so close and his mind flying at the challenges ahead, he didn't want to go through with it. The duel in the face of his current obstacles became an absurdity.

He might just refuse to go.

Thinking of Glaston's smile, Peter knew that wasn't an option. The entire walk back to his apartment he tried finding a way out of his predicament.

***

Avery's carriage rattled to a stop. Peter climbed into the comfortably cushioned compartment and grinned wryly at the agitated expression on his friend's face.

"I don't want to go through with it," Peter announced.

Avery stared at him for a moment, and then looked away, perhaps fighting to be patient.

"We could just tell the driver to take us to dinner," Peter suggested. "I have a yearning for sea bass. We could go to Jardin's; they make an excellent lemon sauce."

Avery toyed with the ends of his moustache. "If you choose not to fight, that's your choice," he replied. "However, as your second, I'm obligated to stand in for you."

Peter would not allow it.

"When we arrive at the field of honor, I'll apologize again to Glaston. You'll naturally apologize to his second. If I do it face-to-face, he'll have to accept."

Peter's words seemed to further irritate his friend.

"First, the Code Duello does not allow for apologies once both parties have taken the field," Avery said. "At least not without a shot being fired. Second, he means to kill you."

"So you keep telling me," Peter said peevishly.

"And if you only you had listened to me . . . "

They travelled in silence for some time. The green landscape rolled by. The sun, hidden behind clouds for most of the day, now blazed defiantly for the hour before it sank below the horizon.

"Why the change in attitude?" Avery asked.

Peter considered telling him about Masterson, but held back. Avery needn't share this burden.

The carriage pulled to the side of the road next to an enormous lawn stretching before a distant mansion. Another carriage was already parked and emptied of its cargo. Standing on the grass were four men. Peter recognized two: Phillip Glaston and his toady, Joseph Comstock.

One of the other gentlemen was tall, with a thick middle and florid face. He boasted an enormous handlebar framing full cheeks. The black bag in the crook of his arm was a sign of his profession; he was obviously a doctor.

The fourth man brought Peter up short. He stared at the face that had held his attention for most of the afternoon. Edward Masterson stood with his hands behind his back, a stoic expression on his face.

"Gentlemen!" Avery called out.

Peter wanted to leap from the carriage and strike Masterson. He forced the anger from his face.

Glaston gave greeting, apparently enjoying the excitement of the moment. He took control of the event and made introductions. The doctor shook his head in disapproval and Peter heard the man's resentment at having been coaxed into participating. Comstock stood solemnly at Glaston's side. He held a handsome wooden box in his arms, its lid secured by an ornate gold clasp. The dueling pistols.

Masterson made a show of solemnity, playing the role of reluctant participant. He shook hands with Avery, then held out a hand for Peter. A long and awkward moment passed before Peter accepted his grasp. They shook once and broke contact.

"Mr. Masterson," Peter said. "We've met before, haven't we?"

"I'm sure our paths have crossed."

"A party, wasn't it? A country affair?"

The suggestion appeared to annoy Masterson. He waved dismissively.

"The afternoon is wearing," Comstock said. "If we're going to get on with this, then perhaps it should commence."

Glaston nodded assent.

Comstock gravely approached Avery and offered the weapons for inspection.

"As the seconds have met and unsatisfactorily attempted reconciliation, we meet here on the field of honor," Comstock began. The man had the voice of a carnival barker.

"I think we might try one last time to reach some conciliatory agreement," Avery protested. Peter was about to add his own enthusiasm for compromise, but Comstock wagged a finger of reproach.

"The Code Duello dictates the seconds will load the pistols before one another," Comstock continued.

"One last time, I think we should settle this without spilling blood," Avery persisted. "We are gentlemen."

Edward Masterson approached, head bowed and arms spread as if seeking apology for what he was about to say.

"I don't approve of this, but no apology can be accepted at this point," he said. "As much as I hate violence, a man's honor has come into question, and must be defended. Without our honor, we are nothing."

Avery continued protest, but Masterson again interrupted. "Mrs. Glaston's worth as an Englishwoman was called into question. That was an intolerable breach of manners. Such an insinuation is considered a blow. Once a blow has been dealt, apology is no longer an option. Unless . . . "

Masterson paused and his eyes locked with Peter's.

"Unless Mr. Styles offers his cane to Mr. Glaston."

Peter's face suddenly warmed at the thought of suffering a public beating. Had another offered the solution, Peter might have bitterly assented. Hearing the words from Masterson's lips maddened him. He felt his cheeks burn. Peter stepped closer to Masterson and they glared at one another. The other men present raised their eyebrows at the intensity of their ill will.

"Mr. Styles has no intention of offering his cane," Peter uttered. He tried penetrating Masterson's thoughts, but all that came back was the same cold silence he always encountered when trying to probe Virgil.

A silver chain about Masterson's neck arrested his attention. It was almost hidden by the man's collar. Peter felt a tingling and knew that whatever might be attached to that chain must be the protective charm keeping Virgil safe from psychic detection.

Peter had originally intended to offer apology and failing that, simply walk away and deal with whatever social consequences the act of cowardice might bring. His reputation would suffer, but Peter didn't worry about that; he was already becoming ostracized for being a public menace, the abandoned duel would just be one more offense. It might even make his lack of character larger than life.

But Masterson's presence changed his mind. He would go through with the duel. Or at least appear to.

Avery loaded the pistols as the interested parties looked on. Did Glaston know Masterson's secrets? Peter eyed the man and detected a struggle to quell a spiking fear. Arrogant as he might be, Glaston had no more belly for this than Peter did. The git had come to kill him, but now Glaston's stomach roiled at the thought. Glaston couldn't do it. He'd aim to wound and consider honor satisfied.

Peter sucked in air, thinking his odds of survival better than before. He felt bad for Glaston, and guilt washed over him. It was Peter's fault they stood at this precipice. He had been an ass.

"Have you ever dueled before?" Glaston asked as Peter was offered his choice of pistols.

"No, I have not."

"I must confess this is my first time as well." The quiver in Glaston's voice stung him.

"The challenger has the right to choose distance," Comstock announced.

"Ten paces?" Glaston asked.

Peter shrugged and both men stepped back, taking a moment to gather their wits and prepare for the consequences of their actions.

Peter summoned Avery and leaned into him. He spoke in a whisper, almost pressing his lips against his friend's ear.

"No matter what happens here, there is something you must do," Peter murmured. "Mr. Masterson has a charm about his neck. You can see the chain if you look closely. You must get it from him."

Avery stared at Peter as if seeing a madman.

"What are you going on about?"

Peter squeezed Avery's bicep and his eyes reinforced the urgency of his message. "Get the charm."

"Why should I do that?"

"Because Masterson is Virgil."

Avery's eyebrows shot up. He rose on his tiptoes so he could see the man over Peter's shoulder. Peter yanked him back down.

"Mr. Styles, the afternoon is failing," Masterson called.

Peter gave Avery's shoulder a slap and turned to face Glaston. The two combatants assumed positions, their seconds watching from midpoint. Peter examined his pistol. It was Parisian, and lighter than expected. He ran his palm along the blue octagonal shaped barrel. The .46 caliber weapon's deadly potential unsettled him.

"On the count of three," Peter called, gesturing to Comstock.

"One."

An early evening breeze kissed Peter's face. He looked about, surprised by the sudden keenness of sense. His eye ran over the landscape, taking in the detail of the beauty around him, heedless of the violence about to occur.

"Two."

He thought about the letter he gave Avery when they were in the carriage. It was to be delivered to his father in the event that the duel went badly. The old man would be disappointed in him, yet again.

"Three!"

Glaston's weapon discharged before the third count. Something punched Peter's chest and he staggered back. He heard Glaston shouting in alarm at seeing the premature shot had struck a fatal blow.

"He's killed me," Peter choked.

Fighting the dizziness and sudden cold, Peter raised his weapon and took quick aim at Masterson. The man stood no more than four paces away. Comstock and the doctor both shouted to halt Peter, but he squeezed the trigger.

Masterson's lips formed a perfect, round circle. His eyes widened and he looked down at the red stain forming on his expensive white shirt. The man dropped to his knees.

Peter stumbled, his vision now blurred and darkened. He landed hard on the rich grass of the Glaston estate. He couldn't breathe and his mouth was so dry.

The doctor rushed to attend to Masterson. He knelt with some difficulty and ripped apart the other man's shirt. Peter didn't need to read the physician's mind to feel his outrage.

Masterson moaned, turning his head from side to side. His face was pale and his features showed the fear now gripping him. Death greedily enfolded the necromancer.

"I didn't think it would be like this," Peter whispered.

"Like what?" Avery asked. His friend was at his side, with tears running down his full cheeks.

Icy tendrils wrapped about Peter and started tugging him into blackness. He fought the panic and the wall of regrets tumbling around him.

"Get the charm," Peter whispered.

"What bloody difference can it make now?" Avery asked.

Peter continued to urge his friend into action. Avery stood and approached the doctor, who had removed his jacket and now installed it under Masterson's head as a pillow. He distracted the physician, loudly imploring him to see after the other wounded man. As the doctor turned and looked Peter's way, Avery yanked the charm from Masterson's neck.

The doctor approached Peter, but after a desultory examination and a shake of his head, he proclaimed both men beyond hope. He returned to Masterson, and Avery came back to Peter.

Avery showed him the charm. It was a flat square of brass, each side less than an inch in length. Several runes marked the surface.

"Keep it safe," Peter said.

"What about you?" Avery asked. He stroked Peter's forehead, the grief on his face painful to behold.

"I'm dead."

Peter surrendered with a laugh and tumbled into the blackness.

CHAPTER XI

*Wherein Ember conducts a scientific experiment
only to encounter another mysterious threat*

JAMES, THE HANSOM DRIVER, CARRIED IN THE LAST OF
EMBER'S EQUIPMENT AS CHIEF CONSTABLE BAKER EMERGED
FROM THE DARKNESS INTO THE GLOW OF SCATTERED
LANTERNS. He examined the large copper contraption she had
erected. His finely manicured fingers ran along a fine coil of silk-
covered copper tubing surrounding an air chamber and his lips
curled into a bemused smile.

"What on earth is it?" he asked, pointing to the device.

"It's a scale," Ember laughed. "It measures current."

"Looks dangerous," he said. Baker turned from the device and
removed his hat to give a proper greeting. "I received your note,
Miss Quatermain," he said. "Although, to be blunt, I'm not sure
about our purpose here."

Worry creased his boyish face and it looked as if he hadn't slept
in some time. She noted a nick on the skin above his collar, evidence
of a hasty shave.

"The two workmen who died were killed by some kind of
electrical discharge," Ember said. "I have a theory about what
might have happened."

Baker turned to the equipment. "And how does this machine
figure into it?"

"I think there's an energy stream running through Paddington.
The workmen inadvertently tapped into it."

Baker scratched the back of his neck. He gave her a skeptical
glance. "The second worker was killed quite a distance from here."

"That's correct," she said, with no further explanation.

"You make it sound like electricity runs like water. If that's so, then why are we still standing about? Why aren't we being roasted like those unfortunates?"

"There are different types of energy," Ember explained. "I don't think this stream can be accessed without the proper conduit."

Baker returned to scrutinizing the equipment. He wandered to a stack of crates where Ember had placed a crystal pentacle. Baker ran his hand over the surface.

"A battery," she explained.

He leaned against one of the crates, exhaling slowly as his eye traveled over the contours of Ember's tight fitting gutta-perhca rubber suit. She felt suddenly self-conscious.

"And that costume?"

"Protection against the electricity," she replied.

"I don't like this at all," Baker said.

His tone concerned her; she could imagine him putting a stop to her activity and claiming safety concerns. She pointed at the device and said, "I need to generate my own energy to disrupt the flow and channel it into the battery. The battery is designed for amplification as well as storage. When I have enough power, I'll reverse the flow and send a burst into the stream. My machines will be able to record information which will help us understand the nature of the stream and maybe see if there are any disturbances through its path."

"You might as well have told me it's magic for all I can understand of it. If we're in some kind of energy stream, Miss Quatermain, then why aren't we feeling it?"

"I think we are. Staying here for a short period of time might make you edgy, perhaps upset your stomach. I think it is capable of inhibiting your thought process, perhaps even producing hallucinations."

Baker remained unconvinced, but the equipment appeared to impress him.

James approached and, with a grunt, set down a large box containing a small boiler. Ember hastily attached a copper wire running from the pentacle to the boiler and made sure none of the other connections had come loose during transport. She had spent the entire night putting this thing together, and she worried her weariness might make for error.

"Anything else, Miss?" James asked.

"No, thank you kindly."

James removed a handkerchief from his pocket and wiped a sweaty brow. He gave her an exhausted salute and disappeared into the gloom.

"Poor James," Ember said. "I had him up before the sun hauling equipment down here."

Baker frowned at Ember, pursing his thin lips. "You're going to send out a burst of energy into some different, unknown energy and see if you can find something wrong. Do I have that correct?"

"You do."

"I'm not as educated as some, but I'm not a stupid man, Miss Quatermain. If you want to continue with this experiment, you'll have to do better. What are we searching for? What does this have to do with the dead workers?"

She produced the map created by memory from the one Timothy allowed her to scrutinize and spread it before the Chief Constable. He leaned over it with interest.

"This is a map of the energy lines throughout Europe," she said. "The original was very old, and it was drawn to provide clues, though not the exact location, to an extremely old artifact. Not the one found in the tunnel, but something quite valuable."

Ember stopped talking and watched him for reaction. He was intrigued, but he appeared to struggle with the implication of all this. She suspected he also struggled with the risk of being the butt of someone's joke. She could only imagine how quickly his skepticism would turn to ridicule if she tried telling him the map gave a clue to finding the Emerald Tablet of Hermes. She didn't think she could bear that.

"You really believe these energy lines exist?"

"I do."

"And someone's used them as markers to hide something?"

"I suppose that's one way to look at it," she said. "And either I follow these lines all over the continent, or I send a signal along them, like a vibration through a spider web, and see what bounces back."

"And you're not afraid of attracting the attention of the spider?"

She gave a nervous laugh. "It was an analogy," Ember said.

"The dead men weren't an analogy."

Ember had no response. She returned to readying her equipment. As she worked, she thought of ways to collect power from the energy stream itself, instead of having to power the device from a steam engine. That would make it easier to transport.

"I'm not saying I'm believing any of this," Baker said. "But I'm willing to see what's what."

He frowned and pointed at her. "If these lines exist, and if this place is going to be jumping with electricity, then shouldn't I have a suit as well? I'm just saying."

"When I activate the device, you'll be standing there. That area is shielded."

"You've thought of everything."

He stepped around her and went to further investigate the safe area.

"I went to see Styles last night," she said.

The Chief Constable's expression changed. He frowned, but held his tongue. Encouraged by his silence, she told him what happened in the street, and waited for his derision. To her surprise, Baker remained silent. Perhaps her account gave him further doubt about being here and letting her proceed with these experiments.

"Well?" she asked.

Chief Constable Baker's furrowed brow smoothed suddenly. "Did he tell you anything worthwhile?"

Ember wanted to tell him about what she encountered outside Styles' apartments, but held her tongue. Once she opened the door to that . . .

"I don't much care for Mr. Styles," Baker said. "I mean to know what he knows about this case. I've put in a request to see the Commissioner."

Baker brooded a moment and approached Ember. "I couldn't sleep last night," he said, "not after what I saw in that field."

She watched him and knew these words hadn't been easy for him to say. Ember warmed toward Baker.

"You're accepting the idea of the walking dead? Of ghosts?"

He squirmed at these words and pinched the bridge of his nose. "I don't know. I'm trying to keep my mind open. I'm here, aren't I?"

Ember smiled and he smiled back. Baker's youth no doubt made him more receptive to the unthinkable.

"We used to think the world flat," Ember said. "Or that if you sailed far enough into the horizon you would fall into a void. But we've learned things and what was once magical is now commonplace in our world."

"Maybe. We live in curious times. I'm just trying to gather facts and see where they take me. Of course, I'll admit this to you, but outside this tunnel, I'd rather not seem so gullible."

Baker had to work hard to fit into a society which valued maturity over fresh thought and calm reasoning over intuition. The police officer absent-mindedly touched an exposed wire. It sparked and threw him back against the tunnel wall.

Ember cried in alarm and rushed to his side. She squeezed his shoulder and put a hand against the side of his face. He turned his head and offered a sheepish expression.

"I'm right as rain," he said.

Her heart pounded at the thought he might have hurt himself. She checked his eyes and found herself staring into them. The moment stretched and the sense of intimacy grew.

Ember stepped back, embarrassed by her forwardness.

"Don't touch anything," she admonished. "This equipment can be dangerous."

"Then perhaps it would be best if we disconnected it," he said. He was playing with her.

"Just don't put your hands where they don't belong."

"That's easier said than done," Baker said. He seemed shocked by his own reply and colored.

His flirtation made Ember grin. The Chief Constable was a reliable man, even tempered, and able to withhold judgment of things he didn't understand. So why did her thoughts keep wandering back to Mr. Styles?

"I appreciate your friendship," she told Baker, who beamed at her words.

Ember directed him back to the shielded area. "I think I'm ready to begin. Chief Constable?"

Baker bit his lip, but went to stand in the area indicated. Ember pulled on the hood of the rubber suit and a pair of insulated goggles to cover the eyeholes. The only remaining opening was a pair of tubes aligned with her nostrils for breathing.

Baker watched with concern.

Before she lost the nerve, Ember started the engine. It hummed, softly at first, then the vibrations became an angry buzz. Energy flowed into the crystal pentacle. Ember watched the battery, keeping track of the indicator built into its face.

The charge expelled would be tenfold what the battery had been fed. She could imagine modifying the device so it could amplify power a hundred times. What a weapon this could be. The idea of being responsible for creating something capable of such destructive power disturbed her.

"The battery is almost charged," she called to Baker. "At least enough for our purposes. When I give word, avert your eyes."

Ember tripped the switch on the battery. Instead of receiving energy, it would now dispel it; not from the five tips, but from a flexible tube inserted into the epicenter.

"Now!" she shouted. She aimed the tube at the end of the tunnel.

The light was blinding. Ember imagined the burst gliding into the streams, shooting along its pathway like a traveler moving through congested London streets. It thrilled her to think how far and how fast the signal would go.

She tripped another switch and once more reversed the flow, only this time she pulled power not from the engine, but from the energy streaming through the tunnel. Instruments which had recorded the energy fluctuations before the blast would now measure them afterward.

The battery warmed. Ember watched with concern as the small needle on its face jumped, indicating an unexpected power buildup. The dampening device wasn't kicking in.

Ember remained calm. She once more reversed the flow and avoided catastrophe by sending the charge back down the tunnel in the form of a blue-white ball of energy. She blinked her eyes, trying to rid herself of the spots in her vision.

What had gone wrong? Where was the surge of energy from?

Ember checked the pentacle, afraid the mechanism had been damaged. Thankfully, it showed little wear, other than some blackening at its tips and a crack in the glass protecting the power gauge. When she got home and took the thing apart, she suspected some of the cells might be damaged or utterly ruined.

Ember rose to announce to Baker the conclusion of the experiment, but saw him emerging from behind the protective barrier with an expression of astonishment on his face.

"Something's coming!" he said with awe.

Ember followed his gaze and at the end of the tunnel five shapes formed from the blackness. Ember's fingers jerked and the pentacle dropped at her feet.

Three women and two men approached. As they slipped forward, their translucent bodies solidified in the glow of the kerosene lanterns. One woman with long chestnut hair spoke in a lilting voice, but in an unknown language. Ember started. Her lips hadn't moved.

The lead woman drifted closer; her eyes were black within black. Ember felt the presence of menace, but her instinct couldn't overcome her wonder at the woman's grace and power.

A lanky male flitted next to Ember, his eyes appraising her with amusement. He looked barely nineteen. Ember swallowed hard, surprised by a sudden rush of emotion. She was embarrassed by her yearning.

Ember tugged off her protective hood and dropped it to the ground. The young male smiled, innocently at first, then lewdly.

The lead female came closer. Although shorter than Ember, her stature didn't diminish the strength she exuded. Ember watched the woman's broad hips and slightly rounded belly, and noted with fascination the shadows playing over her ample breasts. Her breath quickened and a pleasant tingle ran through Ember's body.

"Who are you?" Ember asked. The words strangled her.

The woman reached out and ran the back of her hand along Ember's cheek. Her touch made Ember shudder.

"Pretty," the woman spoke out loud.

The second male approached. This one stood tall, with broad shoulders and thick arms. He possessed a Roman nose and round, deep-set eyes. His hair was the color of mercury, cut short to his scalp. He drew a single finger along the curve of Ember's cheek and traced a continuous path down her neck and chest.

Ember was instantly overcome with the desire to have him take her. Her newfound lust made it difficult to think, but within the flood of yearning was a spark of alarm ignited by the threat these beings posed.

"Where is Apollonius?" the woman crooned.

Ember wanted to answer; she would do anything to please. She wanted to give her heart without question. She felt so small and insignificant, and safe within the presence of a goddess. She wished nothing but to surrender.

Ember fought to clear her mind, to come to grips with what was happening.

These things stimulated her and then fed off the energies released. The violation crippled her; she'd never felt so helpless and so happy to be that way.

"I don't know," Ember said. "I don't know who you mean."

"She has willpower," one of the other women replied. "Look how she fights."

The leader ignored the statement and instead said, "He's been here. I can feel him."

A sliver of rational thought penetrated the haze. These beings came through when the overload disrupted the stream. It punched through their reality and opened a breach to another. Ember held onto that thought, reaching into herself to break free from the woman's influence. She tried turning her head to look for Baker, but couldn't tear her gaze from the leader.

The woman sniffed the air. Her fingertips grazed the air currents, reminding Ember of a blind person feeling her way through the sighted world. The woman paused . . . eyes wide, her brow furrowed.

"He's near," she said to her companions. "Very near."

The woman's eyes scanned the tunnel, but her gaze was elsewhere. Like Timothy, perhaps she was sensitive to the energy flows without the aid of a device.

"Well," she said with finality, "Apollonius knows we're here now. It's been a long time since I've seen my lover."

The woman eyed the equipment with puzzlement. She studied Ember's attire, then peered at Baker.

"This is a portal I've never seen before," the woman said. "We'll have to go exploring."

She waved her hand and the boyish male was on Ember, grabbing her by the hair, he snapped her head back. Her neck stretched taut and she found it hard to breathe.

"Let her go!" Baker shouted. Out of the corner of her eye she saw the Chief Constable rush to intercede. The other two women moved swiftly, with inhuman grace, wrapping arms around him to hold him back.

Baker started to sink. One of the women kissed him and he responded with an erotic groan. Ember watched him writhe with passion, although she could see the embarrassment and shame in his eyes as he gazed in her direction. Another woman held him in place with little effort as the first ran her hands along his chest and down his stomach. Tears moistened The Chief Constable's cheeks.

The young man next to Ember pursed his lips and blew warm breath along her neck. She arched her back at the intensity of the sensation. Although she fought the desires buffeting her, she still wanted him closer. Her hand, almost of its own volition, rose and caressed the side of his face.

Her self-control weakened. Rational thoughts slipped farther away. Another wave of lust rode through her. She craved the touch of the younger man standing at her side. She needed to slide her hands over his lithe form, to feel the muscles beneath his ivory skin. She wanted to taste the strength he possessed.

On the verge of surrender, she clawed back. They would slake their thirst and drain her entirely, leaving little but a mindless shell.

Ember fought through the haze. It was like being underwater and swimming without knowing the way to the surface. She shoved aside the irrational and found the patterns which gave her strength, the predictable flow of cause-and-effect.

She strained for the battery at her feet.

"What is she doing?" one of the men asked.

Ember felt his grip lighten and shouldered him. She dropped and reached for the pentacle. She wasn't sure how much energy remained, but hope drove her to act.

Ember turned the tube connected to the center of the device at the three intruders nearest her and flipped the switch.

The leader screamed as the burst slammed into her. She stumbled back, vanishing entirely. The younger male rolled along the wall of the tunnel before falling into nothingness. Only the third individual appeared able to fight the assault, but like his kin, the blast shoved him back until he winked out. The air rippled where the three creatures had vanished. It was like peeking through warped church glass.

Ember reached out and her hand disappeared to the wrist. It felt like dipping into a pool of icy water. The effect was slightly disorienting and she quickly withdrew her hand. The other two creatures had abandoned Baker and crouched warily, poised to attack. Ember wasn't sure if there was enough charge. She braced herself, hastily moving back down the tunnel as she once again readied the device.

They sprang. Ember hit the switch and a stream of light shot forward, immediately halting their movement. The strange ripple in the air intensified and the two women vanished.

Ember shut down the device. The atmosphere in the tunnel seemed to return to normal and the disturbance between the realities faded. She warily approached the spot where her hand had disappeared and waved at the air, this time without incident.

Baker, on his hands and knees, stared at the ground. He shook his head. With an eye on the tunnel, she made her way to the Chief Constable and knelt beside him.

"Mr. Baker?"

She could see the pain in his flushed face and was torn between giving him a moment of privacy to collect himself and throwing her arms protectively around him. He managed to stand, his face and clothing damp. He avoided her gaze.

"What happened?" he asked at last, his voice a croak.

"I didn't half believe it," she said. "But I think we created some sort of breach. We weakened the integrity of the barrier between this reality and . . . "

He continued watching her and she tried explaining the concept of the energy lines and the existence of multiple realities. He waved a hand to stop her from going further with an explanation.

"What about those things?" he asked. "What were they?"

His voice was hard. She saw the anger riding through his shoulders.

"I'm not sure."

"They were going to kill us," he said. Baker straightened his collar and fixed a button that had come undone. He then ran his hand through his hair, pushing it back into a semblance of order.

He looked at Ember, his eyes traveling over her form. She blushed. She knew he was seeing the two men in his mind, running their hands over her. She turned away.

"I'm not proud of myself," he said.

Ember faced him again and saw his grim expression. Whether he blamed himself for his paralysis or whether he blamed her, she couldn't offer anything to defuse the tension between them.

"I need to get changed," Ember said. She hastened behind a stack of crates where she kept a dress she intended to put on after the experiment, when the protective suit would no longer be necessary.

"Miss Quatermain, what happened here was loathsome," he called to her. She didn't answer, but busied herself unfastening the rubber suit. Her hands shook and she struggled to hold back tears.

"I'm not sure I believe what I saw," he continued. "I don't understand half of this, but what I do know is that we crossed a line."

She peeked around the corner of a crate and studied him. His clenched jaw and worried eyes gave away his inner turmoil. He shook his head and grimaced.

"We definitely crossed a line," he repeated. "Perhaps the less we said about this, the better it would be. Don't you think? I can't imagine anyone believing it anyway, and if they did, well, then there are still details we would be better off omitting. Miss Quatermain?"

"I hear you," she answered.

"Just so we're clear. I don't think this a matter appropriate for open discussion. It won't do either of us any good to share our embarrassment. You were compromised as well as I."

This last sentence was delivered as an accusation.

She didn't respond. Coming around the crates, she avoided looking at the police officer. Her temper soared and she fought to control herself.

"I'll escort you out," Baker said. He waved toward the exit and the formality in his tone let her know Baker wasn't interested in any further discussion. She moved to retrieve the information gathered from the tunnel, but he again gestured.

"Your driver can collect your things."

Ember stopped and retrieved the pentacle. She disconnected it from the engine and tucked it under her arm. Without acknowledging the Chief Constable, she hastened from the tunnel, eager to put distance between them.

CHAPTER XII

EVERAL HOURS LATER EMBER SAT IN HER FATHER'S LARGE ROOM, SLUMPED IN A CHAIR, HER LEGS STRETCHED OUT IN A MASCULINE FASHION. She considered Chief Constable Baker, knowing they would have to talk and smooth things between them. She didn't want the incident in the tunnel to remain a wedge.

She clipped the end of a cigar and struck a match. Through a haze of blue smoke Ember wiggled her fingers and imagined grazing them against the bare chest of the tall male from the tunnel, the one with the strong face and mercury hair. She shook herself from the daydream. What part of the fantasy was a reflection of her own needs and what part was the residue of those creatures' influence was difficult to say.

That was a dangerous path to tread.

These things were more the provenance of Peter Styles. She should go see him again, or perhaps arrange to meet in a neutral setting, with a proper chaperone. She chewed on her cigar as she thought of him, transposing Styles' face on the body of the creature from the tunnel.

Wicked.

Who else could she talk to about these matters? Certainly not the Chief Constable. She couldn't discuss these matters with Josephine. She had few friends, and none she would willingly expose to what had emerged through the rift in the tunnel.

If only Hans were about. She missed his calm demeanor and common sense advice.

"You're like a top, Miss Ember. Someone sets you spinning and off you go, bouncing into the furniture, scratching things up and causing all manner of confusion."

"I know," she said to herself.

"It is not always wise to act before we pause to consider the consequences of our actions," he would have admonished her.

What were the consequences? She mulled over this question. It felt like a tremendous drama was being played out and she had arrived in the middle of the action with little understanding of the plot and the dramatic personae.

She again thought of the Chief Constable. She needed someone else's perspective, and since he had been involved with this strangeness from the beginning, it only followed he should be given the opportunity to further explore the matter.

As she stubbed out her cigar, Ember heard the bell at the front door. Soon one of the servants announced Chief Constable Baker.

"I was just about to send you a message," she said.

Baker entered the room, his uniform immaculate and his hair combed neatly back from his forehead. He looked entirely recovered from their encounter.

The Chief Constable sniffed the air and turned a disapproving eye to the still smoking cigar in the ashtray.

"Miss Quatermain, I wish to offer my apology for my earlier behavior," he said. Baker had difficulty meeting her gaze. He strode about the room as if looking for clues.

"I became emotional and unprofessional," he announced.

Ember tried reassuring him but he waved her off.

"No, it's true. I'm a competent police officer, and I have promise. I am ambitious. However, since this affair began, I've been confronted with things which have challenged my entire world view. I don't know what is, or isn't, true any longer."

Baker pivoted and froze her with a steely gaze. "How is it you don't feel the same disorientation? How do you go on as if it is all an experiment? Doesn't any of this affect you?"

Ember didn't trust herself to speak. What insensitivity! His impertinence stunned her. How could he behave like this? If her father were here, she'd see the Chief Constable thrown out of the house.

"You're a cruel man, Mr. Baker," she managed.

He considered her response and gave it a curt nod. "Two men are dead, and we almost joined them. You exposed us to those despicable creatures, and God only knows what other types of danger. This isn't a game, Miss Quatermain."

She considered punching him in the face. Ember took a deep breath and stepped close to him to show she wasn't intimidated.

"Whether you believe me or not, I didn't know that would happen," Ember said.

"That's my point!" Baker cried. He stopped and caught his breath, quickly apologizing for having raised his voice. He stepped away from Ember and his expression calmed.

"That's my point," he said once more. "Stop playing at things and be more aware of the consequences of your actions."

"You pompous git. You're not angry at me," Ember said. "You're upset with yourself. You lost control in the tunnel and that's unbearable to you. You can't handle feeling helpless."

Baker's jaw clenched and his face reddened. He laughed without mirth and leaned against the mantel over the fireplace. "I made a mistake coming here," he said. "You're a hard woman, Miss Quatermain. However, I'll give you credit for lacking the sort of guile that plagues most of your gender. You speak so plainly, you have no idea when you are being hurtful."

He reached for his cap and gestured toward the door.

"I apologize if I've said anything which gave offense," he said.

The police officer turned and Ember watched him disappear into the hall. She had begged for a confidant, and when he appeared, as if summoned, she drove him away. No, she hadn't. He came to satisfy his ego, to chastise her for her outrageousness and to reclaim the dignity lost in the tunnel.

When she was a child and one of her friends left in anger, Hans always made her chase after to seek reconciliation.

Ember went after him. She called to the Chief Constable as he paused at the front door.

"Chief Constable Baker, wait. I spoke out of turn. I've been unforgivably rude," Ember said. The urgency in her words surprised her.

The police officer turned and gave her an appraising glance. He waved dismissively, but she restated her apology.

"You and I have been through a good deal the last twenty-four hours, Miss Quatermain. I think we're both on edge."

Ember smiled and slipped a hand about the crook of his arm. He raised his eyebrows in surprise, but she noted a slight flush in his cheeks and a tugging at the corners of his lips.

"I have a suggestion to make, Mr. Baker. It's unorthodox. However, before I make the suggestion, you must promise not to take umbrage. I do not want for us to quarrel again."

"If you have a suggestion, then I would hear it," he said.

"I think we should see Peter Styles."

Baker opened his mouth, but shut it again. She could tell he didn't like her idea.

"I know he's a brute, Mr. Baker—which is why I wouldn't think of seeing him again without accompaniment. However, he knows more about this matter than he's let on. I think Mr. Styles could be a valuable ally in this affair."

She stepped closer to him.

"Perhaps you're right," Baker said. He clearly didn't like the idea. "However, I think seeing him will make us both feel better. Whatever character flaws we posses will seem miniscule when compared to Mr. Styles' sinful nature."

"He's not so bad, once you get to know him," Ember said, and wondered why she felt it necessary to defend Styles.

Baker grunted.

Ember retrieved her overcoat and hat, and they passed into the late afternoon.

A cold breeze came through the window of the hansom as they headed across town. Ember sat back and occasionally snuck a glimpse at her escort, and was pleased to know he did the same.

They rounded a corner and slowed in traffic.

"Evening papers! Get your paper here!" a small boy cried. "Queen to entertain Dutch dignitaries! Edward Masterson murdered!"

Ember's heart dropped. She rapped on the ceiling, signaling the driver to stop. Digging out a coin, she summoned the smudge-faced boy for a paper.

"Masterson was the fellow at your father's the night we met," Baker said.

The story was on the second page. Ember scanned the article, eyes freezing on the name "Peter Styles."

The paper fell to the floor of the cab.

Ember pressed a hand to her chest, her body suddenly numb from the neck down.

She bit her lip, hard. The sting, the warmth from the issuing blood, made her surroundings once again feel real. And as the shock ebbed, it was replaced by sorrow.

Suddenly she was crying, unsure who she was mourning, Styles or Masterson. The thought stunned her. Rude, arrogant, conceited—Mr. Styles was all those things, but not evil. She retrieved the newspaper and read the story, studying the details, seeing the event in her mind's eye. Baker watched and held out his hand for the paper when she finished.

"This is horrible business," he said. Baker set the paper on the seat next to him and quietly mulled it over. He turned his hazel eyes on Ember again, and when he spoke, his voice was softer.

"This must be difficult for you, Ember."

She shook her head, trying to make the account of events real in her mind.

"It sounds as if Mr. Masterson didn't stand a chance," Baker observed. "The way Styles shot him was dishonorable. I'll admit his behavior is a shock to me. I wouldn't have considered him a killer."

They had not given instruction to the driver to change their destination, and so within a few minutes they found themselves arriving outside Styles' apartments. Ember looked out the window. The Strand wasn't nearly as intimidating in the afternoon sun as it had been under a blanket of darkness. When she promised Styles she'd return, these circumstances never entered her imagination.

"Are you okay?" Baker asked. His concern warmed her.

Without answering, she took a deep breath and stepped down from the cab, not sure of her purpose. Baker followed and she was grateful for his company.

The few people lounging about gave little notice to her, but one or two slipped deeper into shadow at the sight of a police officer.

A lean boy sat on the steps outside Styles' apartments. He turned a gaunt face as they approached, his eyes almost hidden by a shock of hair. Ogre slept next to the boy, the animal's legs occasionally twitching.

The boy accepted their greeting with a cautious nod.

"I'm a friend of Mr. Styles," Ember offered.

"No, you're not," the boy said. "He don't have friends. At least none that come around. Except for maybe Mr. Tressler."

Something about the boy's impertinence made her smile. He stood and she suspected if the Chief Constable said anything, he would bolt.

"Are you a friend of Mr. Styles?" she asked.

The question surprised the boy. With a moody grumble, he shrugged and finally nodded.

"Did you hear what happened to him?" she asked gently.

The boy's eyes darkened, his body posture became defensive. Ogre opened an eye, perhaps sensing his discomfiture, and realized a visitor stood close by. The animal gave her a familiar growl.

"Is Mr. Styles okay?" the boy asked.

She paused, not sure how to respond. At last Ember shook her head. She put a foot on the step and said, "Mr. Styles is gone. He was killed in a duel."

Pronouncing the words gave them more weight. The boy shook his head and tears welled up in his large eyes. He wiped his sleeve along his cheek and sniffled. Ember placed a hand on his shoulder.

"Mr. Styles was a good man," he said. "Every time he saw me, he flipped me a coin and told me to get in trouble. Sometimes he gave me a book to read and paid me more if I told him what it was about."

She smiled at this, pleased to have something to flesh out what she suspected of the man. She'd never have the opportunity though to get to know him better.

"Guess you'll have to look after Ogre now," Ember said, stroking the animal's head.

"Oh, no, Miss. I can't," he said with great pain. "My mom won't have it. And what would I feed him?"

"He needs someone to look after him," she insisted.

"You do it, Miss. You take him home. Mr. Styles would want to know he's safe."

The dog raised a leg and attended to its nether regions with no regard for decorum. She imagined how Hans would respond were he to come home and find the beast lounging on one of Father's sofas in the great room.

"I'll take him," Ember said.

"Wait," Baker uttered. "You're not serious."

The dog rose stiffly, shuffling forward, lowering its head to be petted. She scratched behind Ogre's ear with two fingers. The poor beast. It was the sort of mutt people chased away or shirked from.

Ember dropped onto a knee, draping her arms around the animal. "Come home with me," she sniffed, lost in taupe fur. "I have more than enough to share."

Ogre leaned into her and the relationship was sealed. Ember turned to the boy. "What's your name?" she asked.

"Arthur."

She opened her small purse and found a coin. She pressed it into his hand.

"What's this for then?" he asked.

"Go get in trouble," she said.

Arthur stared at it for a moment, as though debating whether or not to refuse the prize, but in the end stuffed it in a pocket. Without another word, the boy ran into the fading afternoon, a blur as he rounded a corner.

"What a lost boy," she said.

"Not one to be trusted, that sort."

Ember ignored Baker and turned to face the street. Ogre followed at her heels as she approached the cab. The driver raised an eyebrow.

"Whoa, Miss. I'm sorry but I'm not taking that monster into my cab."

Baker opened the door for the dog. The cabbie, not about to argue with the police, rolled his eyes and turned away.

Ogre sniffed the interior before entering, but finally jumped up and settled in. As they rode away, he put his head in her lap, panting languidly, and giving one low whine, perhaps lamenting the departure from his master's home.

⚷—

Bidding farewell to Baker, she entered her father's house, with Ogre bounding ahead, tail wagging and nose against the ground in pursuit of interesting smells. She marveled at the mastiff's resiliency.

She closed the door and herded the dog toward the stairs that led to her workroom. The animal clumsily maneuvered the steps.

She picked up an old blanket from a workbench and shook it out. Forming it into a kind of nest, she tucked it into a corner. Ogre circled a few times before contentedly flopping down.

A fleeting smile traversed her lips. "I don't think Mr. Baker much cared for you. And I know Father won't, which is probably a plus. And Hans will like you even less."

She reached for a bag on a high shelf, pulling beef jerky from her stockpile. The workshop often caused her to lose time and eating became such a chore, she'd likely not eat at all without the hoard. In the old days, Josephine would have brought a tray, regardless of Ember's wishes, but the newer help cared little for anything but orders. Ember dumped the bag out and Ogre chewed the dried meat down like breathing was unimportant.

Watching the dog eat, she thought of Styles. She didn't haze her recollection of him; he was a misogynist of the worst order, and emotionally unstable. Yet, there was something about him she felt attracted to. The pain and disillusionment hid a special individual, she was sure of it.

Now she would not get an opportunity to know him better.

Ember sighed and tried not to cry again.

Whenever her father caught her moist eyed, he would always encourage her to stop fighting her nature. Tears were a sign of frailty, and an important trait of femininity. He saw them as hope that Ember was not beyond salvation and would someday return to the more suitable behavior for her gender.

Her father was threatened by her intelligence. Perhaps Baker, too. Although Styles never seemed intimidated. Perhaps he hadn't the wit.

Ember caught sight of herself in the cheval glass. With wryness she thought her features would have fit right in with the women in the ladies' fashion catalogues, admired as an example of beauty. Trapped within was the technomancer.

"Maybe the technomancer isn't the problem, Miss Macumazahn," she could hear Hans chide. "Maybe the problem is the jailer."

And perhaps that had been Styles' curse as well.

8—

Ember went to her engine, which James had taken great care to haul back to the workshop. From the rear of the machine, she unlatched a compartment, freeing a scroll of paper with data from the energy stream. Ember unrolled the spool, studying the readings. One of the five lines had a shorter wavelength than the others.

It could be a malfunction. Or it could be something else.

She went over to the modified map of Europe. Maybe the aberrant signal represented something projecting energy, or maybe repelling it. Maybe it represented another breach.

She ran her finger along the map, mentally computing how far the information must have traveled before it returned to them in the tunnel. Her finger came to rest on Switzerland, somewhere on the banks of the river Aar.

Ogre snored loudly in his dog nest.

There was only one thing to do. She'd have to go to Switzerland and conduct another experiment. The airship resting in the barn in their country estate could make the trip in no time.

Oh, Baker would love that. She laughed loudly at the thought, but it was exactly what must be done. And she knew, despite his aloofness, and his resistance to confronting things outside the ordinary, that he would come along.

Ember rose and Ogre followed.

A trip to Switzerland required some preparation. She had to secure funds and persuade one or two of the house-servants to make the trip with them; the idea of just her and Baker making the trip was unacceptable.

She climbed the workshop steps and went to the foyer where she tugged on her overcoat. As she reached for her hat, a knock sounded from the front door. Without waiting for a maid, she opened it.

Josephine stood on the landing, eyes red and swollen with tears. Ember threw her arms around her, then dragged the woman inside.

"Why are you crying? Where's Harry?"

"The neighbor's watching him. I can't stay. I just came to tell you he's taken with a bad fever. I must get back right away."

If Josephine had come for her, then Harry must be very bad indeed. She gripped Josephine's shoulders.

"Let's go," she said. "We'll bring Harry back here and I'll send for the doctor."

Josephine rolled a handkerchief between nervous fingers. "Your father'd have my head."

"If Father's displeased, then he can be damned."

Josephine's mouth hung open. "You shouldn't say such things."

"I'm serious. Harry should be here. The cottage is too far away. I can't stand it."

The old maid gave the matter consideration and finally acquiesced. "All right love, if he can be moved without much distress, then we'll take up residence here for a while. But only until the child is right again."

"We'll go with James. There's no cab faster." Ember gave her another hug, then pushed her back out the door. "James?" she called.

"On my way out the back, Miss," his voice sounded from some other distant room.

All thoughts of Switzerland fell away as Ember hurried the old woman out the door. Maybe the child wouldn't be in too much distress. She didn't like feeling powerless. She squeezed Josephine's hand and they met the cab as it clattered around the drive.

CHAPTER XIII

Wherein Apollonius inadvertently summons lamia

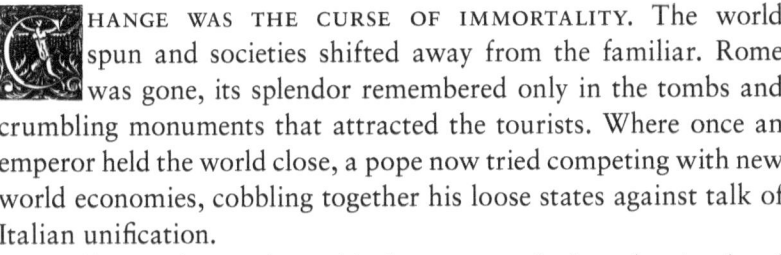HANGE WAS THE CURSE OF IMMORTALITY. The world spun and societies shifted away from the familiar. Rome was gone, its splendor remembered only in the tombs and crumbling monuments that attracted the tourists. Where once an emperor held the world close, a pope now tried competing with new world economies, cobbling together his loose states against talk of Italian unification.

Apollonius shrugged on a black gown, one he kept for ritual and paused before a mirror. He liked the man there, the lean face, the pronounced cheekbones, and long nose. A ruler's countenance. His eyes, black within black, shined with confidence. How many years had passed since those eyes last reflected his humanity? Memories from his other life slipped away, and with them the echoes of his former self faded as well.

He turned and strode down the stairs, a leather satchel in hand. Down a long hall and around a corner, he entered a small room where a man lay on the floor with his hands and legs bound behind him. The man was a laborer from the next village. He was reported missing and local gossip had him running off with a housewife who had also disappeared.

Apollonius bent down and wrapped his freehand around the man's belt. Without much effort, he lifted the prisoner. The man struggled, but Apollonius quieted him with a thought, replacing the fear with arousal.

With an eager step, Apollonius slipped into the night and strode across the property behind the rented manor. He moved with confidence into a wood, pushing through the underbrush, ducking large branches and snapping off smaller ones. He wound his way into the cool dark, destined for a clearing, prepared earlier today—a small nexus of several minor energy lines. They were little more than ripples, easily missed, but useful for what he had in mind.

He dropped the man onto the grass and opened the satchel. Using white candles, Apollonius began melting wax to depict a large pentagram. His mind wandered. Coming to Britain, he supposed life would be simple and carelessly neglected the protections he usually kept in place. The first indication something seemed amiss was the talented young man who followed him through the aether, tapping into his consciousness.

Peter Styles.

The young man surprised him. Although undisciplined, he posed a definite threat. Mr. Styles had displayed through his ability to manipulate the aether that he might have the power to remotely, using the key, tap into the power of the tablet. Provided the key and the tablet were in the same reality. And that possibility put him in the same category as Lysimachus.

No, Mr. Styles couldn't be allowed into this game as a free agent. He must turn him. And when he had Mr. Styles, he would go after another who held his interest, the self-proclaimed necromancer who had almost procured Lysimachus' map in the first place, the one calling himself Virgil.

Virgil could wait; he didn't pose the same threat as Styles. Also, Apollonius now knew something else about the man: his identity. The magic keeping him hidden had been abruptly cancelled. He couldn't feel Virgil's presence, but he no longer felt blocked.

Apollonius now used salt to create a circle and complete the wax pentagram. Next, he again lifted the man stolen from the village and sliced away the wretch's shirt and trousers. He then gently and lovingly lowered the naked man to the ground.

Apollonius pulled out the ancient map created by Lysimachus and uttered a few words of ritual. He thought about the old man, Alexander's favorite, and bristled. Time enough later to fulfill the self-promise to pay back the meddler. Now wasn't the time to be distracted by memories and unresolved conflicts. Just as he sensed the old man here in Britain, so the old man, if he still lived, would sense him. And if that was the case, Lysimachus was even now putting things in place to thwart him. Or maybe it was just an echo of paranoia.

He sprinkled water on the naked man and pressed a palm against the man's forehead. The touch kindled his hunger. He wanted to excite the laborer's life energies and then greedily devour them.

He fought back his urges and instead followed the life energies into the aether. The man didn't generate much power, he was more of a candle, providing just enough illumination to begin a search along one of the many threads. Even with the map, he had burned through several such candles, and still didn't feel any closer to the tablet.

The laborer writhed under Apollonius' touch, moaning and pushing his hips forward. Ignoring the burst of desire, Apollonius rode the man's energies to probe the lines marked on the map.

He was missing something. He knew the tablet to be out there. He had a connection to the stone rivaled only by Lysimachus. Where was it?

The aether rippled. Apollonius used the pentagram to amplify the last of the laborer's energy, but it was like trying to push lightning through metallic mesh. Images bombarded him and he drank them in. The energy lines moved, realities shifted, what was once true, might not be now. Clever Lysimachus. Even with the map, the location of the Emerald Tablet dangled just out of touch.

It was no use. Apollonius threw back his head and with an animalistic cry he halted the search.

The candle winked out.

Apollonius kneeled beside the man on the ground and stroked the side of his face. The poor little fellow was nothing but a husk now.

Perhaps he needed another sort of candle.

Imagine what illumination Peter Styles might provide.

Using Styles' energies to follow the threads through the aether felt like inspiration. Although the map remained a locked vault, Apollonius was confident that with enough energy and with his knowledge of the stone, he could find the hiding place.

Apollonius once more folded the map and secreted it on his person. He prepared to step across the circle and head back the way he had come but was arrested by a blast of foreboding.

He scoured the dark sky. A mélange of scents blew through the treetops. An owl sensed the approach and screeched before taking flight. Apollonius waited, hoping he was wrong. He could flee, but besides the taste of cowardice that would leave him, he would be left looking over his shoulder, wondering if his senses had been correct, or if he had been duped by his own paranoia.

Apollonius had never been a warrior, nor a general. Nevertheless, he waited.

The first to materialize from the darkness was a tall and powerfully built female. The moonlight caught her pale skin and gave her a ghostly appearance. Behind her came a small, lanky woman, who slipped through the grass with a panther's speed and grace. They stopped at the edge of the circle.

The women exchanged smiles as their gaze dropped to the naked figure at Apollonius' feet. The more muscular of the two moved away from her partner, perhaps to distract him, but he realized she had merely moved to make way for two more figures, these male.

The first was magnificent, with short-cropped metallic hair and a gladiator's physique. He slid an arm around the smaller woman. The other man appeared younger, almost boyish. His hair was a shock of curls.

"You're almost one of them," the tall woman said, her tone disdainful. Apollonius hadn't heard Ancient Greek in a very long time.

"Where's your mistress?" he asked.

"Mistress is here," the effeminate male responded.

Apollonius waited and when she at last appeared, the past rushed at him without remorse. Liala materialized from the shadows, her beauty still staggering. Her hips were wide, but not overly so, and her breasts were magnificently full. Chestnut hair fell over sculpted shoulders and framed a strong jaw and well-defined cheekbones. Her eyes, like the others in her retinue, and like Apollonius', were the black within black of the lamia.

"I tasted you," Liala remarked. She smiled and radiated power. Apollonius studied her with appreciation and care.

"He doesn't look like much," the gladiator stated.

"He never did," she said.

Another lifetime. Apollonius recalled the wedding on a hillside in Corinth, overlooking the sea. His student, Missipus, the groom. The bride, a virgin from Perigiali. The perfect couple, a match to bring tears to the eyes of old men and women. Except the bride wasn't human.

Apollonius had seen through the veil immediately and acted, but rashly, without realizing the violence which would follow the unmasking of Liala as lamia. The groom escaped, but she and others of her kind waiting in the gathering fell on the wedding guests.

She punished him by robbing him of his humanity.

Now here she was, Liala, with members of her court in attendance.

Moving around the circle, perhaps probing it for weakness, Liala kept an eye on Apollonius. He could feel her pull, even through the magic barrier. She snickered, perhaps because his trepidation fed her ego.

"It's all like an elaborate web, isn't it?" she said. "One strand vibrates, suggesting trapped prey, and we follow the disturbance and unwittingly step through a portal."

"As you foolishly stepped through it before," Apollonius chided, a reference to how he bested Liala long ago.

The men watched the power struggle with interest. An eager expression stole over the face of the curly haired one, reminding Apollonius of a hunting dog awaiting a command. The two women remained intent and more dangerous than the men. One of them was surely Liala's ambitious second, retained not for her loyalty but because having someone close who would jump at the chance to destroy her kept Liala sharp.

The tall woman with the powerful physique was too obvious and too threatening. The smaller woman was more likely Liala's choice. She had a feral air about her.

"You're still looking for it, aren't you?" Liala asked.

Apollonius didn't respond and his silence appeared to anger her.

"Why does the Emerald Tablet of Hermes mean so much to you—after all this time?" she asked. "How you might have thrived had you abandoned your obsession. If you haven't found it by now, you never will." Liala hugged herself and eyed the night. He saw her shiver. She looked vulnerable; that was her strength.

"What do you want, Liala?" he asked.

She took a step forward as if forgetting the circle, but stopped. "I want you, Apollonius."

He almost responded with a jibe, but instead waited for her to continue.

"Lysimachus must know you're here," she said. "He must have felt you, just as we did. And he'll do what he can to keep you from your search. Maybe not directly, but as we speak, the old manipulator will have set things in motion to make your path treacherous."

She was correct. Liala always used the truth for her manipulations. He suppressed his frustration, not wanting to give her the satisfaction of knowing how she affected him.

"You can't beat him," Liala said. "You don't have the patience of a tactician. Lysimachus has patience to spare. He was Alexander's tutor. Even after being supplanted by Aristotle, he still shaped the emperor. I wonder who he has chosen to shape now."

"I am not worried about Lysimachus." He hadn't meant to speak those words. The lack of self-control further fueled his resentment.

Liala paced the border of the circle. Something tickled the back of Apollonius' neck and he knew she was drawing in power, that she had been stalling in an effort to gather energy. He had the advantage, the center of the circle being the center of the nexus. He opened himself to the energies, tapping into the lines here.

A faint change in Liala's expression showed she felt his intent, as he had felt hers. If he acted first, he might not catch her unaware, but he might minimize the advantage she gained from her followers. First, he would have to break the circle, otherwise the energies would hit the barrier and rebound on him. Liala would know as soon as the circle was gone.

Timing was everything.

The strain of collecting energy was becoming too much for him and he feared an uncontrolled discharge. He locked eyes with Liala and slowed time.

The circle fell away. Its collapse unintentional. The lamia felt it.

Apollonius released the energy. Blue-white light shot from the nexus followed by the smell of ozone. Three of the figures outside the circle were thrown into the air, their bodies surrounded by violet flame. Their hideous screams gave voice to the pain surging through their systems.

Apollonius charged forward. He kept low and shoved through the undergrowth. He could make a stand. He could defeat any one of the lamia, maybe even two, but not the entire pack at once.

Hands gripped his shoulders from behind and pulled him down. He rolled with his attacker—the little huntress. He used his weight to keep her pinioned and maneuvered his forearm against her throat.

She countered not with force, but instead with the cold rush of presence, an old trick meant to distract. She hammered through his consciousness without finesse; this one didn't have Liala's skill. He shoved her from his thoughts and rose up to grip the sides of her head. He twisted it sharply, listening with satisfaction to the sound of snapping vertebrae. Her wounds would mend in minutes if given the chance to heal, but he had no intention of allowing that chance.

He dropped beside her, and whispered in her ear, "Are you there, Liala?"

She would hear him through her pet. This was no time for taunting, but he couldn't help himself.

"I never gave you fealty. I never gave anyone fealty. Not Hadrian. Not Antonius Pious, not Lucius Veras or Marcus Aurelius. None of them! My allegiance has always been to myself."

The last sentence gave him pause.

He lunged, freeing a dagger from its hidden holster. With an angry roar, he sawed through skin, muscle, and cartilage with a surgeon's precision. Bone snapped. He held the head aloft as the body fell to ground.

The gory prize disgusted him. He would take the head and bury it far away. If he left it by the body, Liala might be able to bring her servant back.

Apollonius hastened to the mansion to claim his belongings. Except for the one. He would leave that in its hiding place.

As he ran, he tested the aether to see if he could feel Liala give pursuit. It was too soon. The blast had weakened them. They would give chase, but not before Liala recovered the body of her favorite.

He rolled Lysimachus' map and stuffed it into the lining of a valise. The head was put into a burlap bag to dangle from his saddle. Later, he would bury it in a salt-lined hole.

Apollonius swung onto his mount and, without glancing back, charged into the darkness toward London.

It was time to find Mr. Styles.

CHAPTER XIV

Wherein Avery receives a night visit regarding the death of his close friend

AVERY STUDIED THE CHARM STOLEN FROM MASTERSON'S NECK AND CRINGED AT THE SHAME OF HAVING COMMITTED THE ACT. Although Peter's last request, it was wrong of him to comply.

He ran a finger over the piece of brass, examining the different symbols etched into the surface. The charm was ugly and crudely fashioned. He hefted it and squinted a brown eye as though trying to peer through the metal. No doubt the item was remarkable, perhaps possessing some innate power. Avery wasn't a skeptic. No, his disbelief vanished long ago, while he served as first mate of *The Dolphin*, and with it went any hope that the universe was a well-ordered place, with the people populating it fitting neatly into a grand scheme.

Avery tossed the charm into the air and caught it in his fist. Nothing to do with it for now, he supposed. Avery fell into an easy chair and a bitter expression stole over his face.

"Keep it safe," Peter had said before passing away.

Avery shook his head and wished Peter were here; he had few other people he trusted with his emotions. "You should have listened to me," Avery said in a whisper. He shut his eyes and exhaled slowly, as if his grief and rage could be thus expelled. He was fearful of the dreams; although he hadn't had the nightmares in many years, he always fretted over their return.

He commanded himself to turn away from this train of thought, and yet in doing so, it only seemed to solidify it.

Someone knocked on the door to his flat.

Fear stabbed him. Avery raised an eyebrow and glanced toward the door. It was late and no one was expected. Avery shoved the charm into his pocket as he rose.

"Who's there?"

"Mr. Tressler, I'm looking for a mutual friend."

Avery didn't recognize the voice, but it did little to squash his growing sense of dread. He hastily cast about for a weapon; he started to reach for the sword cane resting in the umbrella stand, but instead went to his desk and retrieved his Colt. He checked the weapon and thrust it into the same pocket as the charm.

"Mr. Tressler?"

Avery squared his shoulders and opened the door to face a remarkable man who at once fascinated and repulsed him. Avery almost let his hand stray to his pocket.

"My name is Stefan Apollonius," the stranger offered with a short bow. "I apologize for the lateness of the hour, however my schedule is pressing. I need to find Peter Styles and I was told you might know where he is."

Another figure stood in the hall behind the stranger. This one dressed in a brown robe tied at the waist with a modest length of rope. The man's face was hidden by a deep hood. A monk? Avery leaned to one side to try and get a better look at the man.

"I stopped by Mr. Styles' lodgings, but no one was there," the stranger continued. "Someone mentioned you were a close friend, so I assumed you would be able to give me some information."

"I'm sorry," Avery replied. He noted the gentleman's foot slip at the threshold, presumably to block the door from shutting, but didn't respond to the action. He turned his attention to the man's face, and found the eyes unsettling. They were black and large, and almost inhuman in their intensity.

"Please, help me," Mr. Apollonius urged. "Mr. Styles sent me a letter warning that I might be in danger. I don't mean to be sensational, but I've seen things that have unsettled me. Mr. Styles said he could help."

The black eyes widened and Avery found it difficult to look away. He should let the man in and perhaps offer him a drink. If he could assist him in any way, then he should do so. He smiled at the fellow, feeling comfort in his presence and opened the door wider for him.

"Come in, Mr. Apollonius."

The gentleman spoke to his companion before entering: "Wait there, Theron. I shall not be long."

Apollonius shut the door, momentarily breaking eye contact. Avery's trepidation returned. The man turned back around and placed a heavy hand on Avery's shoulder. "Where is Peter Styles?" he asked.

Avery took a deep breath before answering. "I'm sorry to inform you that Mr. Styles is dead."

Apollonius dropped his head as if deeply affected by the news. "I am distraught to hear this," Apollonius replied. "My condolences for the loss of your friend. He was a young man. What happened to him?"

"A duel."

Apollonius raised his eyebrows.

"The affair's already in the newspapers, and certainly will receive no small amount of attention tomorrow," Avery elaborated. "Styles and Masterson were fairly well-known."

"I had hoped for Mr. Styles' protection. He had warned me of a dangerous figure. Now Mr. Styles is gone and the threat to my family remains."

Avery was nearly swept along with the passion of the man's words, but his conscience warned him to be on guard. There was underlying corruption in the man's tone.

"Can you tell me the identity of this person who threatens your family?" Avery asked.

"Neither Mr. Styles, nor I have had that information. The villain protects his identity well."

"Perhaps your family is safe, Mr. Apollonius. I believe the man you refer to was the very man Mr. Styles shot."

Avery hadn't meant to say anything else about the matter. His own words confounded him.

"What was this man's name?" Apollonius asked.

"Masterson. However, my friend said he used another name as an alias."

Avery became acutely aware of the weight of Apollonius' hand upon his shoulder. He had an urge to bat the man's hand away, to break contact with him, but couldn't.

"What other name?" Apollonius asked.

Avery knew he had said too much already. And yet, he answered. "Virgil."

A businesslike nod by Apollonius suggested he had known the name all along. Avery tried moving, but his arms hung uselessly at his side.

Apollonius leaned close and spoke in a hushed voice.

"Where does Mr. Styles lie in repose?"

The question shocked him enough to break free of Apollonius' influence. It was like jerking awake from a nightmare. He moved back, wanting distance between himself and the stranger. He considered threatening him with the Colt, but resisted the action.

"I don't know where Styles rests," Avery lied. "I suspect the authorities still have his body."

Apollonius studied him. "He's been given over to his family," Apollonius murmured. "I believe Mr. Styles hails from Southall?"

"Get out!" Avery stood straight as the words emboldened him.

The man's eyes were now an abyss of black, a reflection of the sickness within. "I'm sorry, Mr. Tressler," Apollonius said. "I've overstayed my welcome. I should have been more considerate of your grief."

Without further comment, the stranger strode to the door and stepped into the hall. Avery heard him address the robed figure in another language. Greek?

The voices stopped and a form stepped through the still open door as Apollonius' footsteps receded down the hall.

The person now entering the apartment was medium height, with broad shoulders suggesting tremendous strength. His face was hidden by the monk's robes. Avery shuddered at what stood before him.

Nekroanypomonos!

Fear caused Avery's stomach to roil. His mouth felt cottony and his head suddenly light. He clenched his teeth and let his military training push away the crippling horror assailing him.

The thing swayed slightly. The hood shifted to expose a milky eye and grayish skin. The lower lip was partly torn away and hung as a flap on the chin.

Avery remained still and watched in fascination as the monster took a step to the side, eyes sweeping first one side of the room and then the other. The dead man stepped forward and stopped. Its face was expressionless. Again, the thing's eyes scoured the room as if blind.

Avery held his breath and slipped a hand into his pocket to withdraw the Colt, but stopped as he remembered the dagger Peter had given him. The blade was in his bedroom on the bureau.

He took a step back, moving carefully to minimize any sound. Continuing backward, he left the carpeted area and the wood floor creaked under his heel.

The dead man's head swiveled. It started in his direction. Avery pivoted and broke for the bedroom.

A hand gripped the back of his shirt as he lunged for the bureau. Fabric ripped and the buttons down the front popped off and were strewn across the floor. Avery stretched for the dagger. His fingers closed on the hilt.

Before he could make use of the weapon, an arm closed on his throat and pulled him backward. He tried bracing himself, but his shoes slid along the polished floor. The grip tightened, making it impossible to breathe.

In desperation, Avery stabbed at the forearm, ripping the blade through flesh and muscle. His attacker hissed and released him. It stumbled against the four-poster bed.

Avery spun and leapt on the dead man. He drove the dagger into the thing's heart and twisted the blade. The monster arched its back and clawed at Avery's hands. He yanked the blade free and stabbed again. They slid to the floor with Avery still on top.

The *nekroanypomonos* kicked the floor, jerking from side to side in an attempt to free itself. A final spasm wracked its body and it went limp. Avery said a quick prayer as he slid from the corpse. He felt drained, as if something had sucked energy from him. He now understood Peter's instructions on how the blade channeled energy to sever the ties between *nekroanypomonos* and necromancer.

Free from danger, Avery's wits returned.

The dead man hadn't seen him. He was sure of this. He thrust a hand into a pocket and withdrew the purloined charm. It had hidden Masterson from discovery and blinded the dead to his presence. He gazed at the item with newfound respect.

Avery returned the charm to his pocket and retrieved the knife from the dead man. He stood on shaky legs and removed his shirt to seek a clean one from his wardrobe. As he dressed he was unable to look away from the corpse.

And now he was unsure what to do. There was no one he could call who would believe what had happened here. Avery puzzled over his next course of action and groaned.

"I believe Mr. Styles hails from Southall?" Apollonius had said.

Cursing himself for his slow wits, Avery hurried to the front hall for his coat and hat. He charged from the apartment and took the stairs two at a time. Before stepping outside, Avery paused. What if Apollonius was in the street, waiting to collect his creature? More likely that the necromancer was on his way to Southall to steal Peter's corpse.

Avery thrust a hand into his pocket and felt for the Colt. Apollonius had seemed flesh and blood, but maybe a gun would prove as ineffectual against him as it would be against one of his servants. If it did, there was still the blade.

He stepped into the cool evening air and peered into the shadows for any evidence of threat. The street seemed calm; the only sound was the whinny of a horse attached to a nearby carriage. Avery called to the driver, who raised his face and stared at him for a long moment before gathering the reins and giving them a shake to move the horse forward.

Avery imagined he was a sight. He tried adjusting his cap and straightening his clothes as the driver looked down at him.

"Sir?"

He gave the driver the address for the Styles estate. The driver scoffed at the fare.

"It's quite a ride from here," the man protested.

Avery controlled his impatience and instead slipped the driver extra coin. The man stared for a moment before gesturing him into the hansom.

"Make haste," Avery ordered.

The driver mumbled in protest, but still gave his small whip a crack. The hansom rattled quickly down the street, heading east for the fringe of the great city.

He had always felt anger at Peter for involving himself in action that went against any reasonable moral compass, regardless of the intent. Still, he owed it to his friend to make sure his final sleep was undisturbed.

Avery slumped in his seat and turned his attention to the ominous gray London sky and the purple streaks low on the horizon which announced the advance of night. He shook his head and worried a fingernail. A cold damp wind blew in from the west and reminded him too much of old nightmares which refused to relinquish their hold.

The hansom approached the front of the Styles' estate. The property was well-maintained and old trees grew along the sides of the drive which curved before the front door. Avery alighted from the carriage and slipped another coin into the driver's hand.

"That was well done," Avery said. The driver touched his finger to the brim of his hat.

"Would you be willing to wait for me?" Avery asked.

"You can count on me, sir."

Avery thanked the man and approached the front door. He had expected some sign of trouble, but the house was silent and the song of distant night birds contradicted the worry which plagued him. Doubt fell on his shoulders. He searched for what he would say to Styles' father. Still, the old man knew his son and that alone should help him receive Avery's unexpected and unusual appearance. He rang the bell and stepped back.

A servant soon appeared; a short man with spectacles balanced on his nose. The man studied him with suspicion.

"Sir?"

Avery slipped a card from his pocket and presented it to the man. "Avery Tressler. It is urgent I speak with the master of the house."

The man squinted and pushed the glasses higher onto his nose. He peered over Avery's shoulder at the waiting hansom.

"I'll be back in a moment, sir."

"May I wait inside?" he asked.

"No, sir. I'm sorry."

The door shut. Avery ground his teeth and supposed he should have expected that. He listened to the servant's feet retreating down the hall. While he waited, Avery stepped back from the door and examined the front of the manor again, his eyes keen for anything out of the ordinary. This was a well-loved fortress, with an orderly and lovingly cared for landscape. According to Peter, that's the way his father liked the world; the old man appreciated balance and didn't understand his son's extremes.

Avery met him twice before. The old man was tall, solidly built, with gray hair and clear eyes. He always spoke in a calm manner, with carefully chosen words. The man was affable, and inspired confidence and loyalty.

"My father is England," Peter once remarked.

"And you?" Avery retorted.

"Why, I'm England, too."

Avery had laughed at the remark, but thinking back now there was truth to it.

The door opened and the servant showed him in. Avery waited in a small sitting room at the front of house where a candle was lit for him. The room was sparsely decorated, with a few innocuous paintings on one wall. The fireplace was small, and the two iron chairs before it uncomfortable. The room wasn't welcoming. He decided against sitting and instead paced before the door.

Mr. Styles, esquire, soon arrived, in a heavy dressing gown, hair uncombed and his eyes weary. He offered a hand to Avery and gave him a slap on the shoulder.

"Avery, is there an emergency?" he asked.

"It's about Peter. I need to check on him," Avery blurted out. The words sounded insane. He damned himself; he had intended to first offer condolences and inquire after the old man's health, but the urgency of the last couple hours now had the better of him.

Mr. Styles' eyebrows rose. He stepped back and studied Avery.

"Sit down, man," Mr. Styles said. He squeezed Avery's shoulder. "You look ill. You're not making sense."

Avery sat, his back straight and his hands on his knees. He gathered his wits and tried again. "Mr. Styles, forgive me. I've had a difficult evening. I apologize for my lack of manners."

The older man waved his hand. "You were, I think, one of the few people he trusted," Styles said. "I know this difficult for you. It's been unbearable for me."

Having made this pronouncement, his friend's father sighed and looked away quickly. He cleared his throat and Avery lowered his head to give him a moment of privacy.

"Ah me," the old man said, and the misery in those words struck Avery deeply. "I never lost faith in my son. I knew his failings. I didn't shut my ears to scandal, but I knew Peter, and I knew the good in him. More than he was willing to admit to himself."

Avery could do little but nod. Gratefully his poor start seemed forgiven, but he again considered how to deal with the matter which brought him here.

"His mother died when he was seventeen, and his sister passed away a couple months later," Styles said. "She and Peter were so close; it devastated him. He always struggled to find his way, didn't he? He always took things so hard. He was a slave to extremes."

The old man put his head down again, but he lifted his face and looked warily at Avery.

"What did you mean when you said you needed to check on

Peter? What brought you here?"

There was no sensible way to proceed; he had played this scene over in his mind several times and every approach sounded like a mad raving or an inept rationalization. He shrank under Styles' scrutiny.

"You disapproved of many of your son's associates, and quite rightly, although you respected Peter's independence and didn't interfere. One of these individuals harbored great animosity toward Peter, to the point that he may attempt to interfere with Peter's internment."

The old man's mouth dropped open; he looked horrified at the idea. "Who? Why? Have you been to see the authorities?"

Avery thought of the dead man lying on the floor in his bedroom. "No, Mr. Styles, although I shall do so first thing in the morning. Right now, I just want to be sure Peter's rest is undisturbed."

"Who is this man? Is it Glaston? It couldn't possibly be Glaston."

"No, you're correct. Mr. Styles, I wouldn't have imposed on you unless I thought this a serious threat. These people keep a dark society; they work outside the law, if you get my meaning. I tried to dissuade Peter, but he had his own mind."

"But what you're suggesting is incredible."

"Nonetheless," Avery said. He tried imparting urgency into his words. "I wish I could tell you more, Mr. Styles. You know me, though. You know me well enough to trust I wouldn't come in your time of grief and make such outrageous statements without good reason."

Mr. Styles nodded and they sat in silence, with only the sputtering of the candle to intrude on their thoughts.

"You were a good friend to Peter," the old man said. The firmness in his voice resonated with resolve. "Thank you for posting his letter to me after the duel. I wish your influence had had more impact on him."

The man stood and took the candle from the table near the door.

"I believe you," Mr. Styles pronounced. "I will post servants to watch the body and make sure that I have additional people about the grounds keeping an eye open for strangers. I do not know what anyone would gain from preventing Peter from receiving a proper funeral, but we live in strange times, and my son sometimes kept eccentric company, yourself excluded."

"Thank you," Avery said. "I feel better knowing you take this as seriously as I."

"There are things a father doesn't want to believe about his son," Styles said. "We'll check on Peter together, and we'll both rest easier knowing he is safe. After that, I'll call my man Carter to keep watch."

Shielding the flame, he led them along a narrow hall to a room at the far side of the house. He paused, taking out a key to open a door.

Avery waited.

"Did he ever cross over?" Mr. Styles asked. "I mean, did he ever do anything that went beyond the point of forgiveness?"

Avery knew what the father was asking; he had asked that of Peter many times himself. He gave the answer firmly. "No, Peter may not always have been Christian in his actions, but the only person he truly injured was himself."

The old man received these words with a sad expression. "Well said," he replied. He turned the key and opened the door. As they entered, a groan escaped the old man.

The coffin rested on the floor. Several bunches of flowers were set about its head. The lid was unfastened, and only partially covered the box.

"Dear Lord," Mr. Styles moaned.

Avery continued further, peering into the empty coffin.

"I'll summon the authorities," Avery said this more to comfort the old man than out of a belief that it would do any good.

Mr. Styles stumbled toward the vacant casket, but Avery caught his arm. The old man pressed a palm to his forehead and allowed himself to be pulled from the room. Outside, he leaned against the wall and covered his face with his hands.

"To what end?" Mr. Styles asked.

"To keep him from being buried as a Christian," Avery lied. "To cause more controversy."

The old man smiled and remarked in a voice which could have been Peter's: "To that end they perhaps pay my son more tribute than do him harm. You know more than you're letting on, Mr. Tressler."

Avery remained silent.

Mr. Styles took his hand and squeezed it. "Whatever you need to stop these people, you let me know. Find my son, Mr. Tressler. Bring him back. Let him find the peace in death that he never found in life."

CHAPTER XV

Wherein Ember is accosted by an uninvited guest

MBER STOOD WITH HER BACK TO THE DOCTOR, GAZING THROUGH THE WINDOW AT THE LAST SHREDS OF FRAYING DAYLIGHT.

Two days had passed since she received her nephew, making him as comfortable as possible until the doctor could find time to call.

Ember collected her nerve and faced the bed. It wouldn't do to have Harry see her in distress. Not that Josephine was faring any better at hiding emotion. The old nanny sat in the corner, sniffling into a damp handkerchief. Her worry made her look older, beaten down by time.

Another, more upsetting thought crept into Ember's mind. *That Harry wasn't in any condition to notice them.*

Doctor Roberts hunched over the boy, the ruddy light winking from his stethoscope like a demon's eye.

A sheen of sour sweat coated Ember's fitful nephew, his eyelids shut to slits. Ember went to his side, pressing a palm to damp, matted hair.

"You should keep away," Doctor Roberts said, his voice calm to the point of patronizing. "I don't know whether he's contagious."

Ember withdrew; pained she could do nothing to help.

"He will have to be kept fairly isolated," the doctor continued. "Kept quarantined here. Anyone who touches him must thoroughly scrub their skin. I'll try bloodletting and see if that doesn't ease his condition."

Ember's stomached flipped thinking about the copious amount of bleeding required to flush out a fever.

"Mercy," Josephine whispered. She pressed a fist to her forehead. "Oh, it's all my fault. I shouldn't have let him play with the neighbors."

"Hush now," Ember said.

She stared at Harry, seeing her brother in her nephew's pale face. Even as children, they weren't good together. Her brother was cruel, and her father seldom corrected him.

She heard her father's voice, intruding as Josephine stood between her and Harry.

"Careful there, Jo, you'll break that boy's spirit."

"Harry's spirit is fine, you should worry more about Ember."

The doctor cleared his throat. "We'll also need him to purge, it will do him well to purify his system. And I don't want him eating any meat."

"Is there nothing else to be done?" Ember's voice came out in a rasp.

"Nothing, I'm afraid." Doctor Roberts unlatched the clasp on his medical bag, pulling out a lancing needle along with a glass bell and portable burner.

Ember turned her head.

While Doctor Roberts readied the lancing needle, there came a knock on the bedroom door.

"Excuse me, Miss," the maid Lucy said in hushed tones. "Chief Constable Baker's waiting downstairs to see you."

Ember felt a shamefaced sense of relief rush over her, glad she wouldn't bear the unfolding medical horrors alone.

"Send him up."

Lucy gave a slight nod before disappearing down the stairs.

Doctor Roberts was heating the glass cup when she heard masculine footsteps ascending. The doctor laid the cup aside, picking up the needle. Ember closed her eyes as he made the first puncture.

Baker entered the room. She turned from the sick bed and approached the constable. She held back her tears, but couldn't find her voice. Instead, she pressed her head into Baker's chest and didn't turn back until the bloodletting was over.

She caught the doctor and Baker exchanging concerned glances.

"Ember, go downstairs and have some tea," Doctor Roberts urged. "If you don't get some rest, you'll be the next one to fall ill."

She resisted, but Josephine stepped into the debate and Ember acquiesced. Baker gently ushered her from the sickroom.

Downstairs, she collapsed into her father's smoking chair and considered the cherry wood box on the round table next to her. Were Baker not here, she would light up a cigar, or perhaps borrow a bowl of her father's sweet tobacco. She noted Baker and grinned at his rigid posture; he was old fashioned and not likely to change. When he wasn't being a prig, he could be charming, but he seldom lowered his guard.

The silence continued until it irritated. Ember shifted in the chair and gazed at the ceiling; her imagination filled in the details about what was happening upstairs.

She made a declaration that would have angered her father. "He's my nephew," she said. "Harry's my brother's son."

Baker didn't respond. She wanted to elaborate, to expose the family scandal, but couldn't. Her father's influence stilled her voice.

"I can't leave him," she said. "I can't travel to Switzerland, not while he's in the grips of fever."

Baker looked relieved. She had approached the constable about heading across the channel, pushing him hard to understand what was at stake. Although he resisted her initially, he showed signs of giving in when they discussed it further.

Then the fever worsened.

"I think that's best," Baker commented.

Ember rankled at his answer.

Baker's face remained stoic, but she saw in his eyes that he was pleased at having her back off the plan to once again tap into unseen energies. Maybe it reassured him that she showed signs of vulnerability; perhaps it helped him frame her in a more conventional role.

The doctor appeared, stepping into the room as he untied the strings of a blood-speckled apron.

"Harry needs rest, now," he said. "You, too."

Ember nodded wearily. Baker took the doctor's hand, annoyingly playing the host role for Ember. "Thank you, doctor. We appreciate all you've done."

After Baker showed Doctor Roberts to the door, he came back to the great room and resumed his vigil, as though standing sentry or possibly declaring his territory. Ember knew she was being unfair, but couldn't help herself.

"It's late," Baker said. "You should do as the doctor prescribed and try and get some sleep."

"I don't think I'm quite ready to sleep," she replied. "Nonetheless."

Ember shook her head and flipped open the cherry box. She extracted a cigar and reached in her purse for a small blade. Baker rolled his eyes as she sliced off the end and set the rolled tobacco in her mouth. She watched him as she struck a match and ignited the end.

"Very well, I have to get back to the station tonight," he said.

"Thank you for stopping by Chief Constable. Your presence was most comforting." She punctuated her remark by sending a cloud of bluish smoke toward the ceiling.

"Ember," he started, but the rest of the sentence never made it out. Instead he toyed with his cap before saying, "I'll stop by tomorrow morning and see how you are doing."

He made her feel beastly. She didn't answer, but listened to the sound of his footsteps as he headed down the hall.

"Idiot," she chided herself. Ember threw the cigar in the fireplace and headed upstairs to check on Harry.

Ember shot up with tears in her eyes. She clutched her quilt and still saw her brother, stretched out in a hotel room, his throat cut. The fright of the dreamworld followed her into this one.

"Harry?" she whispered.

She rose and hastened to her nephew's sick room. The boy lay in the same position as when she'd last checked on him a few hours ago. Thankfully his chest rose and fell with steady rhythm, but the horror of the dream still clung to her.

No, it was something else.

Ember searched the room not sure what she might be looking for. She stalked to the window and opened it to peer into the night.

The cool air refreshed her. She leaned against the sash and considered the too familiar image of her brother; after all she had been exposed to these last few days, of course such dreams would haunt her.

A gaslight flickered, as if a momentary shadow eclipsed the glow. Startled, she watched the street, but everything was as it should be. Ember wished the dawn were closer. Still uneasy, she closed the window and locked it.

She was her father's daughter; if her dread proved to be prescient, then she would face the threat better prepared. Ember considered going to her father's room to retrieve one of his weapons. She could shoot a rifle as well as any man. However as her mind went to the creatures in the tunnel, she instead headed for the back stairs to her work room. A bad dream and a shadow in the night hardly justified this growing alarm, however Ember couldn't dismiss the grip of impending doom. She fumbled with a candle and illuminated the workbench where sat a smaller version of the pentacle shaped battery she had used in the tunnel. Attached to it was a tube to funnel and concentrate the discharge.

Ember lifted it by a strap she had secured to make it easier to wield and slipped it about her shoulder. The tube's shell was fashioned of copper but shielded by rubber. She had welded a grip to the tube to stabilize aim.

There had been no time to test it, but she was confident of its functionality. It would prove a formidable weapon.

Ogre lay in his bed, breathing slowly and whining in his sleep. Did he sense the oddness in the house? Did it link into his dreams as well? She almost woke him, but decided against it, not sure what the poor beast might do should the perceived threat prove to be something from the other world. She bit her lip at this thought and hastened up the steps from her work room to the first floor, and slipped into the foyer.

Weapon abutted against her chest, she opened the door slightly, just enough to scour the road. Satisfied no one prowled nearby, she considered stepping outside and doing a more thorough search of the grounds. Instead, she closed the door, moving silently, and hurried to Harry's room. There, she found Josephine, entranced in front of the open window.

Ember slipped across the threshold. She watched her dear old nanny as the fear within her grew. The house felt alien to her; no longer the safe castle of her childhood.

"Josephine," Ember whispered. "Did you open the window?"

The old nanny swiveled to face her and Ember marveled at the strange expression on the woman's face. She bore the dull look of the somnambulist.

"I don't recall, Miss," she said. "I think I fell asleep, but I don't recollect coming in here."

Ember put the back of her hand against the woman's forehead and found it frighteningly hot. The flesh glistened with perspiration.

"You're burning up," Ember said.

Josephine seemed to have difficulty swallowing. She put a hand to her chest and took a ragged breath. A sly smile stole over the woman's lips.

"It's not the fever," she said.

Ember threw a glance at her nephew's sleeping form. She watched him for a moment before returning her attention to Josephine.

"You sit down. I can't have you getting sick, too."

"I'm not sick," Josephine whispered. "Far from it."

Ember set aside her weapon and pulled a comforter from the back of a chair to wrap around the older woman's shoulders. She rubbed Josephine's hands and ushered her toward the door.

"You should go to your own room and sleep, Jo. I mean it."

The old woman's eyes widened and she shuddered, as though overcome by sensation.

Josephine frightened her; the woman wasn't herself and certainly in no condition to be in the same room as a sick child. Ember was about to put an arm around her and shuffle the old nurse off to her own room when a sound made her turn in time to see a pale face appear from the deep shadows beside the wardrobe.

Edward Masterson stepped into the moonlight streaming through the window.

Dressed in voluminous white funeral robes, his arms spread open in invitation. He was transformed. His ruddy skin was now luminous and smooth, his once frosty eyes were now a terrifying but beautiful black within black.

A slow, deep burn swept over her, a painful ecstasy. "Have you made a decision about my proposal?" he asked. She didn't remember his voice being this deep or rich. She wanted him to speak again.

With one sinuous step his hands were on her. Jolting fingertips explored her flesh. Ember's eyes shut as warm yearning spread through her body and she trembled at the sensation of his tongue flicking over her earlobe.

Masterson cupped her face and as he leaned in to kiss her, Ember responded with a low moan. She pressed against him as arousal ignited. His hand slid across her stomach and moved over a breast.

In the periphery of her vision Ember glimpsed Josephine. The woman leaned forward, spellbound by the salacious display. Her eyes were round with excitement and her lips were damp. Arthritic hands manipulated the air in anticipation.

The sight of her old nurse sparked a moment of clarity. Ember remembered her nephew's sleeping form only feet away and found the strength to block Masterson. She had been on the verge of surrender, enticed by a level of intimacy unlike anything experienced before. She teased the fear which played at the back of her mind and drew upon the resolve to protect Harry. Her determination found purchase.

Now or never.

She raised the back of her hand to Masterson's temple and pressed hard, triggering the signet ring to discharge a burst of electrical current.

A normal man would have dropped in a spastic fit.

The action merely startled Masterson. He grimaced and stepped back. His eyes burned with rage and his hold over Ember dropped away. She saw him for what he was now.

Ember bent and retrieved her weapon from where she had placed it before rushing to Josephine's side. Her palm closed on the grip and she squeezed the trigger. A burst of energy lit the room and Masterson was thrown back against the wall with a force which cracked the plaster. A picture frame dropped to the wood floor with the harsh sound of breaking glass.

She rejoiced seeing him in pain.

Masterson pushed away from the wall and flew at her. His speed caught her by surprise. She squeezed the trigger again and the energy burst missed him, leaving a black mark upon the wall. Masterson had fallen to the floor to avoid the blast and now crouched there like a bloated white spider.

The weapon didn't have enough charge for a third burst. Still, she raised it in bluff. Masterson rolled and leapt for the window. He flung the pane upward although he barely raised a hand. He jumped, more like an ape than a man, to the sash and balanced there.

"Clever," he uttered.

"Get out!"

She again felt the stirring of desire, the heightened vulnerability and need to surrender. Ember aimed the tube. Masterson's eyes flashed and he was gone.

"He was a devil," Josephine said. The old woman made the superstitious gesture of knuckling her forehead.

Ember hurried to the window. She searched the night and caught sight of a white blur beneath the lamppost, then the road was vacant once more. The old nanny wrapped Ember in her arms, and tears flowed freely down both women's cheeks.

"I'm so sorry, Miss," Josephine cried. "I'm so sorry."

Ember hushed her, but shared the woman's shame. She looked back at the street and saw Peter Styles in the pale lantern light. Dirt from his grave soiled his shirt and trousers, and a red stain marked where the bullet had entered his heart. He looked up at her with corrupt eyes, black within black.

Her knees weakened and she cried out.

The image vanished. It hadn't been Styles, but only fear gnawing at her mind. This was the beginning of madness.

Her cry of distress had awakened the caretaker in Josephine. The old woman made a hushing noise and wrapped her in a protective embrace. "I wish your father were here," she said. "Mr. Quatermain would know what to do were he home."

"Would he?"

Ember extricated herself from Josephine and approached Harry. It alarmed her that despite the chaos, the child still slept in fever dream. Josephine stood behind her and the silence between them was unifying.

"He's so sick and so small," Ember said. She brushed the damp hair from her nephew's forehead. What would have happened if Masterson had triumphed?

Peter Styles had tried warning her.

Masterson would return, but not tonight. And fortunately, his target wasn't Harry, but herself.

Staying by her nephew's bedside wouldn't keep the child safe. None of them would be safe until she dealt with the threat that had turned Masterson into one of those things encountered in the Underground.

"Go call Ogre up here," she said.

"A fine idea, love. Nothing warns of danger like a dog."

As Josephine left to fetch the beast, Ember checked her weapon. Without the engine, it was spent after two bursts and would require several hours to recharge. With the engine, it could fire continually, or at least as long as the engine ran. She set it aside, confident they wouldn't need any weapon the rest of this night.

Ember leaned over Harry and pulled a cover up to his chin to protect him from the still cold room.

The only thing which could save them would be direct action. The creatures from the Underground had been sent back through the rift she created, which meant another of their kind was out there, one who could raise and transform the dead.

She thought of the dead men in Paddington.

Baker wouldn't be pleased, but they had to go on the offensive, and that meant flying over the channel to Switzerland. She knew who was at the heart of this evil, and to stop him they must keep him from achieving his goal, the acquisition of the Emerald Tablet.

CHAPTER XVI

Wherein Mr. Tressler continues his investigations

THEY APPEARED TO BE LABORERS, PAUSING ON THEIR WAY HOME TO SHARE A QUIET MOMENT OF CONVERSATION. Avery watched them from the safety of the hansom and felt trepidation. Maybe his lack of sleep distorted his judgment. Maybe this perceived threat was little more than the product of an overactive imagination.

"You all right there, Mr. Tressler?" the driver asked.

It was a difficult question to answer.

One of the men outside his apartment glanced up the walk. Avery followed the gaze and saw a third man secreted in the shadows.

Sometimes paranoia wasn't paranoia.

"Sir?" the driver asked.

The owner of the hansom had been well-compensated for spending his night and most of the day at Styles Manor, and in him Avery had found a pleasant companion. Jim Burke was likewise a veteran and had served on the same battlefield. Avery even knew the man's former commander, and disliked him intensely. Apparently, so did Burke. This bond strengthened their friendship immediately.

While Avery never considered himself a snob, he seldom had opportunity to share personal information with someone of Jim Burke's class. However, Burke's style of speech and manner showed him to be of different breeding than his rough exterior indicated.

"My parents once had money," Burke explained. "Before they lost everything my father arranged for me to serve in the military. He hoped I would make connections and find it a stepping stone. You see how well that worked out."

"With your background, I don't understand why you haven't risen above this station."

Burke shrugged. "I like driving. Few people talk to me, and I get to ride about most of the day or night, depending on my choosing. It's freedom I want, and it's freedom I have."

Avery had offered to help him into another position, but the driver waved him off.

"Mr. Burke?" Avery called up to the driver.

"Yes, Mr. Tressler?"

"What do you make of those gentlemen lounging outside my door?"

"They look a bit suspicious, sir. What would you like to do?"

Watching a bit longer, Avery decided they were flesh and blood. Knowing this emboldened him. He nodded to himself and tapped the roof of the hansom.

"I think they're fine," Avery said. "My nerves have me imagining things. I'm going in."

He stepped down and waved goodbye to his new friend. The man smiled and delivered a military salute. "You know where to find me the next time you're in need, Mr. Tressler."

"Indeed, Mr. Burke."

Halfway across the street Avery noted the two laborers were no longer talking to one another, but now faced him. He slowed a step, not sure what to do. They might only have glanced up to see who approached. They might be merely ruffians unconnected to Apollonius. Checking over his shoulder for an escape route, if it came to that, he saw the third man had emerged from his dark niche and now moved to block him.

Avery drew his Colt. The faces of the men before him changed, becoming outright hostile. Each took a step to the side as if to let him through.

"Here now, we don't deserve none of that," one uttered.

"You win, sir, don't shoot."

The men continued moving, separating. Avery heard a step to his rear and remembered the third one. He whirled, ready to fire. Offering a gap-toothed smile, the man raised his hands.

The other two took advantage of the distraction to edge closer.

Avery turned quickly. They were working like a pack of dogs. The presence of the revolver hadn't stopped them, perhaps because they didn't believe he would pull the trigger.

His stomach tightened as he accepted the necessity for violence. He aimed the weapon at the closest thug and would have pulled the trigger had an arm not curled around his neck and pulled him off balance. He surprised his assailant by throwing himself backward. While the grip slackened slightly, the man didn't release him.

The sound of rushing feet drew his attention back to the other two. Avery again tried aiming. He fired the Colt and one man fell to his knees with a bullet in his chest. Avery fired two more shots, but missed both times

"Get the gun," someone said.

Hands worked to pry the weapon from him. Avery tried twisting away from his attackers but the man choking him tightened his grip. Spots swam before his eyes and the Colt tumbled from his fingers.

The man suddenly released him and Avery stumbled forward.

He heard scuffling behind him and turned as Jim Burke blocked a punch and countered with his own.

Avery lunged to retrieve the Colt, but the man who had been trying to rip it from him was already there. They collided and rolled over the cobblestones. Although the other man was younger and stronger, Avery was a trained fighter. He used his arm to block the fellow and elbowed him in the face. The blow stunned the man. A second blow gave Avery the opportunity to grab the gun and roll to his feet.

"Stop and live," Avery called.

Then two villains ceased the attack. Burke released the one, shoving him contemptuously.

"Are you all right, sir?" Mr. Burke asked.

Avery gave the driver a brisk nod and glanced about. He was surprised the neighbors weren't sticking their heads out their windows to see the cause of the commotion. Given the time of day, many of them were probably at work. Still . . .

"With the gunshots, I suspect a constable will be along shortly," Avery said. The two standing criminals nervously checked the street. Seeing their response, he pressed them.

"If you wish to avoid being dragged off to jail, you'll answer my questions. Who sent you?"

The two men's faces darkened as they considered their reply.

"I shan't ask again," Avery said, putting menace in his voice.

"Maybe they're just robbers, Mr. Tressler," Burke suggested.

"If they're just robbers, then we'll wait for the police," Avery concluded. He saw the men exchange glances.

"We don't know no names, sir," one finally volunteered. "The man what hired us is tall, with thick black hair and black eyes."

"He spoke with an accent?"

"Aye, sir."

"What did he tell you to do?"

"We was to nick something you're carrying. A bit of jewelry. He couldn't describe it, so we was to empty your pockets."

"See, common cutpurses," Burke grumbled.

Avery reached in his jacket and felt about for the odd charm. He remembered the dead man blindly searching for him. Apollonius must have guessed why his puppet had been unsuccessful.

He gestured at the mortally wounded man. "Pick up your fellow and leave. I don't care what you do with him, just get him away. If I see either of you again, I shall shoot you."

Burke started a protest, but stopped himself, perhaps remembering his station. The robbers attended to their fallen companion. Each put an arm about their necks and hastened away, dragging the unconscious man between them. Watching them head down the block, he could imagine an observer easily dismissing them as a trio of drunkards sneaking home following a late afternoon revelry.

"Maybe it would have been better to wait for the police," Burke observed.

"If the police were coming, we would have heard them by now."

Avery turned and offered the man a hand. They shook. "Mr. Burke, I am in your debt."

The hansom driver flushed. "I believe you would have done the same for me, Mr. Tressler."

Avery smiled. "Nonetheless," he said, and reached into his pocket to withdraw several bank notes. He tried pressing them into Burke's palm, but the man refused.

"Don't do that," Burke said. "I don't want money for what I did. You wouldn't accept money were our roles reversed, neither."

"No," Avery agreed, feeling properly chastised. "I would not."

Burke smiled at this and delivered an endearing wink.

"I'm not sure what sort of trouble you're in, Mr. Tressler, but if you need me, you know where to find me. I best be going now, unless there's anything further at this time."

"You should get some sleep," Avery said.

The driver examined the gloomy day before straightening his worn jacket. He tugged the sleeve and without another word headed back across the street, his gait comical by the bowing of his legs.

Avery entered the building's alcove and started up the stairs to his rooms. The attack still had his heart racing and his senses were heightened. He didn't think anyone would be in his apartment as a back up to the welcome he received outside, but one never knew.

Avery stopped and listened.

His mind again mulled the puzzle of why Apollonius had stooped to hiring cutpurses. If the necromancer had his friend's corpse, why waste time hiring these lowlifes? Perhaps it was an afterthought. Perhaps the cutpurses were nothing more than an indication of how unimportant Apollonius perceived him to be.

Avery gathered nerve. He placed one hand firmly on the door knob. The other held his Colt. He turned the knob and threw the door open.

Scanning the room, he let out a cry of surprise and staggered back.

A figure sat in a chair by the cold hearth. The man's eyes were hidden by a large hat with a broad brim. He wore a black coat with a gray waistcoat beneath. Where the man's hands emerged from his coat sleeves, his skin was a sickly ashen color.

"Peter?"

The figure stood.

"Dear Lord, no," Avery moaned. He had feared this. Apollonius had taken the body and animated it. Peter didn't deserve such a fate. Avery met the corpse's gaze and found the eyes without spirit. He remembered the dagger now secreted in his boot. He had the means to free his friend, if he had the courage and resolve to do so.

"For God's sake, Avery, put aside the charm you took from Masterson. I can barely see you."

Avery didn't move.

The dead man walked to the mirror above the mantel and peered into it. He stood for a long time staring at himself.

"I suppose I've looked worse," he commented dryly.

Peter turned and again searched the room for him. Avery saw his friend roll his eyes.

"If I were restless dead, would I be addressing you so calmly?"

"I don't know."

"You do, but you're being obstinate."

"Well, if you're not restless dead, then what are you?" Avery demanded.

"I'm not sure."

"You have some memory of what happened. You didn't just materialize in my apartment," Avery demanded.

Peter let out a frustrated sigh. "Avery, I can't continue a conversation like this. Put aside the charm." He closed his eyes and massaged his temples.

Avery made a decision. He dug the charm from his pocket and tossed it onto a table. Peter's expression lightened with a broad smile.

"Much better. Come on in and shut the door."

Peter returned to the chair and put his feet on an ottoman. He leaned back, settling in comfortably and catlike. He gestured for his friend to be seated as well and watched Avery lower himself onto a divan.

"Not all dead are the *nekroanypomonos*," Peter commented.

Avery remembered the corpse in the other room and considered looking in to see if it still remained.

"What did you find when you arrived here?" Avery asked.

"You're referring to the decomposing body that was resting on your bed? You'll notice the duvet is missing. I took care of things."

Avery stared at him, still trying to decide how to handle the current situation. This thing sounded and acted like his friend, but that didn't mean it could be trusted. Peter rose again and approached the window. He put his hands behind his back and stared into the late afternoon. Avery watched him and tried to sort out his feelings. If this were Peter, it would do no good to badger him with questions; his friend would proceed at his own pace. If it wasn't Peter . . .

"And graves have yawn'd, and yielded up their dead," Peter offered.

"Julius Caesar," Avery replied.

"And quite appropriate, since the fellow we are chasing was most likely alive in the time of Caesar."

"Apollonius?"

Peter raised an eyebrow.

"He came to visit me last night," Avery explained.

"But not alone," Peter commented.

"Not alone. Had it not been for Masterson's charm, I think I would be one of the walking dead myself."

"What did Apollonius hope to gain from you?" Peter asked.

"He was looking for your corpse."

Peter grinned, one eyebrow arched mischievously. Avery knew the expression, it was Peter's gaming face. This was the mask he wore before an expensive wager, or before he embarked on something potentially dangerous. Avery felt a pang of anxiety seeing it, but Peter's contagious spirit always won him over, sometimes against his best interests.

"Well, if someone is so desperate to find me, then he should be fairly easy to locate," Peter said.

Avery recalled the man's eyes and shuddered at the memory of the power they held. With a sinking feeling, he glanced uneasily at his friend.

"If you were brought back, then what about Masterson?"

Peter frowned. He gave his head a quick shake. "I don't think there's concern. Apollonius knew him only as Virgil. The charm shielded his identity."

Avery took a breath and shook his head. "I'm afraid Apollonius does know about Masterson," Avery confessed.

"How would he?" Peter sounded mortified.

"I told him."

"What? Why?"

"He had a way about him that made silence impossible." Avery snapped.

Peter considered this and Avery waited to hear the note of blame in his voice. His fear was allayed when Peter spoke again.

"If he can, he'll revive Masterson."

"What would be the point?" Avery asked. "If he raises him, he'll be no good to Apollonius. The *nekroanypomonos* have limited use."

"Unless Apollonius chooses to raise him as something else," Peter said.

"What?"

"Those who return may take different forms," his friend responded. "I am surely evidence of that."

Peter went to the door and peeked into the hall. He threw the door open and gestured for his friend to follow. Avery hesitated and asked where they were going.

"To see Ember Quatermain."

"Do you think that wise?"

"If Apollonius is seeking Masterson, he will be interested in her as well. He obviously wasn't satisfied with whatever he took from the tunnel at Paddington. And considering Masterson's relationship with Miss Quatermain, as well as the fragment she found at the site, he may think there's more to be learned from the young lady."

Avery granted the logic of this line of thought. He again studied Peter. This was his friend; there was no evidence in Peter's words of any change in his nature. Yet his presence left too many questions.

Peter held the door wider, gesturing impatiently.

"Very well," Avery said. They proceeded down the stairs and stepped into the gloom of early evening. Peter strode forward and Avery struggled to keep pace. Here he was, a former military officer who exercised regularly, straining to keep up with a lazy, often slovenly dilettante who, to his knowledge, did little to physically improve himself.

"You're awfully spry for a dead man," he said curtly.

Peter signaled a carriage.

The two friends entered and gave the driver directions. As the carriage began to move, Avery leaned forward. He spoke with affection and concern.

"When I left the apartment last night, I headed for your father's estate. That's where your body was lying in repose. I was desperate to get there before Apollonius."

"And you found the coffin empty."

"Your father is destroyed by this."

"My father is Gibraltar."

"Nonetheless."

"I think it best if my return is known to as few people as possible. I don't think my appearance would be well-received at the club. Also, I suspect it's a temporary development, so it's best if we move with purpose."

The dismissive tone annoyed Avery. He spent a moment taking in Peter's strong chin, high forehead, and piercing eyes. Difficult, arrogant, hedonistic, impulsive, self-absorbed, and possessed of an acerbic wit, dead or alive, this was Peter Styles.

"Regardless of the circumstances, and regardless of the incarnation, I am happy to see you," Avery said.

"But of course you are," he said, placing a cold hand over Avery's.

They both settled back. Peter frowned in contemplation and Avery retreated into his own worried frame of mind.

⚷

Approaching the front door of the Quatermain residence, Avery became uneasy. Miss Quatermain would surely have heard about the duel by now and even though she had a reputation as being liberal, if not eccentric, he doubted she would calmly accept the late Mr. Styles sudden appearance on her doorstep.

"Perhaps you should stay in the carriage while I prepare her," Avery suggested.

Peter tilted his hat forward and rang the bell. The maid who answered regarded them with disapproval. "Miss Quatermain isn't receiving anyone at this time."

Avery reached into his jacket and withdrew a card. He offered it to the maid. "Please give this to your mistress and say that the gentlemen at the door are here on a most dire errand."

"Mr. Tressler?"

"You may tell your mistress it regards the matter of the dig at Paddington."

The door closed.

Avery stood back, considering what he knew of the Quatermain family. He had met the old man a few times; a queer duck, with a dismissive manner. It wasn't rudeness as much as a lack of awareness and impatience with decorum. Miss Quatermain, on the other hand, always struck him as practical and pleasant. She was bright, with an inquisitive nature. Maybe too modern for her own good, but her quirkiness was appealing.

"At least she's all right," Peter commented.

"She's a handsome woman," Avery said, more to himself.

Peter leaned against the door frame and raised an eyebrow. "She's quite remarkable."

Avery thought about the account he had heard of Peter's behavior at their last meeting, and Ember's response. A smile crept across his lips.

The maid returned. Avery noted her manner, thinking the woman seemed uneasy. The two were led down a long hallway, the walls of which were decorated with a discordant collection of art mixed in with different artifacts from the African continent.

The woman opened a door and gestured them in.

Ember Quatermain, in a practical yellow dress, turned to greet them. A thick leather strap crossed one shoulder. It was fastened to a strange pentagonal shape set atop a metallic box. A flexible tube of silvery material extended from one end. Ember held this loosely.

Peter Styles stepped into the room and spread his arms as he bowed from the waist.

"Miss Quatermain, the reports of my death have been much exaggerated," he pronounced.

The woman's eyes widened and her mouth opened slightly. Avery was afraid she would scream. He raised his hands, palms up, as if to offer comfort. Her hands, which he noted with amusement, bore evidence of chemical stains, wrapped around a small bit of jewelry.

It was a pretty bit of crystal.

She gave it a twist.

A brilliant flash blinded him. He cried in pain and surprise, stumbling back into Peter. Then it felt as if a giant hand closed over him, crackling with energy, and shaking him violently before he passed out.

CHAPTER XVII

Wherein a truce is considered

PETER STRUGGLED BACK FROM BLACKNESS, LIKE A SWIMMER KICKING TO FIND THE SURFACE WITHOUT A HINT OF LIGHT. This battle was different than the climb from death. That return was sedate by comparison.

Peter heard voices. Male and female.

"You've killed them." The man's voice sounded familiar. Kent Baker.

"No, the one is still breathing." Ember Quatermain.

"Good God. That's Avery Tressler! You killed Avery Tressler."

"He's alive," she responded evenly. Thank God for that, Peter thought.

He gave up consciousness and dreamed.

⚷

He remembered lying on a wood floor in a small room. The interior was lit by several candles around the edge of a chalk circle. The markings were unfamiliar. If this was necromancy, it wasn't anything he recognized.

Peter struggled to his knees. He tried standing, but his legs failed to cooperate. He looked down at the bloodstained shirt. The bullet hole confirmed his fears. Although it no longer bled, the area about the wound tingled unpleasantly.

Peter pressed a quick hand to his chest for a heartbeat. Unable to find one, he rested a finger against his wrist.

His mind reeled as he dealt with the horror of his current situation. Sanity became a mirror with a million cracks and he wondered it didn't shatter completely.

Peter forced himself to calm. Dead, but not *nekroanypomonos*. That was something, anyway. He drew in a deep breath and exhaled. The action made him feel better, necessary or not, and he continued to do so as he sat on the floor trying to orient himself.

Not all dead who walk are what you have termed the *nekroanypomonos*, the old woman outside his apartment had said to him. Some come back willingly.

Peter thought about that, but didn't delude himself. He might have the freedom denied the restless dead, but someone was playing him like a piece on a chessboard.

Feeling rushed back into his legs. He finally stood, swaying in place, and took a few tentative steps. He smelled perfume, and recognized the scent.

She had followed him from the beginning, staying at the fringe, but avoided taking a direct part in the series of events related to Paddington. He didn't know what role Adala wanted to play in this, but he didn't trust her.

"Mr. Styles?"

Peter followed his name back to consciousness. He opened his eyes and waited until his vision cleared.

Chief Constable Baker staggered back with a cry of horror. One arm rose as if to ward off an invisible threat. He brandished a revolver, the barrel coming to bear on Peter's face.

"Don't shoot," Peter said.

The fear on Baker's face was replaced by a stern expression. "What are you?" Baker demanded.

Ember approached, a hand extended as if she meant to poke him, but Baker interposed himself to keep her at a safe distance.

With an eye on Ember, Peter addressed Baker. "Chief Constable, I'm thinking Miss Quatermain is quite capable of protecting herself. It would seem she is capable of leveling the entire City of London should such an act catch her fancy."

Peter tried shifting but was bound by a thick rope to a wooden chair. Avery sat beside him, likewise restrained, his eyes still unfocused and his jaw slack.

Ember came closer and examined him with caution. He tried to appear as unthreatening as possible. A smile came to his lips, but he suppressed it remembering someone once describing it as feral. He felt like a curious insect under a thick magnifying lens.

Looking back at Ember, he performed his own examination. She was a beautiful woman, by any standards. Her eyes were large and so lively, and he sensed the most subtle curl of those lips could be enormously expressive. A pang of desire surprised him. With satisfaction, Peter found even in death he managed to retain his arousal by the fair sex. And why not?

She extended a hand and pressed his cheek with her palm. He shut his eyes for a moment and leaned in to her touch. She stepped back quickly, her brow furrowing and her eyes beginning to brim with tears.

"You're not like him," she said. He considered the relief in her voice. When she didn't elaborate, he reached out and picked from her mind a rush of emotion dominated by fear and concern for a small child.

"I'm not like who?" Peter asked.

"Masterson."

She bit her lower lip. When she spoke again, her words were barely audible, as if unintentional.

"He was transformed, like the things we came upon at the Paddington tunnel. How is that possible?"

Her words caused Baker to blanch. Peter sensed the police officer had been accosted by something, and the experience had left him ashamed and questioning himself. Through Baker, Peter saw the black within black eyes.

"Lamia," he uttered. He had a difficult time accepting it, but Baker's sense of violation and the surrender of control compelled him to acknowledge their presence.

When he felt the strangeness touching Apollonius through the aether, he had failed to identify it.

"It's what Masterson has become," Peter said.

"How do we know you're not a lamia?" Baker demanded.

"If I were, would I have to work so hard to impress the opposite sex? You felt those things. You know what they did to feed off you."

Ember considered his words.

"You're not a lamia, nor are you like that thing I encountered outside your apartment the other night. But you're not among the living. How can we trust you?"

Peter sought an answer, but it was Avery who spoke. "We're all in danger," he said. "We came here in good faith. If we meant harm, would we have come so openly? I've been attacked by one of Apollonius' creatures and barely survived. He's the enemy. You know that."

Peter felt Ember's mind settle. She gave a curt nod and approached Avery. "I'll untie you, and Mr. Styles."

"I'm not sure that is a wise course of action," Baker objected.

"However, the Chief Constable will keep his weapon trained on you and fire at the least provocation."

"Then I shall be entirely safe," Peter responded.

Baker watched with disapproval as she undid the knots.

"Seriously, Ember, you can't possibly trust them."

Peter rubbed his wrists to improve circulation, but stopped in the realization the action was unnecessary. With his heart no longer pumping, his blood no longer flowed.

The contradictions disturbed him.

Freed of his bonds, Avery tried to stand but staggered to a nearby settee. Ember retrieved a decanter of whisky and poured three fingers into a plain glass. Avery accepted the drink with thanks and drained it quickly.

"What did you do to us?" he asked. Avery ran fingers through his hair.

"I protected myself," she said defensively.

"Thank goodness that was merely a defensive gesture." Avery said. "I feel as if I was beaten by someone quite large. My head is especially tender. Do you have headache powder?"

Ember sent the maid for a packet while she plied him with another three fingers of whisky.

Baker still had his weapon trained on Peter.

"Chief Constable, perhaps you could put that away?" he requested. "If you do, I promise my absolute cooperation. Our interests lie in the same direction."

"Why don't we first hear what you have to say, Mr. Styles, and then we can explore whether or not we have mutual interests."

Peter gave a slight bow and considered how best to present what he had to offer. Unless exposed to the world of the occult, it was difficult to accept that their threat was from a man who had been a contemporary of Alexander the Great. Or to appreciate the existence of the Emerald Tablet of Hermes and what it represented.

Of course, his return from the dead aided his ability to persuade.

Peter cautiously disclosed what he knew of Apollonius and what the man represented, if he could still be called a man. Baker interrupted several times, usually with challenging statements of disbelief. However, Ember listened without emotion, her lovely eyes never leaving him.

When he finished, the room was quiet. Ember leaned over and whispered in Baker's ear. His brow furrowed and he whispered back.

"I have something to show you," Ember said, and left the room.

Baker glowered. The man was protective of Miss Quatermain and obviously had feelings for her which were new and uncertain. Peter frightened him. He should have used his weapon and sent the thing back to its grave.

This last thought startled Peter.

He's right, I am a thing.

Not that he felt any different. Not even wiser.

Ember returned with a long scroll of paper. She summoned them to a nearby table and unrolled it. A map? Peter examined it carefully, trying to make sense of the symbols running along unfamiliar lines.

"What do these represent?" he asked.

"Energy lines. They exist where two realities meet."

Avery joined them. "What do you mean by realities?"

"Perhaps that's not an apt term for it," Ember offered. "This map supposedly shows the location of the Emerald Tablet of Hermes."

This was the map Apollonius had been studying when Peter spied him through the aether!

"It's a very apt term," Peter commented. He nodded appreciatively. "Where realities intersect the barrier between them would be weakest; but also, the energy produced would be a wonderful place to hide something which has its own magical imprint. Finding an object here would require an amazing knowledge of thaumaturgy."

"Or science," Ember said. "I used a machine to send a burst of energy along one of the lines and received a signal showing a disruption somewhere in the pattern. It's sort of interference, like the ripples on the surface of a pond pushing against one another."

Peter digested this.

Ember tapped a spot on the map. "If I send out another signal from here, I should be able to locate the source."

"Switzerland?"

"What do you think?" Avery asked. Baker stepped closer, also intent on hearing Peter's pronouncement. Feeling the constable pressing in, Peter moved back to give himself room.

"It almost feels too easy, wouldn't you agree?"

Avery appeared grim. "The Emerald Tablet of Hermes Trismegistus. I'm not sure I accept its existence, but if it is capable of altering reality as some propose, then I shudder to think of it within Apollonius' hands."

"As some propose," Baker said with a note of skepticism.

"The Emerald Tablet would be like a God stone," Peter said.

Baker was silent for a moment, visibly trying to process Peter's words. Ember was in her own world. She stared at the map and Peter could imagine her mind turning over the facts, perhaps fitting them into a scheme he had yet to consider. Avery looked from one person to the other, a hopeful expression on his face.

"We must stop him," Peter commented as though solving a math problem.

Ember bit her lip and sized Peter up. She had watched him closely the entire time, the distrust dissipating only slightly. Now she eyed Baker, as if looking to him for guidance, as unimaginable as that might be. "We stand a better chance as a team," Peter argued.

"I was brought back here for this, as a counter for Apollonius."

"We don't know why you've come back," Baker said. "Or who had a hand in your return."

The statement troubled Peter more than he let on, but he acknowledged that truth with a sweep of his hand.

"I'm not the enemy," Peter said simply.

Baker grudgingly holstered his pistol. "I don't know what you are, Mr. Styles. However, I am not sure running off to Switzerland is the answer. If this thing has the power you suggest, then perhaps we should follow another course. We have an obligation to notify our government."

All eyes on him, Baker reddened and waved at the map. "If what you're saying is true, this affects national interests. Queen and country first."

Peter could imagine how the government would receive this tale; they'd likely put Baker on leave for mental exhaustion.

"I'm not sure," Ember said.

"There are things here that could be used against us," Baker said. "Your energy weapon, for instance. I think it only right the War Office have some knowledge of its existence. Or the Home Office."

"That's my property." Ember said and Peter was pleased by the ice in her voice. Baker raised his hands in surrender.

"Of course it is," he granted. "I was just using it as an example. Something like that weapon might be valuable to Her Majesty. It's the sort of thing that should be safeguarded for English interests. At least you know the Crown has noble intentions. Actually, a few of the things you've been working on would be better off overseen by Home Office."

Baker's ambition and dullness pleased Peter. The Chief Constable had pushed Ember Quatermain into his camp.

"I shouldn't fret," Peter joined in. "We can safely send a letter to the War Office and never worry about it getting read. Capital idea, Baker. I'll run it over to Pall Mall myself."

"When our actions affect others, we can't afford to rush off and act independently," Baker persisted. "Adults realize they are part of a society and must act for the good of that society."

"Does this pomposity come naturally to you, or is it something you've managed through diligence?"

Baker's face colored. "I can't imagine how you came to be in that duel."

"I think the issue at hand deserves our attention," Ember said. "This is not the time to consider how to involve officialdom in our current challenge. Your presence satisfies that concern, Chief Constable. What we should be discussing is the trip to Switzerland."

"I haven't been to Switzerland in years," Peter exclaimed.

"I was planning on taking the trip alone," Ember said, "but that was before Harry fell ill. I have the necessary equipment readied."

Avery stepped forward. "Well, we can cross the channel tonight and travel by train tomorrow morning."

"I can't just leave," Baker argued.

"I'm sure Avery and I can handle it," Peter said.

Ember waved her hand for attention. "I was planning on taking an airship."

Her statement turned the debate to silence.

Then, Baker cleared his throat. "This is too much."

"I've read the Germans have been working on balloon designs," Avery said.

"You're suggesting crossing the channel by balloon?" Peter asked.

"I have designed a flying machine driven by engine."

"I don't believe it," Peter scoffed.

"It's really not that complicated, Mr. Styles."

Peter almost touched her mind to check the veracity of the claim, but remembered the last time he had explored Ember's intellect. No, if anyone was capable of building a machine which flew it was this woman. He imagined a mechanical monster clawing its way through the heavens and found the concept distressing.

He saw himself stumbling from the beast and falling for an eternity, his body tumbling end over end as the wind rushed against him.

Baker cleared his throat. "Where is it?"

"At my father's country estate."

"And you've tested it?"

"My father used one of the machines to fly to Africa."

"We definitely have an obligation to contact the War Office," Baker said to himself.

Peter gestured for attention.

"Miss Quatermain, I mean no offense, but I'm not sure why we're discussing an air machine when we should be making plans to cross the channel and board a speedy train. I'm not saying your machine won't make it, but I don't think we can afford the risk when there is so much at stake."

Ember's mouth tightened. She wagged a finger at Peter. "We don't know what Masterson knows, or what Apollonius knows. They might be crossing the channel as we speak, heading for the tablet."

Peter agreed. "Which is why we should fly post haste across the channel and board a train, and when I say 'fly', I'm not using the word literally."

"Traveling to Switzerland by boat and train could take almost a week. Traveling via my airship will take less than thirteen hours."

Peter turned to the other men for support. Avery shrugged. "Less than thirteen hours?"

"It will be longer if we crash into the channel or the side of a mountain," Peter griped.

Ember shoved past him. "I'll get what I've prepared for the journey."

As the echo of her footsteps faded down the hall, Peter appealed to Baker's conservatism. "Surely a reasonable man such as yourself finds this notion preposterous?"

The Chief Constable offered little support. How could grown men seriously take to the idea of air travel?

Ember returned, pulling a large bag along the floor. Baker rushed to assist her, but she refused him and bypassed Peter to address Avery.

"These are the instructions for flying the airship," she said, and handed him a thin notebook. He opened it and peered at the neat writing with uncertainty.

"It's easy, really," she said. "You can keep it low and navigate by landmark. Before ascent, you'd best store a few extra tanks of fuel. I keep them in a shed near the platform. You'll need to keep track of that; think in terms of keeping coal supplied to a steam engine. There is a shed near the platform where you may secure extra tanks of fuel. You'll need to keep track of that. It wouldn't do to have the rotors quit several hundred feet from the ground."

"And why are you telling me this?" Avery asked cautiously.

"I can't leave Harry," she said. "You're the one who will have to take responsibility for flying the machine. Peter said you were a ship's captain at one time. Flying the airship won't be horribly different than piloting a water vessel.

Avery pushed the notebook back at her, but she crossed her arms to avoid it.

"Miss Quatermain, I respect your talents," Avery said. "I believe this airship is what you say it is. However, I am not piloting it, nor do I believe either of these men will volunteer."

Thank God. He could always rely on Avery to stand firm. Ember's cheeks blotched with color and she at last held out her hand for the notebook. One didn't need to have abilities to sense the ire behind that smooth forehead.

"We'll cross the channel immediately," Baker said. His tone was conciliatory. "I'll arrange for two men to be constantly stationed outside the house until I return."

Peter and Avery nodded assent. Her eyes remained calm, but the fury in her mind buzzed through Peter's temples. She believed they needed to act in haste and that if Apollonius wasn't already ahead of them, then he couldn't be more than a step behind. She addressed Avery once more:

"If you will give me an hour, I can prepare to go with you. I'll need to talk with Josephine, my housekeeper, and also make other arrangements."

Peter grabbed her hand, warm flesh pulsing under his cold grip. "You're an amazing woman, and no one here doubts your ability or resolve. However, you should trust us to handle this matter. Your place is here with your sick nephew."

Ember pulled her hand free. She brushed a strand of red hair from her face and studied the men crowding around her. Her gray eyes darkened at his words, but she spoke with an even tone.

"I love my nephew, Mr. Tressler. It hurts to think of leaving him before he is well, but he has shown some sign of improvement. Also, Masterson came for me. If I am not here, he will have no reason to return. If he does return, he'll find me gone, and I do not believe he has interest in an old woman or a small child. And there will be two of Baker's men watching the house as well."

Both Peter and Baker attempted to convince her to remain, but she again ignored them and stepped closer to Avery. She put her hands over his and spoke with conviction.

"I'm not deserting my nephew," she said. "Lord knows the boy has already been cast aside by those who should protect him. However, it would be far more irresponsible to ignore the threat posed by Apollonius. You can see that, can't you, Mr. Tressler?"

"You're quite correct Miss Quatermain," he said. "You will do more to help your nephew by piloting the airship and joining our search for the tablet. I'm sure when you return, you'll find him strong and into mischief."

She thanked him and without looking Peter's way, went upstairs.

"Well done," Peter said dryly.

His friend spread his arms in surrender. "She was quite right. A remarkable woman, yes?"

Peter didn't trust himself to respond, and instead headed outside. He heard Baker behind him.

"Mr. Styles," the police officer said. "I'm not keen on this trip, but I'm less keen on you coming along for the ride. Just a warning, you watch yourself. I don't trust you."

Peter sighed. So, this was why he had been re-animated. It was punishment.

CHAPTER XVIII

Wherein our group of adventurers boards an airship to Switzerland

TWO LARGE STRUCTURES LOOMED IN THE NEW DAWN LIGHT BEHIND THE QUATERMAIN COUNTRY ESTATE. The divorced brick buildings were an austere contrast to the flowery courtyard and the white trim adorning the yellow cottage.

"It's a bit of an eyesore, isn't it?" Baker commented as the cab rolled to a stop. He sat with his hands neatly folded in his lap; his perfect posture accentuated the sharp crease in his trousers and the crispness of his collar.

"It's made to be practical, not pretty," Ember said. The structures were an odd hodgepodge of repurposed materials, red bricks, grey stones, and industrial metal.

"So this is your airfield?" Styles noted with wry amusement. He opened the cab door and hopped onto the grass. Then he extended his hand to Ember.

"What did you expect?"

He opened his mouth, a playful expression on his features, and snapped it shut, censoring himself. She ignored him and instead took Avery's hand. Mr. Tressler was a solid man, a bit old fashioned, but the sort of person who could be relied upon in a crisis.

Stepping down, Ember took a moment to inspect the field. A gentle breeze blew across the grass and strummed through the branches of several trees near the out buildings. A flock of birds took to the air, circled, and alighted once more at the fringe of a small pond. No matter how well designed an airship, it would never possess their grace and dignity.

"So, where is this remarkable machine of yours?" Styles asked. There was tension in his voice. He didn't seem able to stand still.

James carefully unloaded the engine and its cart, as well as a bag of equipment. He wiped his face with a handkerchief and looked about his surroundings with bemusement.

"That'll be all, James," she said to the driver. "Go on home."

He tipped his cap and jumped back up into the sprung seat. With a last wave, he took up the reins and began winding his way back down the dust roads.

"What is that?" Avery asked, gesturing to the cart.

"It's the engine I used to send a burst through the line in Paddington. I'm going to do the same when we get to Switzerland."

"Hopefully not with the same results," Baker grumbled.

Ember looked at the constable askance. "I've taken meticulous care to ensure my equipment is perfectly safe. Follow me, gentlemen."

She turned and started up the dusty path, leaving Baker and Styles to lug the equipment bag and awkwardly weighted cart.

The inside of the building was cold, the air fog-damp. Ember pulled on the fur-lined leather jacket she'd left hanging on a wall hook the last time she'd piloted her airship. Despite the total enclosure of the gondola, it would only get colder when their elevation increased.

As Baker and Styles came huffing through the wide door, Ember directed them to place her equipment inside the airship. Both Baker and Styles paused as they came through the wide door together. She watched them take in the sight of the ship as it sat square in the middle of the wooden floor. The side of her mouth curled with satisfaction at their apparent awe.

She turned her own gaze on the vessel, taking pride in the sleek oaken frame and the four enormous rotors set atop the gondola in two vertical stacks. Across the polished hull she had painted the name *Stella,* after her mother. It felt right, and when naming it, she thought her father would give a nod of approval. He hadn't.

"Did you build it yourself?" Baker's voice echoed. "It looks like a water-running vessel."

Avery smiled at that description. "Yes, I can picture that. What a beauty, she is. You're a remarkable young woman, Miss Quatermain."

He approached the gondola and slapped its side with approval. Her cheeks warmed and she shrugged off his praise.

"My father hired some men from the Underground to help me with the heavier construction. They were happy to have the overtime."

"You're fortunate they didn't steal your plans and sell them for tuppence," Baker replied.

She thought about his earlier comments and bit her tongue. If it were up to Baker, he'd have her hand over her designs to the Queen, free of charge.

Peter approached, his eyes wide, and when he spoke, it was in a hushed tone: "When you said 'airship', I envisioned something lighter, something birdlike."

The dread in his voice was unmistakable.

"Are you all right?" Avery inquired.

"Well, it's a bit large, don't you think? It can't possibly fly."

There was no trace of the famous Styles' swagger. She put a reassuring hand on his shoulder and urged him closer to the gondola.

"It will fly. It's been tested."

"Avery?" Styles appealed to his friend.

"The rotors displace air," Avery commented. They rotate so quickly that they push the air back, lifting the vessel up."

"I have smaller rotors on the aft and stern for steering the vessel."

Avery laughed like a child and clapped his hands. He dashed to one end of the ship and expressed more utterances of approval. The other two men watched in stony silence.

"What type of metal are these rotors made of?" Avery called out.

"A new one. It's called aluminum. It's amazingly light and durable."

"I think we're making an error not taking a more conventional route," Baker said.

"I agree with the constable," Peter spoke up. "I'm not keen on the idea of flying."

Ember played deaf to their protests and escorted Avery into the vessel. Behind her she heard Styles and Baker grumbling to one another, but coming forward and dragging the cart with them. They secured it inside a cargo net and went to fetch the rest of their belongings.

Ember shoveled a small amount of coal into a stove, and spent several minutes lighting the fire. Avery watched with interest.

"That's not much coal," he observed.

"We'll only need to stoke it a few times during the voyage," she said. "The ship is quite efficient."

She turned to face the other two men, who were struggling with the mechanism to lock the gondola's door.

"As soon as you gentlemen are seated, we can engage the rotors."

Peter nodded soberly and left Baker alone. He sat down and wrapped a hand around a brass anchor sticking from the wall. Freed to figure it out on his own, Baker slid the lever down and settled in across from Peter.

"Then we're off," Ember announced and slipped into a seat before a polished wooden dashboard. Gauges showed altitude, speed, and engine pressure. A large panoramic window stretched out in front of her. She pulled a lever to disengage the docking clamp and started the rotors. The airship began rolling down the gently sloped floor and through the large open doors to the field beyond.

Her hands danced over the assortment of levers, buttons, and cranks. She increased rotor speed and there was a sharp sense of rising. The ground dropped away and soon they were over the treetops and floating into open sky.

Avery watched their progress with a child's enthusiasm. He leaned against the glass and laughed with childish excitement.

"Very good," he called out. "Oh, very good!"

Peter stumbled from his seat and leaned into the small pilot house. His eyes widened at the view. He shook his head and in a small voice said, "Turn it around."

She almost felt sorry for him.

"Turn it around," he rasped. "I don't like it. We're going to crash."

She gave him a scolding look. "We're not going to crash," she countered. "Look, we're doing fine."

"I don't like it," Peter insisted, his voice rising in volume. Avery and Baker exchanged glances.

Ember turned her back to Peter. He'd get used to it. If he didn't, then it would be a long trip indeed—for him. She turned back to sky and indulged in the thrilling freedom she felt behind the controls of the airship. She shrugged out of her jacket and tugged off her gloves.

"Mr. Tressler, why not help Mr. Styles into a seat in the back? The cushions are much softer there. They might better suit his constitution."

"What does she mean by that?" Peter demanded.

"Don't be difficult," Avery urged. The older man patted Ember's shoulder and then left to escort his friend to the rear of the gondola.

She heard Baker join the discussion and soon he and Peter were at it again.

8—⚊

Peter sat in the passenger chair trying to remain still, small, unnoticed. As a child he dreamed of flying, and now here he was, uneasy at best. The rapid ascent had caught him unprepared, and while he managed to control his restlessness, if he allowed himself to think too long about it, the idea of drifting through the whiteness threatened to tip him into a panic.

The craft dipped and Peter gripped the armrest. He concentrated on relaxing his muscles.

"This isn't the sort of thing you're used to?" Baker said. What a cocky smile the man had. "I mean your type isn't really used to risk taking."

Peter straightened his back and raised an eyebrow. "My type?"

"You're a man of property. When things have gone poorly for you, you've bought your way out of trouble."

"You don't know anything about me, Chief Constable."

"Ah, but I know the type."

Peter didn't have to touch the police officer's mind to experience the man's hostility, although he wasn't sure where it came from. It wasn't just that the man regarded him as a rival; this came from something else.

"I did some research on you after the last time we met," Baker said. "I also took the time to ask around about you."

"Did you? And I suppose this is where you caution that you'll be keeping a close eye on me."

"It is," Baker said. He leaned forward and started to place a hand on Peter's arm, but abruptly sat back. "Some of the things I've heard went beyond a rich boy's spoiled behavior, and you've as much admitted crossing a boundary no decent person would cross. You're a bad one, Mr. Styles. I'm not sure you're any better than this individual we're chasing after."

The venom behind Baker's words made him bristle.

"What astounds me," the Chief Constable continued, "is that people aren't able to see through you. They're dazzled by your wit and likeability."

"But you're not so gullible."

"I am not."

"And yet here we are, the two of us, collaborators. I do hope this won't inhibit your personal advancement."

Baker fell into brooding silence. He wanted to say more in the hopes of provoking a fight, but Peter sensed the man feared coming out on the short end of an argument. He might have felt bad for the man were he not such an ass. At last Baker stood and made his way to the pilot house.

The airship jostled through a rough patch and Peter groaned. Avery sank into the vacant chair next to him. His friend propped an elbow on the wooden armrest and leaned forward.

"Perhaps you and Baker should declare a truce until this is over. He's a boor, but he's a decent man."

"Is he?"

"He has good intentions."

"And good intentions will get you killed every time."

Avery laughed and conceded the point. "Perhaps you should consider Miss Quatermain, then. She needs someone to look after her, and Mr. Baker is more than willing. You can't argue his dedication."

"You underestimate, Miss Quatermain. This same woman laid the two of us out flat and managed to survive an attack by a *nekroanypomonos*. I'd say she needs no one."

"You're wrong there," he responded. "Otherwise, we wouldn't be here. She needs someone decent to stand by her, Peter. Unfortunately, I'm far too damaged to be truly decent and if I'm damaged, then you're positively broken. Not to mention dead."

"And you're saying Baker is decent?"

Avery ran a hand through his silver hair and shrugged. He settled into a contemplative pose and ignored Peter.

"We're about to cross the channel now," Ember called out.

The four of them crowded into the front of the craft and peered below at the dark water and the French countryside. Peter almost enjoyed the view.

"Thirteen hours at the most," Ember said. "We have a straight line to follow and no obstacles in the road. The wind is on our side. Probably won't take us more than eleven."

"Brilliant," Avery nodded with approval and glanced from Peter to Baker with a broad smile. "Someday all of Britain will travel by air. The average citizen will strap on his personal flying machine and be borne aloft."

Peter wasn't sure if his friend was joking, or not. The Age of the Machine was upon them, though, there was no arguing with that. He continued staring at the channel below them and at the several small crafts navigating the choppy water. The bracing smell of the sea penetrated the hinged portals at the sides of the great window. Ember bent over a desk built into one wall and tapped her finger against a map she'd pinned there.

"This is our route," she said. She traced a line from just south of Paris, cutting east across France for the Swiss border. "If Apollonius is heading for this spot, we should be able to beat him handily."

"Don't be so sure," Peter scorned. "Maps may be flat, but the world is not. There are other ways to travel besides the angles and lines marked out by modern geometry."

Baker rolled his eyes and said, "Mystic nonsense. If we could have traveled there through some magical path, then why didn't we?"

The airship shuddered and dropped a few feet. Peter shut his eyes, and grit his teeth. He braced his arms against the entrance to the cockpit as a series of violent shudders shook the vessel.

Ember clicked her tongue. "Turbulence is perfectly normal." Her tone conveyed annoyance. "Up here there are irregularities in wind flow."

"It feels like we're being torn apart," he said.

"Each seat has a strap attached to it. I think it best if we all settle in until this calms down. Mr. Tressler, could you help Mr. Styles?"

"You heard her, Peter. We're in the way up here." Avery offered a stabilizing arm to escort him to the rear of the gondola. Baker didn't turn around, but it was easy to imagine the smirk on his pretty face. With a sour expression, Peter accepted Avery's arm.

"If you're good, I'll tell you about my first time in Paris," Avery said. "I'll even lie to make it more entertaining."

CHAPTER XIX

Wherein our group of adventurers arrives at Reichenbach Falls

PETER ARCHED HIS BACK AGAINST THE CHAIR, BUT HIS MOVEMENT WAS HAMPERED BY A LEATHER STRAP WHICH CROSSED HIS BODY. He unhooked himself and stretched. His ears popped and he tried working his jaw to relieve the feeling that his ears were stoppered.

"Not pleasant, is it?" Baker commented. "Ember says it's perfectly normal. Something to do with the altitude."

The police officer sat beside him and leaned forward. "Mr. Styles, I want to apologize for the rough start you and I seem to have had. I'm afraid all of this has put me on my guard and I'm not behaving in my usual fashion."

"That's quite all right," Peter said.

Baker relaxed slightly, leaning back in his chair and letting his arms come to rest in his lap. Peter wondered if that youthful and angelic face made it difficult for him to advance in a field where a certain toughness was required. Did Baker overcompensate?

"Mr. Styles, may I ask you a personal question?" Baker asked. His tone suggested he struggled to pose it. Peter eyed him warily and gave a slow nod.

"What's it like?" he asked. "What's it like to die? I don't mean to be intrusive, but it's something that one wonders about."

"What's it like to die?"

The question caught Peter unaware. He noted Avery leaning forward as well and carefully considered how to best answer. He thought about the blackness and the sensation of consciousness; but how did one explain being scattered through different points in space and time while remaining whole? How could he convey that while he retained his identity, it wasn't entirely his own? How did he share the beauty, or the horror?

Peter smiled whimsically. "I'm told it's glorious," he answered.

Baker's features first expressed disbelief, then suspicion and resentment. Avery, on the other hand, brayed until his cheeks flamed and tears ran from his eyes. Peter gave Baker a gentle pat on the shoulder and rose.

"I'm sorry, Chief Constable. The truth is I don't have the answers for you. I just know I was brought back for a purpose, and when I've fulfilled that purpose, I shall once more depart."

"And it doesn't frighten you?"

Peter didn't answer.

"It seems a bit rough," Baker said. "It's not fair to give someone a taste of life, and then snatch it back again."

"If you think about it, isn't that really all we have? Just a taste?"

Peter remembered a young woman with shiny blonde hair and green eyes that widened comically when she found something amusing. Maddalene.

"Death is meant to be a mystery," Peter said. " . . . *the undiscovered country, from whose bourn no traveler returns, puzzles the will, and makes us rather bear those ills we have than fly to others we know not of.*"

Baker narrowed one eye at him. "But *you* know, Mr. Styles. You've been and traveled back."

Peter thought about that and approached the pilot house. He didn't begrudge Baker his curiosity. When the man wasn't struggling with his position as a figure of authority, he was pleasant. Although the black and white world within which Baker resided did little to prepare him for the darkness which was about to descend on him. Or maybe it better prepared him. Maybe the grays he and Avery slipped through were the more treacherous path.

Ember turned at Peter's approach and smiled generously. He returned her greeting, but his eyes held a melancholy cast. It made him seem vulnerable, and it made him more appealing.

"How are you holding up?" Ember asked.

He tumbled inelegantly into the co-pilot's chair. "I'm still trying to make sense of the fact that I'm hundreds of feet above the ground.

I don't like it."

"Perhaps it's the lack of control," she countered.

"I don't follow."

"That's the problem," she said. "In some ways, you remind me of my father, Mr. Styles."

"I hope that's a compliment."

"You're both hunters, always eager for action and always looking forward to the next challenge. The lack of control makes you feel like prey."

He tilted his gaze to look up at her with a serene countenance. Their eyes met. He was the first to turn away.

Although Peter's skin had an ashen pallor, and his lips a bluish tinge, she found him undeniably handsome. His features lacked Baker's perfection, but the distinct sweep of his nose, his high cheekbones, and slightly uneven jaw line excited the imagination with their ability to express emotion. Not that she wasn't fond of the Chief Constable, but Peter Styles struck a chord which didn't fade.

The airship shuddered and groaned. Peter made a choking sound as they dropped and braced himself against a brass rail running parallel to the bottom of the control panel. The ship leveled again.

"Why do we do that?" he asked, his voice too loud.

Ember held up her hand, making a wavy motion.

"Think of a ship in the water," she said. "There are swirls and vortexes, and waves slapping against the hull. We can get caught between currents, pushing one way, then another."

"I can swim in water," he complained.

"There's danger in the water, too."

"Pirates," he mumbled.

"Yes, I can see you as a pirate," Ember said. She laughed and he smiled as well.

"Me? A pirate? Never!"

A spark of mischief ignited action. She stood impulsively, removing both hands from the pilot wheel which controlled rudders along the vessel's rear. The ship pitched slightly and Peter gripped his own pilot wheel.

"What on earth are you doing?" he bellowed.

"Giving you control."

"I don't want control. Sit down immediately!"

She moved behind Peter, stooping slightly and offering instruction over his shoulder. "See that lever there? Grab it."

"Payback? Fine, you've achieved it. Sit down."

"The wheel controls the vessel's lateral movement, but that lever controls its altitude. If you want to go up, you need to pull it back slightly."

"I'm not doing this."

"We're descending and it needs correction. If you don't correct it, we'll keep going down, only the angle of descent will increase, as will our speed."

"We're heading into a cloud," he protested with strained panic. "I think you should take over."

Ember stepped back, hands in the air.

"You can go through, around, or maybe try dipping below. Your choice," Ember said.

Peter gripped the lever and she could see the indecision and worry on his brow. He pulled it so they leveled out and steered into the whiteness of a cloud bank. An eerie silence settled over the cabin, except for the steady whisper of wind against the hull and the steady throb of the rotors.

"It's humbling, isn't it?" he whispered.

His comment surprised and pleased her. She gave a slight nod.

They burst through the clouds into a brilliant sky. Peter's mouth fell open and delight animated his eyes. She wanted to laugh with him, pleased to share this moment as she was drawn to the innocent boyishness he displayed. He manipulated the lever as they passed over a farm, lowering the ship so its shadow chased a flock of sheep moving along a hillside. Beyond that a cluster of buildings marked a large farm. Three children, two young boys and an older girl, pointed up at them while an enormous St. Bernard jumped about with excitement.

The airship changed direction and its shadow disappeared from view.

"I'm flying," Peter proclaimed and in his voice she heard awe and accomplishment. Ember hugged herself and remembered the thrill and satisfaction the first time she had so defied gravity.

"When I was a little girl, I was shy around horses," Ember said. Peter turned to look at her, and she felt his full attention.

"They were so huge and powerful," she continued. "My father is quite the horseman, you know, and of course, it is expected any of his offspring will share that passion. One day he lifted me onto the back of a magnificent Arabian and gave me the reins. I was horrified. My father didn't say anything. He slapped the flank and the beast took off."

"You're father sounds a cruel sort."

"He can be, but in this he knew what he was about. As I gripped the reins all my anxiety fled immediately. That's what I experienced when I first took to the sky."

Peter exploded with deep laughter. "I'm still terrified," he called out. "This shouldn't be possible."

Peter frowned and grew contemplative for a moment. "What an odd statement coming from me."

"Flying makes you believe anything is possible," she said. "You could lose yourself up here, just drifting away. It's remarkable."

"You're what's remarkable, Miss Quatermain," Peter said. He moved slightly and she hoped he might be about to touch her hand; however he didn't relinquish his grip on the pilot wheel.

It was dusk when the ship entered the airspace near Mieringen. They descended slowly, the mountains rising to meet them, stretching ever higher until the peaks disappeared above vibrant clouds. The ship dipped and navigated around the mountain bases covered by a dense canopy of broadleaf trees, beeches, and silver firs.

Ember guided them toward a clearing, angling them down slowly. Fireflies burst from the foliage in a wave of blinking yellow light, reminding her of Josephine's stories about the will-o'-the-wisps and the wee folk. The last few days made the nanny's folk tales seem lest fantastic.

"Beautiful," Peter remarked.

"They're like faeries," she said.

"They're nothing like faeries," he said. "Faeries aren't as organized."

Ember poked him, but enjoyed the teasing. She studied the terrain for a secure landing site. The glass of the pilot window misted and they heard the relentless rumble of the nearby falls. It was hard to see much of the countryside; clouds hid the stars and she knew the moon was only a slender crescent. She yanked the lever, bringing all the blades of the rotor into alignment. The craft hovered. She then spun the crank that controlled the landing mechanism and they sank to the ground.

Ember sat and waited, although she wasn't sure for what. She scanned the darkness for anything out of the ordinary which would justify her building sense of peril.

As Peter and Chief Constable Baker nosily undid the safety net and extracted the engine from its restraints, Avery handed Ember her valise with an offer of encouragement. She thanked him and rose with determination.

"Here in one piece, as promised," she proclaimed. Ember slipped past Baker and approached the door to the gondola. She gave the latch a yank and let in the fresh night air. The roar of the Reichenbach Falls was a steady rumble.

"That should mask any sound we make," she said.

"Aye, and it should make it difficult for us to know if anyone else is around as well," Baker said. "We could hold off until morning or perhaps travel to Mieringen and return after breakfast."

Ember might have agreed with him had Peter not spoken up. "I think it's fortunate we arrived at this hour. We can do what we've come for and be gone before anyone's had a chance to notice."

"I think we need to hurry," Avery agreed, stepping between the two men. "Apollonius won't care if it is light or dark. He seems equally at ease in both."

Baker acknowledged the older man's wisdom and set about dragging the engine to the door, where he paused to raise an eyebrow for assistance. Peter ignored Baker's appeal and stepped into the darkness.

"Really?" Baker called after him. The Chief Constable struggled with the engine until Avery came to his aid.

"How do you tolerate him?" Baker asked.

"It's penance."

In a short time they assembled outside the airship. Ember asked Avery to hold up a sheet of copper with silver netting and connected it via a thin wire to a gauge which she carried in one hand.

"This way," she said.

With the lantern held aloft, the party crossed uneven terrain, pausing often to allow her to take measurements.

"The nexus point is close," she announced.

Ember shivered and ran splayed fingers down her forearms. The hairs on the back of her neck felt as if they were rising. She kept an eye on Peter, who lifted his head like a deer that freezes and tests the air at the hint of danger. He squatted and put his palm flat against the earth.

"I felt something by the tunnel in Paddington, but this is far more powerful," he said. "I don't like it."

"What don't you like?" Baker asked. "I can't see or hear anything."

With Avery once again holding up the copper sheet and turning about like a weathervane, Ember checked her instruments. "Stop," she called out. "I think this is it."

She lifted her face to the sky, but the clouds still hid the stars. A fine mist from the cascading series of waterfalls blew in their direction. Hopefully the moisture wouldn't affect their efforts. Thankfully none of the equipment had exposed wires. She tapped the ground with her toe to indicate where Baker should set down the engine.

Ember passed the lantern and gauge to Peter and turned her attention to attaching cables from the miniature steam engine to the modified battery she had used in the tunnel at Paddington. Avery asked questions as she worked and his responses to her explanations displayed a keen understanding of science. His tone was respectful and admiring; too bad her father never showed this level of interest in her work.

"How will you avoid creating another breach?" he asked.

"With this," Ember said. She tapped a small box installed in the center of the pentacle-shaped battery. "It will regulate the stream to minimize the chance of instability."

Baker had been standing quietly all this time, but he now raised his head and studied the surrounding area. "If this energy stream we're in is a boundary of sorts between two realities, then isn't it possible it can be disturbed by occurrences within the realities? Storms, for instance?"

"I imagine there are regular disturbances," Peter observed.

"I suppose a thunderstorm might affect it," Ember conceded.

"Then why don't we see evidence of such rifts?" Baker challenged.

"There may be more than we're willing to admit to," Ember said. "Think of all the times we hear about things which go 'bump-in-the-night.' I imagine some things we consider the stuff of fairytales are the result of a tear in the wall."

"Unicorns and griffins," Avery suggested.

"Mermaids?" Peter offered.

"You laugh, but I've seen mermaids," Avery countered. "And more besides."

Ember bent back to her work. In a few minutes she announced they were ready to begin.

"The sooner the better," Baker said. "I don't like this place one bit."

Ember heard the anxiousness in his voice. Perhaps the energies were having an adverse effect. She thought it best to hurry. She opened the small door which housed the treated coal powder used for fuel and allowed a handful to slide into a waiting bin for ignition. She touched a match to it and watched the little needle which kept track of the pressure within the water tank. It didn't take long for it to climb to the proper level. She threw the switch for the steam and listened to the engine respond.

"Get ready," Ember called.

She lifted the battery and slipped its strap over one shoulder, and then reached for the grip on the tapered tubing. She braced herself and flipped the switch. A stream of energy sliced through the night with an angry buzz.

"A reading Mr. Tressler," she called.

Avery raised the copper sheeting and called out the energy levels. Ember jotted down figures in a small notebook.

"What's happening now?" Baker demanded.

"I just need to plot the energy flow and look for variations in spatial relationships."

"Oh well, then," Baker said, "I understand. Makes perfect sense to me."

Another burst sliced the air and a loud popping followed. Ember's ears felt blocked, then the sensation passed and her hearing became suddenly acute. The popping reached an almost deafening crescendo. Green light bathed them for a moment and it looked as though some sort of dust swirled around their legs.

"What was that?" Baker shouted.

"Faeries?" Peter asked.

The smell of burning rubber told her something on the engine had blown. Sure enough she could make out charring around one of the machine's seams.

"I think one of the internal connections might have given way."

"That noise didn't come from the machine," Baker insisted.

"Can you fix it?" Avery asked.

"Yes, but it's going to take some time."

"Did you get the information you needed?"

"I'm not sure. I wanted to send out signals from a couple of other locations. Maybe it will be enough, but I don't know."

"You can repair it on the way home," Baker said.

Peter held his arm up for attention and the anxious expression on his face made Ember's stomach jump. In the lantern light his features appeared demonic.

"Do you hear that?" he asked.

Everyone stopped and listened, but it was Baker who answered. "I don't hear the falls."

"Could we have crossed over?" Peter asked.

Baker made a strangled sound and whirled to face Ember. She rubbed her temples to calm a sudden headache. "I didn't use enough energy to open a breach," she objected.

The air crackled. She spied a blue white sphere forming across the field. It moved in their direction, picking up speed and expanding as streaks of light formed about its edges.

"Get down," Avery barked. "On the ground. Find cover."

"Empty your pockets," Ember urged. "Rid yourself of any metal. Cast your weapons aside."

Baker's gun spun away from him in the slick grass. Pockets emptied and shining flotsam fell from their persons.

"My watch," Avery cried, slapping his chest. He stumbled to free himself of the watch and chain. The timepiece fell from his fingers as a green glow surrounded the party.

What began as an unpleasant tingling on her body soon escalated to a painful stinging which had her writhing on the ground. She clawed the damp turf and clenched her teeth. The corset hooks warmed under her clothing and the brass buttons burned her leather boots.

She screamed and her voice sounded far off. The world was slipping away, retreating as colors faded into gray, threatening to tumble into blackness.

The chaos slowed and the pain receded.

Ember rolled onto her back and stared up at the low hanging clouds.

The corpse at Paddington had burned inside out, the coins in its pockets fused together.

The giant orb continued burning a path along the ground as it headed across grassland, still spreading and dissipating as it moved.

Ember stood with shaky knees and brushed the dirt from her hair and clothing. The air was thick with ozone and her mouth was dry. Baker helped Avery to his feet, straightening the older man's jacket and smoothing his collar. A nasty abrasion ran along Avery's cheek. Ember winced at it, but Avery didn't acknowledge its presence.

"I can't say I enjoyed that," Peter announced. He checked Avery, but his friend waved him away.

"We were lucky," Ember said. She took a breath and pointed to the edge of the meadow where the earthly comet had formed. "If we had been closer to the point of origin, it would have charred us."

"Like the two men in Paddington," Baker said.

Ember nodded agreement. What had caused the energy ball? They hadn't opened a breach. Or perhaps the boundary here was so fragile that even the small blast she introduced had caused a minor rift? What other atmospheric disturbances might result from tears in reality?

The darkness kept her from seeing distant terrain, but her hearing reinforced her building fear. The rumble of the Riechenbach Falls was indeed gone.

"Maybe the barrier here was unstable to begin with," Ember mumbled. Her voice was edged with fear.

Peter offered. "Or maybe it just moved and we ended up on the wrong side."

"You said you didn't use enough energy to create a breach," Baker said. He stepped close and she could see the panic in his face by the lantern light. He looked ready to explode.

"I didn't, but something's happened."

"If we crossed over, we need to get back," Avery said. He put a hand on Baker's shoulder and his presence seemed to calm the Chief Constable.

Baker's brow creased and he slapped a hand into his palm as he spoke. "We need to get the machine working, then. Yes?"

Ember didn't say anything; it was better to remain quiet than to speak and let them hear the rising anxiety in her voice. If they had stepped into another reality, then merely firing another burst of energy might not necessarily open a breach allowing them to return from where they started. It might instead send them into yet another reality.

"What do you think?" Peter asked. "Can you repair it?"

She answered by using a finger to probe a burned strip of copper.

"I'll need a hairpin," she said. "I pulled one from my hair before the energy ball hit. It's in the grass hereabouts."

Avery groaned but bent a knee and patted the ground. He was joined by Peter and Baker. While they set about this impossible task, Ember shifted for modesty and ran a hand along the base of her corset. She yanked out a wire hook, but found it unsatisfactory for what she had in mind.

"Ah ha!" Avery held up one of his fallen possessions, a watch. He shook the timepiece, put it to his ear, and gave a look of satisfaction.

Ember pointed.

"Do you have any emotional attachment to that?" she asked.

"It's a nice watch," he replied a bit coolly.

"I could use it to help repair the machine."

"I should think Peter has one you could use. Isn't that right, Peter?"

"Actually no," Peter said.

With an expression bordering on petulance, he handed over the timepiece, and turned away as she attacked it. Ember pried off the back using the stiff wire from her corset and extracted a few thin pieces of copper.

"Ideally, I would melt this down into the correct shape, but we're going to have to content ourselves with mashing it into place."

"But it will work, correctly?" Peter inquired.

Ember scraped at the burnt metal within the engine and measured the copper strips against the contact points. They wouldn't be long enough. She remembered dropping her purse to the ground as the energy ball hit and now stooped for it. How could she have forgotten?

Masterson's gift would provide the rest of the needed material. She withdrew the gold watch and set about accessing its mechanism.

"A bit more light, please?" she requested.

When no one responded, she raised her head. The men stood stiffly, their attention focused on something in the gloom. The cloud cover had shifted and some stars were visible, and thankfully familiar. Unobscured, the sliver of moon provided a bit of light. However, peering across the ground, she saw nothing but shadows, and would have turned away had the shadows not moved. They were like great cats tensing before a strike, and she had to stop herself to keep from crying out.

Peter spoke in a soft voice, as if afraid of being overheard: "If we're in a breach, do you think it might be localized? Would it be possible to just walk out of it?"

"I don't know."

"If it's still open for us, we might just head back in the direction of the airship," Avery suggested.

"If it's still there," Baker said. "I don't see anything though."

"We won't know unless we head back a ways."

The men barely spoke above a whisper and she heard the thick tension in their voices.

"I don't think we'll have time," Avery said. "Whatever it is out there is coming."

He reached into a pocket and extracted a revolver. Baker followed suit. Peter casually dragged his heel in a straight line, digging a furrow through the soil.

He raised an eyebrow at Ember.

"Miss Quatermain, how goes those repairs?"

Ember bent back to the engine and forced the metallic strip between the two contact points. It popped out twice, but using the corset wire, she was able to keep it wedged in place.

Peter continued dragging his heel over the ground until he had created a circle around them.

"I still don't see anything," Baker complained. "Maybe it was our imaginations."

"I've been told that reality is subjective," Avery said.

Baker made a dismissive sound.

"Avery, might I borrow that dagger I gave you?" Peter asked.

He took the blade from his friend and sank its point into the circle. He shut his eyes for a moment and uttered a few words which almost sounded like prayer. Ember imagined a slight glow from the spot where the blade penetrated.

She was amazed and delighted by this. He was manipulating power! Her machine collected energy and directed it through copper wires into a battery. Why shouldn't someone be able to handle it without the aid of machine? The blade channeled the energy, but obviously it was Peter who drew the power from the aether.

"What are you doing?" Baker demanded.

"Proclaiming a territory. Using the energy around us to stake ownership."

"You're working magic," Baker said with disapproval.

"You are free to try prayer."

The darkness rushed at them.

Avery fired a shot and the world responded with absolute silence. Whatever was out there was toying with them, or maybe it was taking measure of Peter's defenses.

Ember's heart pounded but she bent back to finish her repairs. One of the pieces of metal snapped free and slashed the pad of her thumb. She ignored the pain and used the other hand to force it back. Clumsy.

Baker cried in alarm and fired several shots.

She couldn't help herself from turning to witness what was happening behind her. Something dark smashed against an invisible barrier. The darkness resolved into a woman's form, crouching low with her fingertips grazing the ground. Her eyes were hate filled.

CHAPTER XX

Wherein our adventurers fend off an attack

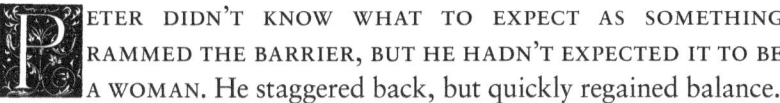ETER DIDN'T KNOW WHAT TO EXPECT AS SOMETHING RAMMED THE BARRIER, BUT HE HADN'T EXPECTED IT TO BE A WOMAN. He staggered back, but quickly regained balance.

A second and third shape darted forward, a smear against the darkness. They rippled and solidified into two male figures; one well-muscled and pale, the other boyish, but with terrifying eyes.

"Lord, no," Baker gasped. The horror in the man's voice made Peter turn. He had mixed feelings toward the Chief Constable, but the man's misery touched him.

"The things from the tunnel," Baker uttered.

Avery gave the man's shoulder a squeeze and locked eyes with Peter to show his concern for the police officer's failing nerves.

Peter returned to the immediate threat. The female singled him out with her gaze and her brow furrowed in concentration. He blocked her and instead directed his energy on keeping the barrier charged and secure. She still worked to penetrate his defenses and he could sense her moving at the borders of his consciousness, testing for a weakness.

"She's the most astonishing thing I've ever seen," Avery whispered. He sounded overcome with emotion.

"Don't look," Baker urged. The man stepped in front of Avery, blocking his vision of the two forms. "They're demons. Succubae."

"They're lamia," Peter said.

Having named them, he now ran through the legends and lore, trying to remember their weaknesses. Creatures of darkness, they hated light. And judging from their inability to cross the barrier he laid down, they were subject to the manipulation of magical energies.

"Avery, how are we doing?" he asked.

His friend's mouth was a tight line and Peter could see the worry in his eyes. After all the man had experienced, the old sailor's resolve was strong. However, he could sense the lamia prying into Avery's mind.

"Ember, how much longer?" Peter asked, trying to keep the tension from his voice.

"I'm almost there."

Another figure came from the shadow, moving with easy, catlike strides. The others showed immediate deference, parting for her.

The woman's presence was palpable. Waves of dark hair rode over bare shoulders and her almond-shaped eyes possessed intimidating wisdom. Her mouth parted slightly and Peter could imagine pressing his lips against her. He wanted to taste her.

She stopped at the barrier and raised an eyebrow.

"This is your work," she said. The voice was deep and musical. He thought of Ulysses tying himself to a mast so he could hear the seductive voices of the sirens.

"The resurrected have limits," she said. "Your talents quite exceed them. Your Maker must have been quite experienced."

Peter didn't trust himself to answer. He knew better than to engage in discussion with a demon, and that's what she was.

"The resurrected?" Avery asked Peter.

She turned her gaze on his friend.

"It's the difference between light and darkness," she said. "Necromancy is unnatural, but not resurrection. It reanimates only temporarily, without stopping the dissipation of the life force. You didn't tell them?"

Peter replied, "They know I died."

"She said 'temporary'," Avery said. "How temporary?"

"The restless dead are kept in their rotting corpse as long as the necromancer wills it. The resurrected tend to be here for a purpose, and once that purpose has been achieved, they are gone again."

"You should have told us," Avery said.

The woman raised her arm and pressed against the invisible barrier. Her distraction had weakened it. The barrier wavered and Peter hurriedly focused more energy to shore up the psychic wall.

"When I first felt you through the aether, I thought you were someone else," she said.

She was trying to distract him while she penetrated his protections. He decided to return the favor. "Apollonius?" he offered.

Her reaction showed his guess correct. She stepped closer and directed her will at Peter. He feared a psychic attack, but she shook her head as if making a decision.

"Apollonius might raise one of the *nekroanypomonos*," she said, "but never one of the resurrected. To do that, he would have to trust you, and Apollonius trusts no one."

The barrier fluctuated again. She had been playing with them, testing her adversaries, but now the woman focused on him and he could feel her warmth spread through his body. He resisted and at the same time tried maintaining the barrier. Failure was too ghastly to bear.

"Come to me," she urged. Her arms stretched to enfold him and her voiced offered irresistible invitation. "Help me instead of Apollonius and I'll use the tablet to bring you back."

The barrier slipped. He struggled to fetch it back, but the continued effort to maintain it had exhausted him.

A triumphant gleam appeared in the woman's eyes. Peter coiled his muscles, ready to spring.

Her eyes flashed and the pack closed in.

Baker uttered a desperate cry. The Chief Constable quickly raised a forearm to fend off one of the males, but was driven to the ground. The thing atop chattered like a hyena.

Avery stepped to intercede, but then stood his ground instead to protect Ember. He retrieved the dagger from the ground as the slender male glided in, and slashed a bloodless tear in the thing's bicep.

Ember stood. She slammed shut the access panel and raised the tube to one shoulder. The machine made a slight chugging sound and tendrils of steam escaped from the exhaust vents.

"Avert your eyes!" she cried.

Peter responded too late and was blinded by harsh light. The air around them reeked of ozone and he again heard a rapid popping and staggered back as a bolt of pain sliced through his forehead.

Unsure if his attackers were likewise disabled, he swung wildly in self-defense. His fist connected with someone and he heard Baker grunt.

"Help him," Avery cried.

"I'm here," Ember called. A gentle grip on his wrist gave him a flicker of hope. Her presence washed over him.

"Stupid of me," he mumbled.

"We have a chance. Come on."

His stomach churned at his vulnerability and more at needing to rely on someone's aid, especially Ember's—though he couldn't say why that made a difference.

He let her lead him swiftly across uneven ground. The back of his neck itched at the thought of someone striking through the blackness. A gunshot made him flinch and he yanked free of Ember, but was quickly grabbed again. "Trust me," she urged.

"That one's down. You've killed him, Baker!" Avery shouted with triumph.

Peter didn't think so; no lead bullet would do the job. Maybe silver? He kept opening and closing his eyes as his vision began returning.

An arm hooked around his neck, pulling him backward and yanking him from Ember's grip. He struggled to free himself as his assailant drained him of energy. The cord between life and death frayed. His consciousness scattered, dispersing into the universe.

When he sank into blackness on the field of honor, the bullet from Glaston's dueling pistol having laid him down, he went willingly into the depths.

This time he fought death's call.

Anger churned and fuelled resolution.

Peter fought his way back from swirling blackness, burning his will into the attacker, burrowing into the woman gripping him about the neck, trying to destroy him.

She didn't think defensively. She relied on her predatory nature, and that was her weakness.

As Peter flanked her, ripping through her consciousness, he heard her name. Liala. Whore to her own father. Eater of children. Eater of souls. Lamia. The invasion of her psyche intoxicated him.

Liala fought without restraint and without cunning. She was a trapped animal. She lashed out in horror and fury, but Peter held on tenaciously until the only way she might save herself was by breaking contact.

Her arm slipped from around his neck and she dropped to all fours.

Peter snapped into the present; his head clear and once again in control of his body. His vision had returned and he noted with satisfaction two attackers sprawled across the ground.

He glanced about and was pleased to see the airship now across the field once more. After the darkness of the breach, the landscape appeared more defined, or perhaps it was his own heightened senses.

Baker had Ember by the arm and was tugging her in the direction of the airship. They were arguing; Baker urging her to seek safety. Avery stood close by, still brandishing the dagger and trying to keep the remaining threat at bay.

Peter moved behind his friend, hoping to thwart any assault to Avery's rear.

"I suggest retreat," Peter urged. Avery nodded assent. Maintaining their defensive position, the two friends began moving toward safety.

The remaining women stayed out of range of Avery's blade, but matched them step for step. Liala watched Peter with smoldering resentment. He had touched her at a personal level. He had seen a piece of who she was, uninvited, and spied something no one had seen for centuries. The sense of violation was unbearable.

"Mr. Styles, once you've found the tablet, what will you do with it?" she called to him. She was maneuvering, looking for an opening, first physically, then psychically.

"Do you think you'll be able to keep Apollonius from taking it?" she asked. "You're no threat to him; you're little more than a nuisance."

The other women had drifted off and Peter watched them with the sinking feeling that while Liala kept him engaged, her minions would head for the airship.

"Avery," he whispered. "Keep moving, no matter what."

Leaving no opportunity for argument, Peter stooped and gripped a handful of soil from the ground. Liala elevated a cautious eyebrow. She crouched, but kept her distance.

"Everything we touch becomes part of us and we become part of everything we touch," he intoned. "And I've touched you."

She took a step closer.

Peter concentrated on the clump of dirt, hoping to infuse it with his presence. Liala wouldn't understand; she manipulated energies naturally, it was part of her nature. She wasn't a thautmaturge. He prayed her ignorance would create uncertainty.

Peter threw the dirt to the ground and shouted a bit of nonsense. Liala would sense his energy spreading from the clump of dirt into the soil and think he had set up another defense. It was little more than a reckless bluff. He didn't wait to see her reaction, but instead turned and bolted for the airship.

He heard the airship rotors. Good, they were going to need a quick ascent.

Avery was almost to the hatch of the ship with the two women still trying to block his approach. He stumbled and one of them dashed in to exploit his misstep. She gripped him by the wrist twisting his arm so the knife fell harmlessly to the ground.

"Avery!"

Ember was suddenly at the hatch, a star shaped device hanging from one shoulder. A tube ran the center of the thing and tapered into a narrow tube. Her hand closed on a grip to steady the tube against one shoulder.

Peter lengthened his strides, shouting as he went, and the two women turned their faces to receive him.

A green-white brilliance shot from the tube. It blasted through the predators and sent them flying across the ground like leaves before a heavy wind. He was about to cheer when he saw the tube turning in his direction. With a derisive cry, Peter launched to one side and barely avoided the devastating energy stream.

Liala, close at his heels, wasn't as fortunate.

"Don't stand there," Avery shouted. His friend waved encouragement, not that he needed any. Peter charged the rest of the distance. Ember pulled a lever as he entered the ship and the door swung up behind him. She handed her weapon to Avery.

"Astonishing woman," he beamed.

"They're not done," she said.

"She's right," Peter added. "We've only bought ourselves a few seconds."

"We have to bump open another breach," Ember explained.

"They'll just travel through it with us," Baker complained.

"I have an idea," Ember said.

Baker held the knife Peter had given to Avery. Something black dripped from the blade and ran along the back of the Chief Constable's arm. The man looked dispirited. His eyes were glossy and his complexion was pale. Peter could hear the fear in the man's voice. His thoughts danced chaotically, streaking out in all directions.

What had Avery once said to him? "We only see a little bit of reality at one time. If we should ever get even a hint of the larger pattern, our minds wouldn't be able to handle it."

Had Baker seen too much?

Ember hastened to the wall. She ran a thin copper wire to a metallic beam which was part of the ship's superstructure. She then connected it to a lead from battery. Holding another wire out for Peter, she indicated that he should do the same on the other side of the ship.

He hesitated.

"We'll create a field within the ship, drawing the energy into the bulkhead," she explained. "The breach will form within and around the ship."

"Or it will cook us," Peter objected.

"If you form a breach within the ship, then isn't there a possibility we'll end up on one side of the breach and the outside of the ship on the other?" Avery asked.

Something rammed into the ship ending all debate. Everyone froze, then galvanized to action with a second collision.

Peter took the wire from Ember, quickly playing it out before attaching the copper strands to the exposed metal frame.

"Run the wire back into the terminal, there. Then flip the switch," she instructed with calm. "Flipping it all the way up will draw in energy quickly. When it starts clicking, push it all the way down in one motion."

"In one motion?"

"It will release the stored energy in a single burst and disrupt the boundaries."

"I've got it," Avery said. He took the wire from Peter and worked it into a terminal.

Breaking glass sounded from the pilot's cabin.

Baker's eyes widened and he whipped around to face the source of the disturbance. He took a step back and the hand holding the dagger trembled. Before Peter could give warning, a form streaked from the pilot's cabin and something drove into Baker, knocking him hard to the floor.

The dagger slid from his grasp.

Peter lunged for the weapon and managed to close his hand on the hilt before being jerked to his feet. His foe was one of the males who he had seen lying on the ground. The man's expression was feral.

Peter turned into him and jammed the blade into the dense pectoral. He concentrated his will as his anger magnified, and sent energy through the twisting blade into the wound.

The creature shrieked and drove him, as it had Baker, into the airship's metal plating. As it tried pressing its advantage by gripping his throat with massive hands, he yanked the blade free and sliced into the thing's arm.

"Get away from the plating," Ember shouted.

Peter twirled free and abruptly slid down the wall. His action surprised his opponent, giving him time to roll to one side of his attacker. He rose, with the things' massive back to him, and shoved the blade into the spine. As it writhed under the blow, he shouldered the howling creature into the plating.

"Now!" Ember called. "Now, Avery!"

Peter rammed Liala's companion again, driving its face into the bulkhead.

The air crackled through the airship. The hairs along Peter's arms and at the back of his neck rose as popping ripped from the stern of the airship and ran along the length of the vessel.

"Wait for it," Ember admonished Avery.

The air crackled and smelled of ozone. Peter gave the brute a final shove.

"Now!"

Peter squeezed his eyes shut and dropped. Screaming sounded over the buzz which filled the cabin.

Peter dragged himself to his feet and offered a hand to Ember, who rose slowly and although she remained uncomplaining, he sensed she had collected a number of bruises. She was a scrapper, obviously as tough as she was smart. And beautiful.

Avery leaned against the bulkhead, a weary expression on his pale face.

"Baker," he said with a gesture.

The Chief Constable lay on the floor of the airship, blood seeping from the back of his head. The side of his face was discolored by bruising.

Ember abandoned Peter and knelt at the wounded man's side. She took his hand and squeezed it. Avery rummaged through a leather sack and came away with a small silver flask. He undid the cap and waved it under Baker's nose before tipping some into his mouth.

"Whisky," he explained.

"How is he?" Ember asked. She directed this question at Peter. Her concern was evident, and the depth of it surprised him. Although she liked the police officer well enough, she didn't have deep affection for him. Yet, he could see her worry plainly.

Peter reached out with invisible hands and picked his way through Baker's consciousness. The man was well enough, and responding warmly to Ember's ministrations. Baker savored her touch in a manner which made Peter resentful for the jealous pang it elicited in himself.

Another presence asserted itself.

Peter shifted and saw Liala's companion stirring. The thing fought through its pain and gathered strength for a renewed attack.

"Avery, open the hatch," Peter said with a note of urgency.

Avery stared as if he hadn't understood the instruction, but following Peter's gaze to where the lamia lay on its side, he rallied and scrambled for the crank. Peter gripped the thing's wrist as cool air rushed into the ship. He dragged it across the floor as it twisted and tried to find something to grip to break their progress.

The creature yanked its arm free. With a shout of alarm, Peter kicked at it, shoving the lamia toward the hatch. He gave a final push and sent the thing tumbling into space.

"Will the fall kill it?" Avery asked.

Peter didn't answer, but noticed they were still rising at a slight angle. He turned and approached Ember, who he noted with annoyance, still attended to Baker.

"The controls?" he asked.

"When we reach eight thousand feet, a mechanism will stop our ascent," she answered. Ember stroked the side of Baker's face.

"How is he?" Peter asked.

"I don't know."

She slipped off her jacket and rolled it up to pillow the wounded man's head.

"I didn't think it hit him that hard," Peter commented. She shot him a vicious glance and retrieved her valise, from which she pulled out a medicine bottle. She shook it once and pulled the cork to wave it under the Chief Constable's nose.

"You're safe," she said soothingly.

He opened his eyes with a cough. The man's face was tremendously swollen; it wouldn't surprise him if Baker had a broken jaw. Peter hated admitting it, but the police officer had stood his ground when things got rough.

Avery approached and threw an arm around Peter, pulling him close and giving him a playful punch. The man looked like a Bedlamite, with his hair made wild by the wind that had blown through the open hatch, and his disheveled state of attire. His jacket hung off one shoulder, and the sleeve of one arm was blackened.

Peter leaned close to his friend and spoke in a soft tone. "The presence of the lamia was no accident," he said. "They are hunting, just as we are, as is Apollonius."

"They are sensitive to the energy streams," Avery observed.

He nodded. "If it was just a matter of being sensitive, Apollonius and his kind would have discovered the tablet some time ago."

Peter thought about that, and about the Liala's offer to restore him. Why would he need her though if he had the tablet?

"You know what you realized at the moment of death?" Adala had whispered to him. He recalled her perfume and her soothing touch upon his brow. "You realized exactly how much you wanted to live. And isn't it a shame no one will appreciate what you sacrificed."

What about Lysimachus? He was the one who had hidden the tablet; surely he had the ability to find it without enlisting Ember's aid. What was his game here? Perhaps his motives were as pure as he represented them to her. Did he realize Adala was making her own power play? And why should Adala trust Peter to find the prize?

Peter straightened. He smoothed back his hair and took a moment to adjust the collar of his jacket and tug at the sleeves. He spotted Avery's dagger on the floor and retrieved it. He offered it, hilt first, to his friend.

"Don't lose this," he said. "I suspect you'll need it again before this is over."

Avery peered up at him and wrapped his hand around the weapon. Peter knew an interrogation was forthcoming, and steeled himself. However a moan from Baker distracted Avery. His friend bent to care for the constable and Peter took advantage of the moment to escape scrutiny by slipping into the control room. He wanted to think over his options and the consequences which may lay before them.

CHAPTER XXI

Wherein Apollonius enacts a new strategy and exploits the most innocent

---

APOLLONIUS SHIFTED IN HIS HORSESHOE-CHAIR AND SULLENLY GAZED OUT THE WINDOW OF THE BORROWED MANSION. He contemplated Styles' return with mild frustration. It was too bad he hadn't the opportunity to turn him as with Masterson. He had been tempted to reach out to him through the aether, but he paused sensing Liala's presence.

Although he still felt Styles, he no longer felt Liala. Curious. He suspected the Quatermain woman's hand in that. First Masterson covertly approached her without permission, and then the irritating Styles sniffed hungrily about. He failed to see her appeal.

Thinking about feminine wiles made him smile at a memory of a former love. He saw her sitting on a marble bench, with the Mediterranean in the background, attired in a simple white tunic.

The image hurt. It rekindled the old question: *What would have happened had he not been turned?* What path would he have followed?

The tablet could give him back everything he had lost. But what if it couldn't, or worse, what if it did, and it no longer mattered?

Apollonius spied Masterson slipping into the room. The man moved cautiously, hooded eyes cast downward. He stopped and obsequiously waited to be acknowledged. Apollonius stared at the flabby skin and sloping shoulders and was again disappointed at Styles' inaccessibility.

"You should have been here some time ago," Apollonius said.

"I am sorry," Masterson replied. The man's insincerity grated. Apollonius never had the patience for gathering followers about him; he had no idea how Liala tolerated it. When Masterson's usefulness ended, so would Masterson.

"The other night you went to see Miss Quatermain," he said. Masterson's face remained a blank mask. Perhaps he should have baited him and seen if he would lie about it.

"You were there and driven out," Apollonius said.

"I was there for you, Master."

"Really?" Apollonius asked. "And why would I want you there?"

"She was at the dig site. She gave me a green fragment."

The words froze Apollonius. He stepped close to his servant and peered at the man. "When were you going to share this with me?" he asked.

"It was nothing," Masterson protested. "It was a shard of soapstone."

Apollonius remembered seeing a piece missing from the box his poppets brought him. It was nothing. Still, Masterson's reticence served as a good reminder why he shouldn't be trusted and why he would be sent back to oblivion when no longer needed.

"What else are you holding back?" Apollonius queried.

"Nothing, I swear."

Three times Miss Quatermain had fended off lamia; not an easy task. Quite remarkable. She had a gift, that one. Somehow she knew about the lines of energy and where they traveled, and somehow she knew how to pass through them from one reality to another. It was almost as if she had a map. And that was unlikely. He had the only map. Unless Lysimachus had drawn up another. Or unless Lysimachus still lived, in one form or another, and had taken her as his agent.

"Tell me about the young lady," Apollonius commanded.

Masterson bowed his head. He raised it again. There was no emotion there. "What would you like to know?"

"Tell me about her character. Tell me about her talents."

Masterson studied him as if weighing whether or not to be completely forthcoming. He began his recitation, speaking haltingly, giving first general impressions of Miss Quatermain and eventually moving into specifics about the young woman and her family.

Apollonius only half-listened to Masterson's guarded narration. He interrupted him.

"It maddens you she and Styles are becoming close, doesn't it?"

Masterson stopped speaking and searched his master's face. His gaze bordered on challenging. The newly turned lamia remembered himself and dropped his head again. His posture remained rigid.

"Ember Quatermain is a unique and useful woman," Masterson said. "I know Styles and what he is capable of. If he has joined with her, it makes things more difficult. It means their chance of finding the tablet before we do increases considerably."

"She rejected you, didn't she? It's not easy to reject one of the lamia, and yet she found you odious enough to give her strength to do so."

Apollonius toyed with proposing he and Masterson visit the Quatermain estate together. He considered the negatives of such an action; it suggested desperation. Although the thought of being able to confront Styles face-to-face was appealing.

Quite a loyal band Miss Quatermain had assembled about her.

"I wonder what Miss Quatermain's Achilles' heel might be. Perhaps she is the Achilles' heel. Or maybe, like Achilles, the heel itself is not truly the weakness."

Masterson didn't stir.

"King Agamemnon took the lovely Briseis from Achilles and bended the warrior to his will," Apollonius continued. "You said she cares deeply for her family. You also said her father was in Africa."

"Mr. Quatermain is in Africa," Masterson acknowledged. "He is a strong willed individual. Dangerous in his own right."

Apollonius waited, letting the man hold onto the illusion that his will was his own. When he spoke, his voice was soft and solicitous. "What would you suggest, Masterson? What would you do if you were in my place?"

"She has a nephew. A small child . . . "

In the great room, Ember sat in her father's chair, watching Doctor Roberts examine Baker. The constable lay stretched out on a divan, resting under the influence of a laudanum haze. Avery and Peter sat near the fireplace, Avery with fidgeting hands and Peter leaning on an armrest.

"He has a fracture of his right arm, and his ribs are cracked. He might have a slight concussion. The Chief Constable took quite a beating," Doctor Roberts commented. "At any rate, I've stopped the bleeding. You'll have to watch that cut on the back of his head. The stitches should do the job though."

The old surgeon glanced about the room as if he expected someone to respond. The silence took on an uncomfortable quality. No one had volunteered information on the circumstances surrounding the injury's infliction. Ember couldn't imagine how the physician would respond to the outrageous tale that was the truth.

The doctor grumbled to himself and finished dressing the wound. He stood and wiped his hands with a fresh towel.

"Of course, he'll need to change the gauze every few days until the wound fully heals. I'll leave this bottle of tincture here. Use it with each new dressing."

Ember nodded. "I'll make sure he follows your instructions."

"And what about you? You look exhausted, Ember. Look at your clothes. Where have you been?"

"Traveling," she said.

The doctor received this with a grunt and waited for more. When nothing was forthcoming, he snorted and gave his head a shake. "I don't know why I should have expected anything more from the daughter of Allan Quatermain. Well, I have another patient here. One who is more cooperative."

The doctor stretched his back.

"If you'll excuse me, I'll look in on Little Harry."

"I'll come with you, Doctor," Ember said.

As they started up the stairs, Roberts spoke over his shoulder. "The Chief Constable is fortunate. He could have been killed. Was it police business?"

"You'll have to ask him when he is more able to answer," she said.

"I hope you're not in trouble," he said.

They headed down the hall to the small bedroom where her nephew slept under a thick quilt. She stood over the boy, staring at him with concern. She touched his forehead. He was still feverish, although not as hot as before—perhaps the child had turned a corner and was on his way to recovery.

She was about to ask the doctor for his opinion, but the man gently moved her aside so he could attend to his patient. She softly tip-toed to a spot by Josephine, who sat at her usual perch in a low-backed chair in a corner. The woman snored gently. Ember stooped to retrieve a comforter that had slid to the floor. She placed it back over the woman's lap. The room felt cooler than it should. She'd have to make sure the fires were stoked, and maybe see to it that the bed warmers were in place.

Doctor Roberts withdrew a long wood tube from his bag and pressed it to Harry's chest. He cocked his head to listen, closing his eyes for a moment. Opening them again, he appeared encouraged.

The doctor nodded cheerfully at Ember. "This is good. Very good."

"He has a good constitution," Ember said.

The doctor grinned and nodded cheerfully. "It's that Quatermain blood. It's the only thing to explain how your father has survived this long."

"Thank you for what you've done for Harry," she said. "He means so much to me."

Doctor Roberts pulled the blanket back up to Harry's chin. He turned and gave Ember an appraising glance. "Ember, when Harry's well enough, you should bundle him up and take a long vacation. Go to the seashore. Or better yet, get away from England entirely. It would do him good, and Lord knows you need the rest. You look stretched thin."

"I'll consider it," she said.

He gave her a paternal wink. "I'll see you downstairs."

The doctor exited and Ember moved to the bedside. She bent over, intent on giving Harry a kiss on his forehead before she departed. She sat on the edge of the bed and leaned over him. Her lips pressed his forehead. She stood and faced Josephine. The nanny was awake now, watching her.

"I heard what the doctor said," Josephine spoke barely above a whisper. "He's right, too. We should all get away from here."

"Soon," Ember promised.

The room temperature was already cooler than it should have been, and now it dropped further. Josephine felt it, too. The old woman's eyes widened and she rose quickly. Ember looked to the window.

"Go downstairs and get Mr. Styles," Ember instructed. Her words were hushed.

The nanny moved swiftly.

Ember considered her weapons. She was sorry the battery was in her workroom. Her fingers closed around the crystal she wore about her neck. She had replaced the chemicals upon arriving home.

Ember took a nervous step toward the window and peered outside. Masterson's return was a very real possibility. The street below appeared as it should. She hugged herself and turned with concern to check Harry.

His breathing was different. His body was rigid and his mouth was open. His breath came in short gasps. She was struck by the fear that he might be seizing. Doctor Roberts had only just left. A servant could be sent to retrieve him.

His eyes opened.

"Harry?"

Ember hurried to the bed. She ran a hand over his warm skin, frightened to see the chilling and unfamiliar stare in her little nephew's eyes.

Harry's breathing normalized. She waited for him to say something, anything to confirm the doctor's cheerful predictions. Instead the corners of his mouth rose in an unfamiliar and corrupt smirk.

Hope fled, replaced by horror.

Ember jerked her hand away from his face.

"Don't stop," the child intoned, but the voice was not his own.

"Harry, darling?"

The boy sat up. He looked about the room and then fixed his gaze on Ember. She moaned and steadied herself against the bed post. Josephine returned, her face red from the run back up the stairs. She stopped, looking first at Ember, then at little Harry, sitting up now and studying his aunt with an icy stare.

"My babies," the old woman cried. She started for Harry, but Ember intercepted her. The woman stopped struggling at the sound of Harry's voice.

"Did you find what you were looking for in Switzerland?"

Josephine uttered the Lord's Prayer and reached out an arthritic hand to touch Harry's face. The child gripped her wrist and squeezed it so the old woman cried out in painful alarm.

"You don't have the tablet yet, do you?" the child asked, turning back to his aunt. Ember shook her head.

"I suspect you're closer to finding it than I am. You've at least had assistance from the person who secreted it in the first place. Although, I am not quite sure why he didn't just go himself, but then I've never been able to understand him. Of course, if he had gone, I'd have known, wouldn't I? Is that it?"

Hearing these words fall from her precious Harry stabbed Ember. She would have screamed had not her nephew's expression changed. He was a child once more, his eyes teary and round. He reached for her, his voice frightened.

"Auntie?" he called.

Ember rushed to enfold the child in her arms. She squeezed him. Josephine put a hand on her shoulder.

"I'm here, love," she hushed him.

Harry clutched at her and his crying subsided. She felt the change in his body before she heard his hot whisper in her ear. "How long shall I give you?"

Ember released the child, almost falling from the bed.

"Leave my nephew," she implored.

"A day? Two?"

"Leave him be!"

Harry's eyes closed and his body twisted in pain. He let out a whimper that most definitely belonged to her nephew, and not to the devil possessing him. Needing to take some kind of action, she threw herself across Harry, holding the child. His pain tortured her. He convulsed, back arching powerfully. Muscles spasming, his arm flailed, making erratic swipes at Ember.

Josephine joined her on the bed, both trying to avoid injury as they struggled to keep the child from hurting himself.

The convulsions stopped.

Harry let out a small laugh.

"Twenty four hours," he said. "I grant you it's not a long time, but I think you perform better under pressure, yes? If you fail to deliver the tablet in that time, I'll kill the boy. And perhaps that's when the fun shall really begin."

Color returned to Harry's face and his breathing evened. He relaxed, his expression morphing from foul to angelic.

"Mercy," Josephine whispered.

Ember turned, hiding the pervasive agony that creased her features.

Behind her, Avery and Peter stood at the open door.

Avery's face wrenched in a grimace of concern as he approached the bed and sank to a knee. With great tenderness he pulled the quilt to Harry's chin and brushed sweat-soaked hair from the boy's face.

Harry opened his eyes and looked about wildly, but calmed as his gaze settled on Ember. She hastened to his side and gave him soft reassurances.

"Just a bad dream, wee one," she hushed.

Still exhausted from fighting illness, and from the psychic attack which she prayed he only remembered as a nightmare, Harry relaxed against the pillow and closed his eyes.

When Harry once again slept, Ember asked how much Peter and Avery had heard.

"Enough."

"How do you fight something like that? Someone that evil?"

Peter watched Avery before answering. "No one is invulnerable," he said. Peter retrieved a handful of ash from the fireplace and marked four points on the wall above the sleeping child.

"East, West, North, South," he intoned.

"What are you doing?" Ember asked.

"Offering protection."

"More witchcraft?" Josephine challenged.

"Magic to fight magic," he said.

"I trust him, Josephine," Ember declared.

She gestured for him to continue. Peter gave the older woman an easy smile and said, "I would not do anything to put him in danger. Believe in me."

Peter then stood before the foot of the bed and closed his eyes. He slowly raised his arms and his fingers moved, as if drawing lines in the air. She remembered his ability to keep the creatures from the other world at bay, and was heartened.

When he finished and crossed his arms over his chest, the only sound in the room was the comforting rhythm of Harry's breathing. Peter dipped his hands in the wash basin on the nightstand and Josephine offered him a towel and took the bowl away.

"Now what?" Avery asked.

Peter scowled and gestured his friend toward the window. Ember followed, bristling at the idea that they might be considering excluding her, for whatever reason.

"You can't protect the child indefinitely," Avery said.

"We won't need to."

"He wants the tablet," Ember said.

"We don't have the tablet."

"Twenty-four hours is impossible," Avery said. "How can he impose such a deadline?"

Perhaps Apollonius knew something they didn't. She closed her eyes and let her mind dance over the image of Lysimachus' map. It was impossible. He couldn't expect them to find in a day what had eluded others for centuries. Or maybe Apollonius supposed they had special knowledge since they were allied with Timothy.

She must contact the old man and ask for assistance. It was very likely he would refuse assistance. He had given her the task to avoid the temptation, or so he said. Perhaps he had placed it beyond his own reach and needed her to find it. That made no sense.

"I need to retire to my work area," Ember pronounced. Her words sounded forced. "I need to study the information I've gathered."

Peter exchanged a worried glance with Avery and stepped close to her. He opened his mouth to say something, but stopped and instead drew her into an embrace.

"We'll beat him," he whispered.

All she could do was offer a quick nod of agreement.

"Trust me," he said and Ember squeezed him hard and struggled to keep from crying.

"I'm so afraid," she said.

"I'd be worried if you weren't, but right now, that's what Apollonius is counting on. Fear is one of his weapons. Go to your workshop and get us something to use against him."

His words buoyed her up. She straightened and calmly approached her nephew to kiss him before departing. Harry stirred. "Twenty four hours," she said to herself.

"Perhaps the answer is closer than we think," Avery offered. The others stared at him.

"Sometimes when we stare at a puzzle it becomes an unbreachable wall. We look away, allow ourselves a bit of diversion, and suddenly an overlooked clue is obvious."

His words struck Ember. An idea played at the fringe of her consciousness and danced away.

A clicking sound traveling across the wooden floor startled her until Ogre padded into the room. The dog froze and curled a lip at Peter. Hackles rose along the animal's neck.

"Here now, old boy," Peter said. "I can't have changed so much as that."

Hearing Peter's voice, Ogre's posture relaxed. The dog wandered over and licked his hand. Peter stooped down, massaging Ogre's back.

"There's a lesson there," Avery said.

Peter nodded and smiled at Ember. "Go on to the workshop. The sands are falling."

CHAPTER XXII

Wherein Ember puzzles out how to locate the tablet

ALONE IN HER WORKROOM, EMBER ALLOWED THE TEARS TO STREAM DOWN HER CHEEKS. Harry had been violated, because of her, and she had been powerless to do anything about it. She gripped an iron paperweight and hurled it across the room. It bounced off the wall and rolled across the length of a slate counter, knocking over glassware.

It was beyond her how anyone could have done that to a child. The image of her nephew's frail body twisting in seizure burdened her with guilt. She considered Peter Styles and his strange beliefs, grateful for his protections, but unsure how long he could keep Apollonius at bay. Poor Peter. It was difficult to see what he stood to gain from any of this when his own time was running out.

Twenty-four hours.

Time.

She lifted a receptor from the battery and, with it, the small box which had recorded fluctuations from the energy stream in Switzerland.

She opened it and stretched out a roll of paper with dots on it. The dots were created by needles discharging ink every time there was a change in stream.

Without much hope, she spread the parchment and studied the black dots. There, the first burst sent into the energy streams and the resulting disruption. Ember marked it. Here, another burst and—a predictable pattern absent of any anomaly.

She couldn't imagine where the anomaly had gone.

Ember bit a fingernail and stared at the dots until they blurred. What if the anomaly detected in the first burst sent from the tunnel had been a one-time occurring energy pocket. Maybe it was entirely natural. Maybe the equipment had just acted up.

She stared at the workbench.

Ember was still not thinking clearly. She tried letting her mind go blank. She put her head down and shut her eyes.

"Twenty four hours," she had said, and Avery had responded: "Sometimes an overlooked clue is obvious."

Those two phrases came together. Ember opened her eyes and reached for her recreation of Timothy's map. Her finger tapped the point where she fired the first burst, then the second.

She returned her attention to the roll of paper, looking at the series of dots representing the energy stream. Even after the burst dissipated, the dots changed slightly over time, almost perceptibly.

A thought tickled her—she recalled the strange globe she'd seen at Timothy's lair and saw the brass framework and copper rods soldered together at the poles.

Ember traced the design in the air and saw her fingers following the unfamiliar markings wrapped around the equatorial band.

Still looking inward, she gripped a mechanical pen and sketched the globe. She drew the symbols and numbers burned into the equatorial band.

Dot-dot-dot.

Tap-tap-tap.

The sphere rotated on its axis to the clicking of gears. Sprouting from the top of the North Pole were slender metal filaments dangling minute crystals. Stars.

Ember watched the filament shift with the rotating of the globe and scrawled the constellations.

Dot-dot-dot.

The world turned, the little diamond stars danced and bobbed at the end of their chains. Instead of imposing order on the gathering information, she let it come together naturally.

Ember's hand froze.

She opened her eyes and compared the map to her drawing of the globe. The pen fell from her fingers and rolled across the workbench.

Good Lord!

Avery had been correct. She gave a triumphant shout and charged up the stairs, taking them two at a time. She ran along the front hall and continued up another flight to Harry's room.

She found Peter and Avery sitting across from one another, their attention focused on a chessboard. Both played with distraction, their worry clearly woven into their expressions as they fidgeted within their seats. Josephine relaxed in her chair, arthritic fingers working the loose skin about Ogre's massive neck. The dog lifted its head as she entered the room.

"Is everything all right?" Peter asked.

He and Avery stood. Ember peered past them to gaze on Harry's still form and offered a quick nod, but she was certain the urgency was apparent in her face.

"We need to talk," she said. "In the hall."

Peter raised an eyebrow but followed her out of the room, with Avery quick behind him.

"I think I know how to locate the tablet," she said in a hushed tone.

Peter put an arm about her and guided Ember further from the room. She was almost afraid to verbalize her thoughts; after seeing Apollonius possess her nephew, she feared he might have the ability to peer into her mind. Thank the Lord he had limits, and thank goodness for Peter for driving him out and keeping him at bay; although she wasn't sure how successful he would be if Apollonius turned all his efforts to penetrating their defenses.

Ember leaned close to the two men and spoke in an anxious tone. "The key is the North Star," she said. "Once you use that as your anchor, you can use the information on the map."

Avery, a former first mate and then captain, showed an expression of incredulity. "You're saying we navigate by the stars?"

"No, I'm saying we navigate using one star. The hiding spot is fixed in another reality that moves relative to our location. Anyone seeking the tablet using a map alone will never find it. One has to also consider another dimension—time."

She watched the two men digest this idea.

"So how do we find it?" Peter asked.

She took the map from the crook of her arm and unfolded it with Avery's assistance.

"We start here," she pressed a fingertip to a spot on the map. "This is May, so we start from the North Star and count over here, then here. It's at the cusp now, you see, second to the right and straight on here."

"So, we use the anomaly first detected at Paddington and triangulate it using the anomaly we detected in Switzerland, and that will tell us where to go?" Avery asked.

"Forget about Switzerland," Ember said, sweeping her hand across the map. "There were no anomalies there."

"But the breach?"

"That was a result of our experiment and a general instability which had been building there for some time."

"But the lamia?"

"They can travel the streams. But forget about Switzerland. Everything has to start from Paddington. We use the original readings and the map will show us which of the stars to navigate from. We'll be able to follow them to the tablet."

"This makes no sense," Peter said, sounding unconvinced. "Apollonius has the same map, I presume. How has he not come up with the same solution after all this time?"

"Because he thinks in terms of space and not time," Ember argued. "Each of these numbers on the map need to be adjusted based on the time of year, and further calculation must be made for other factors. I'm not sure what they are, there's something missing in the calculation. I'm not an astronomer."

"You're suggesting a door will simply open at a certain time and place, and if we are fortuitous enough to be there, we can walk in and claim the tablet?" Peter asked.

"A natural breach should open, yes. It will take time to figure out where and when. And then we can retrieve the tablet."

"I don't know," Peter said. He shook his head and took a step back.

Ember's temper flared at his lack of belief. She thrust the map at him and gave it a shake. "Do you have a better idea?"

"I might," he said defensively. He didn't elaborate and she knew they were empty words.

"Where will this pocket open?" Avery asked. "When?"

Ember started rolling the map. "I don't know. I have to work that out."

"How long will that take?" Peter asked.

"I need a couple of hours to figure it out. But I'm not suggesting we sit around and wait for a door to open, it may be one isn't scheduled close to us any time soon. We don't have time on our side."

Peter chewed his lip and glanced warily at Avery. He crossed the hall and came back again, raising a suspicious eyebrow.

"What are you up to then?" Peter asked her.

"Instead of waiting for a breach to form, we form one of our own. We head into the dark reality where the tablet is hidden."

Avery stared appreciatively. "Miss Quatermain, if only I had met you when I was a younger man. You're a remarkable lass."

Peter, on the other hand, looked with trepidation toward the room where Harry rested.

"We got lucky in Switzerland," he said. "I've glimpsed things through the aether which would drive a man to madness. I am not keen on traveling into another reality."

"We don't have a choice," Ember countered.

Peter's expression softened and he was once again by her side. "Of course we don't."

Avery clapped his friend's shoulder and recited something familiar: "Once more unto the breach, dear friends, once more; or close the wall up with our English dead."

"Let's hope we don't end up on the wrong side of that wall," Peter responded.

Avery nodded and finished the quote: " . . . but when the blast of war blows in our ears, then we must imitate the action of the tiger."

"*Henry V?*" Ember asked.

"Erudite and beautiful, Miss Quatermain."

She blushed and turned to meet the sound of footsteps on the stairs. Chief Constable Baker leaned against the banister, his pale face a patchwork of bandages. His uniform, wrinkled with sleep and torn at the shoulder, smelled of dried sweat.

Ember rushed forward and assisted the police officer into a chair. He protested faintly but accepted her attentions.

"Can I get you water?" Ember asked.

Baker pressed chapped lips into a tight line. He shook his head, the movement bringing a dazed look to bloodshot eyes. He checked their faces and his eyes narrowed. "You all look like you're hiding something," he proclaimed.

Ember kneaded her palms. She couldn't resist reaching out and removing a stray lock of hair from Baker's eyes, and then instantly regretted having done so. His brows rose and his expression softened. She stood back and tried to reclaim her dignity.

"I'm grateful to see you about, Mr. Baker. I feared for your well-being," she said.

The police officer colored slightly and a broad smile came to his face. Their eyes met.

"Thank you, Miss Quatermain."

Peter turned his gaze on her and for some reason she experienced another spark of irritation.

Ember tucked the map back in the crook of her arm and put emotions from her mind. There was too much at stake to waste precious time with stupid distractions.

"Mr. Styles and Mr. Tressler will be able to bring you up to date," she said. Her words came out more brusque than intended.

"Of course," Avery proclaimed. He stepped forward and offered his arm to the police officer. "Come on, Mr. Baker, let's find someplace with a bit more comfort and privacy than the hallway."

Feeling the pressure of getting started, Ember hurried down the stairs.

⚷—

In Ember's absence, they settled into an upstairs sitting room. While Avery hurried away to find refreshment, Peter fell into a chair opposite the police officer and studied him critically. He was a handsome enough man when his face wasn't bruised and cut up. He wasn't clever though, and his ambitiousness was too obvious and bordered on crudity.

Peter grinned at himself. Part of this critique came from his own insecurity. Not that it mattered. Soon the dark leveler would reclaim him. He wondered if he could change that whether his conduct would be any different. Probably not different at all. Convictions born of night faded with daylight.

"Ember Quatermain seems quite fond of you," Peter observed and instantly wished he could take back the words.

Wariness passed into Baker's eyes. "Do you think so? I am quite fond of Miss Quatermain."

Peter felt a rumble of childish resentment and wished he hadn't broached the subject. An uncomfortable silence settled between them and he checked the door in the hopes that Avery would reappear and save him from his discomfort.

"Still, she's a bit unconventional," Peter said. "Although it's nothing some stability in her life won't calm."

"What are you playing at?"

"Me?"

"You sound like someone's father asking after my intentions."

"Now that you mention it," Peter took the opening.

Baker snorted and settled back in his chair. The Chief Constable pulled a cherry pipe from his coat and took time filling the bowl. An irritating expression of amusement remained plastered on his face.

"Mr. Styles, I don't believe you have any right to ask such a question," Baker drawled. "I'll answer it though. I find Miss Quatermain attractive, and if I thought the young lady would be responsive, I would seek an opportunity to court her."

The words, sought and delivered, stung Peter. Jealousy was beneath him, but it still rankled. He wasn't used to the sensation. Baker presented him with a smirk and Peter watched him with growing peevishness.

"Miss Quatermain isn't likely to accept your advances, Mr. Baker. You come from quite different stations in life."

"You think you're more suitable?" Baker asked. "Begging your pardon, Mr. Styles, but I think a bright woman such as Miss Quatermain would realize you're far too selfish to be truly interested in anyone other than yourself."

"How impertinent," Peter said.

"And then there's the matter of your current condition."

His words struck a nerve. Peter stifled an impulse to respond in a biting fashion and instead rose and turned his back to the police officer. Avery entered balancing a tray on one arm and carrying a bottle of wine in with the other.

"I have some fruit, cheese, and bread here," Avery announced jovially. He offered the tray to Peter and then withdrew it with embarrassment. "My blunder," he said.

Peter waved off his friend's concern and removed himself to stand at the window and stare at the afternoon sky. The sky was an immovable sheet of gray. Had spring ever been this slow arriving? Weariness descended on him and he leaned against the sill. How much time remained before he slipped back into the endless darkness? Not much. Not much.

He heard Avery pouring wine into a glass and shifted to watch the two men sharing their repast. He'd been an ass to Baker. The man deserved better. Peter returned to his chair and sat down. His eyes strayed to the fire.

"About that matter we were discussing," Peter said.

The men gave him their attention.

"I was wrong, Mr. Baker. I spoke out of turn. I offer my most sincere apologies."

The Chief Constable nodded once. "No apology needed," he said.

Peter shut his eyes, and tried reaching within, gingerly testing the life spark of his resurrection. It was paler than before.

He considered their arduous task and wondered if enough time had been given him to finish it. He shuddered to think what would happen if they failed and Apollonius gained the Emerald Tablet.

Was the power in the stone itself, or was the power derived from the transformative spell etched on its face? Sir Isaac Newton had allegedly translated it, or at least gained access to a counterfeit.

"That which is below is like that which is above," the translation went. "The sun is its father, the moon its mother, and the wind has carried it abroad."

While the stone undoubtedly possessed the key to power, the legend of its magnitude couldn't possibly be true. It couldn't change reality. If that were possible, then there were no absolutes, and if there were no absolutes, then that made dire suggestions about the existence of God.

Whatever the truth about the tablet, Apollonius wanted it, and that was enough motivation to keep it from him.

Peter walked over to the bottle Avery had provided and splashed a little into a glass. While he no longer needed food or drink, he still had a sense of taste. Peter sloshed a thimbleful around his palate.

"Perhaps if our task is impossible," he said, "we should take a different course of action."

Avery eyed him with a wary expression.

"What other action is there, if we don't secure the tablet?" Baker asked.

"Finding the tablet is urgent only because a threat is hanging over our heads. If the threat is removed, then we may find the Emerald Tablet at our leisure."

"You're going to suggest going directly after Apollonius," Avery said. His mouth was set in disapproval. Peter knew this stern countenance well enough.

"I'm suggesting it."

"It's a terrible idea," Avery said, jabbing his finger at the air for emphasis.

"We may not have other options."

"That's lunacy."

"Besides, I don't know how much longer I have," Peter said. Avery's eyes showed he caught the meaning of Peter's words and his shoulders sagged forward. He let out a ragged sigh.

"I agree with Mr. Styles," Baker said. "A direct confrontation might be the thing to end this. However, I think it foolhardy for Mr. Styles to consider taking on this challenge alone. If he knows where Apollonius might be, then he should tell us. We should all go. I can have several of my men there in no time. We can conduct a raid."

Peter marveled at the police officer's attitude, even after his experiences through the breach he sounded as if he approached Apollonius as a common criminal.

"You do that, Chief Constable, and you'll have the deaths of several good men on your conscience. Any approach at Apollonius will have to be subtle. And unorthodox. I have something in mind; in fact, Apollonius himself opened the possibility to me."

"What possibility?" Avery asked.

"You wouldn't like it, old friend."

"You think you can beat him in a contest of wills?"

"He's corrupt, and probably over-confident at this point. Yes, I think I have an advantage."

"Do you know where he is?" Baker asked.

Peter avoided answering.

"If we stop Apollonius, then we won't have to go after the tablet at all," Avery reasoned. "Leave it where it is, it's been safe these many centuries."

His words were tempting, but Peter shook his head and replied, "No, now that Ember is on the trail to its hiding place, others will follow. There will be no peace. We need to find the tablet and destroy it ourselves."

"You don't mean to turn it over?"

"Who's to say this Timothy character is any better than Apollonius? And how can we trust his motives?"

"Ember trusts him," Baker said.

"I don't. In my opinion he's sent us in his stead to avoid having to deal with Apollonius."

"You neglected answering my initial question," Baker insisted. "How will you find Apollonius?"

Peter hesitated, "By paying a visit to my maker."

CHAPTER XXIII

Wherein Peter confronts the necromancer

PETER MOVED WITH DELIBERATE AND QUIET STEPS THROUGH THE SHADOWS OF EARLY EVENING. He touched the emotions of a group of people passing nearby; weary laborers looking forward to enjoying the warmth of their hearths and the safety of their shelters. He lingered and savored the moment. Moving on he encountered another presence in the form of an old woman close to death. She lingered in the company of a grieving family, sad at the pain she caused them and fearful of the blackness that awaited.

The moon peeked out from a cloud. Peter evaded its light and followed the wall of a tall building. He leaned against the cool brick and studied the edifice across the street. It was a two story Gothic, sandwiched between a pair of older structures. A low wrought iron gate separated the plot from the street, and a paved walk lead to the front door. A black shape stood stiffly by the entrance.

Peter sensed two men down the block. Their thoughts were muddied, and he knew at once they were slightly tipsy. Both were working men. Peter watched them approach the black form. They abruptly stepped into the street, giving the shape a wide berth.

He noted the incident with approval. That's how it always was. Their worlds co-existed, but those who lived in daylight avoided the shadows whenever possible, and vice-versa. And some courageously, or foolishly, strode both paths, and too often paid a terrible price.

Gathering his resolve, Peter crossed the cobbles and the figure at the gate moved to intercept him. It had been aware of him when he was still a good distance away. Now it advanced, stepping out of the darkness.

The guard was of the resurrected. Short and maybe fifty years old at the time of death, he still possessed powerful arms and shoulders, and a thick neck corded with muscle. Faded scars ran along the side of his face and his nose bent to one side, evidence of an old break; a man familiar with violence,

They stared at one another.

"What do you seek here?" the man asked. The voice was amazingly gentle and melodious.

"I'm here for an audience with my maker," Peter replied.

They stared at one another and Peter felt the man's pity.

"Is she expecting you?" the man asked at last.

"I don't think so."

He bent his head in thought and finally said, "Wait here, friend."

Peter watched him turn and pass through the gate to the front door, where the man let himself in. Peter checked the street again, and satisfied no immediate threat existed, studied the door, which he noted was painted dark red. An unlucky color, and a bad omen.

The guard returned and held the gate open for Peter, who gave him a curt bow before passing through. The woman he knew as Adala stood at the threshold, waiting. She stood with her back straight and head up. Her smooth hands were clasped together at the waist. The air around the older woman smelled of lavender and vanilla.

She didn't speak for a moment and Peter knew any attempt to penetrate her defenses would prove futile.

"Hello Peter," Adala said. "You've taken your time coming to see me."

She let him enter and shut the door.

Peter waited for her to pass and followed at a safe distance. They entered a cozy parlor. Many of the decorations here appeared personal mementoes from another country. Perhaps Bavaria.

She sat, back still straight, and waved him into an easy chair.

Peter took a seat and admired a small oval painting of a young girl; he could tell by her serious eyes and pointed chin that this was Adala. Usually when a family commissioned such a portrait the artist went out of his way to portray his model in the most flattering light. Here though was a child in pain. She was beautiful, but her eyes spoke of misery.

"Do you think I was unhappy as a child?" she asked.

She was toying with him, confirming his suspicion of her own abilities, and he resented it. Peter drew forth energy and visualized a door slamming shut. Tension flickered across her features.

Adala reached for a trinket on the table and stroked it. He waited patiently for her acknowledgement, unwilling to give her the satisfaction of showing any sign of impatience.

"Why have you come here?" she asked without looking at him.

"Tell me where Apollonius is."

She weighed his words with a long sigh.

Peter leaned forward, rubbing his lips with the back of his hand, a nervous gesture. "Are you so close to finding the tablet then?" she asked.

He heard a note of eagerness in Adala's voice and once more felt her presence seeping through his defenses. Peter diverted more energy to keeping her at bay. It was difficult; she had brought him back and there was now a bond between them. One she could sever at will, releasing him back into eternal darkness.

"This isn't about the tablet," Peter said.

"It's always been about the tablet."

"The tablet is a lie."

"The tablet is a representation."

She stared contemptuously at him before finally shrugging her shoulders and returning to her seat. Adala's frustration pounded him until it pricked his skin and bunched the muscles about his shoulders and down his back.

She'd wasted countless years searching for the unobtainable. Even should she hold the artifact in her arms it would not be an achievement, only an ending.

"Too bad the tablet isn't like Aladdin's lamp," Peter said.

"How so?"

"With Aladdin's lamp, you only got three wishes."

"Unless the third wish was for three more," she said.

"Or you wished the first to be the only one."

She laughed and shook her head. "If I were only as young as Miss Quatermain," she sighed.

"Is that your wish?"

She flinched at that. Adala shook her head and directed a finger at Peter.

"You can't bring yourself back, even with the tablet," she said. "Only I can do that. "Only I can restore you to who and what you were," she said.

If only she knew the irony those words held for him.

"This is a game to you all," Peter said. "Timothy, or Lysimachus, has his pawn. You have yours. Apollonius has moved one piece after another. Time for the endgame, don't you think?"

"And you're the pawn seeking to become a player?"

"No one can win this," Peter said. "Tell me where to find Apollonius."

Adala reached into a small dish beside her and chose a mint. She popped the hard candy into her mouth. "Apollonius is more than you can handle."

"Whether or not you tell me, I'm done playing. I won't search further."

"Willful child," she said. "Do you know why I brought you back, Peter? Because, even though you may not know it, or admit it to yourself, you're the only player who truly believes in God. Did you know that?"

Adala stood and walked to a table. She drew a quill pen from a ceramic container and dipped it in ink. She scribbled something on a sheet of paper. After waving it in the air to dry, she handed it to Peter.

"You think you've seen the worst," she said, "but you haven't. Not even Apollonius has seen the worst. The work of the well-intended usually brings about the most dire consequences."

"Timothy?" Peter asked.

Adala bent forward and kissed him on the forehead. She smiled and Peter saw a cruelness in her expression.

"Do you know what makes me most vulnerable?" she asked, but answered before he could respond, "You do, my love. If someone wanted to penetrate my defenses, you are the key. A maker is as weak as his or her progeny."

She made a good luck sign and disappeared down a hall and through a door.

Peter climbed into the back of a cab and tried to relax. If only Avery were here; his friend's presence always calmed him. At least he had the comfort of knowing Avery at this moment watched over Ember.

Peter had no illusions about the danger of confronting Apollonius head on, but the boldness of his action might actually give him an edge. Or maybe his leave-taking from the Quatermain residence had been a final farewell.

A slight breeze played on his face and with it came a hint of warmer weather. Perhaps spring was here at last, but not for him.

The cab driver still waited for a destination. Peter's initial plan had been to recklessly gain access to St. Bart's and there, find a closet where he could work a spell and animate one or two of the dead from the hospital's morgue. He turned away from that desperate course of action. He had promised never to delve again into necromancy.

His best chance would be one sudden killing strike.

The stupidity of it appealed to him.

What other choice did he have? Apollonius' attentions were turned on acquiring the tablet and on Ember Quatermain. His arrogance made him vulnerable.

Peter rapped on the side of the cab for the driver's attention and gave him the address on the slip of paper handed to him by Adala.

The ride took him into a dreary section of town, down a narrow street where the only colors seemed variations of gray and brown. Peter shifted nervously in his seat and listened to the emptiness of the neighborhood.

He would challenge Apollonius in an honest battle, as foolish as that might be.

As the cab rolled to a stop Peter saw his destination, a drab warehouse with small windows high above the street. He waited and watched for anything out of the ordinary.

He considered testing the aether for any sign of Apollonius, but if he could sense the lamia, then the lamia could in turn feel his presence.

It could be that Adala had sent him into a trap. She might, if she perceived Peter was no longer useful, or if he now posed a threat. She probably enjoyed the thought of sending him against Apollonius. At some point he was going to have to find out more about Adala and her associates, as well as what her relationship to Timothy might be.

The driver stepped down and opened the door. "Would you be wanting company, Mr. Styles?" he asked.

The driver had the bearing of a soldier. He was large, powerfully constructed, but unattractive, with a flat nose below a heavy brow.

"Mr. Tressler called for me," the man explained. "He said you might require some services outside the ordinary. Name's Jim Burke. At your service."

Peter raised his eyebrows and curled the corner of his mouth. This was the man who had assisted Avery against the thugs outside his apartment; the ones who had been sent to complete the failed task of the *nekroanypomonos*. Good old Avery. Peter slapped the man on the shoulder and warmth flowed over him. The man was sincere and stalwart.

"Thank you, Mr. Burke. I'm not saying I wouldn't enjoy the company, but I think it best if I proceed alone."

The driver blocked his path.

"Mr. Tressler told me something about what you might be facing."

Certainly the cabbie could hold his own in a skirmish, but Peter didn't want to expose him to what lay ahead. Whatever waited in that warehouse would be more than this unfortunate ever bargained for. "I thank you, Mr. Burke, but I'll go in alone. If I'm not out in a half hour's time, then you head cross town and alert Mr. Tressler that I've failed."

Burke again blocked him.

"There's a back way out of that warehouse, Mr. Styles. We could go around that building and come up the alley."

The man stood with his feet set apart. Peter wondered if an act of God could move him from his purpose. He didn't want to waste time on this and the longer they stood here, the greater the chance of someone taking note.

"Do you have a weapon?" Peter asked.

The driver produced a nasty looking dirk from inside his coat.

"That will have to do," Peter said. He held his hand out for the blade and Burke reluctantly handed it over.

"You've seen things, Mr. Burke."

"That I have."

"Well, you'll see things in a few minutes which will challenge your sanity."

Peter bent down and retrieved a sharp stone from the ground, then used one of the edges to scratch symbols onto the metal. There was no time to do this properly, but it was better than nothing. Before he handed the weapon back, Peter pulled energy from the night and sent it into the blade.

"This won't work unless you want it to work," Peter explained. "Once you've seen what we're up against, you'll want it to work. Have no fear."

Burke examined the dirk without comment.

"We'll approach the door together," Peter instructed. "But once we're there, you hang back. If I need help, I'll call for you."

The big man appeared dissatisfied with the plan, and Peter knew he had no intention of hanging back long. They crossed the street, staying in shadows, until they rounded the corner of a dark building.

Peter signaled the driver to stop.

"Someone's been here," Peter observed. He pointed at the trampled grass. With trepidation, he ran a hand along the door, showing the driver where the lock had been twisted off.

"That wasn't done with a crowbar," Peter warned. "That was done with brute strength."

Peter gathered his courage and moved into place. He waved Burke to the other side of the door and eased it open. The old hinges' creak made him wince.

"Well, there's no helping it," Peter whispered.

He placed a hand against Burke's chest and spoke into his ear. "Give a shout if someone comes. Don't be a brave man though, get away if you can."

"You underestimate me, Mr. Styles."

"Perhaps I do, but I've already too much on my conscience."

Peter offered his hand to the big man. They shook and Peter turned to find himself standing face-to-face with one of the *nekroanypomonos*.

CHAPTER XXIV

Wherein our adventurers discover a lost legend

BEING BACK IN THE GLOOM OF THE UNDERGROUND UNSETTLED EMBER. The Paddington tunnel was septic, the infection pervasive. Claustrophobia gripped her as she held the lantern aloft and peered through the gloom. Behind her Avery and Baker spoke softly and sparingly; although she couldn't understand their words, the tone was tense.

The two men caught up to her. Avery stood silently at Ember's side. One hand nervously strayed to the Colt revolver stuck into his waistband. He sniffed the air and made a sour face.

"Smells like the Thames down here," he commented.

"Or something worse," Ember said. She didn't want to go further. The way her skin itched made her shudder.

"I should have brought some men down with us," Baker said. He stepped to the edge of the light. "I wouldn't want to run into those creatures again without being properly prepared."

"What time do you have?" Ember asked.

Avery flipped open his pocket watch. He stared at the face in annoyance and gave the timepiece a shake. He grunted with satisfaction as the ticking resumed. Ember stared at the watch with grave concern.

"What's wrong?" he asked.

"Everything is in motion. Too soon, we step into one reality. Too late, we step into another."

Baker tugged out his own watch. He had insisted on coming with them, and apart from stiffness in his motion and a growing irritability, he showed little ill effect from his wounds. He had a remarkable constitution.

"I wish Peter were here," Avery said.

Ember glanced up; she had been thinking the same thing.

Baker waved at the battery in her arms.

"If we keep bleeding through barriers the good Lord put in place to keep these different worlds apart, then might we not set into motion something that may well prove disastrous?"

"I can't imagine anyone bleeding off enough energy to merge realities," she said.

"But it's possible?"

"The effect is localized. Whatever breach we create is small. And temporary."

Ember turned back to her equipment and worked silently for several minutes. The men watched, occasionally shifting weight from one foot to another. Baker cleared his throat loudly.

"I'm ready," she said. She once again asked for the time.

Ember rubbed her palms together and realized they were sweaty. She dried them and smiled self-consciously. One of Baker's eyes twitched.

"I brought one of my father's hunting rifles down here. It's a small weapon, meant more for a woman, really. It's in that canvas bag Mr. Tressler carried earlier. You can help yourself to it, if you would like."

Baker drew one of Peter's daggers.

"I appreciate the offer," he said. "However, after what I've seen, I think this might serve me better than a woman's rifle."

"Here's hoping Peter's faring well," Avery said. Ember caught the worry in his eyes and had to stay herself from chewing a fingernail.

Ember had emerged from her workroom earlier to find Peter gone and the men reluctant to discuss his absence. Only with tremendous prompting had they finally admitted his fool's errand.

"Peter knows what he's about," Avery had said defensively. "And I've sent someone along to watch his back."

She almost scolded Avery and Baker for allowing him to leave, but the concern in their faces arrested her anger. They couldn't have stopped him. Poor Peter. He had never really been one of them.

Ember once again checked the equipment and switched on the engine. She wired her battery into the machine and attached the tube. Energy crackled from the tips of the embedded pentacle as the machine charged.

"Time?" she asked.

Baker told her, and the stress in his voice made her again wonder if they shouldn't have been more forceful in dissuading him from coming along. She had heard of men losing their courage; if Baker's nerves weren't undone, they were certainly fraying. He was a conventional man who thrived on order. She felt partly responsible for his current state.

Ember took a deep breath and aimed the tube at a spot along the dirt wall where she earlier detected disturbances in the energy flow.

"Get ready," she called. "Avert your eyes!"

She flipped a switch and a ball of energy slammed into the side of the tunnel. Her stomach lurched and she was suddenly disoriented. Avery staggered but quickly regained his footing.

Ember lowered the tube and held up a metallic cone with copper filaments. She pointed it at the wall and checked the attached gauge as it revealed an extreme variance in the energy level.

"It's open!" Ember cried out.

The tunnel remained as it had been, the moment passed in a disappointing anti-climactic fashion. Ember released a breath, but maintained a cautious awareness. She heard the men shift behind her. Baker cleared his throat.

"Nothing's happened," he said.

She didn't move. Something had happened; she was sure of it. Still, her senses told her everything was the same as before.

"Perhaps we should try again," Baker urged. "Maybe it needs to be hit again?"

"It worked," Ember said with conviction.

Avery held the lantern high and took a few cautious steps down the tunnel. He sniffed the air and prodded the dirt with his toe. He reminded Ember of a terrier searching for a rat that had gone to ground.

"Well?" Avery asked. "I don't see anything."

He walked further down the tunnel, his gait less cautious now. The lantern threw weird shadows along the walls. Ember watched with growing trepidation, wanting at once to call him back, but at the same wanting him to test the waters ahead.

"That's far enough, don't you think?" Baker called. "I smell something . . . "

The lantern's glow winked out.

Ember caught her breath and reached for Baker's hand only to find empty space. She heard a scraping sound and a match ignited. Baker had pulled a spare lantern from their bag. He held it up and together they peered toward where their friend disappeared.

"Avery?" Ember called. Baker called as well, cupping a hand to the side of his mouth and shouting with vigor. They both waited for a response.

"I'm heading down there," Ember said.

"You'll do no such thing," Baker sounded frightened. He reached for her but she drew away from him.

"Chief Constable!"

Baker stared into the blackness which had swallowed Avery and back at Ember. His jaw was clenched and a sheen of perspiration shined on his forehead.

"I'm not letting you run into danger," he said. "We're going to do what we should have done from the onset, approach this as a proper police matter. I'm going to get reinforcements, and we're coming back at this systematically."

Ember ignored him and moved forward. She almost lost her footing and saved herself from a stumble only by raking her palm against the rough tunnel wall.

"Miss Quatermain!"

Baker gripped her wrist and wrenched it as he pulled her back. The weight of the energy gun restricted her movement.

"Don't you dare handle me like that," she exclaimed.

"Don't go down there."

Ember shoved past him and gripped the handles of the hand truck bearing their equipment. She pulled with a grunt and dragged the wheels over the rough floor of the tunnel.

"You have no idea where the man has gone," Baker protested, keeping step. He stretched for the cart, but she jerked it out of his reach.

"If you aren't able to assist, then stay behind," she said coolly.

Proceeding down the tunnel the air became denser, humid. A strange breeze played down the passage way. Intuitively she traced a hand across the dirt wall until, taking another step, the wall disappeared.

The air was cool but acidic. Instead of the claustrophobic tunnel, she now stood before a desolate moor with the sky greenish gray. Thick layers of vegetation made the flat ground slippery and strange weeds clung to the ground in clumps and gnarled branches seemed to stretch out like witches' hands.

They had bumped from one reality to another before and opened up breaches in the barriers between the universes, but until now, the world never once looked or felt different. Ember took a deep breath and calmed herself enough to remember Avery.

She cast about and saw him on his knees near a small hillock. He held the flat of his palms to his eyes.

"Avery!"

Hearing his name, he rose like a drunkard and staggered in her direction. He gestured for her to stay back.

"Are you hurt?" she cried.

"Just stay there."

The air cooled at her back and she heard movement. Ember turned in time to see Baker appear. His mouth yawned open in amazement at the change in landscape. He turned in a circle, face to the heavens.

"Dear God," Baker uttered.

Avery stretched out his arms like a blind man feeling for obstacles and moved cautiously in their direction. A twisted root snagged his foot and sent him tumbling. Leathery creatures exploded from the ground as he fell, filling the air with shrill cries, expelling something noxious from their thin bodies. The flock circled once and settled several yards away, disappearing into the ground.

Baker had cried out at the eruption, flinching back as if preparing to flee. His features contorted in dismay as he watched Avery crawling across the soil.

"This way," Baker hissed. The police officer waved frantically, but remained rooted to his spot.

Ember carefully approached Avery and helped him to his feet. She put a protective arm about his shoulder and guided him farther from where the flock had descended.

"I'll be all right in a moment," he said. "Those things keep erupting from the soil. There are these mounds everywhere. I think they're nests."

She handed Avery a handkerchief so he might wipe away the tears streaming down his cheeks.

"I think the spray those bat-like things create is a defense mechanism," she offered.

"Perhaps," Avery agreed. "Blast! My eyes still feel like they're on fire. Give me a moment."

Ember pointed to a spot several yards off and suggested they might move there for safety. Baker took the cart and Ember stayed close to Avery.

"I shouldn't want to meet their predator." he said.

"Nor would I," she agreed. "We need to open another breach quickly. And we better hurry, our window's closing fast."

Baker puffed out a burst of air that lifted the hairs of his moustache. "Why couldn't we have opened it from Paddington?" he asked. Ember thought he sounded petulant.

Avery nodded agreement.

"You know why. I worked it out mathematically according to the map. We needed to jump."

"What if our next jump lands us someplace more dangerous than this?"

"It can't be helped," she said.

Feeling the weight of their mission, Ember pulled the cart to a gentle rise. She lifted the copper cone and took a reading of the area.

"Here we go," she called.

Ember triggered the device and electrical discharge skittered up and down the cart's frame. She aimed the tube and squeezed its trigger.

A fist of energy slammed her to the ground.

Ember writhed in pain. She fought to keep her senses and failed, lapsing instead into uneasy blackness.

⚷

Total darkness greeted her when she opened her eyes and for a panicked moment she feared she might be blind. Ember jerked into a sitting position and pain shot through her skull. Her stomach churned and she fought the impulse to wretch. Her hands burned as if she'd pressed them inside a frying pan.

When her fear subsided slightly, she touched the ground and was greeted by cold stone. Marble? Her palms flamed at the contact and she knew her skin wasn't just burned, but blistering. Nothing to do for it. Ember flexed her hands a few times and pushed back the pain.

She calmed herself and listened to her surroundings. Nothing. The eerie silence of a tomb. She inhaled slowly and tasted cool dry air. The blackness became weighty.

"Avery?" she called.

The dark swallowed her voice.

Ember prayed she wasn't alone, unsure if she could handle that. What would her father do? Ember knew he wouldn't still be on the floor wracked by self-doubt. With that thought, she stood, legs uncertain beneath her, and gingerly reached inside her purse to locate a tiny egg. She pulled it out and twisted the steel ring dividing two chambers within the crystal. A chemical glow quickly illuminated area.

Action fuelled courage. Ember held the crystal high and looked about her. She was in a large chamber, the walls adorned by vivid frescoes. Greek heroes. Perseus held a shield against an advancing Medusa. Nearby, Hercules battled a towering catlike beast, its fangs dripping blood.

Ember searched the shadows for evidence of her hand cart. The electrical discharge had opened a breach and she had fallen through—alone.

The idea of being stranded here pounded at her. She would die of hunger and thirst.

Perhaps the breach was still open.

Ember paced frantically, moving in widening circles around the spot where she had awakened.

She stopped before two enormous statues carved of white marble. The towering figures were perfectly detailed, their powerful bodies reminding her of sculptures seen during a trip to the Athenian Acropolis. The sight of these giants drove the fear from her mind, replacing it with wonder.

The one on the right was definitely male, the one on the left female. At their feet were hundreds of urns, all stuffed with scrolls. The air smelled of cedar oil and nauseatingly sweet myrrh.

She gazed in wonder and read the ancient Greek lettering at the bases of the sculptures. The writing identified the one on the left, the female, as Athena, Goddess of Wisdom. Hermes, the God of Knowledge, stood to her right. Behind them stood other, small statues—all feminine. Nine of them in all. The Muses.

Between Knowledge and Wisdom, and within the semi-circle of the nine Muses, a glass coffin rested on a low dais.

Forgetting her fear, Ember approached the coffin. The light from the egg revealed the opaqueness of the glass along with a stone box at the foot of the dais. The word "Truth" was etched onto the surface of the box in many languages.

Ember's heart hammered in her chest, her throat and mouth were impossibly dry. She took another step closer and peered through the glass at the figure there.

A mummified corpse lay in repose, adorned by a gold crown embedded with gems. A broad belt lay across the middle of its body, a ring next to its hand. Both bore the Greek name: "Caracalla." They were the offering from a dutiful son.

With her nose almost touching the casket, Ember noted the sun carved in the headpiece, with eight faint rays emanating from its center.

"Alexander," she whispered.

She wanted a closer look at the remains of the great man, but uneasiness at invading this sanctuary plagued her. Ember remembered her father's words: "We aren't body snatchers."

A snippet of Shelley's poem came to mind. *"And on the pedestal these words appear: 'My name is Ozymandias, king of kings. Look on my works, ye Mighty, and despair!' Nothing beside remains."*

A buzzing sounded.

Ember first thought it came from around the corpse, but realized it emanated from behind her. She instinctively twisted the egg to seek the protection of darkness.

The air crackled and several electrical discharges flashed purple white. Someone uttered an "oof" and landed on the floor with a heavy thud. Ember waited and heard uncertain footsteps and in a moment pale lantern light challenged the blackness.

"Gentlemen," she called out. "I was beginning to feel abandoned."

Both men turned quickly. Avery's arm was extended, the Colt ready to fire. Baker held the small rifle he had earlier sneered at, and it did indeed look absurd in his arms.

Ember lit the egg once more and saw them relax. The two approached, thankfully dragging the hand cart behind them.

"We were terrified we'd lost you," Avery said. His smile broadened and pleasure shined in his eyes. Baker gave a quick nod, but his attention was on their surroundings. He remained in a crouch and his grip on the rifle tightened.

"There was an unexpected energy fluctuation," Ember said. "It enveloped me. The breach was extremely localized."

"Well, you look no worse for wear."

"I'm afraid I burned my hands," she said.

Avery took her wrist and examined the blisters. He whistled. "That must be damned painful." His concern touched her.

"What is this?" Baker had wandered past them and now stood by the glass casket. His voice sounded strange.

"It's Alexander's tomb," she replied with a sense of pride. "This is extraordinary. It's a marvelous find."

"Wasn't Alexander a king?" Baker asked. "Where are his jewels? His gold sarcophagus?"

Baker stepped closer to the coffin and leaned against the glass. She refrained from cautioning him against contact with the artifact.

"One of the Ptolemys melted down his gold coffin to pay the troops," Ember lectured. "This was a substitution."

"But glass? How has it remained intact?"

"Mr. Baker, I suspect time is different here."

He accepted her statement at face value. His lack of intellectual curiosity further distanced her from the man. He tapped the coffin.

"Still, that crown and that ring would fetch a fortune, wouldn't they?" he uttered.

Quiet reclaimed them. Ember again approached the coffin and the enormity of their accomplishment struck her. They had traversed energy streams and jumped between realities so that they now stood before the remains of Alexander the Great.

Avery must have been thinking the same thing because he put a hand on her shoulder and fondly commented, "You're a remarkable woman, Miss Quatermain."

His comment warmed her.

"Looking at him, Alexander, I feel sad," she said. Even though she whispered, her voice sounded loud and intrusive. "What would Peter say if he were here?"

Avery chuckled. "He'd more than likely say something like, '*Out out, brief candle! Life's but a walking shadow.*'"

She didn't try and identify the line. Instead she ruminated: *Life's but a walking shadow.*

Avery left her side to approach a small stone box at the foot of the platform. He held the lantern up and leaned forward. The wonder on his face made him look childlike.

"The tablet?" she asked.

"I think so," he said. "I'm terrified." The sudden admission made them laugh. Baker came closer and touched the top of the container.

"Open it," he said.

No one moved. "What if it isn't here?" Ember asked.

"It's there," Avery said. "You can feel it."

Baker produced his dagger and slipped it between the lid and the wall of the box. He bit his lip and pried the top upward.

Within was a simple flat green stone. With great tenderness, Avery lifted it from the container.

"It's quite light," he said.

Ember ran her fingertips over the surface. The writing on the tablet was in an unfamiliar language, or quite possibly in code.

"I never thought we'd find it," Avery said.

Ember didn't respond, but her thoughts echoed his.

"And now that we have it, we're going to turn the thing over to Apollonius?" Avery asked.

As she stared at the object she felt torn, still disbelieving of its power. With Apollonius able to threaten Harry, she had no choice but to deliver the prize to him. Truthfully, she hadn't believed in the stone, or if she did, then she hadn't accepted the legend surrounding it. And while she still doubted, even in the face of the things she had experienced in the last several days, Ember now admitted the possibility she was about to deliver incredible power into the hands of a monster.

Ember accepted the tablet from Avery and held it in the crook of one arm. If this stone could live up to its reputation, the one who wielded it would have power to rival God. Impossible. The God she imagined wouldn't allow such power into the hands of a fallible being.

Perhaps it was a test. If someone played at being God, maybe a divine presence would sweep in and punish that person.

She thought of what she had read of the stone and remembered Newton's translation of the *Tabula Smaragdina*. She knew now the wise man had written a bit of vague doggerel to confuse and mislead those who sought this prize.

She wondered how many other guardians the stone had.

Baker rapped the surface of the glass coffin as if testing it.

"What are you doing?" Avery demanded.

"We should take back with us what we can carry. That crown. That ring. We should gather some of those urns as well."

His words shocked Ember.

"We can't," she said.

"Why?"

"It's wrong. We're intruders here. We don't have the right to take anything."

Baker rubbed the bruise along the side of his face and studied his companions. He stepped close to her and spoke in a soft tone.

"Begging your pardon, but think of these treasures lost forever. They will be. No one else will come looking for them, especially with the tablet gone from here. We have an obligation to claim them, don't we?"

When Ember didn't respond, he crept closer and his tone became more urgent. "If this were an archeological dig, it would be our property," Baker elaborated. "Wouldn't it? Isn't that how it is?"

"It's not the same and you know it," Ember said.

She waited for him to present the argument that they should collect these things in the Crown's interests. To his credit, he didn't. Instead, Baker shook his head and appealed to Avery, who thankfully sided with her.

"Constable, I think we're here because we were meant to find the tablet," Avery said. "We were meant to keep it safe. However, I don't believe whatever guided us this way did so for our personal enrichment, nor to further Her Majesty's interests."

"I disagree," Baker said. Ember didn't like his tone. She stared at him. The police officer had been fighting an internal struggle from the beginning. If he wanted to reclaim control and rediscover his authority, now wasn't the time.

"We need to open another breach," Ember said. "The window could close any time, and if it does we'll have little chance to calculate when to make another jump."

Ember turned her back on the constable and approached the hand cart. She examined her machine, quickly scanning it for signs of any burned connections. She took a minute to see Timothy's map in her mind and ran down a series of calculations. The problem was that the original breach was closed now, so if they opened a new portal, they would be operating according to the present reality, whenever and wherever that might be.

They might now be hundreds of years in the past.

According to earlier calculations the window to the original, or home reality, was still open now. However, that time was limited.

Ember turned from the cart to find Baker prying the lid off the glass coffin. He struggled with it, his face grim. A musty smell of dark spice permeated the air. He reached in, fingers closing about the gold crown.

"Stop it!" Ember urged.

He ignored her.

Avery's brows came together and his jaw clenched. He called out to Baker.

"You're better than this, Kent," Avery called. "Put it back, Constable."

The policeman straightened and stepped away from the coffin, the gold band in his hands.

"Neither of you are in a position to order me about," Baker said. "This isn't your decision to make. You have the tablet; this is claimed for Her Majesty."

She found his imperious tone rankling.

"Chief Constable, I don't want to argue," she began.

"Miss Quatermain, I am pleased to hear that."

He returned to the coffin and the treasures within. Ember watched with mounting anger and sputtered as he lifted a huge gem from the mummified figure. This wasn't the man who approached her on the front porch of her father's house only days ago.

She considered the energy streams and knew time was getting away from them.

Ember ignited the engine and listened to it get to speed. She flipped a switch and sent energy into the battery where it could be stored and amplified. She then triggered a blue stream and watched the dust motes churn as cold air suddenly blew into the chamber.

Avery slipped close to the opening portal and pressed his hand into the center. It vanished to the elbow.

Baker watched from his perch beside the dais. He voiced objection but Ember held up a warning hand.

"Chief Constable, I know you've been through a good deal and that you're tired and worn thin. You're a man of responsibility, not a grave robber."

"Miss Quatermain, don't lecture me."

She bristled, but kept her calm.

"I'm about to make you angry, Chief Constable. Mr. Tressler and I are stepping through this breach and if you don't follow immediately, without the crown and jewels, I shall shut it and strand you here."

"You wouldn't," he said.

"You're a good four strides away. We can be gone in one."

"It's a bluff."

Ember stood still, a stony expression on her face.

"If you're willing to take that bet, Chief Constable, then you're a more courageous man than I," Avery stated.

"Mr. Tressler," Baker appealed.

Avery shook his head slowly and approached the swirling dust cloud that marked the breach. He paused before stepping through and said, "Miss Quatermain, I'll be waiting on the other side."

Ember moved the handcart closer to the opening and stared back at the constable. Worry flashed over his face and he cast his gaze about the chamber. He looked back at her and she could tell he knew the threat was empty. But this wasn't about the crown or the jewels, it was about him awkwardly and ineffectively trying to re-establish order. Too many of his basic beliefs had been challenged and failed. He needed to regain some level of control.

Baker relented with a heavy sigh. He gently restored the treasures to their proper places and held his hands up in a gesture of surrender.

"You're a forward thinking woman, Miss Quatermain, but don't consider that a compliment."

"You're an honorable man, Mr. Baker."

"Am I?"

Without another word or a glance in her direction, Baker proceeded to the breach and stepped through.

Ember gripped the tablet tightly and followed. As she stepped from the cool scented air of Alexander's tomb into the damp earthy air of Paddington, she hoped her sudden melancholy wasn't foreshadowing to what lay ahead.

CHAPTER XXV

Wherein Virgil attempts to lead Mr. Styles into another level of Hell

THE DEAD MAN STOOD IN THE DOORWAY. Naked from the waist, its belly grossly distended and its chest and neck sporting purple and yellow splotches. Its blackened tongue lolled over bloated lips.

Burke gasped.

Before Peter could step back, a hand shot out and dragged him inside by the collar. The thing giggled as it rammed him into the wall. Bits of plaster sprinkled the floor.

Burke charged in, the big man ineffectually punching the corpse's kidneys. The *nekroanypomonos* ignored the attack and slammed Peter into another wall. Harder this time. He didn't feel much pain, but instinctively knew damage was done. His arm hung uselessly to his side and his thoughts scattered.

Peter recognized a shimmer of familiar energy rippling his attacker's face. Masterson's touch was unmistakable.

The psychic tendril binding the corpse to its creator was unbreakable, woven with surprising confidence and skill. Becoming lamia had heightened Masterson's abilities.

Burke stood back, seeming at a loss.

"Get out!" Peter shouted.

The *nekroanypomonos* shoved an open hand into Peter's abdomen and grabbed flesh. With the strength the thing wielded, it would close its fist and tear through fat and muscle. Peter acted in desperation. He blasted the psychic connection binding monster and maker. If he couldn't break it, he might at least cause a distraction.

The dead man paused, the fingers relaxed.

Buoyed by the shifting momentum, Peter poured himself into the effort. He threw himself at the link, ripping at the threads until they started to strain and sheer. Energy coursed through him.

The *nekroanypomonos* staggered and Burke leaped. The driver plunged the dagger into the base of the monster's spine. The energy around the corpse darkened, but the thing clung to the braid. With shocking speed, it whirled on the new threat and punched Burke's chest, propelling him down the hall. He dropped to his knees, eyes rolling back in his head.

While the *nekroanypomonos'* back was still turned to him, Peter acted. He gripped the handle of the dagger, and directed energy into the blade, finally severing the connection. The dead man's knees sagged. Peter pulled the dagger out and let the body fall to the floor with a heavy thud.

Burke moaned. He dragged himself into a sitting position, back to the wall. He looked at the corpse with unblinking eyes and moved away a few feet.

"How are you?" Peter asked.

"I'm a bit sick to my stomach and the back of my head feels as if kicked in by a horse. What about you, Mr. Styles? You don't look that well."

Peter helped Burke to his feet and peered into the man's eyes. He considered sending the driver back outside, but didn't want to engage in an argument. Instead he handed the dagger back to the man.

"When you use this," he instructed, "you have to put yourself into the blade. It's not just an extension of your body, it's an extension of your mind and will."

The driver accepted the blade and cleaned it against his sleeve. "I understand," he said. Peter believed him. He helped the man to his feet and they continued into the warehouse.

Where was Apollonius?

Adala had given him this address; she had set him up. She couldn't be working with Apollonius, although her association with Timothy was tenuous. She didn't want the tablet found. She didn't want Apollonius to possess it, nor Timothy. She didn't trust any of them, and so she played one against the other.

Although the power of the tablet teased Adala, Peter never sensed the woman possessed any great ambition. She was motivated by something else; perhaps a need to maintain a balance.

Peter paused outside a door and relaxed until his mind opened. A feminine presence stirred within, and something else. He tried sifting through the confused impressions and sensed Masterson.

Before he had a chance to consider the difficulty of what lay ahead, Peter put a smile on his face and opened the door.

Masterson sat on a large wooden chair on the opposite side of the room. He was clad only in a red dressing gown. Peter remembered the man's face at the duel; the weakness and fear he saw then was now replaced by brash confidence.

A woman huddled on the floor by Masterson's feet, her mouth slightly open and her dull eyes suggesting the influence of drugs. Another woman, quite young, stood in a thin black frock that showed her naked underneath. She rocked from side to side as if in a hypnotic trance.

A third woman stood like a statue. Curly strawberry blonde hair flowed past her shoulders, accentuating a long graceful neck. She had large gray eyes and fair skin. She possessed an uncanny resemblance to Ember Quatermain.

"Welcome to the masquerade," Masterson crooned. The man's eyes shined with excitement.

Two of the women shifted, responding to their master's mood. Peter sensed they were still mortal; he wouldn't risk turning them. Apollonius had more than likely forbidden him to do so.

Burke's desire penetrated Peter's consciousness. Two of the women showed interest in the newcomers. The third, the strawberry blonde, remained aloof.

"Where's your master?" Peter asked.

The question drew a broad grin from Masterson. "He's gone. He has pressing business elsewhere. However, I imagine he'll be along in time. And what about you, Mr. Styles? Where is your master?"

Tremendous energy coursed through this room. Peter started drawing it into him.

The woman in the black frock raised an eyebrow. She reminded him of a sleeper emerging from a nightmare. The smaller woman, the one who appeared in a drug induced stupor, abruptly threw an arm around her sister, not an act of protection, but rather ownership. She turned a cold eye his way and he felt her hatred.

Peter threw a barrier out to protect himself and Burke.

"You're fading," Masterson said. "I can feel it. That's the problem with the resurrected; their return is so brief. If you had been turned by one of us, as I was turned by my master, you'd be able to continually feed."

"By draining from others."

"That is the way of things. It is how Nature operates."

Masterson rose, the robe opening to expose his nakedness. He approached the Ember lookalike and gathered a handful of her strawberry blonde hair. He held it to his nose and inhaled as one might a bouquet of flowers.

"It's what we do," Masterson said. "Mankind. You make it sound vile, but we live by taking life force, whether it's from a grain of rice, a bit of cattle, or from a pretty thing with red hair. Human beings attach too much importance to their standing. Becoming what I've become has helped me understand that.

"I've never been a bad man, Mr. Styles. I just couldn't bear being ordinary."

"You're still ordinary," Peter said.

Masterson's mouth formed a hard line. He touched the shoulder of one of the women and Peter could sense the power being drained. She moaned and bit her lip hard enough to draw blood. He couldn't believe he'd ever fallen under this man's influence. "This fight you're seeking will never happen," Masterson said. "Apollonius will have the *Tabula Smaragdina,* and that will be that. No dramatics."

"When he has the tablet, you think he'll still need you?"

"I'm his servant," Masterson said. Peter heard uncertainty in his former mentor's voice.

A thought intruded, a gentle suggestion. *Lower the barrier.* He almost gave in and dissipated the hastily created protection set down for Burke's sake.

Peter shook free of Masterson's influence. The lamia sensed the shift and lowered his head; waves of malice slammed into Peter as his hand closed on his dagger.

Two of the women charged; the one in black and the smaller one. Peter steeled himself for the attack. The protective barrier had been set against Masterson; the women were unaffected.

One woman passed Peter and lunged for Burke.

The driver tossed his weapon from hand to hand and used a fist to knock the woman down with a blow to the jaw.

The second woman lunged at Peter without regard for personal safety. She shrieked, spittle flying from her lips. He ducked, but she gripped his good arm and scratched at his wrist in an effort to get him to drop his blade.

The barrier dissipated.

With a shout of triumph, Masterson streaked forward.

Peter tossed the woman aside and spun out of Masterson's path like a Spanish toreador. As the lamia went by, Peter latched onto his enemy's neck.

Masterson's presence overwhelmed him. Lustful craving ripped through Peter, demanding violent release. Desire threatened to conquer rational thought. If he were wholly human and not one of the willing dead, the battle would have ended in surrender.

Peter shoved into Masterson's mind and a succession of vivid images battered him.

Here was Masterson as a young man, hiding from his father, who sought to punish him for cruelty against a servant's daughter. Here he was, lost in a library, finding dark satisfaction in solitude. Again, here, the superior outsider, sitting at a table in a pub, the butt of a joke by a group of laborers.

These and a thousand other fragments cascaded until he was Masterson standing on the lawn of the Glaston estate, watching the duel unfold. He sank into horror and self-pity at the unexpected turn of the duel pistol being aimed in his direction. Sweet darkness. And in the darkness the presence of a master and the promise of great power.

Apollonius.

Here was the tie between creator and progeny. Like the thread binding the *nekroanypomonos* to its maker, here was the center of union between lamia master and servant.

And now Peter felt Apollonius, traveling the threads of the aether like a spider tracking its prey. The ancient lamia's consciousness ran from one energy stream to another, tracking a scent with the single-mindedness of a hunting hound.

Like Liala and her brood, Apollonius could see doorways to realities open and close, and he could feel the presence of power.

He hunted Ember!

When she secured the tablet and stepped from one reality to another, he would be waiting for her.

All these images and thoughts occurred in a sliver of a second. In the next instant, Masterson shrugged free and delivered a punch that knocked Peter back several steps.

The world threatened to spin away and Peter barely managed to stay on his feet. He was almost empty. All he had to do to find peace was let go and slip into the sweet darkness, losing himself in something greater.

Peter fought surrender and instead tightened his grip on the blade in his good hand. Masterson drew near and pressed hot lips to Peter's cooling cheek.

"Sleep now, beloved," he cooed. "Your part's not done in this, not by far."

The words lulled him.

"Sleep, and awaken unwillingly."

Peter drove the blade into the back of Masterson's neck and pulled him close. He twisted and held on as the lamia's hands wrapped around his throat and squeezed.

He again dove into Masterson's mind in search of Apollonius. Like a trapped animal, he attacked the link to the master, clawing at the thread and feeding off the psychic energy. Masterson struggled to free himself, but Peter followed the thread through the aether, back to Apollonius.

"Do you know what makes me most vulnerable?" Adala had asked. "You. We are as weak as our progeny."

Peter surrendered his consciousness to the link. He was vulnerable now, but too far in to stop.

What he planned was a final, desperate gesture. Ever the gambler, Peter played his hand and counted on catching Apollonius unprepared.

Ember Quatermain was relieved to inhale the fetid air of the Underground. Although she trusted her calculations, there were always unknowns that might interfere. The egg dimmed, its chemical reaction almost spent. She didn't need it now; Baker stood nearby with a lantern. His entire demeanor suggested defeat. His shoulders sagged and when he was forced to speak, his voice was soft and his words curt.

Avery removed a handkerchief from his pocket and wiped his face. "The tablet of Hermes," he murmured. Avery gave a satisfied grunt and pointed at the object cradled in her arms. "Now what?"

Ember wasn't sure. She tightened her grip on the stone. She didn't sense anything magical about the artifact. It didn't crackle with energy and holding it, she didn't feel any different.

"I'm not sure," she said.

"Why can't we use the stone?"

"How?" she asked.

The question stopped Avery. He scratched his scalp and began to pace. Ember ran her hand over the symbols etched on the piece and tried imposing order on them. Were they instructions?

"How would Peter deal with the tablet?" she asked.

"I'm glad he's not here," Baker said. "This might be too much a temptation for him."

"This time you might be right," Avery responded. His words surprised her.

"I love Peter," he said quickly. "However, he sometimes does things without thinking them through."

She smiled at this. "He does sometimes embrace absurdity," she said.

"Look like the innocent flower, but be the serpent under't . . . "

"And what is that supposed to mean?" Baker asked in an annoyed tone.

"It means no one should ever underestimate Peter Styles."

Ember returned to studying her prize, but inspection yielded little return. "I wish I had Peter's knowledge of this sort of thing," she said. "This is his specialty."

"I don't think possessing the tablet is a guarantee of being able to use it," Avery mused. "It's not Aladdin's lamp, is it? Still, the thing was hidden for a good reason, and the man who bid us to go after it didn't trust himself capable of handling its return."

Avery held his lantern up and gestured toward the tunnel entrance.

"We should hasten back to your father's house," he said. "If Peter returns, that will be where he'll head. We'll check on Little Harry, and discuss our next course of action. We obviously can't just hand over the prize to Apollonius, not without some assurance he won't immediately turn around and use it against us. I don't trust him."

Cold trickled down Ember's spine. She sucked in air and turned on her heel. She was a small child again, alone in the night with her father off on one of his frequent sojourns.

Baker sensed it, too. His eyes were wide with worry and she noted his suddenly tense posture.

"He's here," she uttered.

Avery stepped protectively in front of Ember and gestured Baker to join him. The police officer, still wielding the small hunting rifle, hesitated, then fell in next to Avery. Ember pulled the battery from the handcart and attached it to the little steam engine.

A lone figure stepped into the lantern light.

Tall, with massive shoulders and a solid trunk, Apollonius moved with supernatural grace. His brow was thick and expressive, his nose long, with flaring nostrils. She avoided looking at his eyes, fearful of the intensity of his gaze.

He was tall, with massive shoulders and a solid trunk. His eyes shocked with their intensity.

"I long ago learned not to underestimate the female of the species. Any species," he said. A smile flashed on his lips and he stepped closer. An artist would never have been able to come close to capturing the sheer power of the man's features.

"Apollonius," Avery said.

"Apollonius of Tyana," the lamia corrected him. "Or rather, I used to be Apollonius of Tyana. Now?"

Ember closed her arms more tightly about the stone.

She heard him whisper something in Latin, but couldn't understand the words.

"Gentlemen, step aside, I want to view the beautiful woman who has inspired such courage and succeeded where so many others have failed."

Ember's hope dissipated as both Avery and Baker shifted, allowing the intruder an unimpeded view. His pleasure radiated warmth and her skin was suddenly too hot.

"What a sweet prize," he said. Ember shifted, trying to raise the tube without dropping the tablet. If Apollonius recognized what she might be up to, he gave no indication.

"I used to be jealous of the gods and sought my own apotheosis," Apollonius said. "You, however, have achieved it through your beauty."

Her breath caught in her throat. Ember didn't just hear Apollonius' words, she felt their heat.

"And having achieved it yourself, surely you won't begrudge me the opportunity," he continued. "On that tablet is the gift from

Hermes, the door to final enlightenment. Redemption comes not from sacrifice or prayer, but from knowledge."

Apollonius extended a hand.

A rush of excitement ran through Ember, making her gasp. She wanted to jump forward and fall at his feet. She knew he was in control, and she gladly surrendered. Tears of gratitude streamed down her cheeks.

She dropped the tube. The only thing that mattered now was Apollonius.

He pointed at his prize.

"Ember, my love. Give me the tablet."

CHAPTER XXVI

Wherein a dreadful confrontation is played out

POLLONIUS THRUST OUT AN EXPECTANT HAND. His open palm was a magnet, and Ember couldn't resist its pull. It was as though the dirt underfoot was suddenly frictionless.

His gaze ensnared her.

She struggled to reclaim her will, to resist him, but his shadow wrapped her in sweet caress.

She sank.

Surrender.

Ember reached within herself, trying to find something to give her the means to rebel. Again, she thought of her nephew and the violation of innocence.

She concentrated on releasing the tablet, using her rage to block Apollonius. One of her fingers uncurled. Another.

The tablet fell to the soil with a dull thud.

Apollonius' gaze followed the tablet's descent. The action surprised him, and Ember felt a lightening as his dominating influence lessened a fraction.

Avery jammed a fist into his pocket and pulled free a small brass charm. With this trinket in one hand and a blade in the other, he launched himself at Apollonius.

The lamia's head snapped up, eyes round with astonishment. Too late. Avery crashed into him and they both slammed against the tunnel wall.

Ember suddenly free from Apollonius' will, watched the men struggle, unsure what to do. She turned and appealed to Baker, who stood with the lantern lifted, its light reflecting in his tortured eyes.

She urged the constable into action.

Like a child suddenly thrown into a situation beyond its ability to cope, Baker fumbled with the hunting rifle and took awkward aim. The lantern still dangled from one hand.

Apollonius tossed Avery aside. Her would-be rescuer rolled across the floor of the Underground like a spent toy. She started for Avery, eager to check his well-being, but Apollonius shifted in anticipation.

"What now?" he asked. His thick eyebrows rose and a broad smile spread across his face. Her stomach churned at his enjoyment; at his control.

Avery's blade lay on the ground near her feet.

Ember dove for the weapon but Apollonius stomped on the dagger with his heel. Her body tensed, waiting for the feel of his hands.

The hunting rifle discharged.

Baker's shot hit Apollonius in the shoulder. The lamia gritted his teeth and stepped back. A second shot hit him in the neck.

With renewed hope, Ember bent for the tablet. She gripped the stone and stepped closer to Baker. The barrel of the hunting rifle smoked.

"Let's go," he gasped.

"We can't leave Avery," Ember said.

The fear on Baker's face both stoked her sympathy and her loathing. She looked past the lamia to where her friend still struggled on the ground. He was on his knees now, looking as if he were trying to stand.

Apollonius dropped his hand from the wound at his neck and studied them with cold eyes. He strode the short distance and removed the rifle from Baker's hands. His expression was contemptuous.

He slapped the lantern from the constable's grasp and it shattered on the ground. The kerosene ignited, but it would burn quickly. They had only moments before the plunge into blackness.

Ember shook her head, keeping the tablet hard against her chest. She had no plan now and no hope.

The police officer went slack as Apollonius released him. Baker slid to the ground, his sleeve landing in the burning kerosene and catching fire.

A blur of shadow and Apollonius was on her.

She clung to the tablet, thankful to have it as a barrier between them. He calmly wrapped his fingers about the top of the artifact and yanked it free.

"Hermes' prize," he said. He ran a hand over the stone and closed his eyes.

Ember scrambled past him and dropped to her knees beside Baker. She used her already blistering palms to pat out the flame running up his arm. She sobbed. The bitterness of losing and the fear of what would come next paralyzed her.

Apollonius' body stiffened. He took a step back and peered at a spot down the tunnel. His brows rose and she thought she detected an expression of alarm.

Ember didn't care what might have distracted him, all that mattered was that she acted while she had the chance.

She needed to activate an energy stream.

Ember half rose, moving for the handcart.

Apollonius cried out in pain. Overworked veins stood out on his forehead and his features twisted with anguish. He shook his head violently.

"I'll kill her!" he screamed.

With one arm clutching the tablet, Apollonius darted to block her and grabbed Ember's throat.

He still stared off, as if communicating with something or someone she couldn't see.

His jaw clenched and the air hummed with energy. The Emerald Tablet fell from his arm and landed hard in the dirt. His hand jerked and opened.

Ember sprang. Landing hard on her elbows, she stretched for the tube. Before her fingers could close on it a strong hand lifted her by her hair. Hate filled Apollonius' eyes.

"I've lived lifetimes, Styles," he said. "Did you think you could overpower me?"

She knew now the nature of the battle. Apollonius had been over-confident. He expected any resistance to be physical in nature; he hadn't anticipated an attack at a psychic level. If she could continue to distract him, Peter might have a chance of breaking through his defenses.

Movement down the tunnel caught her attention and she fought the urge to react. Instead she whipped around and pulled free of his grasp. She threw herself onto the tablet and steeled herself against an attack. His boot jammed against her ribs and she cried out. The next blow cracked a rib.

She tried shoving away from him, but he was suddenly everywhere. Apollonius loomed godlike through her consciousness. He consumed her. Nothing mattered. The only emotion left to her was hopelessness.

She sank into a whirlpool, a lost speck.

The blackness lifted and Ember pulled back from the void. It was as if she had been on the verge of drowning and now burst through the surface.

Summoning untapped resolve, she oriented herself.

Apollonius no longer stood over her. Instead he stumbled against the wall of the tunnel, clawing at his back.

Ember cried out in triumph at the sight of Avery twisting a dagger into the base of the lamia's neck.

Ember reached for the tube again and this time her hands closed around the barrel. She raised the weapon and tripped the power.

Nothing.

The battery either hadn't time to properly recharge or a connection had come loose.

Desperation squeezed her and for a valuable second she stared nonplussed at the machine.

Avery clung onto the dagger as Apollonius tried to dislodge him. She considered rushing to his aid, but sensed her efforts to assist would be futile. Her gaze turned to Baker's prone figure. His eyes were partially open, but the man lay in a daze.

Avery spilled over the lamia's shoulder. Both men paused and stared at one another before Apollonius delivered a vicious strike to his opponent's head. Avery sank to the ground, with Apollonius looming over him ready to land a killing blow.

"Stop it!" she shouted. "Please stop!"

Apollonius turned. The savage expression on his face softened a moment as he first glanced at the handcart and then at the tablet still on the ground. He reached for the Emerald Tablet, but his posture stiffened. The arrogance and violence melted from his features and though his jaw worked with strain, his eyes were calm.

"He'll waste no more time," Apollonius whispered. The cadence belonged to Peter Styles. "He'll quickly finish the three of you and take the tablet."

Hearing Peter through Apollonius wrenched Ember's heart; Peter might win this moment, but she knew it was his ending.

Ember gathered her strength and scanned the small steam engine. She heard the regular rhythm of its mechanism. Knowing the machine functioned, she turned her eyes on the connection. The battery still drew power, but the relay to the trigger mechanism hung loose. She quickly wrapped the copper around the contact point.

"Don't!" Peter called out. "You send him through a breach and you've accomplished nothing. He can travel through the streams. He can sense the breaches open and close. He'll come back and hurt you in ways you can't imagine."

"Then what do we do?"

"You kill him. Finish the job Avery started. Cut the cord between him and his maker as I've severed the cord between him and Masterson."

He wanted her to use the dagger.

"Peter," she said.

"You're an amazing woman, Ember Quatermain," Peter said. "I wish I had met you under different circumstances."

She took a long blink. "I wish that as well."

Her voice was thin.

Apollonius' body contorted. His hands balled into fists. Ember watched helplessly as he stumbled.

"I can't hold him," Peter called. "Act now."

She stood and reached for the hilt extending from between the lamia's shoulder blades. She gripped it and felt a shudder pass through Apollonius.

"Goodbye, Peter," she whispered.

Apollonius' scream echoed with the rage and frustration of a hundred lifetimes. Through the point of contact she felt Peter holding on, battling through the aether to break the lamia's tether. Her awareness of the fury of the fight between the two personalities gave her strength.

She twisted the blade and forced her will through it.

Peter offered a final surge of energy and retreated. She could no longer feel his presence. Ember shoved the dagger again and carved through the lamia's psychic core. It unraveled and suddenly resistance ended.

The lamia collapsed. She let the body slump to the ground and pushed the power lever the rest of the way. The temperature in the tunnel jumped as a wave of heat charged past, leaving a foul smell in its wake. A hint of the other side of the breach.

If there was a Hell, then that was where Apollonius was heading.

She slapped the power off and the breach vanished, trapping Apollonius on the other side. The tunnel plunged into darkness.

After a few minutes of stumbling around the cart, she located another lantern and a box of matches. She struck a match and peered down the tunnel.

Apollonius was gone. She knew it. There was no evidence of his presence, no lingering influence.

It was a bitter victory.

She knelt beside Avery and touched his face with the back of her hand. Ember was relieved to see his eyes open. Neither spoke for a long time. Ember left him to check on Baker. She heard Avery following behind her.

The constable lay on his back, eyes closed. She shook her head and tried rousing him. The man could be insufferable, but she felt bonded to him after the events they'd pushed through together.

"Is he alive?" Avery asked.

"He is."

"Thank God. Poor Baker."

Ember looked about. The tablet lay on the ground. She examined the object, thinking about what it had cost in terms of suffering, not just now, but through the years, for all those who sought it.

A mirthless grin formed on her lips.

"Avery, I killed Peter," she said. Having spoken the words, she shut her eyes and felt hot tears running down her cheeks.

"You didn't kill him," Avery whispered. "He was already dead."

He wrapped her in his arms. He offered a moment of comfort and she thought of her father, unable to remember the last time he had made her feel safe. When they separated, he gestured toward Baker.

"We'll strip the machine from the cart and use it to help us get him topside," Avery said. "We owe him that. Then, I'll come down and retrieve the engine."

Ember stared at the tablet and struggled with her emptiness.

CHAPTER XXVII

Wherein Mr. Styles makes a discovery about the Emerald Tablet and has a final dealing with death

PETER STYLES FELL BACK FROM MASTERSON AND ROLLED ON THE FLOOR. His head spun, but the shock of still being among the living was welcome to him, although he wasn't sure how much longer he would remain.

Burke stood over him, the hansom driver's rough features grim with concern as he reached to help Peter to his feet.

"Give me a minute," Peter said.

He assumed tracing the strand from Masterson to Apollonius would be his last act, a bolt of self-sacrifice. However clawing his way into Apollonius' consciousness he had discovered something unthinkable, the ability to feed from the lamia. He attached himself like a parasite and suckled at the life force.

How much additional time had that given him? Not much. And when it ran out, there would be no return.

Two women lay on the floor near one corner of the room. He stared until he was assured they still breathed. A third woman sat with her back to the wall, curled into a fetal position. He thought about the fight and resentment roiled through him.

Masterson stirred.

Peter had hoped cutting him from his master might free him as it did when cutting the tether between *nekroanypomonos* and necromancer. Apparently not.

"Let me help you, sir," Burke offered again. The driver pulled Peter to his feet and stayed by his side until he was steady.

"Mr. Burke, I think you should attend to the ladies. They need your assistance more than I."

"What about him?" Burke asked.

Masterson had shifted position. His eyes flickered open but remained unfocused.

"We should finish him off," Burke said.

The idea of attacking a downed man repelled Peter. However he felt Masterson's energy growing and knew in a minute he would once again begin feeding off the women in the room or possibly turn his hunger on Burke.

The blade used against Masterson to funnel his psychic attack now lay on the floor. Peter retrieved it.

Peter sensed the energies in the room and realized with a start they stimulated his own hunger. Masterson's eyes fixed on him and a faint smile traced the older man's lips.

"You're becoming one of us, Mr. Styles," he croaked. "You've fed off the Master, and now you seek sustenance."

"I won't turn," Peter said.

"We've both died once, Mr. Styles. Was it so pleasant for you that you would run quickly back into her arms?"

Masterson had gathered more energy than he let on. The deceitful creature intended to strike, but Peter moved first, dropping on him and grabbing a handful of hair. He pressed the blade under the upturned chin.

"Virgil, it's a good thing that you're so acquainted with Hell," he said.

Peter drove the blade into the lamia's neck and continued cutting until the head was severed. He felt no satisfaction. His victory over Masterson had been won long ago.

"It's done but for one thing," Peter commented.

"What is that?" Burke asked.

Peter removed a handkerchief from a breast pocket, but paused before using it. His arms and chest were covered in gore. He cast the linen aside and instead wiped the blade on the leg of his trousers. He checked the weapon, his eyes dancing over symbols etched in the steel.

His achievement with Apollonius should have been beyond him.

"Mr. Burke, the next thing I need do, I need do alone. I think the women will be fine, but would you be willing to take them where they can receive attention?"

"You're sure you don't need me?"

"Not now."

"Quite right then," Burke said. "We'll part company. Good luck, Mr. Styles. Will we be seeing you again?"

"Let's hope so," Peter answered and left.

Peter slipped from the warehouse and hailed another cab.

Contact with Apollonius had given him his next destination, an old estate on the edge of a town, a brick building with a deep cellar. Behind one patch of wall he would find a hidey hole, and within that niche, a rectangular green stone. The same green stone taken from the Underground at Paddington. The same stone that acted as a lightning rod for the electrical cloud that came through the breach in the tunnel, and later in the house in Paddington. The stone that completed the Emerald Tablet of Hermes.

The Emerald Key.

With the tablet in another reality, the key had been little more than an arcane curiosity. With the tablet in the same aetherial sphere, it now became something quite different.

Having seen the tablet through Apollonius' eyes, he sensed something he hadn't before, that the tablet wasn't a single piece, and that it was useless without the key. And he knew something Apollonius should have known, he knew why the two items had been cast into two separate realities. One didn't need to actually possess the tablet to access its power. If one had the key, and if the tablet was in the same reality, then the power could be accessed remotely.

Apollonius could have used the tablet without exposing himself to danger.

Time was running short, but there was enough to gain access to the key and to use it to activate the tablet. Adala had been correct, although he often acted to the contrary, he did believe in God. If God allowed the tablet to exist, then it served a purpose.

"Too bad it's not like Aladdin's lamp," he had said during his last conversation with Adala. "With Aladdin's lamp you only get three wishes."

"Unless your third wish is for three more wishes."

"Or unless your first wish is for the next wish to be the last."

CHAPTER XXVIII

Wherein the party of adventurers reunites

ON THE RIDE HOME, EMBER KEPT HER HEAD TURNED TO THE WINDOW. Tears threatened, but she held them back, fighting off a draining emptiness. She should be satisfied, happy to have won safety for her nephew, but instead her spirit was spent.

Avery sat attending to Baker. Leaving the Underground he had hailed a constable to bring around a doctor. The constable argued, insisting the Chief Constable be taken to the nearest physician, but Baker managed to rouse himself enough to make the request a command.

"Bring him to the address the gentleman has given you," Baker ordered.

Avery held the police officer's hand now, offering reassurance and praising him for his courage. His voice soothed Ember. The deep concern and affection comforted her. When this was over, she hoped Mr. Tressler would remain a stable presence in her life.

Ember still held the Emerald Tablet. She was numb, unable to believe what they had accomplished.

She studied the miniscule writing on both sides of the tablet. The words and symbols were dense enough to fill a book. Moses brought two tablets down from Mt. Sinai, and the magic in those stones was in the message they delivered. Perhaps that was the case with the Emerald Tablet of Hermes. Perhaps Apollonius' hunger for power had blinded him to this.

The cab turned the corner and she saw her father's house.

She lowered her head, not wanting Avery or Baker to see the tears that once again ran down her cheek.

They rolled up to the front door and the police officers who had escorted them here now carried the Chief Constable into the receiving room to await the arrival of Doctor Roberts.

Ember left them and hurried up the stairs.

She entered Harry's room and saw her nephew sleeping peacefully. His breathing was normal and his color looked good. She almost waked him, but Josephine rose from her chair, joints popping as she started for Ember.

"How has he been?"

"He's been up and about," Josephine said. "Our Harry is back."

The nurse's eyes narrowed and she put a hand on Ember's arm. "But what has happened to you?" she whispered.

"I'm fine," Ember said.

"You look a sight. You've got bruises on your neck and about your face. And your hands!"

"I'll heal."

The old woman wasn't easily dismissed. She approached her former ward and gingerly touched Ember's face. She wiped Ember's forehead with the corner of a hand towel.

"All over that worthless hunk in your arms. Oh, Ember."

Josephine threw her arms about her and it was difficult not to surrender. When they separated, she approached Harry, instinctively extending a hand toward the child. She wanted to feel his face, but seeing the dirty bandage wrapped around her hand, she pulled back. Ember instead stood for several minutes enjoying a moment's peace.

"I try so hard, Nana." She paused, realizing it was a name she had not called her old nurse since childhood. "I look at him, and think of the things I've seen and done, and wonder if childhood isn't just an illusion. When it ends, and it is so brief, what are we left with?"

"I like to think there is still a little Ember, listening for the sound of a storm so she can run outside and stand in the rain."

"Did I do that?"

"Your father thought you daft."

They both laughed.

With the multitude of realities and the constantly shifting energy paths they created, maybe a little girl with strawberry blonde hair and delicate features still stood in the rain and stared in wonder at the clouds and the lightning. Maybe even in this reality.

"We're all children inside, dear one," Josephine said. "And we still want our games taken seriously."

Ember looked away from her nanny. She thought of Peter Styles. Some people never lost that child.

The hairs along her arm stirred. Energy emanated from the tablet for a brief moment. She almost dropped the tablet as it suddenly warmed.

"What's wrong?" Josephine asked. Hearing the nurse's voice, she knew the old woman felt it as well.

Ember held the tablet from her body. She looked down at the markings, and thought she saw a handful of the symbols glowing.

The moment passed.

The hairs along her arms settled.

Something had just occurred. She had done something without realizing it, or someone else had touched the stone somehow. The sooner she got the tablet to Timothy, the better it would be for all concerned.

Ember kissed Josephine and then bent over her nephew. She hastened from the room and hurried back to the sitting room where she had left Baker. Doctor Roberts had arrived in her absence and stood over the Chief Constable. Avery sat in a chair, his shoulders slumped and his head in his hands.

She approached him and spoke in a casual tone so as to not attract attention.

"Something just happened," she said.

He lifted his head and turned a bleary eye on her. His expression changed and he rose from the chair, stepping close so no one would hear their exchange.

"I felt something upstairs. It was a sudden stirring of energy."

"Apollonius?"

"Impossible," she said.

Consternation hardened Avery's expression. He shook his head and placed a hand on the tablet. "Let me take that burden from you. The doctor needs to look at those hands. Whatever you're expecting, whatever you're worrying about, waiting here is as good a place as any. With people who care about you."

"It's time for this matter to be at an end," she said.

Avery hushed her and summoned over Doctor Roberts.

A few hours later, Ember sat by the window, listening to the quiet sounds of a neighborhood on a calm evening in the early spring. She was exhausted, and fought to stay awake. Baker slept on a sofa, the sound of his breathing comforting. Avery sat next to him, his arm in a sling, and a bandage around his head. He was reading one of her father's books.

The knock at the front door was unexpected.

Ember listened for the sound of the maid in the hall. She heard one set of footsteps on the carpeted floor and then voices. An argument.

The maid pushed through the door, her body framing disapproval. Her eyes were fiery.

"Outrageous," the maid said.

A figure pushed past her. Avery was on his feet, with an enormous smile warming his face. He glanced at Ember, perhaps to make sure he wasn't dreaming, and then back at his friend.

"Well met, Mr. Styles."

"Well met, Mr. Tressler."

The two men embraced. Avery laughed and pushed Peter back to look at him. He slapped the man on his shoulder. Ember watched with amazement, remembering the first time Peter returned when she'd thought him lost. Only now his skin had vitality. She could feel the life radiating from him.

"You're looking horrible," Peter said to Avery.

His friend staggered back and shook his head. "You're looking quite the opposite. Good God, Peter, what have you done?"

Peter's hair was uncombed and his attire filthy and ragged, but his face was without worry. Peter approached Ember slowly. With a gentle touch, he took one of her injured hands and pressed it to his lips.

"My . . . Lord. You're alive," she exclaimed. "You used the tablet. That's what I felt earlier. It was you."

"He used the tablet? How is that possible?"

Peter casually approached a table with a few decanters of alcohol. Pulling the stopper of one containing a rich amber liquid, he sniffed and made a sound of contentment. He poured himself a glass and sipped. He gave them both an expression of approval. "Oh, this is quite good. Would either of you care for some?"

He gazed in the direction of the sofa at the far side of the room. Constable Baker was fast asleep, his mouth hung open. Peter watched him for some time before turning back to Ember and Avery.

"How did you manage to best Apollonius?" Avery asked. "Even distracted, he should have been able to shove you aside. According to you, he dealt with your intrusion easily enough when you first encountered him through the aether."

"Ah, but that was when I was among the living. As one of the resurrected, I found myself able to tap energies denied me as a mortal."

"But how did you access the tablet?" Avery protested.

Peter reached into his jacket and withdrew a rectangular stone of the same material as the Emerald Tablet. He waved it in the air.

"The key," Peter said. "Not only is it the key to the code written on the stone, but it's a psychical key as well."

"But Apollonius had the key," Avery said.

"Ah, but the key can't be used with the tablet in another reality. That is why Lysimachus hid them apart from each other."

"We need to separate them again," Ember said. "We have to give the tablet to Timothy and ask him what we should do."

"I suspect he'll be here soon," Peter said. "He knew it the minute the tablet was in this reality, as did I, as did Apollonius. The arrival of the tablet sent a ripple through the aether that got the attention of anything and anyone attuned to it. I'm sure the old man will be knocking at the door shortly. And I'm sure the old woman, Adala, is on her way here as well. She must have felt our bond sever."

Ember resisted the urge to ask him to elaborate.

Avery didn't have the same inhibition. "What did you do Peter? What aren't you telling us?"

"Mr. Tressler, I suggest you and I head for our apartments. We might bring along Mr. Baker, but even in a healthy state, he's not the best entertainment. We'll get cleaned up, rest a bit, and with Miss Quatermain's permission, return tomorrow evening. I think we should take her to supper. We should all celebrate."

"I'd like that very much," Ember said. "But what about the tablet? What about the key?"

Peter carefully placed the small stone on a circular table.

"When Timothy arrives, give him one or the other, or both."

He linked arms with Avery and pulled him toward the door. "I shall call on you tomorrow, Miss Quatermain," Peter called over his shoulder. "It's been a grand adventure."

Before Ember had a chance to answer, he laughed, twirled his overcoat in a flourish, and disappeared out the door.

Peter and Avery were barely down the drive of the Quatermain estate when they spied a figure turning the corner of the hedge separating the property from the street. The old man stopped at the sight of them and they stared at one another for some time.

"Mr. Styles."

Timothy wore a light coat with sleeves too long for his arms. A formless black cap topped his crown.

"The tablet is in there," Peter said. "Miss Quatermain awaits you."

"But the tablet isn't the only thing required."

Peter leaned close to Timothy. The man bore him no ill will, but he was a difficult read.

"Both await you."

"How curious. I know you are telling me the truth, and yet I detect only a void where there should be great power."

"Ask Adala about Aladdin's second wish when you get the opportunity."

Timothy didn't move. "Shall I tell you my definition for trust?" he asked.

Peter waited.

"It's the absence of fear," Timothy stated. "Simply the absence of fear."

"Then here's to trust," Peter said.

Timothy winked at him. "See? We already have the basis of an interesting relationship. I'm going to call on Miss Quatermain and claim the tablet. Even without its power, it's invaluable."

The old man hummed softly to himself and started up the drive. Peter watched for a few minutes and then continued toward the street.

"The grand thing about adventures is that they are never really over," Peter said to Avery.

"No?"

"No, not so long as children are innocent and heartless." Peter mused. "But then we're all children, aren't we?"

Peter whistled as he walked with Avery, cheered by the prospect of tomorrow and many more fond memories thereafter. The night was turning warm. Finally.

LIMITED HARDCOVER EDITIONS

978-0-9586856-9-6 Love in Vain BY Lewis Shiner
978-0-9803531-1-2 Belong ED Russell B. Farr
978-0-9803531-9-8 Basic Black BY Terry Dowling
978-0-9806288-0-7 Make Believe BY Terry Dowling
978-0-9806288-1-4 The Infernal BY Kim Wilkins
978-0-9806288-5-2 Dead Sea Fruit BY Kaaron Warren
978-0-9806288-7-6 The Girl With No Hands BY Angela Slatter
978-0-9807813-0-4 Dead Red Heart ED Russell B. Farr
978-0-9807813-3-5 Heliotrope BY Justina Robson
978-0-9807813-6-6 Matilda Told Such Dreadful Lies BY Lucy Sussex
978-1-921857-00-3 Bluegrass Symphony BY Lisa L. Hannett
978-1-921857-07-2 Bread and Circuses BY Felicity Dowker
978-1-921857-23-2 Wild Chrome BY Greg Mellor
978-1-921857-27-0 Midnight and Moonshine BY Lisa L. Hannett & Angela Slatter
978-1-921857-37-9 Prickle Moon BY Juliet Marillier
978-1-921857-41-6 The Bride Price BY Cat Sparks
978-1-921857-45-4 The Year of Ancient Ghosts BY Kim Wilkins
978-1-921857-58-4 Everything is a Graveyard BY Jason Fischer
978-1-921857-68-3 Havenstar BY Glenda Larke
978-1-925212-03-7 Angel Dust BY Ian McHugh

EBOOKS

978-0-9803531-5-0 Ghost Seas BY Steven Utley
978-1-921857-93-5 The Girl With No Hands BY Angela Slatter
978-1-921857-99-7 Dead Red Heart ED Russell B. Farr
978-1-921857-94-2 More Scary Kisses ED Liz Grzyb
978-0-9807813-5-9 Heliotrope BY Justina Robson
978-1-921857-98-0 Year's Best Australian F&H EDS Grzyb & Helene
978-1-921857-36-2 Dreaming of Djinn ED Liz Grzyb
978-1-921857-40-9 Prickle Moon BY Juliet Marillier
978-1-921857-92-8 The Year of Ancient Ghosts BY Kim Wilkins
978-1-921857-28-7 Bloodstones ED Amanda Pillar

THE YEAR'S BEST AUSTRALIAN FANTASY & HORROR SERIES
EDITED BY LIZ GRZYB & TALIE HELENE

978-0-9807813-8-0 Year's Best Australian Fantasy & Horror 2010 (hc)
978-0-9807813-9-7 Year's Best Australian Fantasy & Horror 2010 (tpb)
978-0-921057-13-3 Year's Best Australian Fantasy & Horror 2011 (hc)
978-0-921057-14-0 Year's Best Australian Fantasy & Horror 2011 (tpb)
978-0-921057-48-5 Year's Best Australian Fantasy & Horror 2012 (hc)
978-0-921057-49-2 Year's Best Australian Fantasy & Horror 2012 (tpb)
978-0-921057-72-0 Year's Best Australian Fantasy & Horror 2013 (hc)
978-0-921057-73-7 Year's Best Australian Fantasy & Horror 2013 (tpb)

THANK YOU

The publisher would sincerely like to thank:

Elizabeth Grzyb, Christine Daigle, Stewart Sternberg, Cat Sparks, Lisa L. Hannett, Donna Maree Hanson, Robert Hood, Pete Kempshall, Penelope Love, Nicole Murphy, Angela Slatter, Karen Brooks, Jeremy G. Byrne, Felicity Dowker, Kim Wilkins, Marianne de Pierres, Jonathan Strahan, Peter McNamara, Ellen Datlow, Grant Stone, Sean Williams, Simon Brown, Garth Nix, David Cake, Simon Oxwell, Grant Watson, Sue Manning, Steven Utley, Lewis Shiner, Bill Congreve, Jack Dann, Janeen Webb, Brian Clarke, Stephen Dedman, the Mt Lawley Mafia, the Nedlands Yakuza, Shane Jiraiya Cummings, Angela Challis, Kate Williams, Kathryn Linge, Andrew Williams, Al Chan, Brian Clarke, Alisa and Tehani, Mel & Phil, Hayley Lane, Georgina Walpole, Rushelle Lister, everyone we've missed . . .

. . . and you.

IN MEMORY OF
Eve Johnson (1945–2011)
Sara Douglass (1957–2011)
Steven Utley (1948–2013)

www.ingramcontent.com/pod-product-compliance
Lightning Source LLC
Chambersburg PA
CBHW020945260626
47169CB00006B/1828